Resistance

Books by **CJ Daugherty**

Night School
Night School Legacy
Night School Fracture
Night School Resistance
Night School Endgame
Night School the Short Stories
The Secret Fire
The Secret City
Number 10

As **Christi Daugherty**

The Echo Killing
A Beautiful Corpse
Revolver Road

Resistance
NIGHT SCHOOL

C J DAUGHERTY

MOONFLOWER

Published by Moonflower Publishing Ltd.
www.MoonflowerBooks.co.uk

2nd Edition

Copyright © CJ Daugherty 2020

ISBN: 978-1-8382374-5-5

1st Published in the United States 2013

CJ Daugherty has asserted her right to be identified as the author of this work.
This is a work of fiction. All rights reserved. No part of this publication may be reproduced, stored in any retrieval system, or transmitted, in any form or by any means, electronic, mechanical, photocopying, recording or otherwise, without the prior written permission of the publishers.

Printed in the United States of America

Moonflower Publishing Registered Office: 303 The Pillbox, 115 Coventry Road, London E2 6GG

MOONFLOWER

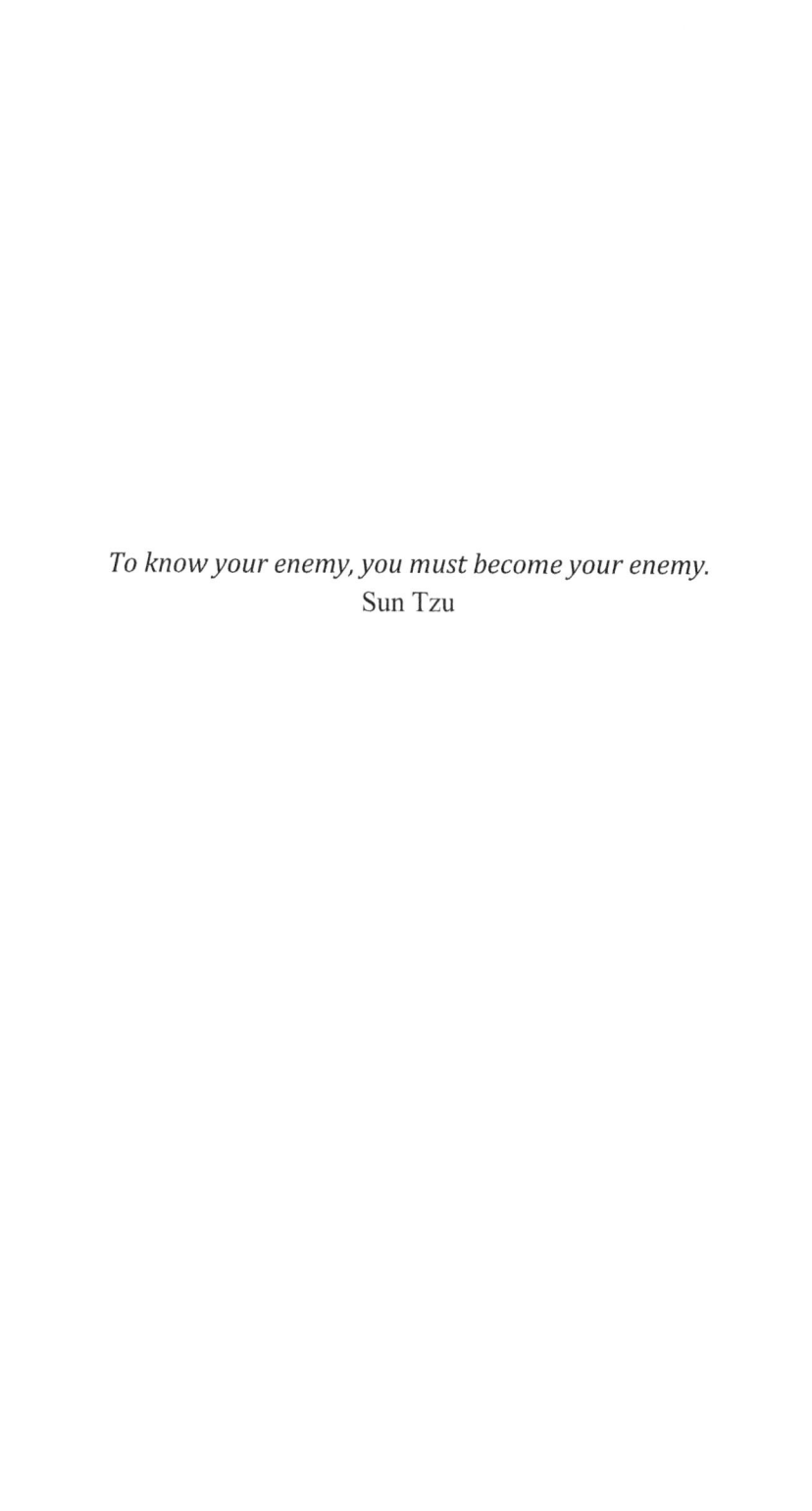

To know your enemy, you must become your enemy.
Sun Tzu

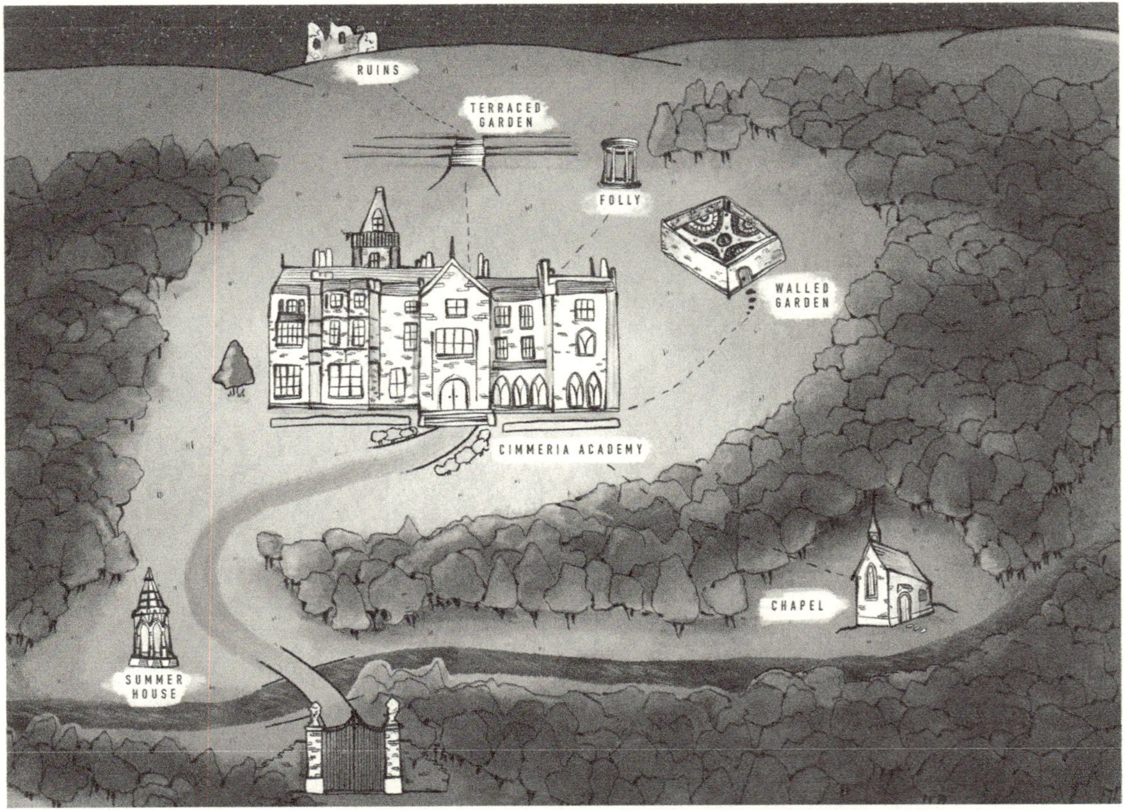
RUINS
TERRACED GARDEN
FOLLY
WALLED GARDEN
CIMMERIA ACADEMY
CHAPEL
SUMMER HOUSE

One

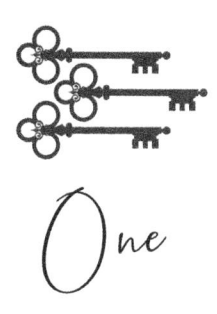

'You must relax,' Sylvain said. 'If you're tense, you'll sink.'

Allie glared at him. Every muscle in her body was stretched tight as a wire. 'I am relaxed.'

They stood in cool, waist-deep water, gentle waves jostling them. The sand was soft beneath their toes. Allie could feel the heat of the sun strong on her skin as she looked out over the cobalt waters.

Sylvain's eyebrows winged up. 'You are not relaxed.' He gestured at her tight shoulders, and hands curled into fists. 'Look at you. We're swimming in the Mediterranean Sea – you act like you're about to be tortured.'

Allie shrugged. She was affecting nonchalance but the fact was, she could hardly believe she was really here. With him. Doing this.

I am in the south of France, she thought, and Sylvain is teaching me how to swim. WTF?

Sylvain was still waiting for her to say something so she muttered darkly about waterboarding.

His lips twitched.

'Here,' he said. 'It's easy. Just … sit.'

Looking around at the utter lack of anything to sit on, Allie squinted suspiciously. 'Sit?'

He demonstrated, lowering his body into the water, which seemed to pick him up and carry him, as if he were relaxing in an invisible chair. Then he leaned back and floated, weightless as a feather. 'See? It's easy.'

Hesitantly, Allie let her body drop into the water as he'd done. The second she lifted her feet from the seabed she sank like stone. Splashing wildly, she regained her footing and turned to him, sputtering and outraged.

'I can't sit,' she said, fuming, 'on water.'

Sylvain tried to hold a sympathetic expression but his eyes danced and his lips curved up.

'That was ... unfortunate.'

'Unfortunate?' Still tasting salt water, Allie seemed to have lost her ability to put a sentence together.

'Look,' he said, stepping closer. 'Try it again. This time I'll hold on to you.'

'Oh no.' Allie, who had just about had enough swimming for one day, stepped quickly away from him.

Laughing now, Sylvain followed her. 'Oh yes.'

Allie tried to run towards shore but the sand and water conspired to slow her and in seconds his hands were on her waist. He pulled her back out as she flailed and giggled with helpless indignation.

'I can't swim. Please don't make me learn,' she implored. 'I hate learning. Learning is stupid. Learning is bad.'

'Learning,' Sylvain said calmly, 'is wonderful.'

He was swimming beside her now and her feet weren't touching the sea floor. His hands were steady on her waist and then she was floating in the water without quite knowing how it had happened.

Treading water, Sylvain turned a slow circle, spinning her easily as she lay flat on her back, staring up at the perfect blue sky.

'See?' he said. 'I knew you could do it.'

'But you're holding me up,' she said.

'No I'm not.'

And he wasn't. At some point he'd let go. She was floating, free.

'I can't believe it,' Allie whispered. But it was true. She wasn't sinking or sputtering. The water held her, like gentle hands. She felt safe.

For just a second, she closed her eyes. It was so quiet and calm, the only sound the swish of the waves reaching the sand, and the sigh as the water returned to the sea. It was … perfect.

That was when the first shot split the air.

The explosive sound ripped through the quiet cove. Allie flinched and started to sink. Before she could go under, Sylvain grabbed her, pulling her close.

His eyes searched the shore.

Clinging to his shoulders, Allie followed his gaze. Everything was just as it had been: soft sand, towering boulders, blue sea. But suddenly it looked different; dangerous.

Irrational anger flashed inside her like fire. This was the first time they'd left the compound since they'd arrived at Sylvain's family home a month ago. Now they'd never be allowed out again. Was this how her whole life was going to be? Constantly on the run?

Constantly afraid.

She thought of Rachel, who she'd left sitting by the pool at Sylvain's family's villa. What if she was under attack, too? They had to get out of here. Get back to her.

She sent up a silent prayer. *Please let her be OK.*

Still holding her tightly, Sylvain began swimming towards a rock jetty that edged the beach, jutting out into the sea. Feeling like a dead weight, Allie tried to make herself as small and light as possible. But he was a strong swimmer and they moved with sure swiftness.

The whole time, they both watched the shore. Nothing stirred.

Then another gunshot rang out.

As the sound echoed off the rocks, Allie and Sylvain exchanged a shocked look. They both knew better than to speak. Without a word, he shifted her to his other arm, putting his body between her and the suddenly deadly shore.

The water seemed colder now; Allie's teeth began to chatter.

Guns. They'd faced a lot of things in England, but never guns. You couldn't outrun a bullet. Or outswim it.

For three months she and Rachel had moved from safe house to safe house. Each more elegant than the last. Each more isolated. Each more lonely.

A few weeks ago they'd arrived in France to find Sylvain waiting for them. Like a piece of home.

And they'd actually been having fun … Until now.

I should have known it couldn't last.

The second they reached the rock jetty, Sylvain navigated to a hidden nook where the boulders naturally shielded them on all sides, like a house without a roof.

They crouched down low, both of them tense.

In the safety of the rocks, Allie felt safe enough to whisper. 'What …?'

'I don't know.' His voice was taut, and a muscle worked in his jaw. 'But I'm going to find out.'

Fear burned Allie's stomach like acid. It must have shown on her face because he took her by the shoulders. His hands were steady and his eyes pleaded with her not to argue.

'Stay here.' Though whispered, the words seemed to echo around them. 'Please, Allie. I'm going to see what's happening then I'll come right back. I promise.'

A visceral frustration shook her. She should go with him – she was trained for this.

But she didn't know how to swim. If she insisted on going too, she'd make things more dangerous for both of them.

She held his gaze fiercely. 'Be careful.'

For a moment he looked at her as if he wanted to say something; instead he pulled her close, hugging her hard. His skin felt wet and cold against hers.

Then he slipped out between the rocks and dived into the water, disappearing with barely a ripple.

As soon as he was out of sight, Allie wanted him back.

Her chest ached. She wrapped her arms tightly across her torso.

People kept getting hurt because of her. First Ruth, then Jo, then Rachel. If Nathaniel got his hands on Sylvain …

Three gunshots rang in quick succession and she gasped, ducking low. A bullet ricocheted off something with a high-pitched whine.

Allie gripped the stone in front of her, digging her nails into a crevice in the black rock. Barnacles were like razor blades beneath her fingertips and she welcomed the pain. It helped her think.

More time passed and Sylvain didn't return. It was becoming difficult to breathe.

She couldn't stay here, could she? He could be hurt. He might need her help.

For a long while she stayed low, torn between rushing out to find him and doing as he'd asked. She counted her breaths.

Fifty-three breaths in. Fifty-four. Fifty-five ...

He should be back.

Finally she couldn't take it any more. She couldn't swim but she could wade or ... walk. *Something.*

She leapt up. At that precise moment, he appeared, dripping from the sea.

Relief threatened to bring tears to her eyes.

Some of the tension left his face as soon as he saw her. He moved swiftly into the safety of the rocks.

'I was sure you wouldn't be here,' he said.

'I can't bloody *swim*.' Helpless frustration rang in her voice and she forced herself to lower it to a whisper. 'What's happening?'

His expression changed, becoming more business-like.

'There are two of them. Our guards are holding them off for now but more could be on the way. We have to get out of here. We need to be fast.' He held her gaze, his blue eyes dark with worry. 'Stay with me – no matter what happens, OK?'

Allie, who had no intention of letting him out of her sight again, nodded vigorously. 'I promise.'

Taking her hand, he bent down low as they left the shelter and slipped into the chilly sea. Fear had heightened Allie's senses – she thought she could see things moving in the water; feel them brushing against her skin.

As he'd done earlier, Sylvain held her close, propelling them through the waves with strong kicks. But instead of steering towards shore, he headed away from it. Slowly, working against the current, they made their way to the end of the rock jetty, and then around it to the other side.

Here, no beautiful beach greeted them. The unsheltered coastline had been battered by waves and wind and allowed to become overgrown with scrub trees and weeds.

Somewhere in the distance she heard shouts. Sylvain's arm tightened around her. Gritting his teeth, he kicked harder. With the waves at their back they glided swiftly towards the shore.

As soon as they reached the shallows, they stood and ran. Sylvain held her hand in a tight grip as they stumbled out of the sea, fighting the force of the waves tugging at their legs as if to hold them back.

When they reached the cluster of boulders that shielded the cove, they stopped to catch their breath. The relentless sunlight bleached the scene in front of them, tinting it all with hazy gold.

From the rocks, Allie could see their guards' SUVs. Just beyond that a flash of bright red – Sylvain's motorcycle.

Shouts erupted in the distance. Unfamiliar voices hurled French words at each other. Allie couldn't see anyone – the guards had to be in the rocks.

'Shh …' Sylvain held up his hand as he listened. Then he turned to her, his eyes urgent. 'They're making a move. Get ready.'

Footsteps pounded across the hard sand. More shouts. A shot was fired.

He pulled at her hand. '*Now*.'

Taking off at a run, they hurtled across the sand. Thorny scrub bushes scratched at Allie's legs, sharp shells cut into her bare feet, but she ignored them, pushing herself to run faster.

The sun turned the sand a brutal white. Her breath burned in her throat.

Ahead of them the motorcycle was like a beacon.

Red. Stop. Danger.

Then they were there. Sylvain leaped on to the bike, reaching back to help her climb on behind him. Shouts erupted behind them and he threw the helmets to the ground – there was no time.

They both knew what would happen when he turned the key, which glittered hot in the ignition where he'd left it.

The attackers would all come running. With guns.

He turned to meet her gaze; his piercing blue eyes were fierce and determined. 'Hold on.'

Two

The roar of the motorcycle's engine was deafening; it drowned out every other sound. Someone could shoot at them and they'd never hear it.

Allie wrapped her arms tightly around Sylvain's waist. His skin felt hot against hers; feverish.

He gunned the engine. The bike shot down the dirt road as if it had been fired from a cannon. It moved like a living creature beneath them and, even clinging to him with all her strength, Allie struggled to hold on, gritting her teeth from the force of the speed.

It felt like gravity was trying to tear them apart.

Sylvain's muscles tensed from the effort of keeping the motorcycle upright and moving in a straight line. The rough dirt road jostled them so violently Allie's teeth chattered.

Then an intersection with a paved highway loomed ahead of them. The road was crowded with late afternoon traffic; they'd have to slow down to merge on to it.

Crouched low behind Sylvain, Allie turned to look over her shoulder. In the distance she saw a dark vehicle roaring after them. It wasn't close yet but it was fast. It would catch up to them when Sylvain hit the brakes to merge onto the road.

But as they grew closer and closer to the busy road, he didn't hit the brakes. And, with sudden cold clarity, Allie realised he wasn't going to.

He was going to turn into that crowded road at full speed.

There was no time to react – to say anything. To try and talk him out of it. Squeezing her eyes shut, she tightened her grip, pressing her face against the bare skin of his back.

They hit the intersection, cutting off a small car that slammed its brakes to avoid crashing into them. Tyres screamed as Sylvain turned the bike sharply. The acrid smell of burned rubber filled the air.

That was when he lost control.

The bike swerved wildly. The road shot up towards them.

Allie screamed and turned her face away just in time to see a lorry piled high with produce swerve off on to the dirt shoulder, sending up a dark cloud of dust and dirt.

Swearing in French, Sylvain fought to right the bike as it wobbled wildly. At the speed they were going, with no helmets or protective gear, Allie knew they'd likely die if they crashed. But there was nothing she could do but hold on. Holding her breath, she clung to Sylvain's waist.

Then, just as suddenly as he'd lost it, he was in control again. The bike steadied. He revved the engine and they tore straight and fast down the road.

Exhaling in relief, Allie lowered her chin to his shoulder. She couldn't tell whether it was her heart or Sylvain's she could feel pounding but a fine sheen of sweat had appeared on his bare shoulders and she was finding it hard to breathe.

He glanced back at her. 'You OK?'

No words seemed sufficient to convey how she felt, so Allie nodded her reply. As their speed picked up, he bent low over the bars. The sea was a blue blur beside them; on the other side fields rushed by, a watercolour of gold and green and lavender. He handled the bike smoothly now, passing cars without hesitation or fear.

She didn't know how fast they were going but had a feeling it must be well over 100 miles per hour. She wondered how Sylvain could see – the wind burned her eyes, whipping her damp hair into a weapon that sliced at her face and the bare skin of her shoulders.

But soon traffic grew heavier and they were forced to slow.

Sylvain swerved, looking for a way out, but found nothing. It was summer time on the French Riviera. Traffic was inescapable.

Still, Allie told herself, at least they'd escaped the gunmen. And by now they had to be nearly back to the house. They'd made it.

Just as she'd begun to relax, though, a black BMW swung into the lane behind them, creeping so close it almost touched the bike's rear tyre.

She could never be certain where it came from. Just, suddenly, it was there; its powerful engine roaring. Tinted windows hid the face of the driver, making the car seem as blank and menacing as a robot.

Allie felt Sylvain's body tense as he studied the car in the bike's side-mirror.

'Is it one of us?' she shouted, her voice disappearing in the wind.

He shook his head very slightly.

Allie's heart sank. It was one of *them*.

By now, she knew what to expect – he didn't have to warn her. She tightened her arms around his waist, bracing herself.

Sylvain pulled into oncoming traffic.

Cars scattered around them like toys in a playground. Discordant horn blasts formed a chorus of rage but Sylvain ignored them, speeding straight ahead.

Behind them, the dark car's engine roared as if enraged.

A shriek of brakes and a crash. Clinging to Sylvain, Allie twisted around to see the BMW knock a smaller car off the road into the scrub brush. Then the driver floored it and headed right towards them.

'Sylvain!'

Hearing the urgency in her voice, he glanced back. Swearing, he swerved hard to the right, on to the narrow, unpaved, shoulder. Pebbles shot out from under their tyres like bullets as they sped along the rough dirt strip for half a mile, passing cars like they were sitting still before careering at last on to a narrow road.

Thankfully, the tree-lined lane was mostly empty. Sylvain accelerated, taking the curves at impossible speeds. Allie knew she should be afraid but she'd seen what he could do. She trusted him to keep her alive.

She kept looking over her shoulder for the black car but it didn't reappear.

Then an imposing metal gate appeared ahead of them. Two familiar dark SUVs sat outside it like sentinels.

The gate was just starting to open. The afternoon sunshine pouring through the black metal was so white and clean it looked like the gates to heaven.

The opening didn't seem big enough for the bike but Sylvain obviously thought differently. He headed for it.

Allie's hands clenched against his waist; she murmured a prayer under her breath. They shot through with inches to spare, skidding sideways on the elegant, flower-lined drive. Sylvain slammed on the brakes to avoid running into the house. They stopped abruptly, and Allie jolted forward against his spine before thudding back hard on to the seat.

Sylvain turned off the engine. The sudden silence was shocking.

Swinging his legs forward, he leaped athletically from the bike and held his hand out to her. 'The gates are still open,' he said. 'We're exposed here. We have to get inside.'

She wanted to do as he said but she couldn't seem to move. Her knees felt like rubber, her stomach churned.

Had they ever been so close to death before?

'I'm not sure my legs will work,' she admitted.

A pleased smile quirked up his lips and he leaned casually against a handlebar.

'It was fast, no? I trained with a Motocross champion. My father insisted as a condition of giving me the bike.'

Allie fought an absurd desire to laugh. How could he be so relaxed when they'd just nearly died?

She swung her legs over and jumped down from the bike. They ran up the steps to the front door.

'I'm glad he insisted,' she said, her voice shaking just a little. 'I like being alive.'

Three

The thing was, the day had started with such promise. It was so sunny the sky was like a sheet of blue glass. It was the day before Allie's birthday, and she and Rachel had a busy schedule of sunbathing planned.

Rachel, of course, sunbathed with her chemistry textbook because Rachel did everything with her textbooks. She planned to go to Oxford and then to medical school, and nothing – not even an attack by Nathaniel that decimated the school and left them both injured – could stop her. They'd both been tutored long distance ever since they left Cimmeria Academy on a cold March night. Over the months, they'd become pretty adept at independent study.

As they sat by the pool that afternoon, Allie had attempted to do her history reading but found it hard to focus. It was only June but already it was summer hot and she kept finding reasons to drop the book.

After all, she thought, lying back on the sun lounger, *do you have to study the day before your birthday? Isn't that a bit like studying on Christmas Eve?*

Overhead, a seabird wheeled in lazy circles, never flapping its wings, only soaring. Not a single cloud shadowed them.

Allie glanced over to where Rachel sat in the shade of a large umbrella, utterly immersed in her work. The scars Gabe had left on her body were hard to see now, and she was glad. Maybe eventually they'd disappear completely.

It had taken weeks after they left Cimmeria Academy for Rachel's nightmares to stop. And she wasn't the only one with bad dreams.

Allie touched the long, thin scar on her own shoulder. It felt hard beneath her fingers and still sensitive. A reminder of what she'd been through. And what she was running from.

It was only really when they came here that they'd both felt safe again.

They hadn't even known whose house it was when they first arrived in a convoy of SUVs, after a short journey by private jet. When the heavy black gates opened, they revealed a grand villa that seemed to absorb the sun into its golden walls. Lush, magenta bougainvillea wrapped around it like a bright blanket.

It was beautiful. But it was just another mansion.

They had been standing in the heat, waiting for the driver to unload their bags, when the front door swung open and suddenly Sylvain was in the doorway, smiling at them like a piece of Cimmeria – like home.

Without even thinking about it, Allie had bounded up the steps and hurled herself into his arms.

He'd just laughed and pulled her closer, as if they hugged each other every day.

'God,' he'd whispered into her hair, 'I've missed you.'

Later, as he showed them around, Sylvain would explain that this was his parents' summer retreat. The grounds held several houses as well as the sprawling main villa, so there was room for guards and staff. High walls and a location at the top of a hill kept it secure.

It was the perfect place to hide and, after a week, Allie and Rachel had agreed they could pretty happily live here forever. In the constant French sunshine, it was easy to forget the chaos they'd left behind. Easy not to worry about Nathaniel and why the guards were constantly around. Why they never left the compound.

Except for today, when Sylvain had shown up by the pool with the tantalising offer of a few minutes of freedom.

'I was thinking of going to the beach,' he'd said. 'Want to come?'

Allie hadn't hesitated. 'Are you joking?' she'd asked. When he shook his head, grinning, she'd leapt to her feet. 'Come on, Rach. You have to come, too.'

But Rachel had shooed them away. 'You go, children,' she'd said, glancing at them indulgently over the tops of her sunglasses. 'I've got learning to do.'

So Allie and Sylvain had gone to the beach alone.

As they'd driven across the French countryside on Sylvain's motorcycle, Allie had absorbed the beauty of the landscape with hungry eyes.

She loved it here.

The only problem was, they'd already been in France nearly a month. That was longer than they'd stayed any place since leaving Cimmeria. At any moment the call could come. Then the plane. Some new anonymous mansion would await them. And she and Rachel would be alone again.

Who knew when they'd come back here? When she'd ever see Sylvain again?

But so far the call hadn't come, and Allie had begun to let herself dream that maybe they could stay. Maybe Nathaniel would never find them. Or perhaps he simply didn't dare mess with Sylvain's father. After all, Mr Cassel was a powerful leader of the French government and one of the country's wealthiest men.

But on some level she'd always known this was just a fantasy. Nathaniel always found her.

Always.

The marble floor was cool beneath Allie's bare feet. After the heat outside, the villa seemed as chilly as a refrigerator. Goosebumps rose on her arms and shoulders.

Above their heads, vaulted ceilings soared up twenty feet; at the top, fans circled steadily with a faint mechanical whirr.

'I have to find Rachel,' Allie said, turning towards the back of the house. But she'd only taken two steps when a trio of guards, clad in black T-shirts and shorts, burst into the room. Stopping in front of Sylvain, they spoke in rapid French as he listened attentively.

Allie, whose French was only so-so, waited impatiently for him to translate.

After a brief conversation the men ran off again. Sylvain turned to her, his brow furrowing.

'Everything's fine here,' he said. 'There was no attack on the house. Rachel is in her room. They've gone to get my parents.'

Allie breathed a relieved sigh. At least Rachel was OK. At least there was that.

But Sylvain didn't look relieved. Worry still creased his forehead. 'What's the matter?' she asked, searching his face for clues. 'Has something else happened?'

He shook his head. 'I don't know. Something they said … I just have a bad feeling …'

He didn't have to finish the sentence. Allie knew that feeling well.

'They're sending us away.' Her tone was matter-of-fact even though her heart ached. 'To the next safe house.'

At her side, his hand found hers. 'I won't let them.'

He sounded determined and, as Allie looked into his eyes, the colour of the French sky, she wished it was possible. But it wasn't. Sylvain could handle a motorcycle like a pro but even he couldn't tell Lucinda Meldrum what to do with her granddaughter.

Even he couldn't keep her safe.

'They'll make us,' she said simply. Then, because it was true, she added, 'I'll miss you.'

He looked at her longingly, as if there was something he wanted to say but he couldn't find the words. His gaze brushed her lips like a kiss.

'Allie ...' he began but, before he could finish the thought, another guard rushed in saying something Allie couldn't understand.

Dropping her hand, Sylvain gave her a helpless, apologetic look. 'My father. I have to go.'

'It's cool,' she said. 'We'll talk later.'

But as he walked away she couldn't suppress the melancholy thought: *If there is a later.*

After Sylvain left with the guards, Allie hurried up the staircase, which curled upwards gracefully in a swirl of delicate white wrought iron. She ran down the airy landing to a set of tall, double doors, which swung open at her touch.

The afternoon sun filtered through the long sheer curtains that covered the floor-to-ceiling windows, giving her bedroom a creamy, apricot glow. A wide, canopied bed, draped in pale linens, dominated the room, but Allie headed straight to the dresser.

Quickly, she pulled a short skirt and a tank top over her bikini. After sliding her feet into sandals, she stopped in front of a door that could easily be mistaken for a closet. She knocked on it lightly.

'Come in.' Rachel's voice sounded muffled through the heavy wood.

Allie opened the door to the adjoining room, which looked a great deal like hers, only with pale yellow curtains instead of peach.

Rachel lay on her bed surrounded by stacks of books. Her glasses had slid halfway down her nose and she blinked at Allie over the top of them.

Allie hated to break the news. Rachel was so happy here. So safe.

But no one is ever really safe, she reminded herself.

Safe is an illusion. A lie we tell ourselves to make it easier to go about our very dangerous lives.

'You better come downstairs,' she said quietly. 'Nathaniel found us.'

'You have to go.' Sylvain's father sat on a stylish armchair upholstered in lush, white linen. Allie, Sylvain and Rachel perched across from him on a long, matching sofa. 'This was a real attack. You could have been killed.' He held his son's gaze. 'You and I both know Nathaniel would have killed you to get to Allie. He'll never give up.'

Sylvain's gaze didn't flicker but, for Allie, Mr Cassel's words were the equivalent of someone opening the cover of an endless, dark well and shoving her down. They echoed in her head.

He'll never give up. Never give up ...

'Where do we go this time?' Rachel's tone was neutral but Allie could sense the weariness she was hiding. They were both tired of running.

His next words stunned them both. 'Back to Cimmeria.'

Allie's heart flipped. Rachel shot her a disbelieving look.

Was it possible? They could go home?

Lucinda had always made it clear they couldn't go back to the school until the situation with Nathaniel was resolved. Which it clearly wasn't. So ... what had changed?

'You're serious?' Allie said. 'We can really go back?'

Watching them from her seat near the tall windows that overlooked the pool, Sylvain's mother seemed unnaturally calm in the face of all this upheaval.

'Every place you've gone to has been discovered eventually.' Her voice was a rich alto. Her French accent made each word elegant. 'For you ... no place is truly safe.'

A slight frown darkened Mr Cassel's expression. 'That is not precisely true.' He turned to Allie. 'Lucinda – your grandmother – has decided you will be safer in England. And –' he hesitated briefly – 'we agree. At least, we think you'll be in no more danger there than you are here. And you can get on with your studies.'

Allie couldn't believe it. She saw Rachel fighting an excited smile and she knew how she felt.

Home, she thought. *I'm going home.*

She would see Zoe and Nicole again.

And Carter.

The very thought of him made her nervous. She'd never got a chance to say goodbye. Never had a chance to sort things through.

Never made up her mind.

'When do we leave?' Sylvain held his father's gaze, his expression intense.

Mr Cassel opened his mouth to reply, then closed it again as if he'd thought better of it.

Allie looked back and forth between them, aware some message was being exchanged but unsure of what it was.

Mr Cassel finally spoke. 'Allie and Rachel leave tonight. If you choose to go with them … then that is when you will go, too, I suppose.'

'Of course I'm going back with them,' Sylvain said evenly. 'You know that.'

From her seat by the window, Sylvain's mother made a small sound. She was still gazing out of the window, her lips tight. As always, she was elegantly dressed – in her white linen blouse and grey trousers; a pale blue pashmina draped across her shoulders, she could have stepped out of a magazine.

But Allie had never seen her look so sad.

'We would rather you stayed here,' Mr Cassel said finally. 'Where we can protect you.'

Sylvain replied to his father in rapid, low French. Allie had been practising but she still only caught only a couple of words. *Jamais* – never. And *comprend* – understand.

His father stood with such abruptness it made her jump. He said something to Sylvain that she didn't catch and strode out of the room.

'What did he say?' she asked, looking at Sylvain.

It was Mrs Cassel who responded, her eyes on her son. 'He said, "Do as you please."'

'*Maman* …' Sylvain began, but his mother held up her hand, her white sleeve falling back to reveal a slim wrist the same tawny colour as his own skin.

'You don't have to explain,' she said quietly. 'I understand. But we love you. And we are afraid for you.' Her gaze moved to encompass Allie and Rachel. 'For all of you.'

An uncomfortable silence fell.

'Well.' Rachel cleared her throat. 'I guess we should pack. And leave you two to talk.' Standing, she gestured at Allie. 'Come on. Those T-shirts won't pack themselves.'

'No, they won't,' Allie agreed, scrambling to follow. 'And the trousers. Someone has to pack those, too.'

Sylvain didn't even glance at them as they hurried up the stairs, leaving a heavy stillness behind.

Allie had already thrown all her things into bags before a guard informed her they wouldn't leave until nightfall. Once they left the safety of the Cassel compound they needed to move fast, the guard explained, and for that the roads had to be clear of traffic.

In the end, it was after ten before they were finally called to the front door where a convoy of black SUVs waited, headlights glowing, engines purring,

Without a word, Sylvain's father kissed Allie and Rachel on both cheeks. He said something quietly to Sylvain in French. Allie saw Sylvain's jaw tighten as he listened. Then he disappeared back into the villa.

Mrs Cassel hugged Rachel.

'Good luck with your studies, Rachel,' she said, in her beautifully accented voice. 'I should like you to be my doctor some day.'

'Thanks for *everything*,' Rachel said. The woman gave her an affectionate smile.

As Rachel headed out to the car, Mrs Cassel turned to Allie.

'Goodbye, my dear.' She pulled her close. Allie breathed in her perfume, a heady mix of exotic flowers and spice.

When she stepped back, Mrs Cassel held her by the shoulders, studying her face as if she wanted to say more. There was something in her warm, hazel eyes Allie couldn't read. Caution, perhaps. Or doubt.

But all she said as she dropped her hands was: 'Be careful, *chère* Allie.'

'I will,' Allie promised. Then something occurred to her. 'What about you, though? Nathaniel knows where you are. He knows you helped me.'

Mrs Cassel seemed touched by her concern. 'We are well protected,' she said gently. 'Besides, it's not us he wants, my dear.'

Her honesty was chilling but Allie was grateful for it nonetheless as she hurried after Rachel to the line of cars.

Sylvain lingered on the front steps. Through the open car door, Allie watched as he talked quietly to his mother. As always, it hurt a little to see anyone so close to their parents. She hadn't spoken to her own parents in months. Phone calls were impossible while she was on the run. She knew Isabelle kept them informed about her. But it wasn't easy to accept that they didn't care enough to insist on speaking to her.

I wonder what it's like to be liked by your own parents, Allie thought. And then she pushed the thought away. It was easier not to think about them.

Mrs Cassel pulled Sylvain into a tight hug before finally letting him go. As he ran down the steps to the car, Allie saw her wipe a tear from her cheek with a quick brush of her fingers.

By the time Sylvain was seated and looking back at her, she'd composed her face. She waved at them with serenely. As if they were just normal kids, heading off to a normal school.

A guard closed the door of the SUV and Allie heard the *thunk* as all the doors locked automatically through the central system.

A thrill of excitement ran through her like electricity. Even if they'd changed their minds now it was too late.

They were going home.

Four

'You have to make your mind up, Allie.' Jo sounded exasperated.

Allie turned to look at her in surprise. They sat beneath the spreading branches of the ancient yew tree in the church yard at Cimmeria. The setting sun had turned the sky a fiery red. It caught Jo's short, blonde hair and tinged it pink.

The colours reminded Allie of something but she couldn't place it.

'About what?' Allie asked.

'Sylvain,' Jo said. She leaned back against the tree trunk with a sigh. 'I feel so guilty. Like it was my fault you got into this.'

'Into what?' Allie was perplexed. 'I'm not in anything.'

'You're in a muddle,' Jo said, and her familiar cut-glass accent made Allie smile. 'You don't know what you want.'

Allie flinched. That was what Sylvain had said to her before she left Cimmeria.

Jo wasn't finished yet. 'You have to choose the one you love.'

'I know that.' Frustration made Allie's voice sharp.

Jo's eyebrows went up and Allie raised her hands in an apologetic gesture.

'Soz, Jo. It's just ... Let me try and explain.'

But how could she explain what she didn't understand? That she cared for two boys and didn't want to hurt either of them. That her relationships with both of them were loaded with the baggage of past mistakes.

That when your own family didn't seem to love you it was hard to love anyone else.

'I guess ... I wouldn't recognise true love if it walked up to me on the street and bit me on the leg. So how can I say I'm in love with Sylvain? Or I'm in love with Carter? I love them both. But I don't know what "in love" even is.'

Jo reached over and took her hand. Her fingers felt like nothing against Allie's skin. As insubstantial as a cloud.

'I can only tell you what I know,' Jo said. 'Love is I care about you. I trust you. I understand you. I want you near me. In love ...' Jo looked wistful, her gaze fixed on some point far away, just beneath the red sky. 'In love is: I would give up everything. Even myself. You, I can't live without.' She turned her wide blue eyes back to Allie; they were filled with tears that glistened like stars. 'Do you understand?'

The bedroom door flew open with a crash, flooding the room with light.

Startled, Allie scrambled back in bed, arms in front of her torso protectively.

Where am I?

'It's true. You're really back.' Zoe's flat, familiar voice steadied her.

Squinting into the glare, she could see the girl's small frame hovering in the doorway like a shadow.

Her gaze skittered around the room.

RESISTANCE

Desk, bookcase, whitewashed floor ... Cimmeria. My bedroom. Home.

It all came to her in a rush. Zoe was right. She really was here.

'Hi, Zoe,' she said, her voice hoarse with exhaustion. 'Long time no see.'

It had been after four in the morning when they'd finally reached the school. Allie had fallen asleep in the car, her head against Rachel's shoulder. Sylvain woke them both when the car stopped at the end of the drive.

Everything had felt dreamlike. The damp and chilly English night. The Victorian, gothic school building towering over them. It was all darker than she'd remembered. More intimidating.

Groggy, she'd blinked up at the school, wondering why no lights were on at all. No teachers came out to greet them.

They'd stumbled up the steps to the front door, but, before they could open the door, a guard had opened it from inside.

Where did he come from? Allie had wondered as the black-clad man stood back to let them pass.

They'd parted at the grand staircase, Sylvain heading to the boys' dorm, she and Rachel to the girls' rooms.

It was so quiet every footstep seemed to echo.

Even though it was the middle of the night, Allie couldn't help but feel disappointed that Isabelle le Fanult, Cimmeria's headmistress, hadn't come to greet them after so long away.

But when she'd walked into her old bedroom she found that someone had made up the bed with crisp, fresh sheets and turned back the duvet. A set of pyjamas with the Cimmeria crest had been left on the pillow. The desk lamp cast a warm glow over it all.

It was all she'd had time to notice before weariness took over. Stripping off her travel clothes, more appropriate to a warm night in the south of France than a cool English summer, she'd fallen into bed.

'You must have got back late,' Zoe said now. 'Isabelle told me to let you sleep but I had to see if it was true.' She looked to one side as if trying to remember something she was supposed to say. Then it came to her. 'Sorry.'

Zoe's odd verbal cadence and her lack of social skills were so familiar Allie felt a rush of affection for her as warm as sunlight.

'I don't want to sleep,' she said, pushing her hair out of her eyes. 'What time is it?'

'Nine,' Zoe said. 'It's Saturday so there are no classes. You missed breakfast. There's a meeting. Isabelle says you don't have to be there.' She paused blinking at Allie. 'You should be there.'

Nine o'clock. She'd only slept a few hours. But she was wide awake now.

'I have to get cleaned up,' she said. 'See you downstairs in ten minutes?'

'Hurry,' Zoe suggested, before flitting away like a bird.

Allie found her dressing gown in its usual place on the door hook, and dug her shower things out of one of the bags she'd dumped on the floor in the night.

The bathroom was halfway down the long corridor and she relished every step. Familiar wood floor. Familiar line of white bedroom doors, each with a familiar number in glossy black. Familiar bathroom with its familiar row of white sinks.

When she returned to her room after a hot shower, she put on the Cimmeria school uniform for the first time in months.

Short, pleated dark blue skirt, crisp, white button-down shirt, blue-and-white tie, knotted loosely at her throat.

Then she studied herself in the mirror – she looked like herself again.

She'd never been happier to wear such boring clothes.

Grabbing a dark blue blazer from the wardrobe, she threw it over her shoulders as she hurried out, slamming the door behind her.

The long corridor was quiet as she hurried to the staircase. Normally she'd expect to jostle against the shoulders of dozens of other girls as she walked downstairs, but this was empty, too.

She ran down to the landing where sunlight poured through broad windows, illuminating a row of marble statues and making the chandeliers sparkle.

Down the sweeping main staircase with its ornate, carved bannister, to the grand hallway, panelled in polished oak and lined with oil paintings in heavy frames, and the hidden, panelled door to Isabelle's office. Past the common room, strangely quiet.

She found Zoe near the entrance to the classroom wing, waiting impatiently at the base of a statue of a rotund, intimidating looking man with spectacles and a ludicrous wig.

'You took longer than ten minutes.' Zoe's tone was accusing. 'We have to hurry.'

Allie, who was used to her abruptness, didn't take offence. She swung into step beside her as they walked into the shadowy hush of the classroom wing.

'What kind of meeting is it?'

'The usual kind,' Zoe said.

'How have things been?' Allie asked. 'Here, I mean?'

'Like this.' Zoe gestured at the dark and empty hallway. 'Quiet. Weird. Wrong.'

Sylvain had already told her the school was down from two hundred and fifty students to fewer than forty. She should have been ready for the emptiness. But she wasn't. It all felt hollow.

This was just the start. Nathaniel was openly courting sympathetic members of the board; he regularly met with Members of Parliament.

He was getting ready to take over.

The thought made Allie's stomach feel tight. If he took over, everything would be lost.

'I'm glad you're back,' Zoe said. Although neither her voice nor her eyes betrayed any emotion, Allie knew she meant it.

'I'm glad to be here.'

The lights were off, but windows illuminated the staircase as they climbed two flights to the top floor, where small classrooms lined either side of the corridor.

Halfway down the hallway, Zoe shoved a door open without knocking. The low buzz of conversation inside ceased abruptly as they walked in.

The room was full of senior Night School students and teachers. As they all turned to see who it was, Allie hung back, suddenly shy.

'Allie's here,' Zoe announced.

There was a pause, then everyone rushed towards her at once. Isabelle reached her first.

'Zoe was supposed to let you sleep,' she said with a wry smile.

Allie was so happy to see her she forgot any hurt at a lack of welcome the night before.

'I wasn't tired.'

Isabelle pulled her into a tight hug. Allie inhaled the familiar scent of the headmistress' citrus-scented perfume.

She smelled like home.

'Welcome back, Allie,' Isabelle said.

Isabelle's dark blonde hair was neatly pulled back in a clip – it hadn't had time yet today to work its usual escape. Her cardigan, the colour of double cream, was soft beneath Allie's cheek.

Only when the headmistress released her did Allie notice the shadows under her tawny eyes; the delicate new lines worry had carved into her forehead. She looked exhausted.

'I need to talk to you about what happened,' Allie said. 'In France. How did Nathaniel—'

But then the other teachers surrounded them, pulling her away.

Isabelle caught her eye, 'Let's talk later.'

Allie couldn't understand why she hadn't already been debriefed. No one had sat her down to discuss what had happened in France. Why she'd been rushed home.

But she didn't have time to think about it as Eloise, the librarian, pulled her into a nervous, barely there hug that ended as quickly as it began. They'd been quite close before Allie had accused Eloise, wrongly, she now believed, of being Nathaniel's spy. Allie glanced at her, wondering how she could apologise for everything that had happened because of her allegation, but Eloise dodged her gaze.

Then Jerry, the science teacher, stepped between them and pumped her hand warmly. 'It's good to have you back.'

After he let go, he took off his wire-framed glasses and polished them with a cloth, smiling in his usual distracted manner as the others took turns welcoming her.

As she smiled and made appropriate comments, Allie scanned the room for Carter. She couldn't see him – but then, the teachers were all in the way.

'Allie!' An elfin girl with huge brown eyes and long, dark hair fought through the crowd to her side.

She pulled her close, strong arms tight around her neck. 'Welcome back!'

'Thanks, Nicole.' Allie grinned. 'It's good to be back.' She glanced down. 'How's your leg?'

'All better.' Nicole stood on one leg and bent the other, demonstrating its wellness. 'Ready to fight.'

The last time Allie saw Nicole was the night Nathaniel attacked the school. Nicole's leg had been broken in the melee.

'I heard what happened in France.' Nicole's French accent thickened as she lowered her voice. 'Thank God you're OK. Sylvain is very good on the bike, no?'

Nicole had grown up with Sylvain; they were as close as siblings. So Allie wasn't surprised she already knew the details.

At that moment, Sylvain walked across the classroom. Like her, he was back in his school uniform – gone were the elegantly loose shirts and chinos he'd worn in France. But he managed to look sexy anyway.

'Yeah,' Allie said, smiling at him. 'He's good on a bike.'

As he stepped up to join them, his eyes turquoise in the light, Allie thought of her dream. Jo's voice. '*Make up your mind.*'

For just a second, her smile faltered. She wished Dream Jo would mind her own business.

In France, she and Sylvain had grown closer as friends but nothing else had happened, in part because they were so rarely alone. Surrounded by a constant coterie of guards, his parents, their staff and Rachel, there was no way even to talk about things that mattered.

Yesterday had been their first real time alone. And Nathaniel ruined it.

'I thought Isabelle was going to let you sleep,' Sylvain said. The way he said it made it seem oddly intimate – like he was somehow *involved* with her sleep.

Allie blushed.

'Zoe …' she said, trying to recover her cool. 'She was my alarm clock.'

The way he arched one amused eyebrow made her think he knew why she'd blushed.

'If someone was going to wake you up,' he said, 'I'd rather it was me.'

Allie's blush deepened. She tried to think of a tart response but her brain wouldn't cooperate.

Looking back and forth between them, Nicole's lips curved up in a knowing smile. She'd been trying to get them together forever.

'Take your seats. We need to get this meeting under way.' Zelazny's voice was like a glass of cold water thrown over their conversation.

The history teacher stood at the front of the room, glowering at them over his clipboard.

Allie was surprised to find she was almost happy to see him. She remembered how he'd stood in front of the school's main door, overrun by Nathaniel's guards, trying to keep order even as the guards dragged students away against their will. Until that moment she'd really thought Zelazny might be Nathaniel's spy at the school. But when she'd seen how frightened he was – how furious – she'd decided it couldn't be him.

As Zelazny continued to complain and bluster, the small crowd began to settle until Allie could finally see the rest of the room. She looked around again for any sign of Carter.

He wasn't there.

She was trying to ignore the pang of disappointment she felt when she spotted a head of glossy, flame-coloured hair.

'Wait,' she said, leaning forward to get a better look. 'Is that … *Katie Gilmore*?'

Nicole nodded. 'Yes – she's been helping us. Her parents are friendly with Nathaniel so her knowledge of how he works has been very useful.'

Allie was stunned. Katie had never been included in senior meetings. She'd helped them out at the end of last year but … only a little.

This was the inner circle. These were the school's elite.

Katie wasn't even in Night School.

But there wasn't time to ask for more information. The room had quietened. Still puzzled, Allie sank into a seat at the back between Sylvain and Nicole as Zelazny yielded the floor to Isabelle.

The headmistress stood at the lectern, looking out at them with tired eyes.

'We've called this meeting to discuss renewed security issues. Now that Allie has returned,' she flickered a smile in Allie's direction, 'the security schedule will change. I'm sure we all are aware that, as soon as Nathaniel finds out she's here, he'll redouble his efforts. Therefore, we'll be enhancing patrols on the fence line and increasing security throughout the building. Effective immediately, there will be a guard in the girls' dorm wing every night, all night.'

Nobody else in the room seemed surprised by the news, so Allie tried not to show how taken aback she felt. There'd always been security at Cimmeria but the guards had kept their distance. The idea of stationing them in the dorm wing to watch the girls constantly was a bit creepy.

As if she knew Allie was thinking this, Isabelle glanced at her. 'The system of placing guards throughout the grounds in key locations has proven effective so we've expanded it. The communication system has also been enhanced—'

'Wait. You're still using it?' Allie was stunned. After Nathaniel hacked the system, she felt certain they would drop it.

'Much has changed here while you've been away, Allie,' Isabelle said. 'Raj has brought in a talented tech expert who's helping us learn to fight Nathaniel on his own level. I'll explain more later.' She turned her attention back to the group. 'Obviously, as per the revised Rules, the new patrol rota will not be put on paper. You'll be told your time and it's your—'

The classroom door opened suddenly. Isabelle's voice trailed off.

Turning to see who it was, Allie froze.

Carter stood in the doorway, staring at her with an expression of utter disbelief.

Five

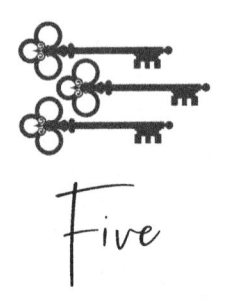

'Carter, you're late again,' Isabelle said with an unsurprised sigh. 'We've spoken about this. And we will speak of it once more, after this meeting. Take a seat.'

But he didn't seem to have heard her. He just stood in the doorway, eyes locked on Allie. He looked furious.

'*Now*, Carter.' Isabelle's voice sharpened.

Wrenching his gaze away, he slunk to a seat at the back of the room as far away from Allie as he could get.

As Allie watched him with increasing dismay, he sat stiffly, staring straight ahead.

He was thinner than she remembered – his cheekbones were too sharp, and his uniform seemed too big on him. His dark hair had grown long; a lock fell into his large, brown eyes and he left it there.

When it was clear he wasn't going to look at her again, she slowly turned back to the front, a worried frown creasing her forehead.

Something was terribly wrong.

It was a strange meeting, and soon Allie was too busy trying to figure out what was going on at the school to worry about Carter. Isabelle was right: much had changed at Cimmeria while she'd been gone.

Nathaniel was only mentioned once or twice and the events in France weren't discussed at all. Even the school's strictly-enforced Rules were no longer the same. The old Rules on electronics and communications equipment had been dropped and new Rules seemed to have been brought in helter-skelter. The guards were in charge. Students were tightly controlled and constantly watched.

The situation felt dangerous and futile. Everyone seemed afraid. Or, worse, resigned.

It was as if the fight was already over.

Why did they bring me back? Allie wondered with a rising sense of panic. *If all we're going to do is give up?*

She'd so longed to come back to Cimmeria – to see everyone again. She'd missed them all so much. But now that she was here nothing was as she'd left it. It didn't feel like the same place.

When the meeting ended, the other students gathered around her.

'Let's go outside,' Nicole said. 'It's nice out.'

'We could play football?' Zoe suggested.

Nicole wrinkled her nose. 'Sports are so boring.'

They settled down to bickering in a way that seemed so comfortable Allie got the feeling they must do it all the time. As they headed to the door, she hung back.

Carter was still in his seat. Isabelle stood over him, speaking in a low voice. He listened without apparent emotion. Neither of them seemed to notice Allie as she stood in the doorway watching them.

Feeling out of place, she hurried into the hall to where the others waited.

Warm summer sunshine streamed through the windows on the landing and they walked together down the stairs just like they used to – Nicole and Zoe chatting in animated tones about the patrol schedule, Sylvain laughing softly at something Zoe said – but it wasn't the same.

Nothing is the same.

Allie blew out her breath.

Nicole shot her a curious look and fell into step beside her.

'It must feel strange being back here again.'

Her voice echoed in the hollow stairwell.

'It's weird,' Allie admitted. 'So much has changed.'

Nicole nodded. 'It's very different now. Ever since the attack.'

'The security is *mental*,' Allie said. 'Is everyone cool with that? It's all very police statey. Which seems, like … not great.'

Nicole considered this. 'I suppose we didn't think we had much choice. Things got very dangerous. When things are dangerous you protect yourself.' She shrugged. 'It's natural.'

They were walking slowly, and Zoe and Sylvain disappeared around a corner ahead. Normally she'd hurry after them but today Allie wanted to take in the familiar beauty of the old school building. Its chandeliers and tall ceilings had always seemed so permanent. Solid.

Now, it all felt fragile.

The sweeping expanse of hallway was lined with old oil paintings in heavy frames showing Cimmeria at various phases in its history. The building grew and shrank, advanced and retreated, brightened and dimmed as they moved.

The school had always been here, she reminded herself. It would always survive.

It had to.

Just ahead of them, Zoe reappeared from around a corner and beckoned with short, impatient motions. 'What's taking you so long?'

Nicole and Allie hurried to where Zoe waited in the stone-floored entrance hall. Sylvain stood near the door talking to a guard. A stained glass window set high in the wall sent shards of gold and red flying across the room.

Nicole and Zoe headed for the front door and Allie began to follow them but Sylvain reached for her arm, pulling her back.

With an apologetic grimace, he said, 'I have to go. Zelazny wants me to meet with the guards for a full debrief.'

'Oh.' Allie tried to hide her disappointment. She felt so lost right now. She needed him or Rachel around to feel normal, and Rachel was nowhere to be seen. But she couldn't say that.

'No worries.' She gave a shrug to show how little she minded.

'I'll come find you later,' he promised.

As he turned back down the hallway, Zoe knocked on the dark wood of the front door. A guard in black opened it from outside. Through the doorway, Cimmeria's lush, green lawns beckoned.

'We'll stay in sight,' Zoe told the guard, then she dashed out into the sun.

Allie's eyebrows winged up.

Since when do we have to ask permission to go outside?

The guard stepped back to let them pass. His expression was pure icy professionalism but his gaze lingered on Allie's face a little too long and she realised he knew who she was. He'd probably talk about her later.

'*I saw her. The one Nathaniel wants ...*'

Forcing herself to pretend she hadn't noticed, she walked down the front steps with her head held high.

Outside, the smooth lawns sprawled in all directions before fading into dark forests. It was sunny but cool – nothing like the brutal heat in southern France – and Allie pulled her blazer tighter around her.

A few other students sat elsewhere on the lawn. At the far edge, some were kicking a ball around.

Nicole and Zoe chose a spot in full sunlight near a flower bed and stretched out on the soft grass. Allie sat down next to them feeling oddly foreign as they chattered about classes she hadn't been to and people whose names she didn't recognise.

'Has either of you seen Rachel?' she asked, when their conversation lulled. 'I haven't seen her since we got back.'

'She went home with her dad.' Nicole gave her a look that said she was surprised she didn't know this already. 'She'll be back tomorrow.'

Rachel hadn't seen her family in months – it made perfect sense. But Allie felt lonelier knowing she was gone.

The others didn't seem to notice her darkening mood. Nicole leaned back on her elbows. Zoe pulled up a blade of glass and blew on it, trying to make it whistle. It just sounded like loud air.

'I'm so happy to feel the *sun*.' Nicole tilted her head so the light fell on the delicate curves of her face, turning her fair skin to gold. 'All it's done for weeks is rain, rain, rain.'

'Did it?' Allie was surprised. 'It's been sunny every day in France.'

'Don't.' Laughing, Nicole held up her hand. 'I don't want to hear how glorious French summers are, I already know. English summers are so horrible. They shouldn't call them summers at all. It's a lie.'

Remembering something she'd meant to ask, Allie turned to Zoe, who was searching the lawn for more likely grass whistles. 'Hey. Why did you tell the guard we'd stay within sight?'

'New rules.' Zoe's tone was matter-of-fact. 'Guards have to know where students are at all times. Can't go into the forest without permission.'

Allie was stunned. Most of the grounds were forested. The students had always had freedom to roam wherever they wished.

'How's everyone taking that?' Looking around, for the first time she noticed all the students were staying on the grass. No one was wandering off down the many forest paths.

'It's OK.' Nicole shrugged and her dark hair shimmered in the light. 'You get used to it.' Opening her eyes, she glanced over at Allie. 'Now that we have some privacy, could you tell us where you've been?'

Allie was surprised. 'You don't know?'

The girls shook their heads.

'We know you ended up in France at Sylvain's place and that's where Nathaniel found you, but that's it,' Nicole said.

'No one would tell us anything,' Zoe's tone was accusing. 'You just disappeared. We came down to breakfast that day and you were just gone. Isabelle wouldn't say where you were. It was all top secret. Were you in France the whole time?'

'No,' Allie said. 'We kept moving.'

'Really?' Nicole's eyes reflected a mix of curiosity and envy. 'That must have been so exciting.'

Allie didn't really know how to explain what it had been like never to know where you were going. To be constantly taken places you hadn't chosen for yourself and knew nothing about. To be held in grand houses you couldn't leave. So she just told them the basics.

When Nathaniel kidnapped Rachel and attacked the school, a number of students were injured. It was clear the stakes had been raised. Nathaniel would stop at nothing in his effort to take control of the Orion Society – the secret organisation that effectively controlled much of the British government – from Allie's grandmother, Lucinda Meldrum, who had overseen it for years.

She wouldn't let go of her grip on power and he would use any weapon he could to hurt her. Cimmeria was one such weapon – Lucinda loved the school and was personally connected to it. Her family was another. He'd already convinced Allie's brother, Christopher, to join him. Now he wanted Allie, too. And he would do whatever it took to get her. Lucinda and Isabelle had decided she wasn't safe at Cimmeria any more – and that her presence endangered everyone there. So early one morning, she and Rachel climbed on to Lucinda's private jet and left, without a clue where they were going.

It turned out their first stop was Switzerland, where they were driven to the mountain estate of a Swiss billionaire who was an old family friend of Lucinda's. They'd been given separate, palatial suites but stayed in each other's rooms every night. Neither of them wanted to be alone. A nurse had come to see them every few days to change the dressings on their wounds; check their stitches.

After a few weeks, they'd been told to pack and they'd boarded the jet again. This time they'd ended up at a vast mansion in Croatia. There, they were greeted by stacks of homework and a letter from Isabelle telling them it was time to get to work.

Croatia had lasted only a couple of weeks.

When they'd been told to pack again, they hadn't actually minded. The big Croatian house had been oddly empty – no one lived there but them, the housekeepers and guards. It had echoed when they talked.

After that they'd spent a few weeks in Germany in a hyper-modern house as big as a hotel where the blinds shut by remote control and they'd never figured out how to make it work. The place after that was Sylvain's house.

'And then Nathaniel found us.' The memory of that hot afternoon – how close they'd come – made her stomach flip. 'If it wasn't for Sylvain—'

Zoe jumped to her feet, cutting Allie off. 'There's Lucas. I have to go.'

And just like that she was gone, darting across the lawn to where a group of students were warming up for a game of football.

Wounded, Allie stared after her.

'Am I that boring?' She kept her tone light but it did hurt a little.

'She's missed you,' Nicole said gently. 'And you know how she is with emotion. She doesn't know how to tell you what she feels.' She looked over to where Zoe was kicking a ball with unnecessary force. 'I think she's upset about what happened to you. It's … hard to tell.'

'I know.' Allie shrugged. 'I don't mind.'

But that wasn't true at all.

'So …' Nicole plucked a wild daisy with a long stem from the edge of the lawn. Then another. 'You and Sylvain …?'

She raised her eyebrows.

Heat flooded Allie's face and she hurried to find more daisies to add to Nicole's collection.

She thought about that moment in the sea just before the gunshots. She'd been certain he was about to kiss her. But he hadn't.

She handed Nicole a flower. 'Sylvain and I are *friends*.'

She emphasised the last word.

'Hmmm.' Nicole began braiding the daisy stems together, forming a fragile chain. 'It's good to be friends.'

Her tone was non-committal but Allie could tell she was disappointed.

Allie decided to switch the topic back to safer ground.

'So Nathaniel really hasn't tried anything here since I left?'

Nicole shook her head. 'Lucinda is fighting with him in London in meetings rather than here with knives but …' She looked at Allie, her dark eyes serious. 'I think she is not winning.'

Her words sent a chill through Allie.

If her grandmother lost, Nathaniel would take over the school and the entire organisation. Isabelle would go. Everyone who really cared about Allie would be gone. She'd have to leave the school. Or stay. And be part of Nathaniel's sickening plans.

'Enough sad talk.' Nicole said decisively. 'This is too depressing for your first day back. We will not lose today.'

Kneeling, she draped her daisy chain atop Allie's hair, a crown of flowers.

'There.' A satisfied smile brightened her perfect oval face. 'Now you look like a fairy princess. Queen Allie of Cimmeria Academy.'

She pretended to bow.

Allie was genuinely touched by this gesture.

'Thank you, French peasant.' She gave a regal wave. 'You may rise.'

Laughing, Nicole leaned back on her heels to study her. 'You look good in a crown.'

Someone called to her from the front steps and she climbed to her feet, shading her eyes with one hand as she peered towards the front door.

'It's Isabelle,' she said, glancing down to where Allie sat straightening her flower crown. 'I'll go see what she wants.'

'You have my permission,' Allie said, still playing queen. 'Sally forth and report back.'

As Nicole hurried off, though, she called after her: 'Tell Isabelle I need to talk to her.'

But neither Nicole nor Isabelle seemed to hear her.

The two disappeared inside the school building. The door closed, and the guard resumed his place outside it, staring out over the grounds intently.

Why didn't Isabelle want to see me? Is she too busy to talk about guns? And Nathaniel?

She leaned back on the grass, considering her options. She could run after them and insist that Isabelle explain what the hell was going on. She really could.

But she didn't move. There had to be a reason why Isabelle was making her wait.

Something must be going on.

The exhaustion of the last twenty-four hours caught up with her and, in the warm sun, her eyelids felt heavy. The soft grass tickled her bare legs. In the distance she could hear Lucas and Zoe shouting and kicking the ball. The faint buzzing of bees in the nearby flower beds formed a soothing backdrop.

Maybe she fell asleep for a while or perhaps no time passed but, suddenly, something blocked the sun. Allie blinked her eyes open to find Carter towering over her.

Six

'Carter ...? What?' She was instantly wide awake.

'I can't believe you,' he said. 'You bloody idiot. How could you be so stupid? Why the hell did you come back?'

'Hey!' Allie protested. 'I mean ... what?' She scrambled to her feet.

'You got away,' he said. 'You were free. And you *came back*? Why would you do that?'

He sounded both angry and genuinely baffled, as if she'd done something unbelievably stupid.

Allie bristled. 'You don't know what happened out there, Carter. I didn't have any choice. And whatever happened to hello and welcome back, anyway?'

He ignored that. 'Oh really?' His tone turned sardonic. 'Couldn't you have run away? I mean, that's your thing, right? Running away. Why don't you do it when it *matters*?'

That one stung.

Blood rose to Allie's cheeks. 'I came back because it wasn't safe out there,' she said. 'That's all. Not because I wanted ...' *to see you* '... to be here.'

This didn't placate him.

'Look around you, Allie.' He flung out his arm and the sweeping gesture took in the quiet grounds, the mostly empty school building, the muscular guards prowling the edges of the lawns. 'Do you feel safe now? Because you're not. Out there, at least you could run. Here, you're in a cage.'

Allie wanted to argue with him – to tell him how wrong he was. But hadn't she felt it all morning? And in that meeting? The insecurity. The futility of their resistance against Nathaniel. The guards watching their every move.

The fight went out of her.

'Look, Carter, all I've done for months is run.' She ran her fingers across her forehead, which was beginning to throb. 'And it wasn't any safer out there. Nathaniel found me. It was … bad.'

A flicker of surprise and concern lightened his eyes. So he didn't know what had happened.

And he cared.

'I don't know if I'm safe here or not,' she continued. 'I doubt it. I'm not safe anywhere. But neither are you. So maybe you should worry less about me and more about yourself. Seriously, Carter …' Her glance slid across his sharp cheekbones, and the tired circles under his eyes. 'What's the matter with you? You look like crap.'

Instantly, his expression hardened. He took a step back. 'What's the matter with me? Nothing. I'm just the only honest person you know. You've got grass in your hair.'

And with that baffling combination of statements he turned and walked away at a rapid pace, kicking at the ground.

As she watched him go, Allie reached up cautiously to touch her hair. Her fingers found the wilted daisy chain Nicole made for her earlier.

'It's not grass,' she said, although he was too far away to hear. 'It's a crown.'

By dinnertime, Allie had given up putting a bright face on things and was in full-on mope mood. Maybe she'd been away too long to just ... come back. It was as if, when she'd gone, life at Cimmeria had closed in behind her, filling whatever gap she might have left.

She walked into the dining room with hesitant steps. At first glance, everything was as it had always been – the room glowed with candles. The tables were set in the traditional way, with crystal glasses, heavy silver cutlery and white linen. But it was mostly empty now. The students easily fit at five round tables. The teachers and guards occupied four more.

In normal times, dinners at Cimmeria were lively affairs with a high, constant buzz of conversation and laughter. But the mood tonight was distinctly subdued. People did talk but it all lacked life and energy.

Spotting Nicole and Zoe with Lucas and Katie, Allie made her way to them.

'Hi, Allie.' Katie smiled at her as if they were old friends. 'Welcome back.'

'Hi,' Allie mumbled without enthusiasm. Katie's smile faded.

An uncomfortable silence fell. Zoe looked from Katie to Allie, frowning.

'Katie's been helping us,' she announced, in a tone that said Allie was being unreasonable. 'She's our friend now.'

Everyone was looking at Allie, waiting for her to say something diplomatic or friendly. She couldn't do it. She knew she was being childish but she couldn't seem to stop. It was as if Katie, of all people, had replaced her in the group.

She fixed the redhead with a cold stare. 'Awesome.'

Colour rising in her cheeks, Katie turned to Lucas and asked a random question about course work in a clear attempt to change the subject.

Lucas shot Allie a disapproving look before answering.

Zoe looked like she wanted to say something else but Nicole rested a hand on her arm and shook her head.

No one talked to Allie after that.

At seven o'clock precisely, Carter and Sylvain walked into the dining room together with Zelazny, who closed the doors behind them.

Sylvain slipped into the empty seat next to Allie, who studiously avoided Carter's gaze.

Seeing her expression, Sylvain leaned close to her. 'Are you OK?'

Allie's lower lip trembled but she just shook her head. She didn't trust herself to speak.

Because Carter was right: she wanted to run away. Only there was nowhere to go.

As soon as dinner ended, Allie made a beeline for the door. She was half-running down the main hallway when Sylvain caught up with her.

Taking her by the hand, he pulled her with him into the shadows under the swooping curve of the grand staircase near Isabelle's office.

'Allie …' he said as soon as they were out of sight. '*Dîtes moi*. What's the matter? You hardly said a word at dinner. You hardly ate. You seem so sad. Did something happen?'

He searched her face as if looking for clues.

Allie dropped her gaze. She couldn't really tell him about Carter because there had always been so much tension between the two of them, and if she explained about Katie it would sound petty. In fact, now that she thought about it, it all suddenly seemed ridiculous and overly emotional anyway.

'I'm sorry.' She sighed, pushing her hair back out of her face. 'I'm just feeling sorry for myself. Nothing is the way I expected and everyone …' She stopped and shook her head. 'I'll be fine. I'm just tired.'

He was standing so close to her she could feel the warmth of his body. It was hard to feel self-pitying when he was looking at her like that.

'You're sure?' he said. 'No one said anything to hurt you?'

Allie gave a wan smile.

'No,' she said. 'I'm being an idiot. I guess I just miss … France. Your place. The way things were. Everything's so … I don't know. Complicated here.'

Sylvain stepped closer; his legs pressed against hers. Now Allie could smell the faint scent of his sandalwood cologne. Feel his breath on her cheeks.

She looked up at him questioningly.

With light fingers, he picked up a loose strand of her hair from the top of her shoulder and let it run through his fingers like silk. Goosebumps sprang up on Allie's arms and shoulders.

'There's something that will cheer you up,' he said. His voice, low and accented, made her shiver. 'It's a surprise. But there's something I have to do first. Meet me outside the back door in half an hour?'

Excited curiosity ran through her. At this moment she wanted nothing more than a distraction.

'I'll be there.'

After Sylvain left, Allie didn't really know what to do with herself. She walked down the grand hallway as far as the library door, then turned and paced back again.

There was no doubt what he had in mind involved kissing. Taking everything to the next step.

And that was fine, right? After all, she was attracted to him. And Carter was obviously not an issue. He'd been a lot of things today, but romantic wasn't one of them.

Why did that matter so much?

She longed to discuss it all with Rachel. She'd know what to do.

'Hey, Allie.' Katie's familiar Chelsea accent stopped her outside the common room. Turning, she saw the redhead hurrying towards her, blue pleated skirt flaring around her perfect legs.

Oh good, Allie thought, despairing.

She braced herself for Katie's wall of sarcasm. But it didn't happen.

Instead, the other girl seemed almost nervous. She kept toying with a delicate gold bracelet that dangled from her slim wrist. The light from the chandelier above them glinted off her hair, making it sparkle like fine strands of copper. Her skin was poreless.

'This is going to sound odd,' Katie began. 'But I just wanted to say I'm glad you're back. And ... I know you don't like me and I don't blame you. I've been a total bitch. I'm sorry ... kind of.' She stopped playing with her bracelet and looked up at Allie with the sharp green eyes of a pedigree cat. 'You were a bitch to me too, you know.'

Briefly, Allie considered defending herself. But she changed her mind. What Katie was saying was true. She gave as good as she got.

'Anyway,' Katie continued, 'then Nathaniel happened and you were like some kind of superhero. I don't know if I ever told you that I thought it was amazing what you and the others did. I don't know how you're so brave. I just ...' She bit her lip. 'I just know that I'm not. Brave, I mean.'

Allie was flabbergasted. Whatever she'd expected Katie to say it wasn't this.

'And now ... the thing is ... I don't want to be your enemy,' Katie said. 'I think we have enough of those right now. So, I'd like to declare a truce. With you. For a while, at least.' She paused before adding, 'When it's all over we can go back to despising each other if you'd like.'

'You want ... You ... To be ... friends?' Allie found it hard to say words that made any sense.

'I know, right?' A rueful half-smile touched Katie's lips. '*Quel* oddity. But you did save the school. And I'm not a complete cretin. Besides, I mostly hated you because of Sylvain anyway. And I'm over him now.'

She smoothed the lines of her skirt with a demure sweep of her hands.

'Is this for real?' Allie finally recovered the power of speech. 'You seriously want a truce?'

'I seriously do.' Katie held her gaze. 'This is not a game. What do you think?'

This was huge. Allie and Katie had hated each other from the first time they met. Katie had been so vicious, so cruel. Allie wondered if it was possible to put that behind her. To try again. But Katie had helped them when Nathaniel came for the students. And everyone else seemed to have forgiven her.

The least she could do was give it a shot.

'OK,' she said after a long pause. 'Truce. But it's weird.'

'Isn't it?' Katie's lips curved up. 'Welcome to the new normal. It's all messed up.'

'Katie! Over here.'

They both looked up to see Lucas waving from across the common room.

Most of the remaining students seemed to be in there, but the room still felt wrong. On a normal night in the old days, it would be packed at this hour. The sprawling space with its tall bookshelves stacked with games and books looked the same, but its leather chairs and sofas were mostly empty. The baby grand piano in the corner sat silent.

Katie waved back at him. 'I should go.' She tilted her head to one side. 'I'm really glad we sorted this out. I think I'll like not fighting with you.'

Without waiting for a reply, she turned and sashayed across the room. From the doorway, Allie watched her walk to where Lucas sat on a sofa. He welcomed her with a jovial insult but Allie didn't miss the way his eyes skated approvingly across her figure.

A frown creased her brow. Lucas was Rachel's boyfriend. Katie and Lucas weren't exactly cuddled up together but they looked awfully cosy.

Something drew her glance to the back of the room. In a dim corner, Carter sat alone in a deep leather chair. A heavy book was open in his lap and he was reading it intently .

A lock of dark hair had fallen forward into his eyes but he didn't seem aware of it. His long legs were stretched out in front of him. He looked older than she remembered. More grown-up.

She wondered if she looked older now, too.

She wished they could just be friends without all this ... *stuff* between them. One of them was always mad at the other one. They were always finding reasons to be upset with each other. While she'd been away she'd missed him more than she'd expected to, and it threw her into confusion. Lying by the pool pretending to study, she'd find herself wondering what he was doing. If he missed her at all.

But Sylvain's constant, attentive presence had made it hard to know how she felt.

Now, with both of them around, things weren't getting any clearer.

Seven

When Allie reached the back door, a dark-haired female guard with a torch attached to her utility belt like a handgun opened it for her before she asked.

'Uh … thanks,' she said, trying not to sound as weirded out by all of this new security as she was.

The guard gave an officious nod and closed the door.

Outside, the sky was cobalt, just beginning to blacken at the edges. A cool breeze lifted her hair.

A few feet away, his hands shoved in his pockets, Sylvain paced the stone walkway. As soon as he saw her, he brightened.

'There you are. Let's go. We have to hurry.'

Allie squinted at him suspiciously. 'Why? Where are we going?'

His lips quirked up.

'I knew you'd hate this part.' He held out his hand. 'Come on. I promise it's OK. It's just a surprise. A *good* surprise.'

She'd never seen him more excited. He was practically hopping up and down with it.

His mood was contagious. Putting thoughts of unfixable Carter and miserable Cimmeria from her mind, Allie took his hand.

'This way,' he said, pointing to the right.

The footpath curved away from the terraced gardens behind the school to the edge of the forest. If you followed it far enough, Allie knew it would bring you to the walled garden. From there you could follow it up the hill to the castle ruins. But Sylvain turned off the path early, into the trees.

'I thought we couldn't go into the woods?' she said.

He gave a mysterious smile. 'I have permission.'

It was darker now – the last of the light had disappeared from the sky. As they moved further into the forest he laced his fingers through hers.

Allie could not figure out where he was taking her. She knew there was nothing ahead of them but forest. The whole thing didn't make any sense.

'Seriously, Sylvain. This is crazy. Where are we going?'

Her impatience seemed to amuse him; he stifled a grin. 'Trust me.'

Just when she was about to demand information, a ghostly glow appeared ahead of them, and suddenly she knew where they were going: The folly.

But why?

Then they stepped through the trees into a clearing and the night lit up.

Allie stopped in her tracks.

Dropping her hand, Sylvain stepped back to watch her reaction.

The folly was a fanciful little structure that served no real purpose – nothing more than a gazebo made of marble with a domed roof, it was intended only to be pretty. A pleasant surprise for Victorians out for a stroll. Inside was a statue of a woman, caught in the middle of a dance.

Tonight it had all been draped in fairy lights. Every piece of marble was enrobed in their sparkling glow. Even the dancing girl held strands of lights in her raised hand like an illuminated veil.

Four steps led up to the statue. And something had been left at the top of the stairs.

Allie turned to Sylvain. In the glow of the lights she could see the anticipation in his eyes.

'Go ahead,' he urged her.

Hesitantly, she walked closer to the folly until she could see what it was.

A cake sat at the dancer's feet, surrounded by candles that flickered in the breeze.

'Oh …' Allie pressed her fingers against her lips.

'There are seventeen candles.' Sylvain had joined her at the foot of the steps. She blinked up at him in stunned amazement. 'Happy birthday.'

Allie was struck speechless. In all the chaos, she'd completely forgotten today was her birthday.

But Sylvain remembered.

Tears burned her eyes, blurring the scene.

It had been so long since anyone gave her a birthday cake. It had to be before Christopher ran away. Last year she'd spent her birthday night out with Mark and Harry in London tagging buildings along a train line.

Mark had painted 'Happy Bloody Birthday, Allie!' on a wall. And that was that.

'I …' Her voice was unsteady, so she stopped talking.

It would have taken Sylvain ages to string all those lights. And the candles. They were the kind they had on the tables in the dining hall – he must have gone back after dinner and sneaked them out.

She turned to him to say something – *anything* – that could convey how much this meant to her, but there weren't words for that. Not any that she knew. So she reached up and pulled his mouth down to hers.

His lips were gentle against hers, questioning. Teasing the corners of her mouth until her lips parted and she could taste him.

She stood on her toes, stretching up to twine her wrists behind his neck, deepening the kiss, demanding more.

She'd wanted to do this ever since she saw him standing on the steps of the house that first day in France with the sky in his eyes.

This had to be right, she told herself. There was no way she couldn't choose Sylvain now. Not after this. It felt right.

Tangling her fingers in the soft curls of his hair, she leaned into him, letting him bear her weight.

Instantly, his arms tightened around her. Supporting her.

For the first time in a long while, Allie thought maybe she was making the right decision.

'It's my dream cake. Chocolate with extra chocolate, sprinkled with chocolate.' Licking icing from her fingers, Allie looked up at Sylvain in the twinkling light. 'Amazing.'

They sat together at the foot of the dancing statue. His arm was draped lightly around her waist and she was snug in the warmth of his body.

'I'm sorry I forgot to bring forks. We have to eat like savages.'

His curious phrasing made her giggle.

'I'm totally cool with being a savage.' She broke off another chunk of cake. 'Tell me again how you got the cake on the plane?'

He bent his head to drop a light kiss on her shoulder. 'Even though we had to leave, Lourdes was determined you should have your birthday cake. So she packed it in a box, which we hid in a suitcase. I had the guards put it in the luggage hold in a place where nothing could damage it.'

Lourdes was the Cassel family cook. The first time she'd met Allie she'd tutted: '*Tu es trop mince.*' (You are too thin.) From then on she was always slipping Allie food – fresh baguettes spread with soft cheese; flaky croissants slathered in jam; vividly coloured macaroons and *langue de chat* biscuits dipped in dark chocolate, which were her favourites.

'Oh, I miss her.' Allie sighed, wistfully. 'I miss France.'

Sylvain's smile faded; his eyes grew more serious. 'We will go back.'

'I hope so.'

The mood had grown sombre and, noticing this, Sylvain cleared his throat and gave a mysterious smile.

'There's one more surprise …'

Reaching into the shadows behind the statue, he pulled out a small box tied with silver ribbon.

'A *present*?' Allie beamed at him. She wiped the sticky icing off her fingers before holding out her hands. 'I can't believe you got me a present.'

He seemed to find her question absurd. '*Bien sûr*. It's your birthday.'

Allie loved it when he spoke French.

The ribbon was made of heavy silk. She pulled at the end and it unfurled, revealing a blue jewellery box.

Her heart fluttered. She was suddenly nervous. No boy had ever given her jewellery before.

The box opened with an expensive creak.

'Oh, Sylvain ...' she breathed.

Inside, a delicate chain of white gold glittered . The chain held two pendants – one a key, ornately designed with swirls and flourishes, the other, an old-fashioned lock, each no bigger than her thumbprint.

Allie couldn't seem to move as Sylvain lifted the necklace from the little pins that held it in place on a satin cushion.

'I had this made for you.' Gently, he moved her hair out of the way so he could place the necklace around her throat. The metal was cool against her skin. 'It is how I feel about you. The secrets in your life ... I want to give you a key to all of them. Unlock them for you. So you can be free.'

Leaning over, he kissed the bare nape of her neck above the collar of her blouse. She quivered at the touch.

Then she turned round until she sat on his lap, legs on either side of his waist. His hands were firm against the small of her back, holding her steady.

She reached up to cup his face in her hands. In the fairy light, his eyes sparkled like sapphires.

She felt a tear trace a soft path down her cheek. 'It's the most beautiful thing anyone has ever given to me. I will love it forever. Thank you.'

'You deserve to have all the jewellery,' he whispered. 'Allie, I want you to have everything.'

Then she pulled his lips down to hers.

Eight

Walking down to breakfast the next morning, Allie couldn't stop smiling. The lock and key necklace nestled against the base of her throat, a constant reminder of last night. The memory of the way she'd kissed Sylvain made her cheeks burn.

In the dining hall, the new air of gloom that she'd begun to associate with Cimmeria hung over the room so tangibly she could almost see it. Allie couldn't face another day like yesterday. Besides, her heart was buoyant. She was filled with joy. Overflowing with love for the universe. So Isabelle had never asked to see her. So she had no idea what was going on, school was depressing and the world was going to hell in a handcart.

Right now she was happy.

The smell of food made her ravenous, and she piled her plate and made a cup of milky tea before going to where Nicole and Zoe were talking quietly with Lucas and Katie.

'I just want to eat all the food,' she said, sitting down. 'Don't judge me.'

Zoe eyed her with mild interest. 'You can eat all you want. You're ectomorphic.'

Her fork already in the air, Allie stopped. 'Wait, doesn't that mean I wear my skeleton on the outside?'

Zoe rolled her eyes. 'That's *exoskeletal*. Ectomorphic means you have a metabolism that tends not to gain weight.'

'Watch me,' Allie said, diving into her eggs. 'I will prove you wrong.'

Once she'd devoured her breakfast she looked around the group. 'So what's on the agenda today? Anything fun?'

The others exchanged blank looks.

'There's nothing to do any more,' Zoe explained slowly, as if Allie was very stupid. 'I told you that.'

Allie made a face. 'That doesn't mean we can't have fun, Zoe.'

Zoe opened her mouth to argue but at that moment Isabelle walked up, neatly clad in a blue skirt and white blouse, a pale yellow cardigan draped loosely across her shoulders.

'Hello, Allie. Could you come with me?'

She'd waited so long for this moment; Allie jumped to her feet and rushed after the headmistress without even saying goodbye to the others.

At last, she thought.

'I'm so sorry I didn't have a chance to meet with you yesterday,' Isabelle said as she walked with brisk steps out of the bright dining hall into the dim coolness of the hallway. 'It was the most hectic day.'

Allie could not imagine what would keep Isabelle so busy she couldn't debrief her about an attack that had made Lucinda change her entire security plan. But she kept her expression steady. She needed to find information. Not get in an argument.

'I wanted to find out how you're settling in,' Isabelle continued. 'Merging back into Cimmeria after time away can be difficult, I know.'

This time Allie couldn't control her sarcasm.

'Especially during an apocalypse?'

The comment didn't seem to bother the headmistress, who pulled a key from her pocket and unlocked a door beautifully hidden in the nineteenth-century carved oak panelling.

'Well,' she said. 'Quite.'

She switched on a light, illuminating the small, windowless office.

Allie looked around hungrily. A large, mahogany desk dominated one side of the room. The wall across from it held a fanciful antique tapestry of a maiden and a knight.

Everything seemed to be right where it had been before she left. At least this room had stayed the same – a familiar oasis amid Cimmeria's chaos..

'Yeah, well.' Allie dropped without ceremony into one of the leather chairs facing the desk. 'Sucks trying to make friends at the end of the world.'

'You already have friends,' Isabelle observed mildly. 'Tea?'

'No, thank you,' Allie said. Isabelle switched on the kettle anyway.

Soon the brewing Earl Grey tea filled the room with a flowery bergamot steam.

'Is Rachel coming back tomorrow?' Allie asked.

'Of course. You both have classes in the morning.'

Relieved, Allie sagged back in her chair. She missed Rachel like a lost appendage.

Isabelle sat at her desk, setting a mug down in front of her. 'Sylvain and the guards have briefed me on everything that happened in France. The attackers work for Nathaniel, of course, although we are still working out some of the details.'

'Who else?' Allie said. 'The question is, how did he find me?'

'I'll get to that in a minute.' Isabelle sipped her tea and studied Allie as if looking for clues. 'They shot at you.'

'Yeah,' Allie held her gaze. 'It was not good. Sylvain saved our arses.'

'And since then?' Isabelle asked.

Allie looked at her doubtfully. 'Since then … what?'

'Are you sleeping? Having nightmares? Panic attacks?'

Allie, who had suffered from all of those problems in the past, flushed. This wasn't what she wanted to talk about. They had, in the past, had very frank conversations about Allie's life. But it was hard to just plunge back into that kind of thing.

'I'm fine.' Allie's tone was cool. 'I've been through worse. I just want to know what's going on with Nathaniel. How he found me. Who the spy is. What we do now.'

'Yes, I'm going to get to that.' The headmistress sipped her tea, a worry line deepening between her eyes. 'But I'm also concerned about what all this is doing to you. You've been through a great deal.'

Allie thought about last night. Kissing Sylvain. The confusing but good swirl of emotions that had summoned. And how, for just a little while, she'd forgotten all of this.

'I'm really OK,' she said honestly. 'I don't know why I'm OK. But I'm OK.'

Isabelle studied her face as if looking for clues, then took a sip of her tea. 'Good. That's the most important thing. If you're fine …'

'I am,' Allie insisted.

The headmistress inclined her head. 'Then we can talk about where we are. What would you like to know?'

Allie didn't hesitate.

'I want to know how Nathaniel found us in France. And I really want to know how safe I am at Cimmeria. Because when those guys were shooting at me I decided I don't want to die.'

A normal headmistress might have found this impertinent. But Isabelle wasn't normal.

'We think it was a coincidence. Nathaniel must have been watching Sylvain's house for some time,' she said. 'There is no other way. Certainly it didn't come from inside this school. It couldn't have. Not one person aside from myself, Lucinda and Raj has known where you were at any point since you left the school in March.'

'Not even the teachers?' Allie asked, surprised. Usually Isabelle's close cadre of senior teachers were told everything.

Isabelle shook her head. 'Not one person,' she repeated.

Allie sat back in her chair.

The idea of Nathaniel just hanging around the Cassels' house, watching Sylvain's family, was ominous.

'Why would he watch them if he didn't know I was there?' she asked. 'What was he looking for?'

'The Cassels support Lucinda. And they are the single most powerful family within the European organisation.' Isabelle's face darkened. 'It appears Nathaniel is broadening his range.'

This was starting to make Allie nervous. 'But if he's watching them he must have a purpose. Are they safe?'

'You've seen the Cassels' security team,' Isabelle said. 'They're extremely well protected.'

Allie remembered the guards standing on ladders to see over the tall walls that surrounded the Cassels' compound, binoculars fixed on the surrounding countryside. The cameras atop the tall solid gates. The razor wire and armoured SUVs.

'Yeah, but …' Allie left the sentence unfinished.

… Nathaniel still found us.

She may not have said it aloud but Isabelle seemed to know what she was thinking.

'They are as safe as it is possible to be right now,' she said gently. 'That much I can promise you.'

'And us?' Allie held her gaze. 'Are we safe?'

Isabelle didn't respond immediately. She drummed her fingers very quietly on her desktop as if deciding what to say.

'I wish I could say yes,' she said finally. 'But I'm afraid the answer is no. You're not. No one here is safe.'

This, Allie hadn't expected.

'If I'm not safe, why am I here? Why bring me back?' Allie couldn't keep the bewilderment out of her voice.

Isabelle gave her a steady look. 'You're here because Lucinda wants you here.'

'Why, though?' Allie asked, her voice rising. 'Why does she want me here?'

Again the headmistress hesitated. 'You'll have noticed we are more … security-conscious now. Things are very tense between Lucinda and Nathaniel. Allie …' She leaned forward, her tawny eyes urgent. 'We're nearing endgame on this. She needs you close.'

Allie thought of Nicole's sombre words. '*I think she is not winning.*'

Her stomach tightened.

'Isabelle,' she asked quietly, 'is she losing this thing?'

There was a long pause before the headmistress replied. 'Perhaps.'

Silence fell. Allie could hear footsteps passing in the hallway outside the door. Someone talking loudly in the distance. A door closing with a hollow thud.

'What happens if we lose?' She could hardly bring herself to say the words. Losing was an eventuality she'd only rarely allowed herself to contemplate, much less discuss. 'What becomes of me and you and' – she swung out her arm in a gesture that took in the grand gothic building around them – 'everyone?'

'That is still to be decided,' the headmistress said briskly. 'We have options. There are ways to finesse this situation and we are looking at all of them but, for now, the fight is still under way and we have to keep our focus on that. It is still possible to win.' She shifted in her seat, leaning forward into the glow of the desk lamp. It highlighted the dark smudges under her eyes. 'I said you weren't safe here because that's the truth, and I never intend to lie to you. You've been lied to enough. But it is also true that you would be much less safe out there. Here, at least, we can do more to protect you. And you can help us.'

'Help with what?' Allie asked, a hint of suspicion in her tone.

Isabelle held her gaze. 'We haven't found the person working for Nathaniel. But we're close.' She paused. 'Very close. We think your presence here could help us … escalate things.' Her tone was cold. 'Because we have to find this person. And we have to stop them.'

Finally, Allie understood why she was back.

For months they'd struggled to figure out who was betraying them. Someone among them was feeding Nathaniel a constant stream of damaging information. This person had helped him try to burn the school down. Let in his henchman, Gabe, who'd killed Ruth and Jo. They would all have given anything to identify the spy and destroy him. But for months they'd tried and failed. And it had cost them dearly.

She straightened her spine. 'What do you need me to do?'

'First,' Isabelle held up a cautioning hand, 'you should know where things stand. While you were away we eliminated all the guards from the list of possibles.'

Stunned, Allie stared at her. 'How? Are you certain?'

The list of suspects had long included a core group of senior guards and the top Night School instructors. Every time they'd tried to narrow down that list, they'd been stymied. The students had all hoped the spy was a guard – someone they didn't really know. Because otherwise it meant that one of their mentors had betrayed them. And that thought was unbearable.

'It was Raj's plan,' Isabelle said. 'He removed all the guards under suspicion from the school while running a thorough background check. At the same time, he planted false information with the senior teachers about your whereabouts. That information made it to Nathaniel, who acted on it, sending a raid party to an empty house in Spain.'

'So ... one of the teachers ...' Allie couldn't seem to complete the sentence.

'One of our three most trusted teachers passed the false information to Nathaniel.' Isabelle's voice was taut. 'Yes. Thinking you would be there. Yes. Knowing Nathaniel might kill you.' She held her gaze. 'Yes.'

Allie cleared her throat, which had suddenly closed. 'So ... it's Eloise, Jerry or Zelazny, then.'

'Yes.'

Allie felt loss. There'd been a time when she would have trusted any of those teachers with her life.

'What do we do now?' Her voice was low.

'Now,' Isabelle said, 'we must be very careful. We believe that, with tensions being what they are, your return will mean the spy will need to communicate constantly with Nathaniel. This will make it more likely they make mistakes.' She leaned back in the shadows; Allie couldn't see her eyes any more. 'When they do, we'll be ready.'

Nine

'I'm back.' Rachel shoved Allie's door open without knocking. 'Did you miss me?'

'Rach!' Leaping off the bed, Allie ran to her, nearly knocking her down. It was late Sunday afternoon. All the things that had happened bubbled inside her until she thought she might explode. 'Never leave me alone again. Swear it.'

'Can I have loo breaks?' Rachel laughed.

'No.' Allie's reply was emphatic.

'Well, that's going to get awkward.' Dropping down on Allie's bed, Rachel looked around the room. 'Can you believe we're here? How was it this weekend?'

Allie's reply was prompt. 'Horrible. And awesome.'

Rachel grinned. 'It's all *and* nothing with you, Allie. Right. Tell me everything. I've been home all weekend eating Mum's food. I've never been fatter or happier so I think I'm strong enough to know it all.'

Sitting in the desk chair, Allie propped her bare feet up on the bed next to Rachel and ticked the weekend's events off on her fingers. 'Everyone is totally depressed. The guards are weird. Sylvain gave me cake and we made out. Carter is angry.'

Rachel focused on the big news first.

'You finally made out with Sylvain? At bloody last.' She sagged back in mock-relief. 'I was so tired of you two circling each other like a couple of hungry lions when we were in France. I thought you'd never get on with it.'

Allie threw a pillow at her. 'You make us sound so obvious.'

'You *were* so obvious.' Rachel grinned, tucking the pillow behind her. 'Look, I'm really glad for you. I came around to Sylvain, you know, after he saved your life, like, four times. I think he's a good guy. I also think he's totally, head-over-heels, crazy in love with you.'

Allie blushed. 'For my birthday … he gave me this.' She lifted the pendant up to show her. It caught the light and flashed.

Leaning forward to look at it, Rachel made all the right admiring noises. 'That is so beautiful. And so you.'

'I love it.' Allie ran her thumb gently across the warm metal before letting it drop back against her skin.

'I can't believe I wasn't here for your birthday,' Rachel said with sudden contrition. 'Dad dragged me out of bed at stupid o'clock. He wouldn't let me wake you. You know what he's like.'

Allie, who did know what Raj Patel was like, thought about telling her how bad the day had been. But she knew it would only make her feel worse.

'It's cool.' She shrugged. 'I got through it somehow.'

'With the help of a certain hot French guy.' Rachel shot her a knowing look. 'Now, I might not have blue eyes and a sexy accent but I did get you a present. Belated-style.' She pulled a box wrapped in pink paper from inside her school blazer and held it out.

Allie grinned at her. 'I love it already,' she said. 'As I love all presents.'

It sloshed as she tore open the paper to reveal a silvery box. It held a heavy crystal perfume bottle that glittered in the light when Allie held it up.

'Oh my God. Is this that perfume I kept nicking at your house that time I came to visit?'

Rachel nodded. 'My mum and I went out to get it yesterday.'

Allie was touched.

'I can't believe you remembered I liked it.' She pulled her friend into a rough hug. 'You old softie. Thank you.'

'Yeah, well. I was going to give you a book but I knew better,' Rachel explained.

Allie spritzed perfume on her wrist and inhaled deeply. It smelled like honeysuckle. 'Yay. I'm safe from words.'

Stretching out her legs, Rachel arranged herself comfortably on Allie's bed. 'Tell me everything that happened. Up to and including kissing. Don't skimp on the dirty details.'

Allie filled her in on her birthday, making it all sound as funny and romantic as possible.

When she finished, Rachel sighed happily. 'That's so wonderful. The cake, the candles ... Sylvain really knows how to do things right.' She cocked her head. 'Not to clash boy topics in an awkward way but ... what about Carter? You said something about him being sad?'

Allie thought of Carter's brooding face. A little light seemed to leave the room.

'He's a mess,' she said. 'He shouted at me for coming back. Like I had an alternative. Like this was all my idea. And he's just thin and ... I don't know. Sad. Not good.'

Rachel's frown was thoughtful. 'Dad mentioned something about Carter having a hard time because of what happened with Jules … and you.'

'Me?' Allie looked up at her in surprise. 'What about me?'

The night before she and Rachel left the school they'd all fought Nathaniel's guards together. Nothing that happened had been Carter's fault. No one could have stopped it. No one except Nathaniel.

Rachel hesitated. 'Something about how he didn't protect you that last night with Nathaniel. And Jules got taken. Dad said he blames himself for everything. No one can get through to him.'

Allie was speechless. Suddenly it all made an awful kind of sense; she could see it all through Carter's eyes.

Carter's girlfriend, Jules, was taken from the school by Nathaniel because Carter got there too late. He couldn't protect Allie during the fight with Gabe and Nathaniel because he was injured. So she ended up cut and bleeding. Then she disappeared.

She and Carter were so much alike. Like her, he had such a sense of responsibility about everything – and keeping everyone safe. He always seemed to think he had to save everyone. Of *course* he blamed himself right now. Super Carter let Jules down. Let Allie down. Let everyone down.

And I didn't help, did I? she thought. *I wasn't here for him after everything happened. Instead I just jetted off with Rachel, leaving him alone with the fallout.*

Guilt unfurled inside her chest.

'Carter wouldn't tell your dad everything,' she said. 'We should find out if there's more to it. Maybe you could ask Lucas?'

As soon as she said the name, though, the mood in the room changed. Rachel tensed and looked away, drumming her fingers anxiously.

'Look, there's something I need to tell you about Lucas. I should have said it before but …' Stopping, Rachel cleared her throat.

Allie frowned at her, puzzled. 'What is it?'

'I did a lot of thinking while we were away,' Rachel said. 'And I decided we weren't right together, Lucas and me. We're breaking up.'

Allie was blindsided.

She'd known Lucas and Rachel were having problems but she hadn't realised it was so serious.

'Is it Katie?' she asked, her voice low and ominous. 'If she cheated with him I'll…'

'No, Allie.' Rachel cut her off. 'Seriously. It's me. Well, it's us.'

She was still avoiding her eyes; Allie wished Rachel would just look at her. It was like she was hiding something.

'What happened?' Allie's voice was so low she was almost whispering. The atmosphere in the room had grown heavy. 'Don't you like him any more?'

Rachel fidgeted with the blue blanket folded at the end of the bed. 'I do like him. He's a great guy, and he was my first real boyfriend but …'

She twisted the blanket harder.

'I guess,' she continued, 'with him, I didn't feel the way I thought I should. I didn't miss him very much while we were gone. And I don't think he missed me either.' At last she met Allie's gaze. 'Sometimes you have to be away from someone to know you don't want to be with them.'

Allie thought about how happy she'd been to see Sylvain that day in France. How much she'd missed Carter. For the first time it made sense that Rachel hadn't stuck around to see Lucas after they'd returned to the school.

Still, there had to be more to it – Rachel's nervousness was out of character.

'Are you … super sad?' She phrased her words cautiously.

The other girl shook her head. 'No. Not like you were when you and Carter broke up. Mostly it feels weird. Like I'd got used to having him there and now he's not.' She waved a hand in the air next to her. 'Like there should be a Lucas-shaped figure here and there isn't. But I'm not crying.'

Not crying? How can she not be crying?

When Allie and Carter broke up she'd wondered sometimes if she would get through it. She couldn't eat. Couldn't sleep … The memory of how that had felt never left her.

So why was Rachel's break-up pain free? It made no sense.

Unless …

'Rachel, is there … you know, someone else …?' Allie's tone was cautious but Rachel's cheeks flamed as if she'd shouted the words. She looked mortified.

'God no. I mean … who could there be?' she stammered. 'That's just … no.'

Allie kept her face blank but her mind was whirling. Rachel's reaction was so weird. Something was definitely up. It must be another guy.

But why wouldn't she tell her? It wasn't like Rachel to keep secrets about dating. They told each other everything.

They'd spent all those months together but now that they were back at Cimmeria she could already feel a new distance between them. And she didn't like it.

That evening, Allie and Rachel walked into the dining hall together. As they passed through the door, Rachel blew her breath out between her teeth in a hiss.

'Blimey. This place is really … not very full.'

'See?' Allie was so relieved to have someone to share this all with she could have hugged her. 'Isn't it weird? And it's not just empty, it's like …'

'Depressing.' Rachel finished the thought for her.

'Totally.'

They made their way across the subdued room to their usual table. Carter, Nicole and Zoe were already there.

'Hey—' Allie started but Nicole interrupted her.

'Rachel!' Jumping up from her seat, Nicole ran over to hug her. 'It's about time you came back.'

'Hey, Rachel.' Zoe waved from her seat then returned to eating a bread roll.

'You have to sit next to me,' Nicole insisted. 'Allie has had enough of your time.'

'You can have her,' Allie said mildly. 'I'm bored of her.'

'Gosh, thanks, Allie,' Rachel said, but she smiled.

Throughout all of this, Carter said nothing. He studied them all from beneath a lowered brow.

'Hey, Carter.' Rachel touched his shoulder as she walked by him.

'Rachel.' He said it politely but Allie could see how isolated he felt. Even surrounded by his closest friends he seemed somehow apart.

She was so deep in thought she didn't notice at first that Sylvain had slipped into the chair next to her.

'You look like you are planning something.'

Startled, she spun round in her chair to face him. 'Hi!'

She'd spoken too loudly; the others turned to look at them curiously. Seeing this, Allie feigned cool. 'I mean … how are you?'

She should have prepared for this moment but she hadn't.

Now here she was with Sylvain and Carter in the same place at the same time and she didn't know what to do. Last night she'd been kissing Sylvain pretty passionately. Carter couldn't possibly know about that and for some reason she was glad he didn't.

How do you handle this? Why are there no rules?

Sylvain arched one bemused eyebrow.

'Fine,' he said. 'Thank you. And you?'

'I'm good,' she said, knowing her awkward tone belied her words.

Sylvain made no move to kiss her and she was grateful for that. But his vivid blue gaze swept the table and Allie knew he was looking for the reason for her odd behaviour. She also knew he'd find it.

When his eyes reached Carter, he went still. Allie could almost hear his mind work as he figured it all out.

Nervousness shot through her veins like caffeine. He and Carter had hated each other for so long, only putting their enmity aside a few months ago to fight Nathaniel. If they started fighting again …

She couldn't face that.

Her mouth had gone dry. She reached for her glass. Finding it empty, she looked around for the jug of water. It was near Carter's elbow.

Defeated, she set the glass down again. She wouldn't ask him. But Carter had seen what she wanted. With deliberate movements, he picked the jug up and handed across the table to her, holding her gaze. His eyes were as dark and limitless as a night sky.

'Thanks,' she said.

He didn't reply. He just looked at her. And in that moment she realised he already knew everything. He knew she was with Sylvain. He'd missed nothing.

She never could fool him.

Ten

On Monday morning school, or what was left of it, began.

Just before eight, Allie walked into her history class to find the room, which normally held twenty students, eerily quiet. She chose her usual seat, conscious of the empty chairs in front of her but somehow unable to make herself sit any closer to the teacher's podium.

A few minutes later, Sylvain's hand brushed her shoulder as he passed and she smiled up at him, grateful not to be alone.

As he took the seat next to her, stretching his long legs out into the aisle, his posture appeared normal, relaxed. But she could sense his watchfulness just behind the easy expression. The teachers were their enemies now. Classrooms weren't safe havens any more.

Four more students arrived before Carter, who entered the room at the last minute. She only caught a glimpse of his dark hair before he slid into a seat on the row behind her.

He'd been silent through the rest of dinner after that brief moment of connection. Since then he'd avoided her. Whenever she walked into a room, he left shortly thereafter. In groups, he stayed as far away from her as he could.

He didn't seem angry. Just distant.

Zelazny walked in, followed by a guard who took a position just outside the door. For the first time since she'd returned to Cimmeria, Allie was glad to see a guard.

She cast a sideways glance at Sylvain. If he was reassured by the presence of the guard she couldn't tell. His expression was inscrutable as the teacher stepped to the front of the room.

Zelazny's small, pale blue eyes swept the sparsely populated room, lingering on Allie and Sylvain.

'Welcome back,' he barked with his usual gruffness. 'I hope you've been keeping up with your studies. Everyone, open your books to page two hundred and twenty-seven …'

He acted just as she remembered. Blustery. Authoritarian. Writing words and dates on the whiteboard in the same spiky handwriting.

Allie scrutinised his every move. Could he have done it? Could he have helped kill Jo?

It didn't seem possible. But one of them had done it.

She knew she shouldn't but she let the memory of that night back into her thoughts: Jo lying on the ground, blood all around her. Arms at an odd angle. So strangely still.

All her muscles tensed and her breaths began to come quicker in short gasps. How could she just sit in this room? One of the teachers had opened the gate to let Jo's killer reach her. Was it Zelazny? Could he have done that? Was she in a room with Jo's killer right now?

She tried to imagine him slipping into Isabelle's office, finding the remote that controlled the gate. Checking his watch. Then pushing the button.

As her thoughts whirled faster, her pulse sped too. Soon her heart was galloping unevenly in her chest.

She hadn't had a panic attack in so long she'd forgotten how horrible it felt.

It felt like she was dying.

Zelazny was still writing on the boards as her chest closed in around her lungs.

All the air left the room. She couldn't breathe.

Allie tried to stay calm. She *had* to learn to deal with this. Because she had to come back here tomorrow. And the day after that.

Closing her eyes to shut out everything, she tried to take a breath but nothing happened. Her lungs would not accept the air.

Her heart thudded so loudly now she imagined everyone in the room must hear it. Or see it through her shirt.

Terrified, she reached out a hand towards Sylvain.

As soon as he saw the look on her face he leapt from his seat and crouched beside her.

'Allie? What is it?'

But she couldn't speak. She was dying.

'What's happening?' Zelazny barked, and it seemed to come from far away.

Through a darkening haze, she heard Carter's voice. 'Move.'

Shoving Sylvain aside, Carter took Allie by the shoulders, lifting her bodily from her chair.

Ignoring everyone else, he locked his eyes on hers. 'Just breathe, Allie,' he said quietly. 'Remember how?'

But she didn't remember. It was as if breathing had become the most complicated thing in the world. She tried to shake her head. Failed.

He turned to Sylvain. 'We have to get her out of here.'

Later she couldn't remember leaving the room. Just that suddenly she was in the hallway. She could hear voices – Zelazny calling after them, students murmuring disquietedly – but it all seemed far away.

The movement helped. Allie wheezed in a thread of oxygen. But not enough. Not nearly enough.

Someone was holding her up. Allie could hear other sounds in the distance but they didn't matter.

'Help her.' Sylvain's voice. Desperate. 'I don't know what to do.'

Then all she could see was Carter. His dark, troubled eyes like pools of deep water. His hands warm and familiar on her shoulders. Supporting her weight.

'You can do this, Allie.' The anger from the day before had gone from his voice. He sounded like old Carter again. Gentle and caring. 'Think of something good. Something you like.' He smoothed her hair away from her clammy face. 'Just breathe.'

Seeing him like this – the way he used to be – made her catch her breath. With that tiny gasp her lungs released a little and she took a short breath.

'That's good,' he said approvingly. 'Try it again.'

Holding his gaze as if only he could make her breathe, she did it again.

'That's two breaths,' he said, and she felt him relax a little. 'You're fine, Allie. You're just fine. Keep breathing.'

Her heart still pounded so frantically she wondered how she could still be alive. But she was.

Gradually her lungs released and air returned to her body. The corridor swam back into view. Now she could see Zelazny in the doorway of the classroom watching her with a concerned frown, students crowded behind him. Jerry had come out of the science room and stood behind Carter and Sylvain, a guard at his shoulder.

'Is she OK?' the science teacher asked. 'Take her pulse.'

Carter didn't lift his gaze from hers. 'She's going to be fine.'

For the first time Allie was really conscious of how close he was standing. She was glad no one was taking her pulse just then.

As if he'd seen this in her eyes, he loosened his hold and stepped back, motioning for Sylvain to fill the space he'd left.

'All right, you lot,' Zelazny barked at the crowd of students. 'Back in your seats.'

Reluctantly they returned to their lessons.

Down the hallway, Allie could hear the bangs of classroom doors closing. The show was over.

Looking pale, Sylvain slipped an arm around her. His worried blue eyes searched her face.

'Do you feel better?'

She nodded, not trusting herself to speak yet. He pulled her into a warm hug. Through his shirt, she could feel his own racing heart – she knew she'd scared him. She'd scared herself.

Over his shoulder she saw Carter looking down at the floor.

Stepping up to Allie, Jerry pressed the back of his hand against her clammy forehead. He lifted her wrist and felt her pulse with his fingertips.

After a moment, he let go. 'Would you stay with her, Sylvain?' he said. 'Get her to drink some water. If she still feels ill, take her up to the infirmary.'

'Of course,' Sylvain said.

After the teachers walked to their classrooms, Sylvain turned to Carter. 'Thank you, Carter.'

His tone was fervent but Allie wished she could stop him.

Don't thank him for helping his ex-girlfriend, she thought. *Don't do that.*

'It was nothing,' Carter said.

He headed back to the classroom without meeting Allie's eyes, and she watched him go.

It wasn't nothing, she thought.

Sylvain kept his arm around her as they walked down the quiet hallway to the kitchen where he poured a tall glass of water.

As she leaned against the counter sipping it, he stood across from her, watching her with caution, as if, she thought, she might catch fire.

'It was seeing Zelazny,' she said, although he hadn't asked. 'Thinking about Jo …'

'I thought so.' His tone was gentle. 'You don't have to explain.'

But she couldn't seem to stop explaining.

'Carter used to have panic attacks,' she said. 'He knows how to handle them.'

It was important that he shouldn't misunderstand what had just happened – how Carter had pushed him out of the way. And leapt to help her when she needed him.

But even as she tried to explain how it didn't matter, her mind kept replaying the scene as if it did. The way Carter hadn't hesitated. How she'd thought she would die until he was there.

'I need to learn how to help you, too,' Sylvain said, interrupting her confused thoughts. 'He might not always be so close when you … when this happens.'

She'd had the anxiety attacks ever since Christopher ran away. She hadn't had one in months, though. Because of that, she'd allowed herself to believe she was done with them.

God, how she hated them. Hated the way her body betrayed her. The way it let everyone know she was afraid.

It had to stop.

Allie set her jaw. 'I'm never doing it again. That was the last panic attack I'm ever having. I'm done.'

Sylvain knew better than to argue.

'That's good,' he said.

'Besides, you've already protected me from bullets and kidnapping,' Allie said. 'You don't have to protect me from everything, you know.'

His expression darkened. 'Yes, I do.'

He crossed the space between them in two steps and then she was in his arms.

'Don't you see, Allie? I don't want anything bad to happen to you,' he said.

Resting her head against his shoulder, she breathed in his familiar scent. 'Bad things always happen to me.'

She said it with a complete lack of self-pity. She wasn't looking for sympathy. It was the truth. Carter knew it already, because he was just like her. Bad things happened to him, too. It was like they were born under the same dark star. But she worried Sylvain didn't understand it yet and he had to. If they were going to be together, he needed to know what he was getting into.

He didn't look convinced.

'I will *never* get used to it,' he said firmly. 'I will stop it.'

His determination warmed her heart. Standing on her toes, she kissed him. His lips were warm and gentle against hers, as if he was cautious – afraid of hurting her.

But she wanted more. She'd felt like she was going to die and now she wanted to feel alive. Wrapping her arms around his neck she pulled him closer, deepening the kiss.

He responded instantly, pulling her closer, opening his lips to hers.

Her hands clenched his shirt and she pushed him back against the counter, pressing herself against him. Demanding more …

At that moment a noise in the hallway – teachers or guards passing mid-conversation – startled them and they leapt apart guiltily. They both struck casual poses, breathing heavily.

When the people in the hallway passed by without coming into the kitchen, Sylvain leaned back against the counter across from her, studying her. He looked feverish and eager.

Allie knew just how he felt. Kissing him made all the doubts go away. All the bad thoughts. All the fear. When she kissed him, all she thought about was her body. And his body.

'I have to be alone with you,' he whispered, and the desire in his voice made her shiver. 'Somewhere we won't be disturbed.'

Right at this moment, Allie wanted that, too. But she knew it wasn't possible. Not now.

'Where, though?' she asked. 'The guards watch everything. They're even in the girls' dorm.'

Sylvain's smile was confident; sexy. 'I'll find a place.'

Zelazny must have told Isabelle about the panic attack because as soon as Allie's last class ended, the headmistress ordered her to the infirmary to be checked out.

Allie, who had spent weeks in the infirmary recovering from the attack that resulted in Jo's death, climbed the stairs with heavy feet.

When she arrived, the nurse seemed unsurprised to see her.

'I guess it's about time we had you back in,' she said with dry humour. 'What have you done to yourself now?'

When Allie told her about the panic attack, she tutted sympathetically before listening to her heart, taking her pulse and generally poking her around.

'Well, you're in better shape than the last time I saw you,' she said finally. 'Your heart sounds strong. But if it happens again I want you to come right back here. Agreed? There are things you can take – medications that can help.'

Allie grimaced. Her parents had put her on medication after Christopher left. She knew how brain pills, as she called them, worked. She was convinced they slowed her down. Make her feel weird. Like she wasn't … her.

Everyone had told her it wasn't true but she knew her own body.

Besides, she told herself, she didn't need them. She'd had her last panic attack. And that's all there was to it.

Mumbling a non-committal reply, she fled down the stairs with the panicked zeal of an escaped prisoner. She was half running along the ground-floor corridor when she saw Rachel heading towards her at an equally fast pace.

'Hey.' Rachel stopped her, a worried frown line dividing her eyes. 'I heard you had a thing. Are you OK?'

'Totally fine,' Allie said breezily. 'Nurse says I'm not sick. I'm just a freak.'

'Well, she is a medical professional,' Rachel joked, but Allie could see the concern in her cinnamon-coloured eyes. 'You haven't had one of those in while, have you? What set it off?'

Allie made a vague gesture. 'It was just seeing Zelazny again. Knowing he might be …'

'Yeah. I get it.' Rachel patted her shoulder. 'I'm glad you're OK.'

Glancing down, Allie noticed Rachel wasn't wearing her required school shoes. Instead she wore a pair of blue-and-white sandals she'd favoured when they were in France.

'What's with the naked toes?' At Cimmeria, only prefects got to wear their own shoes. Jules had been prefect until her parents sided with Nathaniel and pulled her out of the school.

Her eyes widened. 'Oh my God. Jules is gone. There has to be a new prefect. It's you, isn't it?'

'There can be only one,' Rachel intoned, trying and failing to suppress a pleased smile. 'Anyway, yes. Meet the new boss. Isabelle just told me.'

'Congratulations! That's massive!' Allie hugged her. 'Are you going to give me marks?'

'Effective immediately. Detentions all round.' Rachel's tone might have been mild but Allie could see she was flushed with happiness. 'Oh, and there's something else I need to tell you about but I'll tell you tonight. I'm saving it up. A surprise.'

'This is so great,' Allie said, feeling cheerier. 'Yes, our teachers might be trying to kill us. But you're prefect now and you have other fun secrets. It's like things are finally getting back to normal around here.'

Rachel laughed as they headed back out into the corridor, arm in arm. 'Your normal terrifies me.'

Allie shot her a wry smile. 'My normal terrifies everyone.'

Eleven

After dinner that night, Allie went straight from the mostly empty dining hall to the strangely quiet common room with Zoe, her book bag heavy on her shoulder.

'I have so much work,' she groaned, dropping the bag with a thud. 'Don't teachers know we have lives?'

'School is my life,' Zoe said, opening her notebook.

'How awesome for you,' Allie said darkly.

She settled on to the deep leather sofa and pulled out her books, looking through her assignments with increasing alarm. All the teachers had given out work but the worst was history. When she and Sylvain finally returned to Zelazny's class, they'd found him giving everyone a huge essay to write.

'We are looking,' he'd said, his voice jumping a little as he wrote on the board, 'at the age of Empire. Particularly, the structure of government and the ramifications for all citizens …'

He'd droned on for ages.

Now she had a week to write three thousand words on something she knew nothing about.

Muttering to herself, she flipped through her text book, but it was soon obvious it contained far too little information.

'Bugger it.' She sighed, standing up. 'I've got to go to the library.'

'I love the library,' Zoe said without looking up.

Allie couldn't take much more of her earnestness. She headed for the door, leaving her bag behind. 'I'm off. If I'm not back in an hour, send a search party.'

'How could you get lost in the *library*?' Zoe looked baffled.

Allie held up her hands in surrender. Zoe didn't get irony in the best of circumstances – she should have known better.

'It's just a stupid thing people say.'

'People shouldn't say stupid things,' Zoe grumbled.

Relieved to leave the conversation behind, Allie stepped out into the hushed main hallway. Her footsteps echoed around her so loudly it sounded as if she was being followed. By the time she reached the library she was getting jumpy.

The library door opened with a shushing sound, as if quiet just sort of started in the doorway.

All the tables were unoccupied – the green glass desk lamps glowed for no one.

A series of thumps split the silence and she turned to see Eloise piling books on a cart. She had a notepad in her hand as she arranged the books into stacks. It was the first time she'd seen the librarian looking anything other than nervous since she'd returned to the school.

Allie cleared her throat and Eloise jumped.

Now she looked nervous.

'Sorry.' Allie gave an apologetic wave. 'Didn't mean to scare you.'

'Not to worry,' Eloise said, straightening her glasses. 'I just didn't hear you come in.'

'The door …' Allie said, apologetically. 'You should add squeak to it.'

Eloise accepted this with a quick nod.

'Yes,' she said. 'Of course.' As if adding squeak to a door was a completely reasonable suggestion. Then she went back to her work.

Eloise had once been a confident, warm, friendly teacher. She was much younger than the other teachers and had always been the one the students could relate to.

Now, she looked older. She seemed more fragile, too – her nails were bitten to the quick. Some part of Allie did feel for her.

But, fragile or not, Eloise was still one of the three teachers suspected of working for Nathaniel. In fact, Allie wasn't meant to be alone with her at all.

Turning away, she trudged through the forest of shelves. The long, shadowy room was lined on both sides by rows of tall, dark bookshelves. Each soared up at least ten feet. The top shelves were higher than the heavy, metal light fixtures that hung from the ceiling by chains.

Thick, Persian rugs absorbed her footsteps but there was no one to disturb.

She turned into the stacks at the history section. Large, leather books lined the shelves – some as old as the time period they covered. She traced her fingers across the gold-embossed titles looking for something useful, but soon realised the books were mostly about the eighteenth century. A century too early for the purposes of her research.

Her head down, still lost in thought, she turned the corner to the next aisle.

And ran headlong into Carter, nearly tripping in the process.

He grabbed her shoulders to keep her from falling. 'Steady.'

Holding his arms for balance she glanced up at him in surprise.

He was looking down at her with the oddest expression, as if he'd dreamed her up. As if he was contemplating kissing her.

And, for some crazy reason, she found herself wishing he would. She was hyper-aware of the way his leg pressed against hers. She could feel each of his fingers on her shoulders. Feel his breath warm against her cheek.

What is wrong with me? she wondered.

He had Jules and she had Sylvain and *this* was over between the two of them forever. They'd agreed that last term. They were friends for life.

And yet, for a frozen second neither of them moved.

Then the shutters went down over Carter's gaze and he stepped back, disentangling himself from her.

'History essay?' He spoke casually, as if the moment had not just happened. The strange longing look was completely gone from his expression.

'Naturally.' Copying him, she affected nonchalance, but her voice sounded too high and thin. She cleared her throat and tried to force herself to sound cool. 'You too?'

'Three thousand words.' Turning to the shelves, he frowned at the books as if they held all the answers to life's problems. 'Ludicrous deadline.'

From beneath her lashes, Allie watched the side of his face, looking for any sign that what had just happened meant anything real but he seemed utterly absorbed in the book titles.

Dropping her gaze, she exhaled through pursed lips. She must have imagined the whole thing. That wistful look … it was all in her head.

God. Why couldn't she just let them be friends?

'As usual,' she said, turning to look at the shelves, too, although the titles were a blur and she didn't really know what she was looking for.

Pulling down a heavy book, Carter whistled under his breath as he opened it, flipping through the pages.

'The assignment's a bit vague, right?' he said. 'I mean, three thousand words on empire is like … "Give me five thousand words on the history of the world."'

Allie snorted her agreement and chose a book at random. When she opened it, a tiny cloud of dust arose. She sneezed.

'Bless you,' he said solemnly.

As if that were some sort of an insult, she slammed the book shut and turned to him.

'Listen, Carter, I just think we need to talk.'

Clearly startled, he leaned back. 'About empire? Because I had nothing to do with that.'

'No.' She shoved the dusty book back on the shelf where she'd found it. 'About … things.'

'Things?' Carter pulled down another book and looked at it with too much interest.

Now that Allie was in this she wasn't sure what she wanted to say. But she had to keep going.

'When I came back, that first day, you were so pissed off at me and I didn't know why …'

'I have anger issues,' he said. 'I thought you knew that.' His tone was mild but she could see the corners of his mouth twitch.

'Don't make jokes about this,' she protested. 'I just thought we should ... talk about why you were so angry. Or just, you know ... talk. Because I missed you.'

She hadn't meant to be quite so honest but there it was. She'd done it now.

Carter's smile disappeared. He didn't seem to know what to say. For a second he kept turning pages. Then he set the book down and met her gaze with guarded eyes.

'I missed you, too,' he said at last. 'And I'm sorry I seemed angry. I'm an arse. I guess I was just surprised. And ... well. Worried for you.'

Allie's brow lowered. 'Have you ever considered *talking*? That's a traditional method for handling concern in our culture.'

'I know ... I'm sorry about that. Communication hasn't been my thing lately.' He leaned back against the shelves, watching her. He looked like he was afraid of what she might say next.

She knew just how he felt.

'Why were you so ... worried?' she asked.

He made a vague gesture with one hand. 'Because I thought you were safe out there. As you can tell, things are less than safe here. And I didn't know what had happened to you out there.'

'No one told you about the shooting?' Allie said.

His lips tightening, he shook his head. 'I know now. Isabelle told me. And Sylvain filled in the details. I can't ...' His voice trailed off but she saw how his muscles tensed. 'Once I knew ... I understood why you had to come back.'

'Still,' Allie said gently, 'it's not like you to act like that. Not lately, anyway.'

A long silence followed. He didn't meet her gaze. She got the feeling he was trying to decide whether or not to reply.

'While you were gone ...' he began at last. He paused before starting up again. 'Lately, I guess I haven't been in a great place mentally.'

His frankness took Allie by surprise.

'Because of Jules?'

His eyes met hers and glanced away. 'Because of Jules and a lot of stuff.'

'You know it's not your fault ... right?' Allie said.

His face darkened. 'You know Jo's death wasn't *your* fault. Right?'

His words were as quick and painful as a snake bite. Allie drew in her breath.

Instantly contrite, he raked his fingers through his dark hair. 'God, Allie, I'm sorry. That was uncalled for.'

'It wasn't fair.' Her voice quivered and she knotted her hands at her sides. 'Was it?'

He reached out his hand as if to comfort her but stopped at the last minute and rested it on a shelf instead, like he'd always meant to put it there.

'No,' he said. 'It wasn't. I seem to be ...' Biting his lip, he tapped his knuckles against the shelf. Allie got the feeling he'd like to put his fist through it but was restraining himself. 'I seem to be unfair a lot lately.'

'I know what that's like,' Allie said. 'You know I do.' She took a step towards him – invading the wide circle of personal space he'd created. 'You can talk to me about this stuff, Carter. I really do understand. Probably more than most people. Like you get my panic attacks. I get this ... stuff.'

Her sudden proximity seemed to make him nervous. He backed away, pretending he was just shifting his weight from one leg to another.

But when he replied, his voice was soft and filled with pain. 'I know, Allie. But I just … can't.'

It was the way he said her name that did it.

After they'd broken up he always said it quickly, like he couldn't wait to get it over with. Like he didn't like the taste of it.

But this time he lingered over it. Stretched it out.

Allie's throat tightened.

She wasn't imagining this – something was happening here.

But it couldn't be. They were done with that.

I'm losing it, she thought. *He loves Jules. I'm with Sylvain. And I am being incredibly stupid right now.*

Carter was still talking. 'It's hard to bring things up sometimes. When there's no … solution.'

It occurred to her that she wasn't entirely certain what he was talking about. But they were on dangerous ground now, and she needed to pull them back to safety before they went too far. And did something they'd regret.

Because a voice in her head kept telling her to kiss him.

'But I think there *is* a solution.' She talked fast, before she could change her mind. 'We just have to figure it out. I think we need to get Jules back here, somehow. That would make everything better.'

Carter looked at her as if that wasn't the response he'd expected. But as soon as she said it, Allie realised she was right. That was the answer to everything. If Jules was back, Carter would be happy. And then she could be happy with Sylvain. And she and Carter could be friends again. They wouldn't be confused into thinking there was something romantic between them when they'd been so careful to make sure there wasn't.

Jules would fix everything.

'I'll figure something out,' she said, nodding to herself.

His eyes distant, Carter turned back to the books. 'I should have known Allie would come to the rescue.' His voice was cool; enigmatic. He pulled out a thick book and handed it to her, signalling the end of the discussion. 'This looks like a good one.'

She flipped it over in her hands. The title was *Conquering the World*.

―――

For the rest of the evening Allie couldn't get that moment with Carter out of her mind. It was impossible to think about the British Empire when she kept hearing him say her name in that way.

'*Allie*.' Like a caress.

She had to have imagined it. She just had to.

But had she imagined how she felt? The way her heart leapt when she saw him?

This couldn't be happening.

When it was finally time for Night School training she was glad. All her nerves were stretched tight. She wanted to kick things. And hit them hard.

She was eager to get back to work. After what happened in France – and the things she'd learned from Isabelle – she wanted to know more ways to defend herself. More ways to elude Nathaniel's guards.

The next time they came for her she wanted to surprise them with her sheer arse-kicking skills.

She'd trained while she was away but training on your own wasn't as effective as the whole Night School group dynamic, which made her push herself harder. She just hoped she hadn't fallen behind the others. That she was ready for whatever they were working on now.

Just before nine, she headed down the basement corridor towards Training Room One with Zoe, who was in a much better mood now. After learning what had happened that morning, she'd been researching panic attacks and was telling Allie everything she'd learned in animated detail.

'And when your heart does that thing it's not dangerous,' she explained. 'It just feels like it is.'

'Yeah, it's a totally un-dangerous heart attack,' Allie agreed. 'Like a giant coronary joke.' Still talking, she opened the door to the girls' dressing room. 'I love giant …'

As she stepped into the room her voice trailed off. She stopped walking so suddenly Zoe ran into her.

'Giant what?' Zoe asked, looking over her shoulder. Then she stopped, too. 'Oh.'

Across the room, Rachel stood next to Nicole. Both were in black leggings and tops, black running shoes. Full Night School gear. Allie's eyes travelled from Rachel to the empty hook on the wall behind her. Above it, one word had been freshly painted: *Patel*.

Nicole and Rachel were both watching her with hopeful smiles. But as Rachel clocked Allie's expression, her smile turned uncertain and then faded away entirely.

'Surprise?' Rachel said.

Twelve

'What the hell is going on? ' Allie had gone cold inside, as if someone had shoved a shard of ice into her heart. 'Rachel, what have you done?'

Rachel held up her hands. 'I wanted to surprise you. I talked about it with my dad this weekend. He worked everything out with Isabelle.' Her voice was calm but Allie could hear the nervous tremor just beneath the surface of her words.

'Then un-work it. Because this isn't happening.'

Allie's tone was ominous. Inside, she was reeling. How could Rachel do this? She wasn't athletic. She was a brain. She'd be putting herself in danger, and for what? To fight Nathaniel? To fight *Gabe*?

She didn't stand a chance. They'd kill her.

'Allie.' Nicole's voice was quiet but her expressive eyes held a warning. 'Rachel has the right to make her own decisions.'

'No, she doesn't,' Allie snapped. 'Not when it comes to this. I won't have her here, Nicole. She could get hurt.'

'I've already been hurt, Allie.' For the first time, Rachel sounded angry. 'And I couldn't fight back because I didn't know what to do. I was just Nathaniel's victim. His *toy*. Waiting for someone to come and save me. Waiting for *you* to save me.

Waiting to watch him cut you. And to see Gabe nearly break Nicole's leg ...'

She shuddered at the memory and an angry tear streaked down her cheek. Dashing it away with the back of her hand, she took a shaky breath.

Allie was stunned. She'd spent three months with Rachel and she never once mentioned she was considering joining Night School. Had she just been sitting there the whole time keeping secrets? About Lucas? About Night School?

Had she told her the truth about *anything*?

'If I'm staying at Cimmeria, I have to learn how to defend myself. And I'm going to,' Rachel continued defiantly. 'You can't stop me.'

The rush of anger and fear made it hard to think clearly and Allie pressed her fingers against her eyelids. There was no way this could be happening.

'Maybe not,' she said, dropping her hands. 'But I'm bloody well going to try.'

Whirling, she ran from the room, hurtling down the dim corridor almost unaware of the tears pouring down her cheeks. Her steps were sure but inside she was reeling. How could Rachel do this? How could she betray her like this? Nathaniel would ... he would ...

She rounded the corner, so blinded by anger and fear she couldn't see where she was going. She'd made it to the foot of the stairs when someone grabbed her arms, pulling her back. She struggled wildly to free herself but the hands held on to her.

'Allie, *stop.*'

It was Carter.

Still she fought back, hitting his shoulders with her fists.

'Let me go, Carter. Let me go. Let me go.' But he didn't. Instead, he pulled her into his arms and she collapsed against his chest, sobbing, repeating over and over again, 'Let me go.'

He held her until her tears finally quietened. Then he guided her up the stairs to a darkened alcove where they could talk in private.

'Now,' he said when they were settled, 'what the hell is going on?'

They sat side by side on a stone bench. Allie felt sore from weeping – as if she'd cried with her whole body. In one hand she clutched a tissue he'd handed her.

Her voice shaking, she told him everything. The hook on the wall. The look on Rachel's face.

When she finished, he swore under his breath. 'I can't believe she'd do something so bloody stupid. And what the hell is Isabelle thinking?'

Somehow, the fact that he agreed with her made things worse. It meant she was right about how dangerous this was for Rachel.

'We can't let her do this, Carter,' she said, fighting back a fresh flood of tears. 'Gabe will kill her. I know he will. I've got to go and talk to Isabelle. And tell her … tell her …'

He took her hand, folding it in his. Allie couldn't remember the last time they'd been this close without tension between them. It felt natural to be here.

But his next words took her by surprise.

'Or not,' he said.

Dropping his hand, she blinked up at him. 'What do you mean?'

'Look, I love Rachel as much as you do,' he said. 'But think about it. She's not the most physically fit student at Cimmeria, right?'

Still puzzled, Allie nodded. 'She hates exercise.'

'So …' He looked down at her, his dark eyes fathomless in the shadows. 'How's that going to work out for her in Night School?'

Allie considered this.

'It'll be hard,' she said, still not getting it. 'It's hard for everyone.'

'Raj is our lead trainer. You know he's not going to go easy on her just because she's his daughter, right?'

Finally realising what he was getting at, Allie sat up straighter, her gaze fixed on his. 'No. He'll be harder on her. Much harder.'

'Precisely. And Rachel will not handle that well.'

'She'll hate it.' Allie's heart lifted at the thought. 'She'll quit.'

For the first time she felt hopeful.

'OK,' she said mostly to herself. 'That could work. But in the meantime … she's in danger the whole time.'

'We'll all keep an eye on her,' Carter said. 'Seriously, these days we almost never leave the building to train, anyway.'

He had a point. And even though she didn't want to see it – she didn't want Rachel in Night School for five minutes – Allie knew he was right. They could get through this.

Wiping away the last of her tears, she looked up at him. 'When did you get so smart?'

His lips quirked up. 'I've always been smart. You just weren't paying attention.'

She had to smile at that. Despite everything.

It struck her that this was the third time in one day she'd ended up in Carter's arms. Fate kept throwing them together.

She cleared her throat. 'Thanks, Carter. I was totally losing it. I don't know what I would have done …'

'No worries,' he said, as if it meant nothing at all that twice today he'd picked up the pieces and put her back together. 'I was just there. That's all.'

He glanced at his watch then stood, and turned back to face her. 'Now. Let's get down there. And start making Rachel hate Night School.'

After throwing on her Night School gear, Allie rushed into Training Room One. She was late and the dimly lit room was already a buzz of activity.

Working in pairs, black-clad Night School students practised complex means of attack and self-defence. As she entered the dim, cube-shaped room, they were in the middle of a manoeuvre she hadn't seen before. The training pairs were punching, kicking and twisting in and out of each other's grip.

The move was more intricate than anything she'd ever tried. The windowless room was already too warm and smelled of sweat. She scanned the fighters for familiar faces.

Carter and Sylvain were both talking to Zelazny at the back of the room. As if he'd felt her gaze, Sylvain looked up. She saw him observe her puffy eyes, the tracks of her tears. His brow knitted.

Allie shook her head and mouthed, 'I'm fine' at him. Then turned to find Rachel.

She was across the room with Nicole.

She looked so odd in Night School gear. So wrong. It was like she was in a play, pretending to be an athlete. She stood, red-faced and awkward, as Nicole showed her the basics of the move. Already sweating, Rachel appeared perplexed by the instructions.

Good, Allie thought. But her heart felt hollow. She hated seeing Rachel suffer.

Nothing about this was good.

When she couldn't stand to watch any more, she turned to look behind her. Jerry Cole and Zoe were practising nearby, and Allie headed towards them. The instructor wasn't tall but he was strong. His moves were pure power, but Zoe was more agile. Her birdlike quickness meant she easily eluded his kicks, but she couldn't knock him down either.

'OK,' Jerry said, holding up his hands and laughing. 'I'm defeated. You have destroyed me, Zoe.'

'Awesome.' She air-punched happily.

'Uh ... hi,' Allie said, walking up to them.

'You're late.' Zoe's tone was accusing.

'Yeah ... sorry.' Allie cast an apologetic look at Jerry. 'I got held up. It won't happen again.'

She saw him take in her red nose and puffy eyes.

'Everything OK?' he asked.

Feeling stupid, Allie nodded. 'Yeah. It's just a ... thing.'

For a second she thought he might challenge that, make her explain more. Then he seemed to decide against it.

'As long as you're OK.' He stepped back. 'You'll be training with Zoe.' He gave the smaller girl a jovial shoulder pat and she grinned up at him. 'So you'll need to be one hundred per cent. She's ruthless.'

His laidback attitude was not at all what she'd expected. In the past, being late to Night School would earn you a week's detention and a public chiding. At least.

Things really had changed around here.

The other students were still practising around them. Raising his voice to be heard over the rumble of conversation and the thudding of bodies against the floor, Jerry said, 'I understand your strength is back to normal now.'

'Yeah.' She held up a fist half-heartedly. 'I'm ready to rumble.'

He shot Zoe a warning look. 'And you are not allowed to hurt, kill or maim, remember?'

Zoe nodded so hard her ponytail bounced. 'No actual damage.'

Jerry walked Allie through the technique the other students were practising. It wasn't quite as complicated as it looked, but it wasn't easy either. Hand to wrist. Foot to shoulder. Bend back. Twist. Hand to wrist. Repeat. Try not to fall down.

After they'd tried it a couple of times at half speed, he seemed satisfied. 'Zoe can show you the other things we've been working on lately. Wave me over if you need help.' He gave her a smile. 'We're all glad to have you back in training, Allie.'

'Thanks,' she said shyly.

When he'd gone, Zoe turned to her, cocking her head to one side. 'Want to fight?'

Allie grinned at her. 'Absolutely.'

They were working through the third manoeuvre when Sylvain and Carter walked up to them. Sylvain looked solemn.

'Carter told me about Rachel,' he said. 'I can't believe it.'

Allie made a helpless gesture.

'She shouldn't be here.' Zoe's tone was condemning. As if Rachel had broken some fundamental rule.

'She seems to be struggling,' Carter said, and they all turned to look just as Rachel tried to kick Nicole but ended up in a heap on the floor.

'She's terrible,' Zoe said. She glanced at Allie. 'She's even worse than you were when you started.'

Allie didn't reply. She kept her eyes on the pair as Nicole helped Rachel up.

'We thought we'd practise with you.' Sylvain said, drawing her attention back. 'Is that OK?'

'Sure,' Allie replied without thinking. Then she realised what he was saying and looked up in stunned surprise. 'Wait. You two are *training partners*?'

'I told you we've been training together,' Sylvain said mildly.

'Yeah,' Allie looked back and forth between them, 'but you didn't tell me you'd made it official.'

'What can I say?' Carter said with a cynical smile. 'Opposites attract.'

Allie didn't know how she felt about this new development. There was something unseemly about her former and current boyfriends becoming partners.

As they resumed training, she found it hard to focus with them so close. Whenever they talked, or one of them laughed, she looked up to see what was happening and Zoe would kick her in the face.

'You're dead,' the young girl explained helpfully each time this happened.

After a while, though, she got into the rhythm of training – distractions fell by the wayside. She'd always liked the sheer physical effort of it, the knowledge that she could fight back. Or get away if she needed to.

While she'd been away from Cimmeria she'd followed a strict training regime provided by Raj. She was very strong.

Still, working with Zoe wasn't easy. The younger girl's moves were accurate and lightning quick. When she swung her foot towards Allie's throat, her leg was a blur.

Periodically, she and Zoe took a break to watch Carter and Sylvain practise. Their methods were the same but their sheer physical strength made it look more brutal. Carter swung his foot up with the strength of a tank. Had he wanted it to, that move could have thrown Sylvain across the room. Or broken his neck.

When it was Sylvain's turn he was as graceful and lethal as an armed dancer. Instead of a simple swing move, he leapt from the ground in a spinning circle, his foot ending up perfectly positioned in the middle of Carter's throat.

'Great moves.' Raj Patel walked up to them with a smile and held out his hands to Allie. 'Welcome back. We've all missed you.'

He pulled her into a warm hug, patting her on the shoulder. 'Looks like you've been keeping up with your training while you were gone.'

Allie flushed with pride. 'Every day.'

'It shows,' Raj said approvingly. He gestured at the room, where the other students were still working through the move. 'You'll see we're trying new things now. These are moves designed to disable a fighting opponent long enough to give you time to get away.' He added ominously, 'Or longer.'

'Longer?' Allie asked.

'You could kill someone with these moves, Allie,' Raj explained simply. 'We teach you both the kill moves and the disable alternatives.'

Allie tried to hide her dismay. They'd always focused on self-defence and evasion techniques – ways to avoid being kidnapped or hurt. That sort of training was priceless for the children of billionaires who, as Allie had learned, were always soft targets compared to their well-protected parents.

But they'd never learned methods of killing their assailants.

'Wow,' she whispered. 'That's intense.'

It was Sylvain who answered. 'We haven't got any choice,' he said. 'It's kill or be killed with Nathaniel, you know that.'

'And I'm here to make sure none of you gets killed,' Raj said. 'Now,' he looked around the small circle of students, 'I think you should switch.'

They stared back at him blankly.

'Zoe's a great training partner but Allie needs to know how to kick someone taller than her,' he explained. 'She needs to know how to fight a man. So –' he made a swirling motion with his hand as he walked away – 'switch it up.'

Allie avoided Carter's gaze. There was no question who she should train with.

It was clear he knew this, too, because he waved Zoe over. 'Come on, Shortie. Show me what you've got.'

'Don't call me Shortie,' she complained.

As they set up on the adjacent mat, Allie wondered if the slight twinge she felt was disappointment.

Smoothing all doubt from her face, she turned to face Sylvain. 'Ready?'

Unaware of her inner turmoil, he smiled. 'Of course.'

Raj was right – the move was different with someone physically larger. She had to work harder to tilt her body to the angle needed to kick. Had to adjust her responses. It took several tries to get it right. By the end, though, her aim was unerring. Her bare foot ended up just beneath Sylvain's chin. Right where it was supposed to be.

'Nice.' He pretended to bite the arch of her foot, and she laughed and stumbled backwards away from him.

Out of the corner of her eye she saw Carter cast a quick glance at them. There was something raw and conflicted in his expression and she looked away quickly.

This whole training-together thing wasn't going to be easy.

Unable to stop herself, she looked over at Rachel and Nicole, just in time to see Rachel try the same kick she'd just done and lose her balance again. Nicole moved to help her up but Rachel's face was flushed with embarrassment and frustration. Jerry walked over to speak to the two of them quietly.

He didn't seem to be criticising them. Instead, he appeared to be offering gentle guidance. But even from across the room Allie could see Rachel's misery.

When training ended, Allie took a quick shower and threw her school uniform back on in her usual haphazard style. With her blouse half buttoned and her tie dangling from her hand, she hurried towards the door. But as she passed through the main dressing area, she stopped in her tracks. Rachel and Nicole sat in a corner, talking quietly. Both still wore black training clothes. Rachel's head hung down in a posture of defeat, Nicole's hand rested on her shoulder.

Sympathy unfurled inside Allie's heart.

She knew she should make this all harder for Rachel. After all, that was the plan, wasn't it?

Right now she should give her the cold shoulder. Make her feel lonely and isolated. Do whatever it took to convince her she couldn't do this.

But seeing her like this tore at her heart.

When she walked over to them, Nicole shot her a warning look.

When did Nicole become Rachel's protector? Allie wondered. *Isn't that my job?*

'Look,' she said, 'I just wanted to say' – *I'm sorry. Don't do this. Be who you are, not who I am* – 'I'm sorry about how I reacted earlier. It wasn't … fair.' As she spoke, her hands twisted her tie into rope. 'I know it's hard. I hated my first Night School session, too. It gets better. I promise.'

Rachel's face was red with exhaustion and failure but at Allie's words a light seemed to fire in her eyes. Her bottom lip trembled.

'Thanks, Allie. And I'm sorry—'

Allie held up a hand. 'Don't. *I'm* sorry. I was pissed off at you because I'm scared for you. You know why. You know everything. I don't have to tell you. Just …' She hesitated. There was so much she wanted to say. But Rachel looked exhausted. Now wasn't the time. 'Let's talk about it tomorrow. OK?'

Rachel bit her lip and nodded. 'OK.'

Allie walked out of the room feeling better and worse. Better because Rachel didn't think she hated her any more. Worse, because she'd just made it easier for her to tough out the worst week Night School had to offer.

I'm such an idiot.

When she stepped into the corridor, Sylvain was leaning against the wall across from her, one foot propped up behind him. One of the younger Night School students was talking to him, his face aglow with a kind of hero worship. His gaze lowered, Sylvain was listening patiently.

As if he'd sensed her presence, he glanced up, and his eyes met hers.

He said something to the student. With a disappointed look, the boy turned away.

Pushing himself from the wall, Sylvain walked to her.

'How's Rachel?' His voice was low.

Allie thought of the way Rachel had looked at her just before she walked out the door.

'She's hanging in there.'

Talking softly, they walked down the long, basement corridor then climbed the stairs up to the ground floor. Their shoes squeaked on the polished wood floor.

When they reached the foot of the main staircase, they stopped. Sylvain pulled her close. Shutting her eyes, she leaned against him, waiting for him to say goodnight. To kiss her and tell her he'd see her in the morning.

But that wasn't what he said at all.

'Meet me on the roof,' he whispered against her cheek, his breath making all of her nerves come alive. 'At midnight.'

Thirteen

Half an hour later, Allie paced her bedroom with quick impatient steps. Every few minutes she stared at the clock. Time advanced with aching slowness.

Eleven forty-five ... Eleven forty-six ...

She knew what was ahead. Knew what Sylvain wanted up on the roof.

Her heart fluttered with nerves. It had been the most confusing day.

She thought of the look she'd seen in Carter's eyes. The wistfulness she'd thought was there for just a moment.

Then she forced herself to stop thinking about it.

She looked at the clock again.

Eleven forty-seven.

She couldn't wait any longer.

It was late enough.

She switched off the lights.

In the darkness, she made her way to the desk and climbed on top of it. The window was already open.

With easy assurance, she stepped out on to the ledge.

It was a clear summer night – cool but not cold. The air smelled faintly of pine and Allie took a deep, steadying breath as she balanced three storeys above the ground.

She'd performed this feat many times since coming to Cimmeria. The danger of it, the thrill of being one step from oblivion, was like an old friend and she smiled to herself as she felt her way across the face of the building.

You can forget how dangerous anything is if you do it often enough.

Sliding her feet along the ledge, she traced her fingertips across the rough brickwork, feeling for indentations that could provide a grip.

She was heading for a spot where the roof dipped low enough to make access fairly simple. But to get there she had to pass two windows. The first was Rachel's.

When she reached it, the window was open but the lights were off. Feeling a bit guilty for not telling Rachel what she was up to, she slid past it with silent steps.

She was just about to move on when she heard soft voices floating through the window.

Allie's brow furrowed. Who was Rachel talking to in the dark?

She stopped on the far side of the window to listen. The voices were both female. But they were speaking so quietly it was impossible to make out words. Then she heard a soft peal of musical laughter, like bells ringing. She knew that laugh. Rachel was talking to Nicole.

A quick pinprick of jealousy pierced her.

She knew she was being unreasonable. Nicole and Rachel were both science geeks and they'd always had a kind of steady respect for each other's intellect.

Now that Rachel was in Night School, they must be getting closer, that was all.

As she hurried away from the window, Allie told herself that this was a good thing. Nicole was brilliant in Night School. She was really looking out for Rachel.

But the voice in her head wouldn't be quiet.

I'm right next door. Why didn't Rachel come to me?

The next window she passed was closed. Through the glass all she could see was the wooden shutter inside. Cimmeria had lots of empty bedrooms now.

Just beyond that was the low dip in the roof. Making her way to it, she reached up to get a grip on the tiles.

At that precise moment, someone reached down and grabbed her wrist.

Allie stifled a scream.

Instinctively she pulled back, losing her balance. Her heart pounding, she teetered on the narrow ledge, scrambling for a foothold.

But the hand on her wrist was solid as stone.

'Allie, it's me.' In the darkness above her, Sylvain peered down at her. 'Jump. I'll pull you up.'

Allie didn't move. His grip was strong but death waited below her if his hand slipped. Her life would be in his hands.

Her heart pounded a staccato rhythm.

'Don't let go.' She warned him.

His eyes were locked on hers. 'Never.'

Jump.

Still, she hesitated. She didn't know why she was afraid. If Sylvain was basically her boyfriend now, shouldn't she trust him more than anyone?

Taking a deep breath, she jumped.

Using her upward velocity as an aid, he pulled her on to the roof with such ease it felt like flying.

She landed hard on the slate tiles beside him.

He steadied her, one arm around her waist. Her body pressed against his as she sought her balance. The jump had sent adrenaline racing through her bloodstream, heightening her awareness of every point of contact between them. She felt as if she was pressed against a flame.

Swallowing hard, she tried to act normal.

'Bloody hell, Sylvain,' she complained. 'You scared the life out of me.'

'I thought you'd seen me,' he said. Loosening his hold on her, he motioned for her to follow. 'Come over here. The night is so clear. The stars are incredible.'

A breeze blew her hair as she followed him up one of the roof's steep peaks.

'Are you certain we're OK up here?' Allie whispered as they walked.

'It's safe,' he said. 'No guards.'

'I haven't been up here in ages.' She stepped cautiously over a loose ceiling tile.

'It's not easy to be alone now,' Sylvain said. 'We're constantly watched. But I noticed the guards don't patrol the roof. This may be the only place.'

They stood at the base of a gigantic, Victorian chimney that soared ten feet above their heads. Sylvain leaned back against it with insouciant style. He might have been standing beside a swimming pool instead of on the roof of a school in the middle of the night.

His confidence was undeniably sexy. Butterflies swirled in Allie's stomach.

'The security is weirding me out big time,' she said, keeping her voice cool. 'There's a guard in my corridor. Creep factor high.'

'It's much worse than it was when I left to go home,' Sylvain conceded. 'It had begun then – there were more guards. More obsession with security. But it wasn't as intense. Now, everyone is so paranoid. They see Nathaniel around every corner.'

'Totally.' Allie agreed. 'And yet Isabelle says there hasn't been an attack since I left. So why are they being so intense? I mean, yeah, he *is* evil and he is out to get us. But there's no need to freak out about it.' She made a flippant gesture. 'We've all been here. Done this.'

Sylvain considered this. 'It's because of what they are hearing from Lucinda in London. I understand why they are afraid. But they are giving up too much freedom in exchange for safety.'

He gave a resigned sigh. 'Besides, if one of our teachers is working for Nathaniel, what good would a thousand guards do?'

A cool breeze lifted Allie's hair and she shivered, stretching the ends of her sleeves down over her hands.

'It's so hard to believe.' She looked up at him; the shadows hid his expression. 'I wish we knew which one. I hate being suspicious of all of them.'

'Raj's team is working on it,' Sylvain said. 'They will find him. And soon, I think. Raj says they're close.'

'Isabelle said the same thing.' Allie's voice was impatient. 'But how do we keep just going into their classes when one of them wants us dead?'

'We look out for each other,' he said. He reached for her hand, pulling her closer. 'You know, I watched you train tonight. You were vicious. Focused. You can take care of yourself. You know that, right?'

His words made her face warm.

'Yeah,' she said. 'I guess I'm doing OK.'

'More than that,' he said. 'You're one of the best we've got. They should send you after this spy. Whoever it is.'

Allie tried to imagine fighting – really fighting – Zelazny or Jerry. Or worse, Eloise. But she couldn't. They'd always been her authority figures. Essentially one step away from family.

Suddenly she didn't want to talk about this any more. It was too depressing. The betrayal and the lies. The awful cost of it all.

She leaned against Sylvain's body and he wrapped his arm around her, enveloping her in his warmth.

'We'll find him, Allie,' he said. 'Whoever it is. We will find him.'

His lips were very close to hers now. She held her breath in anticipation of the kiss. Instead, he turned her around until her back rested against his torso.

'For now, though,' he whispered the words in her ear and his breath tickled her deliciously, 'we have this.'

He pointed up. Allie followed the line of his hand.

The universe gleamed above them.

'Oh ...' she breathed. 'It's so beautiful.'

With no moon to outshine them, the stars filled the sky with an unbelievable brightness.

It wasn't dark at all.

She leaned back to see better; he tightened his arms around her waist, securing her. He was so close she could feel his muscles move. When he breathed, his breath stirred her hair.

'They say it takes so long for light to travel that the glow we see when we look at the stars happened millions of years ago,' he whispered. 'Looking at the sky is like looking back in time. Many of these stars are dead now. Burned out.'

The thought sent a melancholy shiver through her.

'That's sad,' she said. 'It makes me feel so … temporary.'

'Everything is temporary,' he said into her hair. 'Even the stars don't last.'

His fingers traced light patterns on her forearm. The delicate, swishing movements were maddening. He was touching only her arm but she could feel that touch in her stomach.

'I don't want to be temporary …' she whispered.

Then his arms were around her pulling her close and they were kissing with all the stars spinning above them.

His lips were firm against hers at first, demanding. But when she tangled her arms around his neck he grew gentler. Teasing her lips with his until she parted her lips to him with a gasping breath.

His hands ran down her spine, flattening against the small of her back, pressing her harder against him. As she pulled his head down to hers to deepen the kiss, his fingers found the hem of her top and slid underneath it.

Now his hands were warm against her skin. Curious. Stroking up her spine and down again until she found it hard to breathe.

His lips traced a line of heat across her cheek and down along her jawline. Allie leaned back in his arms, letting him support her weight entirely as he planted delicate, butterfly kisses on her throat.

The necklace he'd given her – the lock and key – hung around her neck. He picked it up with a light touch.

'I'm glad you're wearing it,' he said.

'I love it,' she whispered, breathless.

He pulled her back to him, wrapping her in his arms. He held her tight – so tight she could feel the hammering of his heart. With her secured like that, he lowered his body down to the roof tiles, bringing her with him, until he lay flat on his back with Allie on top of him.

She looked down at his face. In the starlight his skin appeared incandescent – like it was illuminated from the inside. His blue eyes sparkled like sapphires.

They were both short of breath by now. They'd kissed before but this was different and they both knew it. Everything was more intense. They were completely alone up here. They could do anything they wanted.

There was no one around to stop them.

Allie's heart raced. Reaching down she traced the lines of his cheekbones with her fingertips. The straight cut of his jaw. His full lips parted at her touch and she traced them, too.

'Allie, I love you.'

All of Allie's breath seemed to leave her. She looked at him in shock.

'Sylvain ...' she whispered. She knew what she was meant to say now.

I love you, too.

Only she couldn't say it.

She wanted to. But her lips wouldn't form the words.

The moment hung there, half finished.

'From the moment I met you,' he whispered, breaking the silence. 'From the moment you sat down at the table that night and looked at me with those eyes … You were so full of fire. So full of honesty. I didn't want anyone in my life. But I *needed* you.'

Allie's heart hurt. She knew this – she'd always known. And she cared about him, too. Very much. They'd fought back from a dark place together. Forged something quite wonderful out of it.

So why couldn't she say it back? What was the matter with her? He was beautiful. He was perfect.

Confusion roiled within her but there was no time to think about it before they were kissing again.

He was more passionate now. His hands stroked her body, touching her everywhere. Her hips. Her stomach. Nobody had ever touched her like this but she wanted him to. She wanted to be wanted.

Then he reached for the edge of her top and started to lift it.

Her body tightened.

Instantly, he stopped; searching her face with his eyes. 'Tell me.'

Flushing, Allie dropped her gaze. 'It's just. I've never …'

'I know,' he said gently.

Somehow this made her feel worse. She scrambled up until she was sitting, facing him.

How did he know? Was it written on her *face*?

She was mortified.

She knew he was more experienced than her. She could just tell. Sylvain was the first boy she'd ever properly kissed.

Then there had been Carter. Things had gone a little further with him but not much.

Like everyone, Allie wanted to know what the fuss was all about. What it was like to really be with someone. At the same time, though, she was afraid. Once they'd done it … what happened next? Where did you go from there?

Seeing the look on her face, he took both her hands in his and held her gaze with steady eyes.

'I think it's obvious I want to do everything with you,' he said, and she blushed again. 'But there's no rush.' He ran his thumbs lightly across the backs of her hands. 'We will take all the time you want.'

Allie looked at him narrowly. Wasn't that something boys just said before they started pressuring you to have sex with them?

'What if I take forever?'

He held her gaze with earnest eyes.

'I would wait forever for you.'

Fourteen

The next morning, Allie went down to breakfast early hoping to talk to Rachel, but she wasn't in her usual place in the dining hall. Between classes she scoured the hallways for her wavy, dark hair, but it wasn't until lunchtime that she saw her, walking down the corridor with a heavy bag of books. She moved with odd stiffness. Allie guessed her muscles must be sore from training.

When she saw Allie, her cheeks coloured and she dropped her eyes.

Allie's heart sank but she was determined. 'Do you have a minute to … talk?'

'Sure,' Rachel said, but her tone was flat and she didn't make one of her usual jokes.

They found a quiet window seat on the landing. It was a sunny day but grey clouds hung at the edges of the sky like a threat. Allie looked out at them as she tried to decide what to say.

The air smelled of cooked food but Allie hadn't been hungry all day.

It was funny how hard this was. She'd discussed it with Sylvain last night after all the kissing, and thought about it more when she couldn't sleep later that night.

She'd thought she knew just what she had to say. But now that Rachel was here, she wasn't sure at all.

'I want to apologise again for the way I acted yesterday,' she said finally. Rachel shook her head as if to stop her but she kept going. 'It must have been scary for you and I just made things worse. I'm sorry. But –' she stared at the clouds again – 'I just ... don't understand what's happening.'

Rachel looked puzzled. 'I don't know what you mean.'

'I mean ...' Allie took a shaky breath. 'You hate Night School. For as long as I've known you ... you've hated it. You tried to talk me out of joining. You got mad at me when I did join. And you and your dad argued about it all the time. And ... I guess I just don't understand what happened to change everything.'

'I told you,' Rachel said. 'After what happened with Nathaniel I decided I needed to learn how to look out for myself. He'll come back. Night School can teach me to how to do that.'

'You could take a self-defence class, Rachel.' Allie couldn't keep the exasperation from her voice. 'They offer kick-boxing in the gym. There are other options. You don't have to join a group you've always hated. You've always believed everything Night School stood for was wrong.'

'I know. But I guess ...' Rachel dropped her gaze. 'I've changed my mind about what I believe. I've seen what Nathaniel can do. What he wants to do to the whole country. And I've decided that the thing I used to hate is better than the thing that could replace it.' She cocked her head to one side. 'Does that make sense?'

It did, but Allie wasn't ready to accept it. 'I don't get how you can change what you believe. You either believe or you don't. That's how it works. You can't just switch like that.'

A red flush crept up Rachel's neck to her face. 'Of course you can change your beliefs.' She looked at Allie accusingly.

'You've changed your beliefs while you've been here. You used to think Night School was creepy then you found out more about it and before I knew what was happening you joined it.' She folded her arms. 'If you can change, I can change.'

'Yeah, but I discussed it all with you.' Allie was finally getting to the crux of the issue. 'I didn't just spring it on you. "Look, Rachel! I've changed everything I ever believed but decided not to tell you. Surprise!"' She waved her arms. 'We were away for nearly three months. We talked all the time – like, for hours. And you never told me you'd decided to join Night School. Or to break up with Lucas. Two of the biggest decisions in your life and you never even mentioned them … Why, Rach?' She couldn't disguise the hurt in her voice. 'Don't you trust me?'

'Of course I trust you.' Rachel looked as if the suggestion horrified her. 'More than pretty much anyone except my parents. And I'm sorry I didn't tell you. I thought about it but … I guess it's hard …' Biting her bottom lip, she looked across the landing. 'I just didn't want to make a fuss about it.'

Allie's expression must have betrayed her disbelief because Rachel sighed and tried again.

'Lucas and I were having problems before we left. The whole thing with him not being included in the group was hard for him and he felt like I didn't back him up. But … it wasn't hard for me. And that's when I started thinking about it. I've never had a boyfriend before so I didn't know how I was supposed to feel. I just knew I was supposed to feel more than *that*.'

Her words summoned an image in Allie's mind of last night. Sylvain whispering, 'I love you.' How she couldn't reply.

She tried to push the memory away, focusing on Rachel, who was still talking.

'We hardly wrote each other letters while I was away. In his last note he suggested that maybe things weren't working out and I –' she glanced at Allie – 'I was relieved. Then we rushed back and everything happened quickly. Now I guess he and Katie are having a thing and …' She wrinkled her nose in distaste. 'I mean, seriously. Whatever.'

'And you didn't want to talk about this before because …?' Allie nudged her.

'Oh, Allie,' Rachel sighed. 'I love to talk about other people's private lives but I hate to talk about my own. You know that. I didn't mean to offend you.'

But Allie knew Rachel too well. She knew that was the sort of answer she'd give a grown-up. The kind of answer she'd give when she didn't want to offer a real answer.

She remembered that giggle she'd heard through Rachel's window last night. She had a feeling Rachel was talking about all of this with Nicole.

Suddenly she felt lonely.

'I wasn't offended.' She said stiffly. 'I was confused. And I guess …' She looked down at her scuffed school shoes, too sad to pretend it didn't hurt. 'I guess I'm afraid of losing my best friend.'

Rachel reached for her arm. 'Oh no, Allie,' she said. 'You're not losing me, I promise. Please don't think that.'

Allie swallowed hard. 'Are you sure? I just feel like you're making these big decisions and I'm just … not part of it, all of a sudden.'

Rachel took her hand. 'Here's the truth, Allie. I'm going through a thing right now. And I'm not sure what it is. But I think I just need a little time to get my head around it. And I may not tell you everything but I am still your best friend, I swear it.' Her voice thickened. 'I hope you believe me.'

This sounded more like the real Rachel, and the tightness in Allie's chest loosened just a little.

'I do,' Allie promised, although she wasn't sure she did. 'But what are you going through? I wish you'd let me help.'

Rachel hesitated. Her cheeks were bright red now. 'I can't ... talk about it.'

And there it was again – this new barrier between them.

Frustrated, Allie pulled away but Rachel reached for her arm again. 'I *will* tell you. I promise. I just have to get my brain around it first. I'm not sure how I really feel. Do you know what that's like?'

'Yes,' Allie admitted reluctantly. 'You know I do. But, Rachel ...' She searched her friend's face. 'I want to help you if you're going through something. I wish you'd trust me.'

Rachel's eyes were bright with unshed tears. 'I do trust you, Allie. Please believe that. It's me I don't trust. Just ... don't give up on me. OK? I couldn't bear it if you gave up on me.'

Allie's conversation with Rachel bothered her all day. What had she meant when she said she was 'going through a thing'? And if it was as big a thing as it seemed to be, why wouldn't she tell her what it was?

This, combined with her confused feelings about what had happened with Sylvain last night and a distinct lack of sleep, meant she struggled through her lessons.

At the end of English class, Allie was gathering her books when Isabelle walked up to her. 'Could I have a word?'

She sounded serious.

Allie's heart skipped a beat. *Did someone see us last night?*

They would be in so much trouble. Maybe the guards had some sort of monitoring system up there. CCTV.

Catching her eye, Sylvain gave her a concerned look. Allie made a helpless gesture in reply.

As he brushed by her, he murmured. 'I'll wait outside.'

When the room was empty, Isabelle leaned back against a desk and crossed her arms. 'Are you well? You seem unfocused today.'

Allie's tension evaporated. This was just about the not-paying-attention thing. She could handle that.

'I had trouble sleeping last night, I guess,' she said. 'I'm just a little tired.'

That was sort of true anyway.

Isabelle appeared to accept this. 'Good,' she said briskly. 'I'm glad it's nothing serious. But I don't want to see you fall behind so early bed tonight.' She gathered her books into a pile. 'Also, there's a senior Night School meeting in the chapel in an hour. It's one of the real ones so it's very important you should be there.'

Allie frowned. 'One of the real ones?'

Swiping a stray strand of hair out of her face, Isabelle looked at her with surprise. 'Oh, didn't I mention this? We talked about so much in my office but I must have forgotten to explain. You see, we have several meetings a week to which we invite the teachers. And other meetings when we do not invite them. The meetings without any teachers are the only true meetings.'

Allie's jaw dropped. 'So that meeting I was at the other day was …'

'A decoy.' Isabelle said as she loaded her books and papers in a glossy black briefcase. 'We use those meetings to share less valuable information and to plant disinformation for Nathaniel. None of the teachers know this, of course. It's crucial that they continue to believe those meetings are, in fact, senior Night School gatherings. The meeting this afternoon will have only the people I am truly certain about and will address what's really happening.'

Allie was taken aback. She could see the intelligence of it but it also showed how bad things had become. How afraid Isabelle really was.

Something else the headmistress said nagged at her.

'I thought students weren't allowed to go to the chapel any more.'

Snapping the case shut, Isabelle headed for the door. 'You have special permission. Raj will take care of that.' She paused, looking back at Allie sternly. 'Don't explain yourself to anyone, even the guards. If anyone asks what you're doing, refer them to Raj. And for God's sake don't get into a fight with them. We mustn't attract attention.' As she walked out of the room, her last words floated over her shoulder. 'And be on time, please.'

Fifteen

As soon as she left Isabelle's classroom, Allie ran up to the girls' dorm and dumped her books in her room. Then she went looking for the others.

Secret meetings? She thought as she galloped down the stairs. *And no one thought to mention this before?*

Everything finally made sense.

All this time she'd been wondering why everything at Cimmeria was so weird. Now she felt like she understood what was going on. Everyone was putting on a show for the spy. The whole school was basically in disguise, while a small group of select people knew the truth about everything.

And she was about to join them.

She searched the common room and library before thinking to try outside. She found Zoe, Nicole and Carter lounging together on the front lawn.

When she saw Carter, Allie's heart gave a traitorous jump. She could have kicked it.

'Hey,' she said, walking up. 'You guys couldn't mention the secret meeting thing at some point?'

Her voice was louder than she'd intended and they all looked up at her in alarm.

'Shhh!' Zoe raised her finger to her lips and shot her a withering look.

Wincing, Allie held up her hands.

'Sorry.' She sat down next to them and lowered her voice to a whisper. 'Why are you all sitting here? Why don't we just go?'

She gestured in the direction of the path that led through the trees to the chapel.

'We have to go in small groups,' Nicole explained *sotto voce*. 'One or two at a time so the teachers don't notice. The guards provide cover but we have to be cautious.' She gave a shrug. 'We're very good at it now. It's easy. Just ... do what we do.'

Not for the first time Allie felt like an outsider at her own school. They'd all worked out this system while she was gone. They all knew the new Rules. And she didn't.

Zoe and Nicole began to chat about something that had happened in one of their classes. Allie looked over to find Carter watching her. His dark eyes were enigmatic as ever but something about his expression told her he understood how she felt.

'You ready for this?' he asked.

'Until twenty minutes ago I didn't know this existed. So ... no,' she said. 'But I'm not going to let that stop me.'

His lips twitched upwards and he nodded, looking off into the trees. 'That's my girl.'

His words made her breath catch in her throat. She dropped her gaze and ordered herself not to be stupid.

That's my girl... It was just a throwaway comment – he hadn't meant anything by it.

So why did it make her feel so wistful? The storm clouds Allie had noticed when she was talking to Rachel earlier that day had now begun to gather in earnest, blocking the sun. The wind began to pick up just as Sylvain arrived to join them.

As he walked up, he glanced at Zoe. 'Isn't it time?'

She nodded and climbed to her feet. Then she darted into the woods like a swallow.

Puzzled, Allie watched her small form disappear into the trees.

'What just happened?' she asked, looking around the group.

'She always goes first.' Sylvain sat on the grass next to her and leaned back as if they were normal students enjoying the last of the good weather before the rains came. 'She's the fastest so if there's any problem she can circle back and let us know. She's like a scout.'

Nicole smiled indulgently. 'She loves it.'

After a few minutes, Carter glanced at his watch and shot Sylvain an enquiring look. Sylvain nodded.

'Our turn,' he said. He climbed to his feet in one graceful move before reaching down to offer Allie his hand. The rising wind ruffled his tawny hair and he smiled at her with his eyes.

Allie let him pull her up. To her surprise, though, when she was on her feet he didn't let go of her hand. She couldn't remember ever holding hands with him before when they weren't running from something.

His grip was strong and warm – her hand felt good in his.

They'd taken a couple of steps together before she remembered to say goodbye to the others.

She turned to call over her shoulder, 'See you there, I guess.'

Nicole gave a jaunty wave. '*Bon voyage* ...'

Allie let her gaze stray to Carter and her stomach flipped – the storm seemed to be captured in his eyes – he looked tormented.

In the woods, everything was calmer. The light filtered softly through the branches. Sound was muffled – even their footsteps were quieter on the soft dirt of the footpath. The air smelled of cool juniper and rich, damp earth.

Allie walked with her head down. She couldn't get the look she'd seen on Carter's face out of her mind. He'd seemed so lonely. So lost.

Was it because of her? Seeing Sylvain hold her hand?

She shook her head to chase the thought away. It couldn't be. Carter loved Jules. Still, she needed to focus on her boyfriend, who was right here with her.

Luckily, Sylvain was willing to help with that. As soon as they were deep in the woods, he stopped and pulled her close.

'I can't believe I haven't kissed you since last night,' he murmured, lowering his lips to hers.

The kiss was soft and gentle, filled with promise.

This was real. This was what mattered.

The wind lashed the branches above their heads, sending pine cones tumbling around them like hard rain. They both ducked.

'The sky is attacking us,' Allie said. 'We better go.'

Lightning crackled in the distance and Sylvain glanced up at the sky. '*Alors*. We should hurry.'

They set off at a steady jog down the curving woodland path. Ferns grew tall on either side, brushing softly against Allie's legs as she ran. She'd been down this path many times. It was as familiar to her as any hallway inside Cimmeria.

The branches whipped back and forth in the wind, their motion dizzying. In the distance, something caught Allie's attention. It was no more than a shadow but something about it didn't make sense. It seemed to move in opposition to the wind.

As she slowed her pace and squinted into the dimness, a sudden strong breeze parted the branches.

Her heart began to pound.

That was no shadow.

She watched the figure of a man, clad in dark clothes, disappear behind a thick clump of trees.

Allie pulled Sylvain's hand. When he met her gaze she pressed her finger to her lips and pointed to where she'd seen the movement.

Instantly alert, he turned to look in the direction she indicated. He let go of her hand and dropped down into a crouch peering intently into the woods. But she could tell he saw nothing.

'I don't …' he whispered, glancing up at her.

Then the man moved again. It was little more than a flicker of darkness amid the green.

'There,' she whispered, crouching down next to him.

Close together, they peered into the forest. The trees, shaken by the rising storm, danced around them.

She felt Sylvain's body tense as he saw the figure. But then he relaxed again just as suddenly.

'A guard,' he said. He sounded absolutely certain.

'Really?' Allie peered into the woods. But the man had disappeared. 'You're sure?'

Sylvain stood up straight; she followed suit.

'I got a good look at him. I've seen him with Raj before,' he said. 'I'm not really surprised. The guards know there's a meeting this afternoon. Raj probably asked him to keep an eye on us. Well, on you, anyway.' His face grew more serious. 'Do you realise you're followed all the time now?'

Allie's stomach dropped. She shook her head.

The guards were everywhere, yes, but it had never occurred to her they might be there for her. But now things clicked into place. Guards in the corridors, on the lawn, on the stairs, in the classrooms and the dorms… she couldn't remember the last time she'd turned around and not seen a black uniform somewhere within view.

They began walking down the path again, more slowly now.

'I know you don't like it but as long as you're safe,' Sylvain said, 'that's what matters.' Allie knew he was right, but the incident still left her feeling invaded. She was watched all the time? What about last night on the roof? Sylvain was certain they weren't watched but… What if they had been?

The idea made her queasy.

Ahead, the chapel wall loomed into view. Its ancient stone covered in grey lichen but just as sturdy as when it was first constructed centuries ago. Here the path curved left to follow the line of the wall. Nearby Allie knew there was a stream, crossed by a stepping-stone bridge. But they didn't go in that direction. Instead, they carried on to an arched wooden gate. Sylvain held it open for her, latching it behind them with a metallic clatter.

Beyond the gate a small, stone chapel stood, surrounded by the dead.

The church was overlooked by an ancient yew tree, huge and eternal, its gnarled roots so old they'd climbed out of the ground like a tangle of prehistoric vines.

This was Allie's favourite place at Cimmeria. Some part of her longed to climb the tree's long branches as she and Carter had done in the old days, and hide from the world.

But those days were over.

The grass stood high in the churchyard; some of the shorter gravestones were overgrown. Even the tallest were half hidden.

Allie looked around in dismay. It wasn't like Mr Ellison to let things go.

'Why is it like this?' she asked, gesturing at the graveyard.

Sylvain followed the direction she indicated with muted interest. 'There aren't enough people around to help the groundskeeper. He let the churchyard go to seed so he could focus on his other work.'

His explanation made Allie's heart heavy.

She knew Mr Ellison would hate letting it go like this. He cared about every bit of his job.

It was only a little thing, but it bothered her.

It bothered her more that Sylvain didn't seem to know his name.

She wanted to tell him Mr Ellison was more than just a groundskeeper – he was a wise and caring man. He'd helped her deal with her grief after Jo died. He'd raised Carter after his parents were killed.

But Sylvain was standing in the chapel door, looking at her expectantly.

Now wasn't the time. Hiding her doubts, she followed him inside.

Sixteen

It was dim and cool inside the church. Allie squinted into the shadows.

Dust motes danced in the faint light trickling through the stained-glass windows. A single breath could send them spinning.

She could make out the medieval paintings on the walls but it was too dark to see the damage Nathaniel's knife had done the previous winter.

A small group had gathered on the front pews near the altar. As her eyes adjusted, she saw Zoe and Isabelle. Raj Patel stood nearby with a woman she couldn't remember seeing before.

Allie's brow creased. She turned a slow circle as if expecting to see more people in the dusty corners, but the small chapel was otherwise empty.

Could it be that Isabelle trusted so few people? Behind her, the church door crashed open. Everyone fell silent as Carter and Nicole stumbled in. Nicole's hair blew around her face in a dark cloud as Carter pulled the door shut with effort.

'The wind's really picking up,' Carter said over his shoulder as he forced the door into place. 'I think it's about to storm.'

Allie's eyes were drawn to the words painted above the door behind him in gothic lettering. It was the school's motto.

Exitus acta probat.

The result justifies the act.

'Everyone is here.' Isabelle's voice echoed off the stone walls, forcing Allie's attention to the front of the chapel. 'We should begin.'

They filed into the pews like churchgoers; the headmistress stood by the altar, a huge iron candelabra towering over her left shoulder, unlit. Through the windows, Allie could see the trees swaying beneath swirling clouds. The air felt pressured. Heavy with anticipation.

Isabelle began without preamble. 'Lucinda has been in touch to say Nathaniel is increasing his efforts to force the board into a no-confidence vote. Our supporters have received threatening phone calls, their children have been harassed. One MP who supports her was denied a seat in Cabinet.' Her serious gaze swept the small gathering. 'The Chancellor has openly joined with him now and, although the Prime Minister is hedging his bets, he's stopped taking Lucinda's calls.' She sighed. 'I must be honest with you. It looks bad.'

Nobody seemed surprised by this. Her next words, though, caused a stir.

'It would appear Nathaniel is aware that Allie has returned to us. He's contacted Lucinda directly asking for a parley.' She hesitated, as if deciding how much to reveal. 'For a variety of reasons she has declined. This may be why someone attempted to break into the school grounds last night.'

Allie's heart stuttered. Next to her, she felt Sylvain's body stiffen.

'Are you serious?' Carter's tone was sharp.

Isabelle nodded. 'Very.'

Concerned voices swirled around Allie, but she tuned them out. She thought of the person she'd glimpsed in the woods. How some part of her had been disappointed it wasn't Nathaniel. Wasn't someone she could fight.

Even now she knew she should be afraid, and she was. But she was also eager. Ready to fight back.

'What exactly happened?' Nicole's French-accented voice pulled Allie back to the conversation. 'How close did they get?'

'Raj,' Isabelle said. 'Please explain.'

The security chief stepped forward. His familiar face made Allie feel better instantly. Rachel's father was the kind of man who exuded calmness in all situations. The more severe the crisis, the calmer he seemed.

'There was an attempted intrusion last night, just after two in the morning.' The Yorkshire accent he'd never lost stretched every word. 'Someone tried to open the gate using a remote electronic device. Luckily, before any damage could be done, the hack was blocked by Dom, here.' He gestured at the woman Allie had noticed earlier. She sat on the front row with her back to the rest of the group.

She leaned forward to get a better look at her.

The woman was younger than she'd first thought, probably no more than twenty, and slim, with short-cropped black hair, smooth skin the colour of coffee and stylish narrow glasses.

As Raj talked, she sat, legs crossed, in a relaxed posture, but Allie noticed she tapped her fingers in a subconsciously nervous gesture.

At the front of the room, Raj was still talking. 'When we reinstituted tech a few months ago, Dom thought to put a block on every electronic device on the grounds, including the front gate. They all respond only to signals directed to them from inside the school building,' he explained. 'At the same time she programmed a tracker into them, so any attempt from outside the school is logged and traced. Thanks to her, we know which device was used, and where the signal came from.'

'Awesome,' Zoe whispered approvingly.

'Where did the signal come from?' Carter asked.

Raj motioned for Dom to answer.

Thunder rumbled in the distance.

Dom stood and turned to face them. Her clothes were androgynous – skinny trousers, a loose, white shirt and what looked like a man's blazer, worn unbuttoned with the sleeves rolled up. She seemed out of place in this setting.

'It was a short-range device, so it would have originated from just outside the gates – either the woods or the road.' She had an American accent. 'The individual could have been on foot or in a vehicle but they didn't stick around long enough for us to find out. We sent the guards out immediately and they were already gone when they arrived.'

Allie studied Dom with curious eyes. This was the new tech everyone was talking about. For some reason, she'd expected her to be a guy. She'd also expected her to be older. And much less cool.

She seemed to know what she was talking about, but Allie was nonetheless surprised Isabelle had allowed her into the inner circle so quickly.

She glanced around the group – everyone sat still, watching Dom with respectful expressions. Whoever she was, and wherever she'd come from, she'd won them all over.

'Are you certain they were trying to get into the grounds?' Sylvain asked.

Dom turned to him.

'Not necessarily,' she conceded. 'We can't be sure of their plan. They could have been testing our defences. Or merely trying to unnerve us. Either way, they left frustrated. Our security system held.'

'This is the first attempted incursion in three months.' Raj nodded to Dom, who sat down quickly as if relieved to be finished talking. 'Given what you've heard from Lucinda, we believe this is no coincidence. It's more likely this is the beginning of the next phase.'

'You mentioned a parley,' Allie said. 'Why isn't Lucinda meeting him? Isn't that the only way to resolve this?'

Isabelle and Raj exchanged a look she couldn't read.

'She cannot accept his conditions,' the headmistress said after a brief hesitation. 'It would be too dangerous. They're still negotiating.'

Before Isabelle could elaborate, Carter spoke. 'You're increasing patrols?'

Raj inclined his head. 'We've cancelled all non-emergency leave.'

Allie thought of what it had been like here a few months ago. Nathaniel's guards dragging students out of the school. Hiding in the cellar for hours. Emerging to find the school empty; Rachel kidnapped, Jules gone.

'It's starting again,' she said. 'Isn't it?'

The others turned to look at her.

When Isabelle responded she chose her words carefully. 'Nathaniel indicated to Lucinda that he intends to take the school. He will not give up.'

It had grown darker inside the church. Outside heavy clouds blackened the sky. As Allie looked through the window, the first rain drops hit the roof like fists knocking.

The storm had arrived.

⁂

When the meeting ended, Allie gathered with the others by the door. They needed to leave in small groups again and they were waiting for Raj's signal. The rain still fell and the air smelled damp and musty.

'Who is this Dom person anyway?' She kept her voice low. Dom was with Isabelle and Raj by the altar.

Zoe blinked at her owlishly. 'She's a genius.'

Allie made an impatient gesture. 'Yeah, but where did she even come from? Why does everyone trust her so much? What kind of name is "Dom"?'

'She's from the American organisation,' Nicole explained quietly.

'Oh,' Allie said. 'She's from Pegasus?'

Zoe rolled her eyes. '*Prometheus*.'

'Allie.' Across the chapel, Isabelle was waving her over to where she stood with Raj and Dom. 'Could we speak with you?'

Leaving the others at the door, Allie walked down the aisle. Her footsteps seemed loud in the hushed room.

'What's up?'

Raj waited for Isabelle to speak. No one introduced her to Dom, who studied Allie with eyes that seemed to miss nothing. Up close she looked even hipper. Suddenly Allie's school uniform seemed juvenile.

'We've just been discussing how much to tell you,' Isabelle said quietly. 'I'm generally opposed to alarming you unduly but Raj and Dom disagree, so …'

Whenever people don't want to tell you something, the thing they don't want to tell you is always bad.

Allie's stomach tightened.

Seeing the concern on her face, the headmistress held up a cautioning hand. 'Please don't worry. It's all under control. We just … need to talk to you.' Isabelle's eyes swept the church as if ensuring no one could overhear her. 'We think you should know what's been happening behind the scenes. The reason Lucinda refused to accept Nathaniel's invitation to meet. It was because of the conditions he demanded.'

Even though she'd said not to worry, Allie knew her well enough to recognise the anxiety in Isabelle's eyes, and the way her hands moved restlessly at her sides.

'What conditions?' she asked.

'You.'

The word seemed to hang in the air.

'He insists you're at the parley,' Isabelle continued. 'Obviously, Lucinda sees this for the trap it most likely is and has refused. But he's not backing down. They're at an impasse. Because of this, we expected Nathaniel to retaliate. Last night's attempt was just the start.'

An awful sense of trepidation settled over Allie. Parleys were meetings between enemies, intended purely for negotiation.

There was no logical reason for Nathaniel to want her there. Unless this wasn't really a parley.

It was typical of him to use trickery and lies. To play games with people's lives. He never seemed to tire of it. When it came to Cimmeria – to her – he was a machine. He came back and back and back. Relentlessly. He didn't care who got hurt. Who died. He would never give up. Never stop.

It had to stop.

Feeling suddenly tired, she raked her fingers through her hair, pressing her fingertips hard against her skull.

'So now more people will get hurt because of me,' she said tonelessly.

All they'd been through over the last year, all the running and hiding, the fighting and dying. And for what? Nathaniel was inches away from taking over the Orion Society. He was so close to victory he must be able to taste it. And once he won, everything was lost. He would reshape the country in his image. Behind the protective curtain of the powerful organisation he could do whatever he wanted. Use his power to hurt people who couldn't fight back. Change the government. Change people's lives. They would never know his name. Never recognise his face. He would live in the shadows, a puppet master pulling the strings.

'That's where we come in.' Raj leaned forward to catch her gaze. 'We're working very hard to keep him out, and we'll continue to do so. We've been successful for three months ...'

'I've been *away* for three months.' Allie's anger boiled over and her voice rose. 'He's been too busy chasing me around the world to mess with you.'

'Allie, there's no reason to overreact ...' Isabelle began but Raj kept talking as if she hadn't spoken.

'We've brought in extra guards,' he said, as if this changed everything. 'And we're increasing the number of patrols.'

In despair, Allie lowered her head to her hands. Was he delusional? More guards? More patrols? The grounds were vast and wooded, with hills, lakes and forests. You could hide an army out there. And sometimes it seemed Nathaniel had. Last time he'd brought a helicopter. What were they going to do if it came back?

Throw stones at it?

'It has worked before, Allie,' Isabelle said.

Allie whirled on her. 'It has *failed* before, Isabelle. And it will fail again this time.' She looked back and forth between them, cold with anger. 'You keep doing the same things over and over again hoping people don't die this time. I just don't …'

Her raised voice echoed off the old stone walls. Across the chapel the others turned to stare at them.

She cast them a desperate look. That was enough. Sylvain and Carter crossed the room to join her and the others followed right on their heels.

'What's happening here?' Sylvain looked around the group for an explanation.

'Tell them.' Allie turned to Raj and Isabelle, her hands on her hips. 'Tell them how you're going to stop Nathaniel with more guys in black. Tell them your amazing comms system will keep us alive when he comes for his revenge. They deserve to know what's about to happen.'

'What exactly is going on, Isabelle?' Carter stepped forward until he was standing beside Allie.

'It's insane,' Allie said.

'You're being childish,' Raj retorted, his tone sharpening. 'This is the system.'

'Can someone please explain—' Sylvain began.

'Stop this.' Isabelle's voice echoed off the stone walls. They all fell silent. 'This conversation is pointless. This is the way it has to be. We don't have any alternative.'

'Yes, you do.' It was Dom's voice. They all turned to her. Her gaze was on Allie. 'The alternative is standing right in front of you.'

Disbelief spread across Isabelle's face – clearly she hadn't expected this rebellion. 'Lucinda has made it clear she won't allow Allie to attend the parley and I agree with her decision—'

'What? Nathaniel wants to have a parley with *you*?' Carter said to Allie. 'Why would he do that?'

'He doesn't want to meet me. He wants to meet Lucinda. But he says he'll only do it if I come, too,' Allie explained patiently. 'Because he's a mentalist.'

The others exchanged a look.

'A trap,' Sylvain said. 'It would be a perfect time to snatch her. No arms. No guards.'

'Exactly.' Isabelle appeared relieved, as if she'd just won the argument.

'Not every trap catches its prey,' Dom said.

'Many do.' Raj shot her a narrow look. 'Too many to just take a chance with Allie's life.'

'It's my life,' Allie protested. 'It should be my decision what to do with it.'

Dom kept her focus on Raj. 'What are you going to do?' she asked him quietly. 'We can fend off more attacks, keep him out for a while – days. Weeks maybe. Not months. No system is unhackable – you taught me that. If he keeps trying, eventually he'll get in. Then it's game over. We lose.'

Allie looked at Dom in surprise. She worked for Raj but seemed to feel perfectly comfortable openly disagreeing with him. Most of his guards were of the 'Yes, sir!' variety. This one was clearly different.

Raj's jaw was set. 'If we bring in extra guards, cover every inch—'

'You would need a thousand men.' There was no rancour in Dom's voice, only calm rationale. 'Have you got a thousand men?'

'Enough.' Raj, who never raised his voice, nearly shouted the word. His face was red with frustration. 'She can't go. It's too dangerous.'

Turning to Allie, Dom scrutinised her, as if she was a car she was considering purchasing. 'Well, I'd say that's up to her. She's not a child. And from what you've all told me she's extremely capable. There's no reason to assume she'd fail.'

Uncertain, Allie stared back at her. Nobody stood up to Raj like this. Ever. But Dom seemed to see herself as his equal.

How does she know whether I'm capable or not?

Dom's voice cut through the haze of her thoughts. 'What do you say, Allie Sheridan?' The daylight was fading and it was hard to read the American girl's eyes behind her glasses but Allie could hear the challenge in her voice. 'Everyone tells me you never back down from a fight. Want to try and save the world?'

Allie's gaze skated from Raj to Isabelle, waiting for them to argue, but they'd both fallen silent. Isabelle looked unhappy.

Somehow Dom had done it – they were letting her choose.

Now that she had the choice, though … what did she want?

It *was* a trap, she was certain of it. Although it wasn't like Nathaniel to be quite so obvious. Still, there was no reason for her to be present unless he had something planned.

Something awful.

But if she didn't go to him, he'd come to her, and she knew from brutal personal experience that was worse.

Trepidation made her pulse race.

She thought about Jo and Ruth, about Nathaniel with a knife to Rachel's throat. About how the knife had felt when it parted the skin of her arm, and her visceral fear when Gabe raised a brick over Carter's head to finish him off.

In the end, though, they'd stood up to Nathaniel – the students and guards together. They made him back down. There had to be a way they could do it again – only this time, permanently. He wasn't a god, after all. He was just a man. A delusional, obsessed man.

If she could talk to him – find out something she could give him that he wanted – maybe she could stop this. Or even if she couldn't, maybe she could make it better in some way just by being there.

If she kept hiding and did nothing, how would that do any good? Nathaniel would attack, Raj would parry, more people would get hurt. Maybe even die. And it would happen over and over until finally they were defeated. Then Nathaniel would have what he wanted anyway, and what would have been the point of anything?

Yes, she was just a kid and he was a rich and powerful man. But a tiny twig can stop a clock ticking. A speck of dust can do a lot of damage to a delicate machine. She thought of Sylvain's voice the other night on the roof.

Jump.

She held Dom's gaze.
'I'm in,' she said.

Seventeen

Next to her, Sylvain let out his breath. Carter turned to look at her, concern written on his face.

'Awesome,' Zoe muttered.

Instantly, Isabelle and Raj began to argue. Dom appeared composed as the voices swelled around her.

'We should go, I think,' Sylvain said quietly.

He was right – there was nothing to be done. The leaders would fight it out now. But Allie's mind was made up. One way or another, she was going to that parley.

The adults didn't seem to notice the students leaving the chapel – no one tried to stop them. Outside, the air was cool and smelled clean. Allie took a deep breath. Now that the decision was made, she felt lighter; a bit dizzy from her own bravery. Tilting her head back she let the soft summer rain fall on her face.

The others were still oddly silent; she could sense their disapproval.

They were well into the woods before Nicole broke the silence.

'We'll have to prepare.'

She seemed to be avoiding Allie's gaze. 'We know how Nathaniel and Gabe fight. How they operate. We will need to be ready to defend Lucinda.'

'And Allie.' Sylvain's face was creased with worry.

'And ourselves,' Carter said.

'Will we all get to go with her, I wonder?' Zoe asked, looking around the group.

'We'll go.' Nicole's voice sounded tight and Allie turned to look at her more closely.

Rain clung to her dark hair and ran down her face like tears. The set of her shoulders, the tight line of her jaw, told her she was upset. 'We don't have any *choice*.'

She emphasised the last word.

No one argued with her. Only Zoe didn't seem to know what she meant.

'What?' Allie scanned the closed faces around her. 'Are you all mad at me for agreeing to go to the parley? What else was I supposed to do?'

'I'm not mad,' Zoe said. 'I'm excited.'

Allie ignored her. 'Nicole?' The rain grew heavier. Water ran down her face in rivulets, trickling down the collar of her soaked blouse. 'Is there something you want to say?'

The French girl kept her eyes on the ground. 'I think you make these decisions that affect other people's lives and you don't think about what it means. It's dangerous. *You're* dangerous.'

Stung, Allie looked around the group for support. Sylvain stared into the distance, his jaw tight. She could see his disapproval in the tense line of his shoulders.

When she met Carter's gaze, he held out his empty hands in a gesture that said '*What did you expect?*'

Anger flared in her chest. Nicole had basically stolen her best friend and now she was going to take everyone else, too?

No way.

'Well, maybe you'd just rather hand me over to Nathaniel so you can all be a little safer.' Allie's tone was cutting. 'Or maybe you'd like to just side with him now and get it over with. Cimmeria could always use another spy. I hear the pay is great.'

She heard someone's breath catch. Nicole looked shocked.

'Allie,' Sylvain said. 'Don't—'

Allie whirled on him. 'Don't tell me what to do. I hate that.'

He flinched away from her.

Without a word, Carter walked away, leaving them to fight it out. Somehow, this bothered Allie most of all.

'I don't get it,' Zoe said, clearly puzzled. 'Why is everyone pissed off?'

'Forget it, Zoe,' Allie snapped. 'It doesn't matter.'

※

The rain finally stopped that evening but the skies stayed grey. The tensions didn't ease as the hours passed.

At dinner that night the mood at the table was decidedly icy, and Allie couldn't wait to get away. As soon as the meal ended, she pushed back her chair, but before she could stand up, Sylvain leaned over to whisper in her ear, 'We should talk.'

His tone was curt, and her heart sank. She didn't want to fight about this with him. She wanted him to back her up. To understand that she had no choice.

To trust her.

But it was clear there was no getting around it. With reluctant steps, she followed him out into the hallway and up the staircase to the relative privacy of the landing.

At the top, the tall windows had been left open to let in the damp air, cool and fresh from the rain. His expression unreadable, Sylvain led the way into a nook, hidden away behind a tall marble statue.

'What is it?' Allie said, eager to get this over with. 'Is it about what happened today? Because I don't really want to talk about it.'

He looked at her steadily, blue eyes blank and cool. 'Don't you?'

His challenging tone threw her off balance. No matter what she did, Sylvain never got angry with her. She didn't think she knew how to argue with him.

'No …?' she said, her hesitant tone betraying her sudden uncertainty.

His gaze didn't falter. 'I would think you would want to defend your position. Tell me why everyone else is wrong,' he said. 'And you are right.'

Heat rose to Allie's cheeks. This was worse than she'd expected. He seemed genuinely upset.

She needed to change tactics.

'Ok, I've obviously upset you. And, like, everyone. So, that can't be good.' She tried to look as conciliatory as possible. Noble, even. 'I'm sorry if you think I made the wrong decision.'

He didn't wait to hear any more.

'Allie, you could die.'

His words cut across her faltering logic and she stared, at him, wide-eyed. All her excuses evaporated.

'If you go to the parley, Nathaniel could kill you. That may be his plan. And if we go with you, to protect you, we could die, too. Nicole could die. I could die. Carter could die. Do you understand that?' His tone was measured but his words stung. 'I need to know that you understand what you are committing us all to do, without asking us what we think. What we want. Whether we are ready to die.'

A sudden image of Jo, blood encircling her body, flashed into Allie's mind.

She breathed in an audible gasp, and jumped to her feet. 'I have to go.'

But before she could turn away, his hand flashed out and grabbed her wrist.

'You should stay and listen to me, Allie. If you won't listen to anyone else. At least listen to me.' She struggled in his grip, not wanting to hear any more. 'Please, Allie. This is important.'

'I *know that*.' Tearing her arm free from his grasp, she stared at him reproachfully, her chest heaving.

How dare he imply that she didn't know this was dangerous? How dare he talk to her like she didn't know what dying meant?

Did anyone know better than her?

She knew if she said half the things in her mind right now he'd never forgive her and she'd never forgive him. She had to get away, before more damage was done.

Hands clenched into fists, she raised her chin and forced herself to keep her voice low.

'I'm sorry you're angry at me, Sylvain, but I can't do this.'

Then she spun on her heel and fled.

After that, Sylvain kept his distance.

He wasn't alone.

Nicole avoided Allie in the hallways, which meant Rachel avoided her, too, as they were so often together. Isabelle and Raj were similarly cool and distant, and the issue of the parley had not been brought up again. It was as if they'd decided not to discuss it with her.

Carter seemed to disapprove of the entire situation, and Allie rarely saw him. She got the feeling he was avoiding everyone.

As the days passed, she went through the paces of classes and training, but she did it mostly on her own. She felt cut off and isolated, but she wouldn't back down. The meeting between Lucinda and Nathaniel had to happen. It was their only chance. And she had to be there, whether the others liked it or not.

Only Zoe seemed immune to the disharmony in the group, and she stuck resolutely by Allie's side.

One night during Night School training, Allie found an excuse to ask her what she knew about Dom.

'She's cool,' Zoe enthused, aiming a kick at the side of Allie's head. 'She invented some new software for computer monitoring – Raj says the Secret Service use it.'

Ducking the blow, Allie feinted in a zigzag pattern, coming up, arm raised, poised to attack. Zoe blocked the blow with vicious quickness.

Jerry, who'd been watching them spar from a distance, walked up to them. 'Beautifully executed, both of you. I've never seen it done better.'

Relieved that at least one adult wasn't angry at her, Allie smiled at him gratefully. 'Thanks.'

'Keep it up.' Patting Zoe on the shoulder, he walked on to the next pair of students.

Zoe accepted the praise without hesitation. 'He's right. We're freaking awesome.'

Wiping the sweat from her forehead, she picked up a bottle of water from the mat.

Allie looked across the room to where Rachel and Nicole were practising the same move. Nicole's moves were fluid and easy. By contrast, Rachel looked awkward and jerky, recoiling as if afraid when Nicole practised her kick. Raj was watching them, too, and Allie saw him shake his head in exasperation. But Nicole just rested a hand lightly on Rachel's arm and said something that made her laugh, then demonstrated the move again.

It was the right way to work with Rachel – the way Allie would have done it herself.

Again, she felt a knife stab of jealousy.

'She dropped out of Harvard after one year.' Zoe was still talking about Dom as she took a swig of water. 'She was already minted from the software so she didn't see the point in staying there.'

Around them, Night School students kicked and punched each other in complex, violent manoeuvres.

'Isabelle said Raj brought her in. How do they know each other?' Allie asked.

'Dom went to school here. She was an exchange student.'

'Seriously?' Allie couldn't hide her surprise. Nobody had ever mentioned Dom was legacy.

'Raj was her Night School instructor and mentor,' Zoe explained. 'But when they took all the computers away she went back to America. Or at least, that's what everyone says.'

Allie knew that would have taken guts. Nobody just walked away from Cimmeria.

If Dom was the kind of person who trusted her instincts like that, it made sense that she would want Allie to do the same.

Jump.

As she thought it through, her gaze fell to where Carter and Sylvain were practising together – they made the complex series of moves look more violent and potentially deadly than anyone else in the room. They swung at each other so hard she winced, but each pulled back at the last second, just before a foot could hit a neck, or an elbow cut deep into an eye socket.

The force they were using made it hard to believe they weren't genuinely angry, but between rounds she saw Carter make a joke and Sylvain crease up with laughter.

It struck her they were at ease with each other in a way they were never at ease with her.

There was always something between her and each of them – a kind of force field of sex and love.

They didn't have that with each other. So they could just be friends.

And there's that jealousy again.

With a sigh, she turned her focus back to Zoe. 'So why did Dom come back to Cimmeria now?'

'Because I asked her to.' Raj's voice made them both jump and they spun round to see him standing behind them; his expression was dark. 'We needed her help. But right now I'm not convinced that wasn't a mistake. Zoe, your kick is coming from your lower back, not your abdominals. Work on that.'

As he strode off with silent steps, Zoe said in tones of reverence, 'He walks like a ghost. It is *amazing.*'

When training ended that night, Allie began to follow the others out to the dressing room but Sylvain walked up to her.

'Could you wait a second, please?'

She looked up at him in surprise. They'd barely spoken since their argument.

'Sure,' she said cautiously. 'What's up?'

He looked around the room. The other students were streaming out into the changing rooms. 'It's... Well. I will explain in a minute.'

She searched his face for clues but his blue eyes were unreadable. As the room emptied, Carter came over but stayed some distance away, hands shoved in his pockets. Allie tried to catch his eye but he seemed to purposefully avoid her gaze.

Then Zoe, Nicole and Rachel came to stand with them, too.

'What's going on?' Allie asked suspiciously. 'Is this an intervention or something?'

No one smiled.

Only when they were completely alone in the training room did Sylvain answer her question. 'If you're going to the parley, we have to prepare.'

Allie was confounded. 'I thought that was what we just did. Isn't two and a half hours of kicking the crap out of each other preparation?'

'It helps,' Carter said. 'But you've dealt with Nathaniel before. You know what he's like. He doesn't play by the rules.'

Walking to the edge of the room, he crouched down and felt for something underneath the rubber matting. After a moment, he pulled out two objects Allie couldn't quite see.

Then he turned round. In one hand he held a lethal-looking dagger. In his other he held a gun.

The blood drained from Allie's face.

Unnerved, she stared at the knife. The scar on her arm throbbed.

'Carter,' she whispered, 'where did you get those?'

'Don't worry. They're fake.' Sylvain seemed pleased by her reaction. 'Raj got them for us to work with.'

'But,' Carter said, 'they're very good fakes.'

With a casual flick of his wrist, he tossed Sylvain the gun; Sylvain caught it with one hand.

Allie looked around the room – Rachel and Nicole both avoided her gaze. Zoe was watching the weapons with excited anticipation. Nobody seemed surprised by what was happening.

'What's happening here?'

Still holding the gun, Sylvain turned to Allie, his blue gaze steady. 'We're going to practise with the weapons Nathaniel will mostly likely use. We need to know how to protect ourselves from them.'

Carter pulled the dagger from its sheath with a soft *snick*.

The weapon glimmered silver in the dim light. Allie couldn't take her eyes off it.

It might be a fake but it looked lethal enough.

'It's unsharpened.' Carter dragged the blade across his forearm, holding up his arm to show off the unblemished skin.

Taking the knife from him, Zoe turned it over in her hand. She touched the end experimentally with the tip of her finger.

'You could do some damage with the pointy bit,' she announced.

'No stabbing, then,' Rachel said faintly. 'We should probably make that a rule.'

Rachel looked a bit green but not disapproving or upset and Allie couldn't understand why. This was exactly the sort of thing she hated. Why wasn't she protesting?

The cool clarity of realisation hit her like cold water. They were trying to convince her she was wrong about the parley the same way she'd wanted to convince Rachel she was wrong about Night School – by letting her go ahead with it. Hoping she'd drop out.

Dropping her hands to her sides she curled them into fists.

'OK then.' Her voice was tight. 'Let's do this.'

Eighteen

'Go for the wrist.' Carter's voice was sharper than the knife in his hand. Allie gripped his wrist hard but he twisted his arm until, somehow, the knife ended up pointed at her throat.

'You're dead,' he said. 'Try again.'

Sweat ran down Allie's face, stinging her eyes. They'd been practising with the weapons for nearly an hour. She'd already been tired at the end of normal Night School training. Now her muscles felt like rubber.

Across the room, Rachel pointed a gun at Zoe, who promptly kicked it from her hand, sending it flying through the air.

Clutching the hand she'd kicked, Rachel grimaced at the younger girl. 'Uh … that's great, Zoe. You live. I, on the other hand, need extensive reconstructive surgery.'

'*Yes*.' Zoe gave a victorious air punch.

'Again, Allie.' Carter drew her gaze back to the blade. 'You have to get better at this.'

Tightening her jaw, she squared off against him again.

'Fine,' she said through gritted teeth. 'Let's go again.'

He slashed the knife towards her abdomen and she jumped back fast – too fast. She tripped over her feet, falling hard on to the mat.

Rage, white hot and blinding, rushed through her veins like fire.

Bounding back up she advanced on him, so furious she could hardly see him. She swung a vicious kick at his neck.

Sylvain stepped between them, blocking the blow with his arm. 'That's *enough*.' He turned to Allie. 'Watch your temper.'

Shooting him a resentful look, she ran a tired hand through her sweaty hair.

'Look. I know why you're all doing this,' she said. 'You can just … stop it. It won't work.'

'We're doing this because we want to help you,' Nicole said.

Too tired to play games, Allie shot her a withering look. 'That's bollocks and you know it. Let's just be honest now, at least. Raj put you up to this, didn't he? Because he wants me to change my mind about the parley.'

For a second, no one spoke.

'We did talk to Raj about this, yes,' Sylvain said carefully. 'He thought it would be a good idea if we did the first training without warning. So you could learn to react instinctively.'

As she looked into his cool blue eyes, Allie's heart seemed to contract in her chest.

'Sylvain …' Allie didn't know what to say. He was almost her boyfriend. She had the necklace he'd given her safely tucked away in her room so nothing could happen to it in practice. He'd told her he loved her. And yet he let her walk into an ambush?

The sense of betrayal made her ache.

'I can't believe you …' She couldn't seem to find the words. 'Why didn't you just come to me?'

'Would you have listened?' he asked.

Her shoulders sagged. 'You could have tried to find out.'

'Hang on, Allie.' Ever the peacemaker, Rachel stepped between them. 'Sylvain did suggest other options but my dad thought it was best this way. He thought it wouldn't be as effective if we went to you separately. He said this would remind you what it's like, dealing with Nathaniel. How he always does what you don't expect. We didn't like it but …'

'You did it anyway.' The words came out as a whisper.

Hopelessness swept over her.

Do I have to fight everyone all the time? She wondered. *Even my friends?*

Her gaze darted to where Carter stood apart from the group. He'd said very little, and looked unhappy but he wasn't exactly taking her side, either.

Rachel was still talking. 'You agreed to the parley without really taking time to think about it. We wanted to kind of … shock you. To make you realise how serious this is.'

'You think I don't know this is *serious*?' Allie's voice rose sharply on the last word and Rachel flinched.

Allie wanted to say more but she stopped herself. She needed to look at this rationally. These were her closest friends. She'd obviously made a terrible mistake or they wouldn't have gone to such extremes to show her how they felt. She'd scared them. Made them feel helpless.

Wrapping her arms across her torso, she looked around the cluster of familiar faces. Everyone in this room had been hurt by Gabe or Nathaniel. Some more than others. Nicole had been beaten up and her leg badly injured; Carter had been knocked unconscious and could have been killed; Rachel beaten and cut, Zoe beaten, Sylvain beaten.

No wonder they were unhappy that she'd just agreed to drag them back into this without consulting them. It must have looked like she didn't care about how they felt. Like she was putting them all in danger again on a whim.

All her anger seeped away.

'I'm sorry,' she said softly. Across the room, Carter's head shot up and his eyes met hers. 'I get it … OK? You can tell Raj I get the message. Let's just … talk this through tomorrow. We'll prepare properly. We'll be ready. And I won't –' Tears burned the back of her throat. She had to force herself to complete the thought. 'I won't do anything you don't all agree to.'

She needed to get out of here. The room seemed too small all of a sudden. She stumbled towards the door, blinded by a haze of tears.

'Allie …' Sylvain reached out towards her but she brushed his hand away.

'I have to go.'

The next day was grey and steamy. The air felt oppressive; so warm and heavy you got the feeling you could slice it.

After her last class, Allie headed down the main staircase. Her movements were stiff, and each time her book bag thumped against her hip, her muscles objected.

All day, no one had said a word about what had happened. They were all staying clear of her.

While she understood their motives, she wished they'd given her more credit. And she wished they understood why she'd said yes to the parley. That there was no other way.

After all, it wasn't like she was completely self-destructive. She knew perfectly well the parley was a trap. And she had no intention of getting caught in it.

Dom was right. Not every trap catches its prey.

Besides, she thought as she passed a team of security guards, *right now the school is as much a trap as the parley.*

Hell, life's a trap, when you stop and think about it. No one here gets out alive.

She'd nearly reached the bottom of the staircase when Zoe raced up to her, grabbing her hand.

'Quick,' she said, pulling at her. 'Isabelle wants you.'

'Oh God.' Allie sighed. She really wasn't in the mood for one of Isabelle's lectures right now. 'Do I have to?'

Zoe looked at her like she was crazy. 'Yes.'

Reluctantly, Allie turned towards Isabelle's office but she didn't hurry her steps. Every time they'd spoken since the meeting in the chapel, Isabelle had tried to change her mind about the parley. There was no doubt she was in on last night's plan.

On the ground floor, she made her way down the hallway to the office under the stairs and raised her hand to knock.

The sound of raised voices inside the room stilled her hand. Frowning, she leaned forward to hear what was happening inside.

'It's a terrible idea, Lucinda.' Isabelle's voice was sharp.

Allie's heart jumped. Her grandmother was here? Now?

Even with her ear pressed to the door, she couldn't hear what her grandmother said in reply, her voice was too low. But whatever it was she said made Isabelle angry.

'She's a child,' Allie heard Isabelle say. 'She should be worrying about her A-levels, not her life. I won't let you put her through this.'

After that, she lowered her voice, and her words were lost in the thick oak panelling.

Wondering what Lucinda had said, Allie knocked. The conversation inside ceased.

'Come in,' Isabelle said after a moment. Her voice had regained its normal air of calm authority.

The door sprang open at Allie's touch and she hurried in. Everything in Isabelle's office was in its usual place – the large desk dominating one side, the low file cases and cabinets.

But other than the headmistress, it was empty.

For one perplexed moment, Allie peered into corners as if her grandmother might be hiding behind something.

She cleared her throat. 'Zoe said you wanted to … see me?'

'She's here,' Isabelle said to her desk.

'Oh good. Allie, thank you for joining us.' Lucinda's voice emerged, thin and tinny, from a mobile phone resting on the green leather blotter in front of Isabelle. 'I thought it was time we had a chat.'

Nineteen

'Have a seat please,' Isabelle said.

Feeling oddly nervous, Allie perched on the edge of one of the leather chairs facing the desk and shot her an enquiring look. The headmistress looked as if she wanted to speak but then she stopped herself and instead gestured at the phone.

Even when she wasn't physically present, Lucinda was in charge.

'Allie, I hear you're doing very well, readjusting to Cimmeria life.' Her grandmother's powerful voice sounded almost comically small through the phone's minute speakers. 'I'm not at all surprised.'

Again Allie's eyes flitted up to Isabelle's face, searching for clues as to what was happening here. The headmistress kept her gaze lowered, giving nothing away. But Lucinda's next statement answered Allie's unasked question.

'I've asked you here to discuss our plans for the parley with Nathaniel. I understand you have been informed of his requests?'

Allie nodded, then remembered her grandmother couldn't see her. 'Yes.'

'And you think you should come with me?'

Allie hesitated – it sounded like a trick question.

'Ye-es …' she said with more caution.

'You are fully aware of how dangerous Nathaniel is. What he's capable of. And what he wants,' Lucinda said. 'Yet you still want to take this risk? Why?'

Across the desk, Isabelle lifted her golden brown eyes to meet her gaze. Last night's tense training session flashed into Allie's mind again. She remembered how sickened she'd felt seeing the knife in Carter's hand.

Whatever she'd said at the time, and however angry that had made her feel, in some way it had worked. She was much more afraid now than she'd been when she agreed to go to the parley.

And yet she still knew in her heart it was the right decision.

Jump.

'You're going to the parley. You'll be taking a risk,' Allie reasoned. 'Why shouldn't I?'

'We are not the same,' her grandmother's voice said. 'I am trying to fix a problem I had some hand in creating. You, on the other hand, are purely innocent in this. Each side wants to use you to their own ends.'

Allie saw Isabelle's eyes widen in surprise.

Each side wants to use you …

It was oddly comforting to hear an adult verify what Allie had long believed. But it still stung.

'I know that.' Allie tried to sound cool. 'I'm not a complete idiot. But maybe I'm not the pawn you all think I am. If I don't go, I can't change anything. If I'm there, I have some control over what happens to us.'

'Will you?' Lucinda sounded unconvinced. 'Even if you come, I'll still be in control of what happens. You'll just be there to prove my willingness to cooperate. To convince Nathaniel that I'm really listening to him. That doesn't seem worth risking your life.'

'Oh, please.' Allie couldn't keep the bitterness from her tone. 'If I don't come with you, he won't talk to you. If you two don't talk, he'll attack the school, hurting people I care about.' She tightened her lips. 'He'll never give up. When you look at it that way, I don't think I actually have a choice. But no one else is dying because of me. I'm going with you.'

When she spoke again Lucinda's voice was quiet. 'Isabelle thinks you're not ready for this. I think she underestimates you.'

The headmistress kept her gaze lowered. Allie felt suddenly protective of her.

'She doesn't underestimate me,' she said. 'She wants to protect me.'

'And you don't want to be protected?'

Allie didn't hesitate. 'I want to fight back.'

A long silence fell. Allie stared at the small, plastic phone.

'Parleys are, by tradition, non-violent. You leave your weapons behind. As you can imagine, I do not expect Nathaniel to honour this noble tradition. Therefore, we are deciding now how best to stay safe. Guards must be with us every step of the way.'

Lucinda's tone was brisk and business-like. The decision had been made.

Excitement and fear ran through Allie's veins, heating her blood. She was actually going to do this. She was going to the parley.

'We will not go in alone and we will have a plan,' Lucinda continued. 'Whatever that plan is, I'll expect you to follow it.

Regardless of what happens to anyone else. Regardless of what Nathaniel does. You will be allowed to accompany me only if you give me your word. No matter what happens that night, you follow the plan.'

Allie's throat tightened. How quickly it all became real.

'I'll follow the plan,' she said. 'I promise.'

'Good,' Lucinda said. 'Nathaniel will have endless annoying demands and will no doubt choose an utterly inappropriate location. He always does. As soon as a date is set, you will be informed, but I imagine he'll give us little notice – he likes to catch us off-guard. So be ready. Are you practising?'

Allie blinked. 'Practising ...? What?'

'Self-defence, of course,' Lucinda said. 'Isabelle said you've begun training with weapons.'

Allie's gaze shot up to Isabelle; her returning glance was unapologetic.

'Yes,' Allie said with dry understatement, 'we're using the weapons.'

This seemed to satisfy Lucinda. 'Good,' she said. Then her tone changed. 'Isabelle, do you have the item we discussed?'

The headmistress bent down and retrieved a package wrapped in brown paper from beneath her desk. 'I have it here.'

'Would you be so kind as to hand it to Allie?'

Expressionless, Isabelle held the package out across the desk. Allie rose to receive it.

It was heavy, and perfectly rectangular.

She held it gingerly. 'Should I ... open it?'

'Of course,' Lucinda said. 'How else will you find out what's inside?'

Carefully, Allie split the seam of the paper with her fingernail. The heavy paper fell open to reveal a battered book, its pages worn from use. The cover bore no lettering. It had the musty smell of age.

Intrigued, she opened it. Inside was a hand-written family tree, which seemed to go back to the twelfth century. Exploring further she discovered each page was topped with a name, faded with age, and a description of when that person lived, who they married, when they died.

'If you are going to fight with your family, I thought it was time you learned who you are fighting for,' Lucinda said. 'This is the book of our family. My great-great-grandfather had it written, and each generation has filled in pages since. My father gave it to me. Now I'm giving it to you.'

Allie, who had only learned Lucinda was her grandmother a few months ago, knew very little about her own family. Her mother had kept her heritage from her until Nathaniel made that impossible. Since then she'd told her only the bare minimum about herself.

Few things meant more to her than finding who she really was and where she came from. But how could Lucinda have known that?

This book was one of a kind. Hand-made. A priceless family heirloom. It might answer all her questions but it was also a huge responsibility. Her grandmother was sending her a message. Telling her she trusted her.

She swallowed hard.

'This is important,' she said, looking at the phone. 'Valuable. Are you sure you want me to have it?'

Lucinda didn't answer right away. But when she did, all she said was, 'I think it's time for you to have it.'

Allie closed the book carefully and wrapped it back in the protective paper. 'Thank you for trusting me. I'll take very good care of it.' Her voice was fervent. She meant every word.

'I know you will,' Lucinda said.

Back in her bedroom later, Allie turned the pages of the book with careful fingers. The paper was thick but soft to the touch and the page ends were uneven, as if they hadn't been cut by a machine.

She could see now how the handwriting changed periodically. The first half of the book was written in a spidery, swooping hand, and included names like Lord Charles Alton Finley-Gaston. His birthdate was 1681. Underneath, the book noted the years he'd served in Parliament. And the date of his death: 1738.

His wife was Mary and they'd had three children, two of them already dead by the time Charles passed away. One, Thomas John Finley-Gaston, survived. When she turned the page, his name headed the next entry.

Only now he was *Lord* Thomas John Finley-Gaston. Born 1705. Died 1769.

His children and grandchildren filled the pages after that.

This is my family, Allie told herself. She was trying to feel the things other people felt when they talked about their ancestors – a kind of possessiveness; a clear connection.

But the names meant nothing to her. She might as well have been reading the books in the library downstairs.

She felt nothing at all for these long-dead men.

Flipping forward in time, she passed increasingly familiar names. Names she'd read in history books. A prime minister here, a chancellor there. Then suddenly a long name stared out at her, written in a confident, no-nonsense handwriting that slanted sharply to the right: Baroness Lucinda Elisabeth Eugenie Gaston St Croix Meldrum.

Each word was clear and clean – no embellishments.

The page held a description of her life, her role as first woman chancellor, head of the World Bank, UN advisor. Beneath that, her husbands were listed, along with Allie's mother. Like the book's other pages, the information was all straightforward. But there was something about it that bothered Allie. She was at the bottom of the page before she realised what it was.

The page was written in the past tense.

Dread twisted inside her like a blade. Slowly, she turned to the next page. When she saw what her grandmother had written at the top of the next page, the blood drained from her face.

Lady Alyson Elisabeth Gaston Sheridan

Twenty

The words swam in front of Allie's eyes.

How could Lucinda do that? Allie felt betrayed. She couldn't be in this book. She wasn't one of the dead old men trapped in its dusty pages. She was young.

She was alive.

Suddenly she didn't want to read any more.

Closing it with an emphatic thud, she wrapped it back in the anonymous brown paper and slipped it into the bottom drawer in the desk, beneath a pile of old assignments.

When it was hidden away she wiped her hands on her skirt, as if to remove any traces it might have left behind.

She didn't want that book. She didn't want any of this. She'd figure out a way to give it back to Lucinda. To tell her she'd made a mistake.

Allie's whole life was ahead of her. Nathaniel might have tried to kill her but he'd failed.

She didn't belong in the family book of the dead.

All the next day Allie waited for word from Lucinda about the date of the parley but none came. The day after that was the same: nothing.

Each day when her lessons ended she ran to Isabelle's office to ask for news but the headmistress just shook her head.

'They're still negotiating terms, Allie. This part takes time. It could be weeks. Spend that time focusing on your studies, and on getting yourself ready.'

But it was increasingly difficult to pay attention in her lessons. To care about homework. It all seemed absurd compared to what was happening outside the school grounds.

And what lay ahead.

The air between Allie and Sylvain was still clouded and heavy with unspoken recrimination. She never saw him alone, and she got the feeling he was avoiding her as much as she was avoiding him. In groups he was studiously polite to her. But their conversations were stilted.

It was hard to believe that just over a week ago he'd told her he loved her.

Allie had taken to studying in the library. Nobody else used it these days – most students preferred to study in the common room, or out on the lawn on sunny days – so she often had it to herself.

Eloise was slowly thawing towards her – Allie wondered if the librarian somehow knew that she was the one who'd accused her of being the spy. But she was afraid to ask. She was just glad she didn't look so afraid every time she saw her now.

One afternoon she was alone at one of the tables, working with only desultory interest on a science project in the glow of the green-glass desk lamp, when someone dropped into the chair across from her. She looked up, into Carter's dark gaze.

'Hey.' His tone was casual, as if they always chatted like this.

'Hey back,' Allie said, and she saw the flicker of surprise in his eyes.

That was how they'd always greeted each other back when they were friends, before everything happened. It was a weighted phrase. A Carter and Allie code. It meant, 'Everything is OK. I care about you.'

Allie swallowed hard, her chest felt suddenly tight. She didn't know why she'd said it. Their relationship was such a mess, especially now. She waited for him to shut down, to withdraw. To walk away.

Instead he leaned forward, one hand sliding halfway across the table top towards her.

'I've been wanting to talk to you,' he said, 'about the other night.'

Allie steeled herself for more criticism. Carter had kept his distance ever since that night and she was certain he was angry at her.

But he wasn't.

'I want to tell you I'm sorry,' he said. 'I should have warned you what they were planning. I let Raj and the others talk me into it.' He held her gaze with steady eyes. 'I was wrong.'

Allie let out a breath she hadn't realised she'd been holding. There was no way for him to know how much this meant to her. She'd felt so lonely ever since that night. So conflicted.

'Thank you,' she said with real feeling. 'That means a lot.'

'You have every right to make your own decisions,' Carter held her gaze. 'Don't let anyone try and talk you out of what you think is right. Not even me.'

Heat rose to Allie's face. Every word he said was like a balm to her soul. But she had things to apologise for, too.

'I still think I was wrong,' she said. 'The way I just made the decision about the parley without asking you and the others what you thought. I felt like it was my decision to make but you guys are in this, too. It's going to be dangerous. I should have talked to all of you first. It should have been a group decision.'

All the tables around them were empty, and the rest of the library was in shadow. Allie knew Eloise was somewhere in the back, shelving books. But here, in the dome of light cast by the desk lamp, it felt safe and private.

'I think I owe everyone an apology. Including you.'

Carter's eyes darkened. 'No one should blame you for that. Isabelle should never have put you on the spot like that. It wasn't fair to you.'

Their eyes met and held. Carter's dark gaze was limitless, conflicted. He looked as if he wanted to say something else. Then he straightened, withdrawing his hands from the table in a movement too casual not to have been deliberate.

The spell was broken. Hurriedly, Allie picked up her pen and toyed with it as if it was the most interesting thing she'd ever seen.

'I've got to go find a Gertrude Stein book for that English essay,' he said, pushing back his chair. 'Although I don't really see the point. Her poems make about as much sense as a fish with a shotgun.'

She forced a smile. 'That's cool. Luckily, I have the wonderful world of physics to keep me company …'

Her tone was light but her voice was thin. As he walked away, she watched him from beneath lowered lashes. His long, loping stride was as familiar to her as her own breath.

She felt lonelier now than she had before he sat down.

Allie was so confused about what she wanted and why she wanted it, she didn't know what to do. She longed to discuss all of this with Rachel but things between them were too fragile right now.

That was another thing she needed to fix. Somehow.

So she'd have talked about it with someone else but … who was there to talk to? Nicole was still angry at her.

And Zoe was … Zoe. She'd just look at her like she was mad.

There wasn't anyone else to ask. In the *world*.

Not any more.

Oh God, Jo. I miss you so much.

Gathering her books she made her way to the common room, hoping to find more focus. But she was just as miserable there as she'd been in the library.

She was so deep in self-pity she didn't hear Katie walk up to her.

'God. All my teachers are such bastards,' she announced, dropping on to the other end of the sofa without waiting for an invitation. 'I wish they'd get real jobs.' Barely glancing at Allie, she pulled out a text book and began flipping through the pages. 'They will work us to death.'

Tapping the end of her pen against her chin, Allie eyed her speculatively.

She's probably still inherently evil. But nobody in this school knows more about boys.

Glancing up, Katie caught her staring.

'What?' Her green eyes narrowed. 'Do I have something on my face?'

Although tempted to say yes just to watch her squirm, Allie shook her head.

'I just … I thought I could …' She made herself say it. 'Could I ask you a weird question?'

Katie brightened visibly. 'Please tell me you want makeup tips. I've been dying for you to ask me.'

Allie paused. 'What's wrong with my makeup?'

'Oh, Allie,' Katie said, shaking her head mournfully. 'Everything.'

On some level Allie wanted to discuss eyeliner for half an hour and forget all about Sylvain and Carter and *life*. But she couldn't forget.

That was the problem.

'It's not about makeup,' she said. 'It's a random thing just about, like … boys.'

Katie pursed her lips. Leaning forward in her chair, she lowered her voice. 'I've noticed things are weird between you and Sylvain. What's going on? Is it a sex thing?'

'No, it's not a sex thing,' Allie glared. 'It's … well, it's something else. And we're not having problems.' She added the last line hastily. 'We're fine.'

That wasn't true but … whatever.

'Well, what is it, then?' Katie looked as if she couldn't imagine a problem between couples that did not involve sex.

Allie was already regretting this conversation. But she had to talk to someone.

'It's not about me and Sylvain,' she lied. 'It's for someone else. They asked me and I didn't know what to say because … anyway. I didn't know. And I thought you might.'

Katie studied her steadily.

'What does your … friend' – she emphasised the word – 'want to know?'

'OK, so …' Allie couldn't look at her. She kept her eyes on her hands, which were twisting the hem of her short skirt into a knot. 'If a boy tells you he loves you and you can't say it back, does that mean you don't love him? Or are you just … I don't know. Weird. Or something.'

Katie's smile faded. 'Oh. A real question. Right.'

As she paused to mull this over, Allie sat miserably, wishing she'd never brought it up.

When Katie finally spoke again, her tone was surprisingly thoughtful. 'It could mean she doesn't love him back. Sometimes it does. There's nothing like someone telling you they love you for you to realise you don't feel the same way.'

Allie's heart sank. *How could I not love Sylvain? Is that even possible? He's beautiful and he kisses like* fire. *And he loves me.* Katie was still talking, warming to the topic.

'On the other hand, it could also mean you're— Sorry. I mean, *she's* not ready for that kind of commitment yet.' She looked at Allie seriously. 'It's a really big deal. If you say you love someone then suddenly everything gets super intense. You could really like him but maybe he just said it too soon.' She seemed pleased with her own assessment. 'Tell your friend to take her time. Nobody should rush anyone into "I love you." Frankly, I'm surprised Sylvain would put pressure on you like that.'

Allie, who was still processing all of this, replied automatically.

'He's not pressuring me—' Realising what she'd said, she blanched. 'I mean, she's ... I didn't mean ...'

Katie wore the serene countenance of the victor. 'Of course he isn't. He's far too mature for that.' Allie got the feeling she enjoyed her new role of romantic advisor. 'Love is a big deal, Allie. You can't say it if it's not right. I don't think I've ever said it. Not yet.'

Allie mumbled some sort of garbled thanks, and Katie beamed at her.

'If you ever need more advice, come to me,' she said brightly. 'I'm like a sexpert.'

If Allie had thought talking about this would make her feel better, she'd been wrong.

She felt utterly confused.

How could she not love Sylvain? They were perfect together.

But then, if she did love him, why couldn't she just say so?

And why did she feel so empty when Carter walked away?

After Night School that evening, the group stayed behind for more weapons training. Allie waited until it was just the six of them before standing up. She'd thought about this all afternoon. It was time to settle this. And get things back to normal.

'Before we get started, there's something I want to say. What happened in the chapel – the way I agreed to the parley without asking you first – that was wrong. And I'm sorry.'

She saw Rachel's eyes widen. The cautious approval on Nicole's face.

The puzzled boredom in Zoe's expression.

'I know it made you all angry and upset, and I don't blame you. Please believe me.' With her eyes she sought out Sylvain's face. His expression was hard to read. 'I won't do anything like that again. I promise. We're a team. We decide things together.' Tugging at the hem of her black exercise top, she stepped back. 'That's all I wanted to say. I hope you can forgive me and I'd really like us to get back to normal. If we can.'

She saw Zoe roll her eyes as Rachel and Nicole both rushed over to give her a hug.

'That was a lovely thing to say,' Nicole said. 'I'm sorry about what I said the other day. It wasn't fair.'

'And I'm sorry we listened to my dad,' Rachel said. 'I should have known better.'

'It's cool,' Allie insisted. 'I deserved it. And … to be fair, if your dad was trying scare me, it bloody worked. I'm terrified now.'

When the girls walked away chatting, Sylvain came over to her.

'I know that must have been hard,' he said when no one else could hear . 'I'm really proud of you. And I'm sorry about everything. I handled it all badly. But I was afraid for you.' He paused. 'I wish there was a way to take it all back.'

His tone was fervent, but he kept his distance. As if he wasn't sure she'd welcome his touch.

The caution in his eyes hurt her.

Allie wished she knew what to do. They'd been so close while they were in France. But, somehow, after they came back to Cimmeria that changed.

Everything was so confusing here, it was so easy to lose your way. Maybe that was what had happened.

Breaking the space between them, she rested her hand on his arm. 'No, *I'm* sorry. I was selfish. I didn't think. And I really just want us to go back to the way we were before everything happened. I miss us, the way we were.'

Some of the tension left Sylvain's shoulders. Taking her hand in his, he lifted it to his lips.

'I miss us, too,' he said softly. 'Let's be us again.'

But even as Allie smiled up at him, some part of her knew that wanting something and having it are two very different things.

Twenty One

Over the days that followed, Allie had little time to worry about Sylvain. Night School training became increasingly intense. Raj ratcheted up the pressure, assigning difficult martial arts. Extending training hours. Demanding more of them. All the students were training with weapons now, and tensions were high.

Each night he and the other trainers circled the room barking out criticism and demands. And always he wanted them to be faster. Hit harder.

Allie didn't mind. She poured herself into the physical effort of training. Running until she was exhausted. Kick-boxing until her muscles felt like jelly. Practising the precise vicious movements of martial arts until every part of her ached.

It was the only time her mind was quiet. The only time she didn't doubt herself. Didn't worry about Sylvain and Carter.

And Rachel.

Rachel was falling further and further behind the Night School group. Everyone knew she wasn't cut out for it but she stubbornly refused to give up.

Allie couldn't bear to watch her have to fight so hard.

It was worse on the nights when Raj trained with them. As she and Carter had expected, he was tough on his daughter.

'Your kick isn't high enough, Rachel,' he said one evening as she tried again to swing her leg up to Nicole's neck. Rachel took the criticism with stoicism. But Nicole's disapproving eyes were fixed on Raj as if she was willing him to stop.

'You have to be fast or you're just giving your enemy another weapon to use against you,' Raj continued. 'It's all pointless if you're just giving someone a part of you to twist or break, leaving you weaker than you were before.'

Rachel had been struggling with the move for some time by now. Most of the other students had completed the move and they stopped to watch the scene play out.

'I'm trying ...' Somehow, Rachel's tone remained reasonable. But her face was red from exertion and embarrassment, and perspiration rolled down her cheeks. Her long, curly hair was pulled back in a pony tail that bounced with ironic perkiness as she tried the move again.

To be fair, Allie thought with a sigh, it was a simple move. All she had to do was block the fake gun in Nicole's hand with her forearm, then swing a kick under the French girl's chin to knock her back.

The others had got it the first time.

'Try again.' Raj's voice was icy. 'Try harder.'

As Allie watched, wincing at Rachel's awkward moves, Carter joined her. They exchanged worried glances.

'She's not getting any better ...' He whispered the words in Allie's ear. The warmth of his breath sent shivers down her spine.

'I know,' she said as Rachel prepared to try again.

This time Rachel's kick went too high. Nicole had to jump back and Rachel nearly toppled over from the effort.

'Not good enough,' Raj said through gritted teeth. 'No one leaves until you get this right. We'll stay here all night if necessary.'

Jerry said something to Raj too quietly for Allie to hear, but Raj waved him away. 'No. She has to get this.'

Carter shot Allie a telling look.

'What's the problem?' Zoe walked up to join them. 'It's an easy move. I don't get it.'

They all studied Rachel's stance critically, hoping for a way to help her as she tightened her jaw and tried the move again, still panting from the last failed attempt.

'Is there anything she's doing wrong?' Allie murmured, half turning towards Carter so he could hear her. 'Is she not planting that leg?'

He shook his head glumly. 'It's just conditioning. Strength.'

This time, when Rachel swung, her foot ended up in the correct place, and Nicole feinted to one side, swinging up with her fist, which Rachel blocked.

Allie sagged back with relief. They'd done it.

Looking pleased, Nicole patted Rachel on the shoulder.

'That was adequate.' Raj's tone was dismissive. 'You must do better.'

But every person in the room knew Rachel couldn't do better. And Allie had no idea what to do. If she was allowed out in the field in this condition she'd get killed.

Something had to give.

After practice that night, Allie walked out of the dressing room at the same time as Carter and they fell into step together. She cast a sideways look at him. He was looking ahead, frowning to himself, as if thinking about something troubling.

'What the hell are we going to do about Rachel?' Allie asked quietly.

Carter shook his head. 'We've tried everything. She needs to drop out, for her own sanity. But she just … won't.'

'I wish I knew how to convince her.' Allie said. 'But I yelled at her so much at the beginning, now she just dodges me whenever the subject comes up.' She gave a regretful sigh. 'And I don't blame her.'

'You had your reasons,' Carter said.

Allie considered this. 'Sometimes I think I'm not really a people person.'

This surprised a wry chuckle out of him.

'I wouldn't worry about that if I were you,' he said. 'I don't like most people and I get along just fine.'

For a while after that, they walked down the narrow basement corridor in companionable silence. The fluorescent strip lights above them buzzed quietly and cast the scene in a greeny-yellow glow.

'Can I ask you something?' Allie said.

He shot her a sideways glance. 'Sure.'

'Are you scared?'

He arched an eyebrow.

'About the parley, I mean,' she said. 'It's going to be messed up, right? However much we train and prepare. It doesn't matter. It's going to be bad.'

Carter shook his head. 'Not scared. More like … I'll be glad when it's done.'

Allie nodded to herself; that was exactly how she felt.

'I just wish I knew for certain everyone would be OK,' she said.

They'd reached the foot of the basement stairs. Carter leaned against the handrail, studying her thoughtfully.

'You know this isn't your fault, right?' he said. 'All this …' He waved one hand. 'It's not because of you.'

Allie, who very much thought it was her fault, bit her lip.

'I get what you're saying but … still. Maybe I could stop it if I just … I don't know.' She could hardly bring herself to say the next words. 'Did what Nathaniel wanted. Joined his side.'

Carter blew out his breath. 'I knew you were thinking that. I could just sense it.' He held her gaze. 'Look, Nathaniel is just using you as a focus point because it drives Lucinda nuts. What he really wants is the school. The organisation. Orion. Everything. He'd be doing this whether you were here or not.'

His words made sense but Allie still couldn't accept his logic.

'I get it. But I … feel like I've dragged all of you into this.' She glanced at him and then away. 'And I hate that. It's so dangerous—'

'We've all made up our own minds about this, Allie. The same as you. And we can change our minds. Whether or not I go to the parley is my decision, not yours.' His words were sharp but there was gentleness in his tone. 'And if something were to happen to me, it would be on me. Not you.'

Allie's eyes shot up to his. 'Nothing's going to happen to you.'

A long look passed between them. 'OK,' he said with quiet intensity. 'Nothing's going to happen.'

A shock of connection like an electrical current jolted her. Their eyes locked.

She thought she saw something in his gaze – desire. And it made her legs feel strangely weak.

Jump.

A sudden burst of harsh laughter from the corridor made her start and she spun around. But it came from the distance – a group of Night School students further down the hall.

When she glanced back at Carter, whatever she thought she'd seen in his eyes was gone. He just looked a little bored.

With a sigh, he lifted himself off the wall. 'It's getting late. I've got to go.'

As he loped up the stairs, she flushed, mortified by her own confused thoughts.

I am losing it.

After giving Carter a good head start so she was certain not to run into him again, Allie climbed the stairs to the girls' dorm deep in thought. In her mind, she replayed their conversation over and over again.

The more she thought about it, the more idiotic she felt.

All he'd done was say something nice. Like friends do.

What if he'd noticed how she'd misconstrued it?

The very idea made her cheeks flame.

She hated herself.

She and Sylvain had something – something real. When he kissed her, she melted. And now they were back on track. Why couldn't she just let it happen?

Why couldn't she just let herself be happy with him?

She and Carter had once had a thing but it was over long ago. Now he was trying very hard to be her friend and she was being unbelievably stupid and messing everything up for everyone.

What really scared her was the thought that, if she wasn't careful, she'd lose both Sylvain and Carter. She had to get it together.

Her mind was so occupied she hardly noticed where she was going, but it didn't matter. She could walk through Cimmeria with her eyes closed and never hit a wall.

She reached the elegant first-floor landing with its tall windows and graceful statues without looking up. As she turned left towards the stairs leading up to the top floor her trainers beat a soft dirge against the oak floors.

At the top of the stairs she waved absently at the guard, who sat in her usual chair shoved back against the wall, and headed down the long, narrow corridor lined with white doors, each with a black number painted on it.

By now she'd convinced herself Carter hadn't noticed her strange reaction.

Maybe everything would be fine.

Her thoughts were in such a hectic whirl by the time she reached her room she was on auto-pilot. She barely noticed she'd opened her door – force of habit dictated how far she turned the handle, how hard she pushed.

Inside, she flicked the lights on with careless familiarity. Dropped her bag to the floor in the usual place.

Only then did she realised someone was standing in front of her.

She stopped breathing.

'Hello, Allie,' her brother said. 'I thought you'd never get here.'

Twenty Two

'Christopher ...?' Allie's lips wouldn't move. The word came out in a terrified whisper.

He stood in front of her desk, his back to the open window.

'It's me,' he said, turning his hands over as if that proved it. 'And I'm not setting anything on fire so ... please don't call for help until you hear me out.'

Allie's heart was racing but it seemed hard to move. It was like she'd walked into a dream. A nightmare.

Christopher was really *here*?

There'd been a time when talking to him was the only thing she wanted. Now she was afraid of him. And angry.

When she'd first found out he'd joined Nathaniel she wouldn't accept that he was lost to her forever. Eventually, though, she'd had to let him go. She'd had to accept that he'd chosen the other side in this battle.

Now here he was again, right in front of her, smiling that familiar guilty smile. Like he'd just broken something and wanted her to promise not to tell Mum.

Resentment and hurt made her stomach churn.

'What the hell are you doing here?' Her voice was low and ominous. 'How did you get past the guards?'

He gave a short laugh. 'It wasn't easy. Look, I'm sorry to show up like this but I had to talk to you.'

He sounded calm but Allie saw his Adam's apple bob with nervousness. In fact, now that she was aware of it, she could see the tension in his shoulders, his arms, the way his hands kept moving.

His fear gave Allie strength. Reminded her where she was and all she'd learned.

He *should* be afraid.

She studied him steadily, letting him see her suspicion. Making it obvious. 'Did Nathaniel send you? What does he want?'

His fingers twitched.

'Nathaniel doesn't know I'm here. If he finds out ...' His voice trailed off as if what would happen was unsayable. Unthinkable.

A cool breeze blew in through the open window behind him. Outside Allie could see no moon or stars – nothing but darkness.

Her eyes narrowed. 'Now, why would you take a chance like that? I thought you were his loyal subject.'

'I was.' He leaned back against her desk. 'I mean ... I believed him. I do, still, believe him.' He rubbed his hands across his face. 'It's just got confused, Al. It's all confused.'

Allie couldn't hide her incredulity. This new Christopher... where had he come from?

'What's confused?' she asked, her voice sharpening.

'Me.' Christopher looked down. 'He told me the truth about us ... our family. And I thought he could make it all better. Give us what we deserve. But then he did things – really bad things. And now I don't know what I believe.'

Allie, who knew all about the bad things Nathaniel had done, didn't know what to make of any of this. Her brother seemed genuine. But for all she knew, this was an elaborate act. Part of some trick Nathaniel had devised.

If there was one thing she'd learned in the last year it was this: everyone lies. Even people you love.

'Don't say "us".' Her tone was clipped. 'You didn't do anything for me. This was all about you.'

He didn't argue.

'Fine. I know you're angry. And I don't blame you. But you have to understand. That guy ... Gabe?' Christopher searched her face for signs of recognition.

Allie gave a terse nod. Oh yes. She knew Gabe.

'He's crazy. And Nathaniel knows it. He's dangerous as hell, but he keeps him around like he's some sort of ... I don't know. Human handgun.' He shook his head. 'He wasn't supposed to hurt your friend Ruth at all. Or that other girl ... what was her name?'

For a second Allie couldn't speak. She curled her hands into fists until her nails dug deep crescents into her palms.

'Jo,' she said.

'Yeah.' It was clear the name meant nothing to Christopher. He didn't know any of the people Allie loved. 'Nathaniel was furious about that. But he kept him on.'

Hearing this, Allie wanted to cry. To scream. But she stilled that urge. Because she needed to know more. She kept her voice even.

'Why?'

He held her gaze. 'Because he scares you.'

Allie heard herself give a bitter laugh and she tried to stifle it.

'That's a bloody bad reason to hang out with a psychopath.'

'I know. That's the whole *point*.' He raked his fingers through his hair. He looked agonised, and she studied him with new interest. Could he fake this?

'There's more. Other things. I think what he wants is right but …'

'What?' She couldn't stop herself. 'To run the world? To be some sort of mental emperor? You think that's okey-dokey but killing a few people … now, *that's* wrong? Bloody hell, Christopher.'

Her voice dripped sarcasm and he looked at her narrowly.

In that moment he looked so much like their dad, Allie caught her breath. Same pale blue eyes. Same disapproving expression.

'Come on. You think it's OK for Lucinda to run the country now but if Nathaniel did it that would be wrong?' He straightened and took a step forward. 'Why shouldn't he run things? Why shouldn't *we*? Anyone with the energy and the ideas and the family history …'

She bristled. 'What does family have to do with it?' Her voice rose. 'Are you saying you have to be related to us to have power because –' she made a rolling gesture with her hand – 'Sheridans make awesome prime ministers? Or something?'

While they argued they'd moved closer together without Allie noticing. Now she was too angry to care. She had to stand on her toes to be eye level with him – she didn't remember him being so tall.

'Meldrums,' he corrected her, using their grandmother's last name. Allie thought about the book in the drawer, filled with the names of their forefathers, all of whom had lived lives of wealth and power because of who they were, rather than what they'd done. Or how hard they'd worked.

'You know what? That's not even her real name,' she snapped. 'That's her favourite husband's name. So if you're looking for a name to hang this whole world-domination thing on you might need to dig a little deeper. Find out who we really are.'

'All right. All right.' He held up his hands in surrender. 'Let's not fight. Just wait until you hear what I have to say. Then I'll go, I promise. I can tell you don't want me here.'

'Make it fast.' There was ice in her voice.

He took another step towards her. He was too close now. But Allie didn't want to show her fear and back away. She forced herself to hold his gaze.

'You're planning to go with Lucinda to the parley with Nathaniel,.' He spoke low and fast. 'Don't go. It's a trap.'

Allie sighed. Had he seriously come all the way here just to tell her the most obvious thing in the world?

'Oh for God's sake. Of *course* it's a sodding trap. You think I don't know that?'

He shook his head. 'It's a good trap, Allie. And it's not for you.'

That stopped her. She stared at him.

'Who is it for?'

He answered her question with a question. 'Who is Nathaniel's biggest problem right now?'

'Lucinda.' The word came out as a breath.

His expression told her she was right.

'So, if it's Lucinda he's after, why don't you want me to go?' Her voice stayed neutral but internally she was calculating how long it would take her to get to Isabelle's room and get her to phone Lucinda.

'Because once she's gone,' he said in the same voice he'd once used to help her with her homework, 'who's left to protect you?'

His words seemed to hang in the air between them.

What was he saying? That Nathaniel would come after her as soon as Lucinda was gone? And since when did Christopher even care about that? It wasn't like she hadn't been hurt already.

The scar on her arm gave a warning throb.

'I don't get it,' she said. 'You're warning me about Nathaniel. Telling me you want Lucinda to win. Whose side are you on?'

The question seemed to throw him. He hesitated before replying.

'I guess I'm on my own side now. Because I can't be a part of what Nathaniel's doing any more. But I can't be with you either, can I? Because you don't trust me.'

His gaze challenged her.

'How could I trust you?' Her throat was suddenly tight. Her voice wavered, just a little. 'How? You chose *his side*. He killed people I love. And you were right there with him.'

'So here we are.' He seemed to say this mostly to himself. As if some suspicion had been verified.

Then he straightened. 'What if I told you who the spy was? Would you trust me then?'

Allie froze. *He knows?*

She fought to keep her expression neutral.

'I wouldn't even believe you,' she said.

'But surely you want to know who it is …' Christopher took a step towards her, but now he was far too close and Allie scrambled back, running into the wall. She raised her fists.

'Don't come any closer,' she warned him.

He stopped instantly. Pain flared in his eyes.

'God,' he said. 'You really hate me, don't you?'

Allie wasn't about to apologise for that. 'What did you expect?'

'But don't you see?' He held her gaze. 'We're all we have now, you and me. Our parents don't care. No one else cares …'

His words hit her with the force of a fist, throwing her off-balance.

Was he right? Was he all she had?

For a split second she remembered the wounded girl who first came to Cimmeria Academy. Abandoned by her family. No friends. Alone in the world.

But she wasn't that girl any more. She'd worked *hard* not to be that girl. She thought of Rachel and Zoe, Carter and Sylvain.

When she spoke, she was surprised by how strong her voice sounded. 'Maybe I'm all you have. But you're not all I have. I am *surrounded* by people who care about me.'

'Are you?' His eyes were cynical. 'Or are you just surrounded by people who love your grandmother's power? Tell me this. If Lucinda Meldrum weren't your grandmother, would you be here? Would one person at Cimmeria Academy be your friend? Would they even know your name?'

Allie hated that there was a kernel of truth in those awful words. Hated that it made her doubt her friends.

'Get out.' She hissed the words.

When her brother didn't move, she advanced on him, her movements slow and deliberate. With each step she was judging the angle. The trajectory. Where to grab him to throw him off balance.

'Get the hell out of my room or I'll throw you out.'

'Allie …' He took quick steps away from her. 'Come on. At least let me tell you who—'

But she didn't want to listen any more.

'I swear to God, Christopher, I will throw you out that window. And if you don't believe I can … just try me.'

Deciding she was serious, he turned and ran to her desk, leaping on it in an easy, athletic move. Now she had to crane her neck to look up at him.

She took a careful step back. They both knew he had the advantage.

But all he did was talk. 'You know I'm right. In your heart, you know. I wouldn't ever hurt you. Don't go to the parley, Allie. Don't trust anyone. Be careful.'

With that, he jumped on to the ledge outside her window, and disappeared.

'That was all he said?' Isabelle leaned back in her chair. Her long, dark blonde hair hung loose over the shoulders of her white dressing gown.

When she crossed her legs, the ankles of her pyjamas peeked out beneath the hem of her robe. Something about that made her seem vulnerable.

Allie nodded. 'The parley is a trap for Lucinda.'

'I'm most interested in why he felt inclined to tell you this.' Lucinda's tinny voice emerged from the telephone propped up on Isabelle's desk. 'If what he said was true about Nathaniel, he risked his life to tell you this. Why the sudden change of heart?'

'I don't trust him, Grandmother,' Allie said, looking at the phone as if it could see her.

'I trust your instincts,' Lucinda said. 'But I want to know more. And also, he's my grandson. If he has left Nathaniel then he's alone out there. He could need my help. Isabelle, ask Raj to have someone find and follow Christopher for a while. See where he goes, what he does.'

Isabelle made a note on the pad in her lap. 'I'll do it first thing, Lucinda.'

'What about the spy?' Allie looked at the headmistress. 'Do you think he was telling the truth? Does he know?'

'Perhaps. Or Nathaniel could have intentionally planted information with him. It's a shame he didn't tell you a name, at any rate.,' Lucinda said.

Remembering how angry she'd been, how she wouldn't even allow Christopher to tell her, Allie winced.

'Still, there's been some progress on that front from elsewhere,' Lucinda continued. 'One of my contacts at MI5 from my old government days has been in touch. She's no fan of Nathaniel. She's looking into the situation for us now. I'll get back to you as soon as I know more.'

'Thank you, Lucinda.' Isabelle closed her notebook.

'I presume the guards have checked the grounds thoroughly?' Lucinda asked. 'I don't think Christopher would be foolish enough to come back, but still. I'm not sure I want Allie alone in her room tonight.'

'We've stationed a guard on the roof above her window. Another will be outside her door,' Isabelle said.

'Excellent. Then I'll leave this in your capable hands. Let's speak again tomorrow.' Lucinda ended the call without another word.

Allie stared at the silent phone. A guard on the roof and one at the door.

I'm a prisoner now.

Twenty Three

The next morning seemed to crawl by. When she was meant to be studying, Allie instead made notes about the things Christopher had said to her. She kept going over it in her mind.

She'd told the others about it at breakfast. The whole time she spoke, Sylvain kept his gaze fixed in the distance. The only sign that he was anything other than calm was a muscle flickering in his jaw.

When she finished, Carter looked furious. 'So all their security and he just waltzes into your *room*? What the hell is going on around here?'

'They can't secure this place,' Nicole said. 'We all know it. It's too big. Too rambling. If someone tries hard enough …'

'They'll get in.' Rachel finished the sentence. She looked pale. 'I was in the next room; I didn't hear a thing. Oh, Allie, I'm so sorry.'

Allie shook her head. 'It's not your fault, Rach. I didn't scream for help. Anyway, there was a guard in the hallway the whole time.'

They all started speaking at once then.

'They should …'

'Isabelle …'

'We should try …'

Sylvain's voice cut through the chaos. 'This is too dangerous.' He turned to Allie. In the light streaming through the huge windows, his eyes were lavender. 'Isabelle must do something.'

'There's a guard on the roof above my room now,' she said. 'And outside my door. No one's getting in. Or out.' She gave a harsh laugh. 'I'm being held prisoner for my own safety.'

'What a mess,' Rachel murmured.

⁂

After breakfast, Sylvain caught up with Allie as she walked up the stairs to chemistry.

His eyes searched her face. 'Are you really OK?'

'I'm really fine,' she said. 'He didn't hurt me.'

Sylvain took her hand, and laced his fingers through hers.

'He could have. You were alone with him.'

His hand was warm against hers. Solid. She squeezed his fingers.

'I know. But he's my brother and I guess …' She sighed. 'I just don't think he'd hurt me.'

They'd reached the classroom now and they stood outside the door as the other students hurried to their lessons. A guard stood nearby, his dark uniform crisp and clean. He kept his attention focussed elsewhere, pretending he couldn't hear what they were saying.

Guards had followed her down to breakfast this morning, too.

Glancing at him, Sylvain pulled her closer and whispered, 'If anything happened to you ... I don't know what I would do.'

He looked beautiful in the soft morning light, all tawny skin and aquamarine eyes.

'Nothing will happen to me,' she said. 'I promise.' Around them, classroom doors had begun to close. The guard moved closer.

Feeling his eyes on her, Allie pulled back. 'We should go in.'

Sylvain didn't argue.

After taking their usual seats, they talked in whispers about the guards until Jerry Cole walked in, calling for silence in his usual mild fashion.

The science teacher seemed even more disorganised than usual. His papers were crumpled and out of order, his wiry hair needed combing and his glasses were crooked, as if he'd rushed to the room.

'Today we're talking about ...' He rifled through his papers as if he had no idea what he wanted to talk about today. Eventually he found the one he wanted and held it up triumphantly. 'Gauss's Law of Gravity and ...' Stopping again he searched for another page. 'Oh dear, where has everything gone?'

The students tittered at his confusion. He smiled at them over the tops of his glasses. 'I didn't sleep last night, gang,' he said. 'So this may be one of those classes where you explain string theory to me and I grade the inventiveness of your descriptions.'

Allie cast a surreptitious glance at Sylvain from beneath her lashes. His lips were curved into an unselfconscious smile as he watched Jerry try and get it together.

He looked even better when he smiled. She had to love him back.

That evening, the group gathered on the lawn to compare notes. It was July now, and it stayed light until late in the evening.

Two guards stood about ten feet away, keeping watch.

By now, Allie hardly noticed them. They'd followed her all day.

After kicking off their shoes and loosening their ties the students sat in a circle on the soft grass.

The thrill of Christopher's sudden reappearance had faded by now, and for a change, they weren't talking about Nathaniel or Christopher at all. They were complaining about their homework.

' …then she said, "You can read fifty pages by tomorrow, can't you?"' Nicole sounded vexed. 'And I said, "Of course. Because this is my *only* class …"'

The others made soothing noises of sympathy.

'Is it just me?' Allie said. 'Or is Zelazny going a little crazy? Look at this.' With an accusing look, she held up her assignment page so they could see the length of it. 'If he's the spy, he's trying to kill us with coursework.'

'All the teachers are a little intense,' Carter said. 'Like they sense something is … going … on …'

His voice trailed off as he looked past her shoulder. Everyone twisted around to see what had drawn his attention.

The guards who had been standing behind them had taken off running to the school. They were talking into microphones Allie couldn't see.

From everywhere, guards poured onto the lawn, where they conferred before taking off into the building. In the distance, Allie heard cars roaring up the drive at top speed.

'What the actual hell …' Allie said, as nerves began to tighten her muscles.

'Uh-oh,' Rachel whispered.

Sylvain, Zoe and Carter leapt to their feet. The others scrambled to do the same.

A guard Allie remembered from Night School training ran across the lawn towards them. He was shouting but they couldn't understand what he was saying until he neared them.

'Everyone *inside*. Now.'

Without pausing to grab their books or shoes they took off across the lawn. Around them, Allie saw other students doing the same. Everyone poured towards the school. Guards stood at the door urging them to move faster. Nobody screamed. There was no panicking. This was Cimmeria, after all. But everyone moved fast.

The grass was soft and cool beneath the soles of their feet. The sky was blue and innocent overhead. They might have been playing a game in other circumstances.

But this was no game.

Allie didn't know what she was running to or from, but she was alert and focused. She glanced back for Rachel, and found Nicole was already at her side.

Carter and Sylvain flanked Allie, matching her step for step. Ahead, Zoe had already reached the front steps and zipped into the building.

'Go, go, go!' the guards by the door kept shouting.

By the time she reached the entrance hall, Allie was moving so fast her bare feet skidded on the stone floor. She steadied herself without breaking stride. Down the hallway, she saw guards and teachers herding students into the common room.

She started to follow but someone called her name. Turning, she saw Raj in the doorway to Isabelle's office, gesturing to them urgently.

With Carter and Sylvain beside her, she ran over to him.

Raj wore the cool, tense expression she remembered from other disastrous evenings. 'In here.'

When everyone was in, he shut the door and crossed the room to where Isabelle stood at her desk. The headmistress held her mobile phone loosely in one hand. Allie noticed her hair was dishevelled as if she'd been running. And she thought her hand trembled slightly as she pressed it against her forehead and nodded at something Raj had said.

The small room was crowded with Night School students and guards but the atmosphere was hushed. Nobody said a word.

With so many people in such a small space it was almost instantly hot and stuffy. Allie was squeezed in between the two boys. She could just see Zoe, but there wasn't room enough for her to turn to look for Rachel and Nicole. She assumed they were behind her.

'Whatever's happening,' Carter whispered, 'it's bad.'

She heard Zoe mutter, 'I can't see anything.' Then watched her elbow her way to the front with what looked like unnecessary violence.

'I need you to stay calm,' Isabelle said.

The room went deathly silent.

'The situation is this,' the headmistress continued. 'The person among us who has been working for Nathaniel has been identified.'

Allie's breath caught.

A murmur swept the room and Isabelle waited for it to fade.

'I can't tell you how right now but I can assure you our evidence is correct. He is on the run. He knows we are looking for him. We believe he is hiding in the building or very close to it. Raj?'

He, him, Allie thought, feeling slightly dazed. *It's not Eloise.*

Raj leaned forward, pressing his hands on the top of his desk. 'We need you to help the guards sweep the building to find him. Time is of the essence. You will be divided into teams of three.' His steely gaze moved from face to face, as if he spoke to each of them individually. 'You are to follow the usual protocols but the person we are looking for is very dangerous. Highly trained. If you find him you are not to try to capture him yourself but wait for the guards. Am I clear?'

The students nodded their agreement.

'The person you're looking for is Jerry Cole.'

Twenty Four

Everyone shouted at once.

'*Jerry?*'
'What?'
'No.'
'It *can't* be.'

As the uproar rose, Allie stood in absolute silence. The news was like a wave curling over her head. Poised to draw her under.

It was *Jerry*? Kindly, jovial, science-loving Jerry?

Her brain wouldn't accept it.

But then, across the crowded office, Isabelle caught her eye. The pain on her face was so raw the faint hope provided by disbelief evaporated instantly.

Isabelle was careful. And she wouldn't look so haunted if she wasn't certain.

Allie's stomach ached as if someone had punched her.

She thought of Jo, blonde and bright and so alive, pointing at Jerry. 'Isn't he just yummy for an old man?'

It was Jerry who opened the gate that night. Jerry who lured Jo to her killer.

We trusted him, she thought. *And he helped to kill her.*

She needed to sit down. The room was airless. Hot. She felt dizzy.

Her heart was thudding in her ears and it was too loud to be healthy.

'*It won't kill you ...*' Zoe had said of panic, but at that moment she almost wished it would.

How could she live in the kind of world where this could happen? Where someone could pretend to be so kind and then do such awful things?

How does anyone live here?

The world is uninhabitable. It is full of monsters.

A tear ran down her cheek and she brushed it away. It was becoming hard to breathe and she knew if she didn't focus – if she let panic take over – she'd be a burden to the others. She needed to control her pain. Direct it where it would do some good.

At the front of the room, Raj was still talking and she forced herself to listen. He was calling out names and assigning locations. It felt distant, as if it was all happening to someone else. The words blurred together like some unknown language.

Then he'd finished and everyone was moving, and Allie wasn't sure where she was supposed to go. Someone touched her arm and she looked up to see Sylvain's blue eyes watching her with concern.

'I'm sorry,' she said, pulling herself together. 'Whose team…?'

'You're with me and Zoe.' His French-accented voice was low and preternaturally calm. 'Are you OK?'

Straightening, she gave a terse nod to show she was fine, although she wasn't fine at all.

'We are certain he is in or very near the main building,' Raj said. 'But we can't be certain where. So we need to search floor by floor, room by room. The guards are already doing this, your job is to assist them. Act as additional eyes and ears.'

Someone opened the door, letting in fresh air. Allie tried to take a deep breath but her lungs felt tight.

'Take a comms device on your way out.' Raj raised his voice to be heard over the low rumble of conversation. 'If you see anything at all, report back immediately. Do not engage.'

As the students began to file out, accepting small, handheld radios from guards at the door, he called after them. 'And remember: Under no circumstances are you to try and take him alone.'

Later, Allie wouldn't be able to remember leaving the room. All she knew was that suddenly she was walking down the wide main hallway alongside Sylvain and Zoe, as fury slowly grew inside her.

Jerry has to pay.

The school felt oddly empty, inhabited only by the dark shapes that slipped out of Isabelle's office and fanned out across all levels of the rambling building, silent as wraiths.

Movement had calmed Allie's nerves. The methodical process ahead of them – the ultimate goal – gave her purpose. She breathed normally.

Speed was essential; there was no time to change into Night School gear. The polished wood floor was cool and uneven beneath Allie's toes. Like Zoe, she was still barefoot. Their group was to search the ground floor of the main building. As they walked, Sylvain explained in a whisper what Allie had missed – the guards had already been through this quadrant so they were simply mopping up. He almost certainly wasn't down here. The non-Night School students were being kept in the common room, so they headed past it to the nearest room – the dining hall.

By common consent, Sylvain took the lead. Allie and Zoe stood back on either side of the doorway as he turned the handle.

Allie's heart rate accelerated. All her muscles tensed. She was ready.

The door swung open on silent hinges.

Inside, the vast room was dim, illuminated only by the evening light that filtered through the huge windows on the far wall. The round tables were bare, heavy chairs neatly pushed in.

They branched out, Sylvain heading left, Zoe right.

Cautiously, Allie walked down the middle of the huge room. But there was no place to hide here. No closets or hanging fabric. It was clearly empty.

Crouching, she peered under the tables. Nothing but wooden legs.

She straightened again. The three exchanged glances. Zoe pointed to the double doors at the end of the room leading into the kitchen. Nodding, Sylvain hurried towards her and Allie followed suit.

She tried to imagine what she'd do if she found Jerry – he was the best of all the teachers. Highly trained. Lethal. Muscular.

Her teacher.

How would she fight him?

I'd just do it, she decided with cold determination.

But the idea scared the hell out of her.

This time, Zoe went first – springing through the doors in a clean, athletic leap.

Industrial-sized dishwashers burbled in a corner. Giant refrigerators hummed. But the room was empty.

They searched the low cupboards and looked under the gigantic butcher block. Nothing.

Sylvain cocked an eyebrow and she nodded.

The next room along the corridor was the great hall.

It was Allie's turn to go first. She waited until the others were in place before reaching for the door knob. The metal felt cold beneath her fingers but it turned easily. The door swung open without a sound.

The long, elegant ballroom could hold several hundred revellers. It was easy to imagine them now, swirling across the polished oak floor, drinking champagne, laughing. Empty, it had a hollow, ghostly feel. There were no windows here – the far end of the room was lost in shadows.

Allie's chest felt tight.

Again they spread out under heavy, metal light fixtures. They glowed like a thousand candles when lit. Now, they were dark and cool.

The room was virtually devoid of furniture, which made searching easier. They kept pace with each other as they walked down the length of the ballroom. The floor felt clean and smooth beneath Allie's bare feet, as if it was swept every day, even when it wasn't used.

At the back of the room, stacks of chairs and a few tables had been pushed to the side, waiting for the next gala event. Moving in near perfect sync they all crouched low to look beneath them.

Nothing. Not even dust.

There were no closets here or cupboards. No places to hide. So when they reached the back wall they turned in unison and headed back out again without a word.

The hallway was still and silent.

The next door along was a utility closet Allie could never remember noticing before. It held mops, buckets and other cleaning supplies, and reminded her uneasily of the place where she'd hidden in Brixton Hill School the night she and Mark were arrested. An event that led her here, to this day. This moment.

A split second in time that changed everything.

What if that never happened? she wondered as they closed the door again. *What if I'd never gone out that night to tag the school? Where would I be now?*

But there wasn't time to dwell. They were nearing the last door in the hallway – the library.

By now their routine was set. Allie and Zoe flanked the entrance. When they were in place, Sylvain stepped forward and reached for the handle.

They all heard the noise at the same time. A faint crash. The sound of exertion or struggle muffled by the thick wood of the door.

The moment seemed to freeze. Allie felt Sylvain's body tense. Next to him, Zoe frowned and cocked her head, alert but tiny, like a bird poised for flight.

Then Sylvain threw his shoulder against the door, and they all spilled into the room.

At first they could see nothing but the forest of bookshelves that towered above them and sprawled out in all directions beneath the dim, antique lighting. Instinctively, Allie started to move, but Sylvain flung out his arm, stopping her and Zoe. For a split second they stood still. Then they heard it again. The sound of flesh against flesh, of breath forced out, a stifled cry. The thud of something falling.

'That way.' Zoe pointed with eager assurance across the room.

They took off at a run, sticking close together this time. They were nearly to the mid-point of the library when they saw Eloise and Jerry. They were just outside the study carrels – in fact, one of the carrels still stood open, light and colour pouring through its small, carefully disguised door.

That's where he hid, Allie realised numbly.

The two were fighting viciously. Eloise's long, dark hair had come free of its clip and flowed down her slender back as she swung a kick at Jerry's neck. Her aim was unerring but Jerry was fast and he dodged her foot with frightening ease, bobbing up with his fist raised.

He said something then that Allie didn't hear and Eloise whirled, elbows out like pikes. This time she connected, striking him hard in the chest. He winced but still rolled out of reach when she sliced a punch to his face.

That was when he saw them.

Allie saw his gaze skitter across their faces and she thought, for a second, a hint of regret shadowed his eyes.

'Get him,' Sylvain said.

The three hurled themselves across the room. Zoe, always the fastest, reached him first, shooting in to aim a sharp, well-placed kick at his lower back, but he dodged her with ease, swatting her away.

As she realised what was happening, Eloise's eyes widened.

'Get back!' she shouted.

Their presence had distracted her, and that gave Jerry a break. Moving fast, he lifted a nearby study table as if it weighed nothing at all then threw it at them with such force it splintered when it hit the ground.

They scattered. A small piece of flying wood hit Allie like shrapnel, slicing the skin on her thigh, but she ignored the sting and spun round, looking for the science teacher. He was nowhere to be seen.

'This way!' Eloise called, running towards the back of the room.

Behind her, Allie heard Sylvain speaking urgently.

'In the library. Now! Now!' Tension made his accent thicker and it took her a second to realise he was talking into his radio. She'd forgotten she had one.

Her heart hammered against her ribs as she ran through the stacks towards the sound of Eloise's voice. She'd lost Zoe after the table was thrown, but there was no time to do anything except run.

As she spun out of the stacks to the open space at the back of the library she heard Eloise talking, her voice low and taut.

'You stole everything I cared about,' she said. 'Everything that mattered. If it takes all my life I will make you pay for that.'

They were by the back door. Eloise was blocking Jerry's escape with her body. Zoe buzzed around them like a fly, looking for a moment of weakness to get a blow in. They both ignored her.

Sylvain stood in the shadows across from Allie, watching intently.

Eloise was their teacher. A Night School instructor. This was her play.

Jerry's attention was focused on Eloise. He didn't look angry or bitter. He looked regretful.

'I'm so sorry, Ellie,' he said. 'I never meant for this to happen.'

'Bollocks.' Eloise spat the word at him. 'You chose Nathaniel over me. You never loved me. Every word you ever said was a lie.'

The science teacher shook his head hard, no longer trying to get to the door. 'No, no, no. I did love you. I do. I meant everything—'

At that moment, seeing him distracted, Zoe launched into a whirling kick, aimed at the back of his head.

But Jerry was the one who taught them that move. And he was also the one who taught them how to defend themselves against it.

Spinning, he knocked her back with a strong counter-kick and, before she could regain her balance, swung a punch at her jaw. The blow made an awful cracking sound.

Zoe's body flew through the air, crashing into a table, before crumpling to the floor, where she lay horribly still.

Twenty Five

As she watched Zoe fall, Allie couldn't seem to move. Her legs felt heavy. The world turned hazy. Around her, everything blurred together. Eloise turning to Zoe. Jerry fumbling with the door. Sylvain shooting past in pursuit of him.

Then she was running to Zoe's side, her steps heavy and slow. Eloise was already there, fingers pressed against Zoe's neck, whispering to herself as she searched for a pulse.

'Come on, Eloise. Find it. Find it…'

Behind them, footsteps pounded the floor. Guards stormed into the room shouting orders and commands.

'Where is he?' one of them shouted.

A cool evening breeze blew through the open door leading out on to the grounds.

Jerry was gone and Allie couldn't seem to care.

'Zoe,' she whispered, stroking her face with tentative fingers. Her skin was cool and pale as marble. Her eyelashes lay on her cheeks like dark feathers.

Unconscious, she looked like a little girl.

'Zoe,' she whispered again, her voice breaking. 'You have to wake up.'

But she didn't move.

RESISTANCE

All Allie could think was: *Dead like Jo.* She kept hearing the sound Jerry's fist had made against Zoe's chin. Seeing the way the blow had twisted her head to one side. And she felt herself dragged again towards the pit of despair, which it had taken her so long to escape last winter. It was some time before she understood what Eloise was saying to her.

'She's alive, Allie.' The librarian gripped her by the shoulders and Allie wondered how long she'd been saying it. 'She's alive.'

But Zoe was so still, so pale, Allie couldn't believe it. Jerking free of Eloise's hands, she shook her head stubbornly, biting back a sob.

'Her neck,' she said. 'It could be broken.'

Eloise's lips were tight. 'Stay with her. I'll be back.'

After the librarian left, Allie became more aware of the activity around her. Guards ran in and out of the door, their booted feet like muffled thunder on the thick, Persian rugs.

She clung to the younger girl's hand, shielding her body with her own. Numb, she watched as the nurse returned with Eloise to place a protector carefully around Zoe's neck. Then she walked alongside as the guards lifted her on to a stretcher and wheeled her up to the infirmary.

After that, she waited for her to wake up. The other students came and went. First Nicole, and Rachel, later Sylvain and Carter. Even Katie came for a while and fussed about, pouring glasses of water Zoe wasn't awake to drink and that Allie refused to touch.

By ten o'clock, they were all gathered in the infirmary, ignoring the nurse's muttered complaints ('Give the child some space …') and talking quietly as they waited.

The room contained four old-fashioned white iron beds. Zoe lay in the one closest to the window, which had been cracked open just enough to let in a light breeze. Allie sat next to her, still holding her hand.

She was only thirteen. She looked so small beneath the white covers.

The faint smell of antiseptic in the air reminded Allie sickeningly of the two weeks she'd spent up here last Christmas after Nathaniel tried to have her kidnapped.

She wouldn't leave Zoe alone up here. She knew what that was like.

As time ticked away and Zoe remained unconscious, the others arrayed themselves on the empty beds and talked about the evening's events. It was then that Allie learned what happened in the minutes after Zoe was hurt.

Sylvain had run out after Jerry but lost him almost immediately. 'It was as if he disappeared,' he said bitterly. 'I was right behind him. I don't know how he did it.'

'He had a plan.' Nicole gave a discouraged shrug. 'Maybe he planned this long ago.'

The guards launched a search of the grounds before abruptly calling it off. A short while after that, the students heard cars roaring down the school's long drive.

No one had seen Isabelle, Raj or the other senior Night School instructors since then, and rumours were swirling about where they were and what had happened.

The students had been released from the common room – a sign that the threat was believed to have passed. But everyone was still baffled as to what, exactly, was going on.

Allie absorbed all of this information without releasing her hold on Zoe's small hand.

The doctor had told her Zoe was fine. Told her it was a concussion and trauma but that her neck and skull were fine. Her reflexes good. Pupils normal. Breathing regular. That she would wake up when she was ready. But Allie didn't believe it.

She didn't dare hope. All hope does is make everything hurt that much more when it all goes wrong.

Still, she was glad the others were with her. Their familiar voices wrapped around her like a warm blanket.

'I can't believe it's Jerry,' Rachel said, repeating the sentiment they'd all found themselves saying.

'I always hoped it was Zelazny.' Nicole sighed.

'Well, I'm glad it wasn't.' Sylvain's voice was gruff. Zelazny had been his Night School mentor, and they were close.

Allie thought of Eloise, no longer nervous, fighting Jerry like a tiger.

'How's Eloise?' she asked. The others looked at her in surprise. She had barely spoken this whole time. 'She fought Jerry hard.'

'No one knows,' Rachel said. 'She's disappeared along with Isabelle and Raj. But she seemed fine right after everything happened. Just … really pissed off.'

This wasn't hugely surprising. Eloise and Jerry had been together for a while, only breaking up after the librarian was accused of being the spy, and he didn't defend her. She had a lot to be angry about.

'Do you think she knew before?' Nicole mused.

'You mean that he was working for Nathaniel?' Carter seemed surprised by the question. But Nicole nodded.

'Especially after what happened when she was accused,' she said. 'He let everyone think it was her. She must have had some idea that he wasn't what he said he was.'

'Maybe she just thought he was a bastard,' Sylvain suggested.

They all considered this. It seemed feasible, if unlikely. When you really care about someone, it's hard to believe they're capable of something truly bad.

Zoe gave a soft groan and Allie spun back round. She had more colour in her cheeks and, after a second, stirred beneath the white blanket.

'Is she waking up?' Rachel asked. The others drew closer to see.

'What hit me?' Zoe murmured, one hand flying up to touch her jaw.

'Jerry.' Allie pulled the covers up to her shoulders before glancing at the others. 'Someone go tell the nurse she's waking up.'

Sylvain ran to the door.

Zoe's eyes fluttered open, taking in the room and the faces around her.

'Oh bollocks. It wasn't a dream.'

Her voice was thick. Someone handed her a glass of water and Allie put an arm around her narrow back so she could sit up to take a sip.

Her shoulders felt as fragile as bird wings beneath her arm.

Zoe blinked up at her. 'Did he get away?'

A sudden urge to cry made it impossible for Allie to speak. All she could do was nod.

''Fraid so, Shortie.' Carter reached out to pat her wrist.

A touch of colour came back to Zoe's cheeks.

'Bugger. I can't believe I forgot to guard my left flank. That's *basic*.' Laying back down on the bed she let go of Allie's hand. 'Bloody hell, my head hurts. What did he do to me?'

Rachel grinned at her. 'You've got a pretty bad concussion. It makes you sweary. Who's the prime minister?'

'That stupid guy.' Zoe groaned. 'With the face.'

'That's the one.' Rachel nodded, satisfied. 'I don't think you damaged your brain more than it was damaged already.'

'It feels like my head is exploding,' Zoe said, clutching her hair.

The nurse bustled in. 'I can help with that.' After taking her pulse and listening to her heart, she handed her two white tablets. 'Take these.' As Zoe obediently took the painkillers from her hand, the woman glowered at the others. 'Now, I'd thank you all to give her some space now, please. She needs quiet.'

But as they filed out of the room, obedient at last, Allie lingered, drinking in one last view of Zoe, alive and complaining.

Zoe cocked her head to one side, astute eyes assessing her expression.

'Did I scare you?'

Allie exhaled audibly, and smiled.

'You scared the crap out of me.'

Zoe looked wanly pleased. 'Awesome.'

When the students reached the foot of the stairs, a trio of guards stood waiting.

A muscular woman in black gear with long blonde hair pulled back in a braid scanned the group as if looking for someone.

'Allie Sheridan?'

Allie, who was last to come down, pushed her way through. 'Here.'

'Isabelle would like to see you.'

The woman looked familiar – Allie had vague memories of seeing her around the grounds. But she still studied her uncertainly. Isabelle had never sent guards for her before.

'What's going on?' Sylvain joined Allie. His tone was even but his mistrustful eyes watched the guards closely.

The guards turned their attention to him.

'I couldn't say.' The female guard's tone was cool. 'But it is important.'

'Where's Isabelle now?' Rachel appeared at Allie's other elbow. Her tone was conversational but her gaze suspicious. 'We haven't seen her all night.'

The woman looked nonplussed. Clearly she hadn't expected this. 'In her office. But she's busy.'

'Well, that's too bad,' Carter said, as he and Nicole joined the others to encircle Allie. 'Because we need to talk to her.'

'We don't have time for this,' one of the male guards said, impatiently. But the woman held up her hand.

'Give us a second.'

The three guards retreated to confer.

After a short while, the female guard returned. Her expression was hard to read.

'One of you can come with her,' she said, 'But that's all. The rest stay here.'

Her tone brooked no opposition.

'You go with her,' Carter said to Sylvain. 'I'll stay with Rachel and Nicole.'

Sylvain nodded his assent.

Allie ran a tired hand through her hair. 'Do you really think it's a trap? This is all so weird.'

'Yes, it is.' Carter's tone was dark.

He and Sylvain exchanged a worried glance. Rachel and Nicole were huddled close together.

'Stay nearby,' Sylvain whispered to Carter. 'I don't trust anyone right now.'

'I hear you,' Carter said.

The others dropped back as Sylvain and Allie followed the guards down the dark hallway. It was late now – Allie had no idea how late, she'd stopped caring hours ago. But the building had a hushed, late-night feel, thick with danger.

She was still shoeless and her feet were cold. She wondered if her shoes still lay out on the grass where she'd left them. She was tired but wide awake at the same time, adrenalin coursed through her veins like a drug.

When they reached Isabelle's office, one of the guards rapped twice on the heavily carved door. It swung open immediately. Raj Patel stood in the open doorway, backlit by a warm glow of light from within.

His eyes took in Allie first, then her companion.

'Sylvain – what are you doing here?' he asked brusquely.

Allie stepped forward. 'I want him here.'

Raj looked over her shoulder at the blonde guard. She held up her hands. 'She wouldn't come alone. I knew you needed her here fast. I didn't have much choice.'

Raj rubbed his hand across his cheeks, fingers rasping against stubble. For the first time Allie noticed how worn out he looked. His eyes were bloodshot.

'Fine. Inside. Quickly.'

Dom was already inside, sitting in one of the chairs in front of Isabelle's desk, her laptop open in front of her. Her gaze was fixed on the screen, intent.

What is she doing here? Allie thought. Her stomach had begun to churn.

Isabelle was at her desk talking quietly into her mobile. She gave them a harried glance. 'Sit down everyone. Quickly.'

Stiffly, Allie lowered herself into the chair next to Dom, who didn't look up from the screen.

Sylvain perched on a low cabinet at the back of the room. Raj stayed by the door. Otherwise, the room was empty.

Isabelle pushed a button on her phone and set it on her desk. 'Everyone is present, Lucinda. Allie is here with Sylvain Cassel.'

'Good.' Allie's grandmother's voice rose from the device, resonant and authoritative even through the medium of the small speaker. 'Thank you all for coming. Allie?'

'Uh ... yes?' Allie sat up straighter in her chair.

'I understand you and another student were very brave this evening in your attempt to stop Jerry Cole, and your friend was injured.'

In her head, Allie heard again the cracking sound Jerry's fist made against Zoe's face. Unconsciously, she flinched.

'I thought,' Lucinda continued, 'under the circumstances, you'd like to be here when we caught him.'

Allie blinked. 'Caught who?'

'Jerry Cole,' her grandmother said.

Twenty Six

Confused, Allie looked around the room, waiting for someone to explain what was happening. She couldn't understand what her grandmother was talking about. Nobody here seemed to be catching anyone.

'I don't understand …'

Dom looked up at her. 'I'm watching him,' she said. 'Right now.'

Her narrow spectacles glittered in the light.

Everyone else in the room had gone very quiet.

'How?' Allie asked.

'Tracking device. In the ankle of his trousers.' Dom turned back to her computer. 'Very tiny. Impossible to detect.'

She spoke with the careful precision of a well-educated American – like the scientists Allie had seen on the news. She found this comforting, somehow. The tech sounded capable. Knowledgeable. Like she could put an astronaut in space. Fix broken things.

'Where is he?' Allie's voice was cold as ice.

'Here.' Dom pointed at a red dot on her screen, moving slowly and steadily. 'He is on a train to London.' She turned her wrist; a heavy silver watch gleamed. 'He arrives at Waterloo Station in seven minutes.'

'My guys are there, Allie. Waiting for him.' Raj spoke with the curious calmness he always displayed when an operation was under way.

Allie turned in her chair so she could see his face. 'Jo liked Jerry, Raj. She *trusted* him. Don't let him get away.'

Holding her gaze, the security chief inclined his head once. She knew he understood. He'd cared about Jo, too. They all had.

'Jerry,' Dom said, typing, 'is not going anywhere. Look.' She pointed to the screen. Five green dots had appeared around the red dot. 'See the green dots? Those are our guys.'

It took Allie a second to realise what she was saying. 'They're on the train with him?'

Dom nodded.

As she stared at the screen, Allie's heart beat out a rhythm so fast and uneven it hurt.

Pressing a fist against her chest, she pushed back at her heart's painful pounding as she watched the screen.

'Isabelle,' Sylvain's voice was preternaturally calm. 'What the hell happened? How did you know it was him?'

The headmistress cleared her throat.

'Lucinda's MI5 connection was very helpful,' she said. 'With access to extensive information, she checked all of the suspected teachers' backgrounds more thoroughly than any of us ever could. Zelazny and Eloise both checked out – everything was just as it should be. With Jerry, though, there were … issues.'

'What kind of issues?' Sylvain asked.

'His banking and financial records are perfect, up to a point,' the headmistress explained. 'In fact, everything's fine up until seven years ago.'

Sylvain frowned. 'What happened seven years ago?'

'Before that point there are no records,' Isabelle said. 'No birth certificates. No taxes. No bank accounts. Seven years ago, as far as we have been able to determine, there was no Jerry Cole.'

A stunned silence followed her words.

Allie felt a chill, as if a breeze had blown through the windowless office.

'How is that possible?' Sylvain's tone was sharp. 'How did this go unnoticed until now? What about *our* security checks?'

It was Lucinda who replied. 'It would appear our Jerry Cole is an invention. His work history, his references, everything he brought when he applied at Cimmeria Academy – cleverly falsified. A brilliant job, really. Nathaniel used the best for this. And, to answer your question, Sylvain, we do very good background checks but nothing as thorough as MI5. We did not, for example, check his DNA.'

As they talked, Allie kept her eyes on Dom's laptop. More green dots had appeared on the screen. Catching her eye, Dom tapped them. Allie nodded to show she understood. Those were Raj's men in the station. Waiting.

'And so … all this time ….?' Sylvain couldn't seem to get his head around it and Allie couldn't blame him. Betrayal was awful. She knew that better than anyone.

'All this time he waited,' Isabelle said, 'pretending he was one of us. Reporting back to Nathaniel. Watching us. Using us.'

Allie kept her eyes on the dots. All that mattered now was catching him.

'How did he know to run?' Sylvain asked. 'Did you confront him?'

'No,' Lucinda answered. 'By the time we went to look for him, he was trying to find a way out. Somehow he must have realised we knew.'

The red dot was very close to the other green dots now. Allie found its progress hypnotic. She could imagine the train with its passengers, mostly normal people going about their everyday lives. Jerry would be pretending to be one of them, maybe holding a book open on his lap.

But knowing Lucinda's guards were after him. Knowing she'd send everything she had.

She hoped he was afraid.

She knew Waterloo Station as a grey, teeming place. Noisy and cavernous. Patrolled, as all big London train stations are, by armed police. Most of the police were now on Nathaniel's side.

Raj's guards would have to grab Jerry quickly and hustle him away before they could notice.

Lucinda was still talking. 'The guards were sent to—'

'He's arriving at the station.' Dom's voice cut her off. 'Now.'

Lucinda fell silent.

Raj spoke into his phone. A voice crackled on the other end. He looked up at them. 'Everyone's in place.'

Allie stared at the dots. The red dot was still moving slowly, inexorably. The green dots had gathered behind him.

She thought of the way trains pulled slowly into stations. The long pause before the doors opened. Then the rush to exit.

Suddenly the red dot moved in a different direction, quicker than before.

'He's running,' Dom said.

But it was futile. Allie watched the red dot stop. The green dots surrounded him.

Dom turned to her, her expression unreadable. 'They've got him.'

Raj's phone crackled again.

'Copy.' His tone was coolly vindictive. 'Well done, all of you. Bring him in.'

Allie still stared at Dom's screen. The green dots were all around the red dot, and they were moving briskly. Escorting him from the station.

She felt numb.

They'd finally found the person who betrayed them. But it all felt too late.

***

Late that night, the students gathered with Isabelle and Raj on the front steps. Eloise and Zelazny joined them.

The sky was clear; a crescent moon shone above them amid a circus of stars.

It had already been a long night. After leaving Isabelle's office, they'd gathered the others to tell them what had happened. Allie let Sylvain do the talking.

Now they stood together, waiting. Carter and Sylvain stood at the edge of the group with Raj, who seemed to be explaining something to them. Rachel and Nicole held hands, as if to give each other strength.

Allie stood alone, shoulders high, hands clenched at her sides.

Then she heard Zoe's piping voice.

'Is he here yet? Did I miss it?'

She whirled in surprise.

The younger girl dashed out of the doors, skidding to a stop when she saw the crowd.

'Oh good. I'm not too late.'

She looked pale and a purpling bruise had spread across one cheek. Her hair stood up at the back as if she'd just jumped out of bed.

'Zoe?' Allie said. 'How did you get out of the infirmary?'

Zoe made a face. 'That stupid nurse would not let me go. So I waited until she left then I escaped. I'm so glad I didn't miss it.'

'Are you OK, though?' Rachel said doubtfully. 'She probably wanted you to stay in bed because you, like, need to be in bed.'

But Zoe brushed that off. 'I'm fine. The pills she gave me were *amazing*.'

The rumble of engines cut through the night and they all fell silent. A few minutes later, headlights appeared and were fractured by trees into chaotic rays that seemed to spin and soar.

Six dark vehicles rolled up the curving drive, their tyres crunching on the gravel. The engines fell silent.

As the guards climbed out of the Land Rovers, Raj walked among them, shaking every hand.

'Good job,' he kept saying. 'Well done.'

In the crowd of black-clad men and women it was hard to find Jerry – he wasn't very tall and there were so many of them. Only when they marched him to the building did Allie see him.

He looked exactly the same. Glasses crooked. Wiry, uncontrollable hair.

He still looked like their friend. Their mentor.

But he was neither of those things.

The group parted silently so Jerry could pass. As he went by, his eyes scanned the crowd as if he was searching for someone. Allie assumed he was looking for Eloise.

But then his gaze locked on hers and she froze.

She couldn't read his expression in the dark, but she felt like his eyes were judging her, condemning her. She wanted to get away but couldn't seem to move; to free herself from that awful glare – until Carter stepped in front of her, arms crossed, blocking his view.

Allie's lungs felt compressed. She shivered as Jerry was hustled into the school building, disappearing in the shadows.

Carter spun round, searching her face. 'You OK?' he asked. 'What the hell was that about?'

She shook her head.

Sylvain joined them, his face tight. He met Carter's gaze. 'I didn't like that look.'

'Me neither,' Carter said.

'Was that the real Jerry?' Zoe asked. 'And the one we knew before was the pretend?'

But no one knew the answer to that question.

After the guards and teachers disappeared, the students stood in a tight cluster on the front steps, unsure of what to do. The night seemed darker now, more oppressive.

'I'm not tired,' Zoe announced.

'No,' Nicole said, looking around the group. 'None of us are.'

'Common room,' Carter said. 'It's after curfew but no one's going to care.'

They trooped down the empty hallway to the big student living room, with its deep leather chairs and sofas, and bookcases piled high with board games. The baby grand piano stood quietly in one corner like a reminder that this was supposed to be a place where people had fun.

They settled near the back and talked in quiet tones.

'He didn't look roughed up,' Carter said, glancing at Sylvain. 'I was surprised by that.'

Sylvain gave a shrug that said he didn't care whether Jerry was roughed up or not. 'Raj said he didn't fight.'

'Why didn't he fight?' Zoe asked. Everyone looked at her. 'I mean, he didn't want to get caught, did he? So why not at least try to get away? There would have been other people there. He could have ... done things.'

There was some truth to this and the students looked at each other with growing unease.

'You don't think ... did he *want* to be caught?' Rachel looked queasy.

'And be brought back here.' Nicole finished the thought, her eyes dark with worry.

'But why?' Allie asked. 'They'll have searched him, so he can't have brought anything. He'll be kept under guard, so he can't escape. So ... why come back?'

No one had an answer to that.

'Either way,' Nicole said, 'poor Eloise.'

'I know ...' Allie thought of the teacher's grim determination as she fought the man she'd loved. 'He broke her heart.'

'He broke everyone's heart,' Rachel said softly.

Isabelle had told them what would happen next – Jerry would be questioned, then she and Lucinda would try to trade him back to Nathaniel.

'In exchange for what?' Allie had asked, wondering what on earth they would want from him.

Isabelle's reply had been simple. 'Peace.'

She and Lucinda were going to try to use Jerry to buy an end to this battle. Or at least to buy time to negotiate. They believed there must be a connection between the two men. Something powerful enough that Jerry would be willing to give up his very identity for more than half a decade to hide at Cimmeria under an assumed name.

The students talked for hours in the near dark. Their conversation was largely circular, returning repeatedly to Jerry and betrayal. Zoe finally fell asleep with her head on Allie's knees and her feet on Rachel's lap.

As she watched her sleep, her chest rising and falling with each slow, regular breath, Allie felt a wave of protectiveness for her so profound it shook her. She had to find a way to keep her safe. To keep them all safe.

Dawn had just begun to break when they heard footsteps in the hallway. Isabelle rushed in, looking around until her eyes lighted on them. In the darkness it was difficult to make out her features.

'There you are.' Her tone was curt, as if she'd found them playing truant. 'Allie, come with me please. I need you.'

Allie didn't ask any questions.

With slow, careful movements, she extricated herself from beneath Zoe, who didn't wake, but turned over on to her side and curled up into a ball.

As she brushed past Carter he caught her hand in his. His grip was warm and reassuring.

'Be careful,' he said.

His touch made her feel braver. She raised her chin.

'Always.'

Twenty Seven

Isabelle led the way down the darkened hallway to a narrower corridor, then through an innocuous-looking door into one of the school's old servants' staircases. The winding stone stairwell smelled of damp and dust. The deeper they descended the cooler it became.

Funny, Allie thought. *It's meant to be hot in hell.*

The headmistress didn't speak as they entered the tangled spiderweb of cellar corridors beneath the school building. Flickering wall sconces were the only light. Things moved in the air around them.

Allie hoped it was just particles of dust.

In the gloom, it was impossible to keep track of where they were but, finally, they turned a corner and a cluster of guards appeared ahead of them, in front of an ancient, arched door.

Raj and Dom broke free of the group and walked over to join them.

'We're keeping him in the old wine cellar.' Isabelle's voice sounded odd, as if they were in the middle of a conversation only she could hear.

Up close Allie could see the headmistress was exhausted. Her face drooped and dark circles like bruises underscored her eyes. Strands of hair had crept free of the clip and hung loose around her face.

Raj, too, looked tired. None of them had slept in more than twenty-four hours.

'There was no other place secure enough,' Isabelle concluded.

Only Dom seemed untouched by everything that was happening. Her masculine, pin-striped shirt was crisp. Peeking out from beneath the turned-up hem of dark brown trousers, her brogues gleamed.

Catching Allie's look, she answered the question she hadn't asked. 'He's asking for you.'

Even though she'd expected something like this, the verification made Allie's pulse quicken.

But she kept her expression calm, responding with a nod. 'I thought so.'

'So far he's refused to talk to us.' Raj rubbed his bloodshot eyes. 'He says he'll tell us what we need to know … but only if he speaks to you first.'

Allie's mouth went dry.

She'd known Jerry since she first arrived at Cimmeria. Once she'd have trusted him with her life. Now she was afraid of him. Afraid of what he'd come back to tell her.

But she knew there was no way they'd ask her to do this if there was any alternative.

Straightening her spine, she met Raj's gaze. 'What's the plan?'

He gave her an approving look. 'Go in there. Listen to what he has to say. Promise him whatever you have to – you won't be held to any of it. We need you to try and get through to him. Find out what he's told Nathaniel. What Nathaniel has planned for the parley.'

'He's ... secured,' Raj added. 'He can't touch you.'

'Nonetheless, stay near the door,' Dom interjected. 'Keep your distance from him. We don't know what he's capable of.'

'Yes we do,' Allie said flatly. 'He's capable of murder.' She turned back to Raj. 'Anything I should look out for? Questions I should ask?'

'Just try to get him to talk. Anything he says could prove useful.' Raj's almond-shaped eyes, so like Rachel's, held hers with a steady confidence that warmed her. 'Then get the hell out of there as quickly as you can.'

Allie could sense his faith in her. His belief that she was capable of dealing with a situation as difficult as this one made her feel stronger. Braver.

Six months ago they wouldn't have let her anywhere near this room.

Dom pointed to a laptop set up near the door. On the screen Allie saw a figure, huddled in a chair. Jerry's hands hung at his sides and his head was down, hiding his face.

'We'll be watching,' she said.

When she walked towards them, the guards drew back to let Allie pass. She could see the curiosity in their eyes. The recognition.

Here comes Allie Sheridan. The one Nathaniel's obsessed with, she imagined them thinking. *What is it about her that's so important?*

She imagined she must look disappointingly ordinary to them in her short school skirt and rumpled white blouse. Certainly she didn't look like she could take on a man who'd fooled everyone for years.

And maybe she couldn't. There was only one way to find out.

The guard nearest the door opened it for her then stood back. Dressed all in black like the others, he was tall, with short-cropped brown hair. Her gaze flickered up to his. He gave a respectful nod. As if she was one of them.

Returning the nod, she turned back to the open doorway. Then, with cautious steps, she walked inside. The room was windowless and cool, walled in stone. It was bigger than she'd expected from looking at Dom's screen – long and narrow – and completely devoid of furniture save for one wooden chair at the far end of the room on which Jerry sat.

His head was still down, obscuring his face, but she could see now that his wrists were handcuffed. The cuffs were secured with long chains to a hook fixed to the wall.

They were taking no chances.

A guard stood just inside the door, his hands behind his back, watching him.

Allie took another step and another. The teacher didn't look up. He was so still she wondered if he was unconscious.

She was just beginning to wonder if she should say something when he spoke.

'Guards out.' His voice was a low growl.

Goosebumps pimpled Allie's skin. That didn't sound like Jerry at all.

'No talking,' he said, still not looking up, 'with them here.'

Allie turned to the guard. He met her gaze and asked a question with his eyes.

Her throat felt suddenly tight.

If the guard left, she'd be alone with the man who'd helped to kill Jo. Who'd put her own life at risk many times. But if the guard didn't leave, she wouldn't learn anything. Couldn't help anyone.

After a brief hesitation, she made up her mind.

She nodded her answer.

The guard rapped once on the door and it opened. He stepped out. It closed behind him.

Now she was alone with the man who'd betrayed them all.

At the thought, Allie started to feel panicked. A bit dizzy. Her lungs threatened to stop working.

I can't do this. I can't do this.

Then, in her head, she heard Carter's voice. '*Just breathe.*'

She breathed.

When she spoke her voice rang out, clear and strong. 'You asked to see me. I'm here. Let's talk.'

'Allie Sheridan.' Slowly he raised his head.

His wire-framed glasses were gone – they must have taken them away. Maybe they were just a prop anyway. He had a bruise on one cheek but looked otherwise unscathed. His normally clean-shaven face had a day's growth of whiskers, which gave him a vaguely disreputable look.

'Why did you want to see me?' she asked, trying to sound tough.

He laughed then and the sound made her skin crawl. It was a bitter, angry laugh.

'You have caused a lot of problems, young lady.'

Anger unfurled in Allie's chest. She fought to keep her voice even.

'How have I caused problems?'

'Everything could have been so different,' he said, shaking his head, 'if you'd just done what you were supposed to do.'

'And what was that?' She was surprised by how unafraid she sounded.

'Walk away from here,' he said. 'Join your brother. Join Nathaniel.'

'You're right. I didn't do that,' she said. 'So you killed people. You killed Ruth and Jo …' Her voice hitched and she steadied herself before continuing. 'And attacked Rachel and me.'

He made a dismissive gesture and the chains rattled. 'Gabe did those things, not me.'

Allie shot him a contemptuous look. 'You helped.'

'It's a war, Allie.' His tone said he thought she was being obtuse. 'People die in wars.'

'It's not a war.' Her voice rose. 'It's a family disagreement. Nobody should have died. Nobody should ever die for money.'

He laughed again.

'You're so naïve. Money is all anybody dies for these days.' He settled back in the chair and scrutinised her. 'But you're young. You'll learn.'

'Thanks for the *lesson*.' She spat the word out, as if it tasted bad. 'Is that all, Jerry? Because I think this is a waste of time.'

When she took a step towards the door, though, he jerked in the chair as if startled.

'No, wait.' His voice was urgent. She turned back. 'The reason I had to see you … I have to warn you.'

The temperature in the room seemed to drop.

'Warn me about what?'

'The parley,' he said. 'Nathaniel has a plan.'

Now, Allie thought, *we're getting somewhere.*

'What is the plan?'

He grimaced. 'I can't tell you that.'

'You have to,' she said. 'Or you'll never get out of here.'

'I can't,' he said deliberately, 'help you.'

Furious, Allie took two steps towards him. 'Then why am I here? Is this some sort of a game, Jerry? You want to warn me? Then warn me. Because we're busy …'

'Oh yes,' he growled. 'I know how *busy* you all are. I know everything about you, Allie. And so does Nathaniel. We know your weaknesses and your strengths. What you're willing to part with and what would destroy you.' He smiled, his lips stretched tight across his teeth. 'We know it all.'

Allie felt sick. This man looked and sounded nothing like the science teacher she'd known and trusted. That man was kind and thoughtful. This man was filled with violence and hate.

It was impossible to reconcile the two. She knew she should walk out of the room now. There was nothing to learn here. But she didn't.

'Why Jerry?' she asked, unable to stop herself. 'Why did you do it?'

For a long second he studied her. When he spoke, his tone was bitter. 'Your grandmother will tell you why, when she figures out who I am. She made me everything I am today.'

Allie's heart stuttered. *What did Lucinda have to do with him?*

She tried to keep her confusion out of her expression.

'You must really hate her,' she said, 'to be willing to kill children as some sort of twisted revenge.'

'I didn't kill *anyone*.' He shouted the words, leaning towards her, stretching the chains as far as they'd go. She could see through his shirt the way his shoulder muscles bulged.

She forced herself not to flinch. He couldn't reach her. But her eyes strayed to the hook in the wall. It was holding firm.

'Don't worry,' he said, following her gaze. 'I'm well secured.' Calmer now, he settled back in his chair. 'I am not a killer, Allie. My part in all of this was purely information. I was here to help Nathaniel understand his enemy.'

'Maybe if Jo hadn't died that would have worked as an excuse,' Allie said with cold deliberation. 'But she did die. And you knew exactly what you were doing. The risks you were taking.'

A brief silence fell.

'Maybe you're right.' He ran his hand across his jaw; the chains clanged. 'That was a bad night.'

'But you stayed loyal to Nathaniel even after that.' Allie couldn't let this go. She needed to understand. 'Why, Jerry? Jo liked you. You knew what Gabe might do. Knew how vulnerable she was. And yet you still delivered his notes to her. You opened that gate.'

His eyes looked yellow in the harsh fluorescent light. But he didn't shout this time.

'She was a good girl,' he said. 'I'm sorry it happened like that. Nathaniel thought Gabe was in control. He was wrong.'

'You were *both* wrong.'

Allie had heard enough. Jerry obviously had nothing to tell her but excuses and vindictive self-justification. She took a step back.

'Wait,' he said again. 'You have to know about the parley.'

'Then *tell me*.' Allie seethed with frustration.

He leaned forward and spoke urgently. 'Don't go to the parley alone. Nathaniel will make you agree to go alone – don't do it. Take someone with you. Someone you really trust. You won't get out of there otherwise.'

Allie's mouth went dry. What did he mean she wouldn't get out?

'What is he planning?' she asked. 'Tell me.'

Jerry shook his head. 'I can't tell you any more than that. I'm sorry. But please believe me. It's important.'

Allie studied him doubtfully. 'I don't get it. If you hate Lucinda so much, why would you help her granddaughter?'

He held her gaze and, for just a split second, he was Jerry Cole again, science teacher, Night School trainer and all-round nice guy. His eyes were warm and distracted.

'I have my reasons for hating your grandmother. But I have no reason to wish you harm. Just … take my word for this, Allie. Take someone you really believe in with you. You'll need them.'

Seeing that flash of the old Jerry, Allie's heart ached. Why couldn't he have been who he said he was?

It's so hard to believe in anyone when everyone lets you down.

Behind her the door opened, creaking on its old iron hinge. Apparently Raj thought this discussion was over.

Allie took a last long look at the science teacher. He peered at the door behind her with hungry eagerness. As if he hoped it was opening for him. For his escape.

She thought of Jo and Ruth – lives over so young. Of Sylvain beaten and bleeding. Carter nearly dead. The scars her own body now bore. And she didn't walk to the door.

Instead, with purposeful steps, she crossed the room until she stood within reach of the man complicit in all of it. Then she drew back her hand and slapped him with such force her hand burned.

His chains rattled as he took the blow. When he lifted his face she could see the shape of her palm rising red on his face. And the cool calculation in his gaze.

'That's for Jo,' she said.

She was almost at the door when he spoke again. 'Remember, Allie. Someone you believe in.'

'Screw you, Jerry.'

This time she didn't look back.

Twenty Eight

'I really trusted him. How could he be such a bastard?' Jo looked over at Allie, cornflower blue eyes wide.

The sun turned her short blonde hair into a golden halo.

'Who? Gabe?' Allie was confused. For some reason she couldn't remember how this conversation had started.

Jo gave her a withering look.

'Jerry, of course. God. And I had such a crush on him.' She gave a rueful sigh. 'Honestly. I had the most appalling taste in men.'

They were walking through a meadow. The sun was so bright it seemed to wash out the sky. The ground was soft beneath their feet. Yellow and orange wildflowers grew tall enough to brush their knees. It was wild and beautiful all at once. Like Jo.

Allie looked around, suddenly aware she was lost. 'I don't know this place. Where are we?'

'I love it here.' Jo's dimples deepened. 'I come here all the time. It's peaceful.'

A warm breeze ruffled her hair. Around her the flowers yielded to the wind, bending gracefully, like dancers.

'But Jerry ...' Allie said. 'Is he as bad as he seems?'

'Oh yes, Allie.' Jo's expression grew serious. 'He's very dangerous. Please be careful.'

'I will,' Allie assured her. A sudden sense of fear pierced her heart. Something bad was going to happen. She reached for Jo's hand but she was just out of reach.

'You must,' Jo said. 'Please, Allie. Don't end up like me.' She looked down.

Allie tried not to follow her gaze but she couldn't stop herself. She had to look.

On the front of Jo's white dress a red stain blossomed and grew. Soon she was soaked in blood. It ran from her fingers in streams. Puddled on the ground ...

With a strangled gasp, Allie sat straight up in bed. She looked around wildly, tears wet on her cheeks.

Morning light poured through her window. The sky outside was blue. It was going to be a lovely day.

And Jo was still dead.

※

The next day was Saturday but this was no ordinary weekend. As word spread of Jerry's betrayal, the atmosphere at the school grew increasingly anarchic. Teachers avoided students. Students simmered with rage, as if all their instructors were guilty by association. They felt betrayed.

Allie knew just how they felt.

The senior Night School instructors remained absent – busy, Allie suspected, with Jerry. She passed Dom in the corridor at one point but the tech didn't notice her as she hurried by, a laptop bag over her shoulder, oval face intense.

Night School training had not been resumed. In fact, all normal school activities had ground to a halt. No one studied. Students gathered in whispering clusters, sharing rumours, which grew wilder as the hours passed.

'I heard Nathaniel's coming here,' Allie heard a tall, blond boy say. They were in the common room and he was at the next table, playing chess with a group of friends. As he spoke, he moved a pawn. 'And Lucinda's giving him the school.'

'That's not what I heard,' a dark-haired girl replied.

They were all, Allie thought, about year ten. She'd seen them around but they weren't in any of her classes.

'What did you hear?'

She lowered her voice so far Allie had to strain to make out her words. 'I heard Nathaniel's going to raid the place to get the science teacher back. That he said no one would stop him.' She studied the shocked faces around her with grim satisfaction. 'He uses guns.'

Allie knew she could have stepped in and told them they were wrong but … were they? What did she know, really? Jerry hadn't told her much of anything.

Besides, the other rumours were even worse. Jerry and Zelazny were in it together. Six teachers had fled overnight, taking student records with them. Nathaniel had placed cameras in the school and watched their every move.

Given all of that, Allie wasn't at all surprised when Katie dropped down on the sofa next to her and fixed her with a determined look.

'I've been picking my way through the gossip,' she said by way of hello. 'Is it true you spoke with Jerry Cole?'

Allie tensed. She'd had this conversation many times today and she wasn't wild about having it again.

She glanced around to make sure no one was listening, but the chess players were far too involved in their own conversation to notice, and the other students were too far away to hear.

'Yeah,' she said cautiously. 'I talked to him.'

'And he really confessed to being Nathaniel's guy?'

Allie nodded.

Katie exhaled audibly. 'Jesus. I can't get over it. He just …' She waved her hand and her pearl and diamond ring glimmered. 'He never seemed like anything other than a typical trustworthy boring science geek. It's super creepy to think the whole time he was …'

'Watching us,' Allie finished the thought. 'I know.'

If she'd expected Katie to pick a fight or somehow diminish the impact of what Jerry had done – what Allie had been through in the last few days – she was wrong. Katie seemed just as shocked as the other students were. Just as demoralised and angry.

'The rest of the gossip sounds like bollocks to me,' Katie said. 'No other teachers are involved, are they?'

Allie shook her head. 'Just Jerry.'

'They're quite sure?' Katie pressed her.

'Lucinda and Raj …' Allie tried to decide how to put it without mentioning the MI5 connection. 'They were very thorough.'

The redhead seemed satisfied by this. 'If Lucinda's involved they would have gone straight to the top,' she said. 'What happens now?'

'They're setting up a meeting with Nathaniel.'

Katie arched one perfect russet eyebrow. 'Let me guess. You have to be there. Because Nathaniel's obsessed with you and your brother.'

Allie gave a tired shrug. 'Welcome to my world.'

Across the room, someone laughed. Allie glanced over, wishing she thought anything was funny right now.

Tapping one perfectly manicured nail against the smooth skin of her knee, Katie considered this.

'It isn't though. Your world, I mean,' she said. 'It's mine.'

Allie gave her a puzzled look. 'I don't get it.'

'You don't really know these people,' Katie explained. 'But I do. I've known them all my life. Nathaniel's been a friend of my parents since I was little. He was at my eleventh birthday party.'

The very idea was so stunning, Allie couldn't disguise her shock.

Katie made a wry face. 'Imagine how much fun that was for me – I asked for a bouncy castle and cake. Instead I got caviar and the Orion board of directors.'

Allie was speechless. It had never occurred to her that Katie would know him personally. She always talked about her parents like they were separate entities, rarely encountered. But, as a child, she would have been home more. So of course she would have known Nathaniel and Lucinda – all the people Allie had never heard of until a year ago had been part of Katie's life all along.

'What I'm saying is –' Katie leaned forward, her green eyes clear as sea water – 'if I can help you prep for this – get you ready so you know what to expect – I'd like to do it.'

Getting over her surprise, Allie found her voice again.

'Thank you,' she said with genuine feeling. 'I'd like that. It would help. He weirds me out. I always think I'm ready for him and then when I actually see him – ' she remembered facing him in the castle yard; the way her hands had trembled – 'I just lose it.'

'Ask me anything,' Katie said. 'I'll tell you all I know.'

Across the room, someone was striking a key on the baby grand piano. Just the same mournful low key over and over again.

'Will you stop that?' Allie heard someone say. The sound ceased.

All she knew of Nathaniel was what she'd seen. He looked ordinary – medium height, dark hair, neither very handsome nor ugly. If you passed him on the street you wouldn't look at him twice.

He didn't look evil. He looked like someone's dad.

'I guess I'd want to know what makes him tick,' she said. 'If I knew, like, how his mind works, then I'd know how to get under his skin. How to throw him off balance.'

Katie nodded briskly. 'He's very into organisation. Everything always has to be perfect. The crease in his trousers is very straight, if you see what I'm saying.' She warmed to the topic, looking over Allie's shoulder as if she could see Nathaniel in the distance. 'And everything is always the same. If he's writing something down he has this way of tapping his pen twice on his notepad before writing – always twice. Never more or less. In fact, he does everything the same way each time. Brushing dust off his shoes with the same weird wrist flick, when there's, like, no dust there to start with.' Seeing the look on Allie's face, she gave a self-deprecating shrug. 'When I was a child I often had very little to do besides study my parents' friends. I used to make a game out of it. Observing them like a Sherlock Holmes. Pretending I'd be questioned about it later.'

Allie blinked at her. This was a side of Katie she'd never seen. A surprisingly likable side.

'So, he's got OCD or something.'

'Quite,' Katie said. 'Like, he does this thing when he's really cross.' She held up a milk-pale arm. 'He twists his cufflinks three times, like this.' Demonstrating, she twisted her fingers with quick, precise moves.

'Good. I can look out for that,' Allie said. 'Did he ever talk to you much? I mean, directly?'

Katie paused to think about it. 'There was one moment I'd mostly forgotten until recently. My parents used to have meetings at the London house. There'd be all these boring business people around and, usually, I'd just play upstairs. But sometimes I'd sit on the stairs to watch them and sort of … eavesdrop.' She made a face. 'I was an odd child, I know. But seriously, grow up in *my* family? You learn to make your own fun.

'Anyway, one time I was sitting on the stairs. I must have been … twelve, I think. It was right before I came to Cimmeria. And Nathaniel saw me. I remember he walked up to me and he called me Katherine – nobody calls me that. It's my mother's name. He said, "And how are you, little Katherine?" And I corrected him, you know, like little girls do. I said, "My name is Katie." He seemed to find that funny. Then he said, "When you get to Cimmeria, I'll teach you some manners." And it scared me.' She paused. 'I think because of that I kind of expected him to be here when I arrived, but he wasn't.'

'Only he kind of was,' Allie said.

Katie held her gaze. 'And now he's teaching us some manners.'

'Do you know why your parents are on his side?' Allie asked. Katie's expression darkened, and she hurried to finish the question. 'I mean, did Lucinda do something to them to piss them off so much that they'd—'

'Side with the devil?' Katie cut her off. She sounded sardonic and angry now. Allie worried she'd gone too far. But then Katie gave a resigned shrug. 'With my parents it's always about money and power. My father lost a fortune in bad investments when I was little and he's been trying to claw his way back ever since. My mother would kill a human being for a title.' She appraised Allie, her apricot-pink lips curving up. 'You've already got one of those, I hear. Lady Lanarkshire, isn't it?'

Flushing, Allie dropped her gaze. 'Bloody Rachel. I knew she wouldn't be able to keep it a secret.'

'My mother would be so jealous.' Katie sounded almost wistful. 'I do wish we were still speaking so I could tell her. She'd just love to have you to dinner then. Or *for* dinner. Whichever. Envy is her main character flaw. And mine, to be fair.' She turned stern, lowering a glare at Allie. 'Why should *you* have a title if I don't?'

For a split second, Allie wondered if she was serious, but then the redhead grinned again.

'Oh, I forgot. Because my mum used to be a receptionist at one of my dad's companies. That's why. She's new money all the way. God, she'd hate that I've told you that.' She settled more comfortably on the sofa. 'I really must try and think of more scandalous things about her to tell you.'

Allie had to laugh at that. She was starting to like this new, mischievous Katie.

'I can't believe you're being so nice to me.'

Katie didn't blink. 'I can't believe you're letting me. Why aren't you snapping my head off?'

'I don't know,' Allie admitted. 'I guess it's like you said – there are other people to fight with right now.'

They studied each other for a moment, considering this new alliance. Then Katie grew more serious. She leaned forward, lowering her voice. Allie noticed the chess players had departed at some point without her realising it.

'Look, Allie. This meeting. If Lucinda wants Nathaniel to back off … it won't work. You need to be ready for that.'

The warmth in Allie's chest faded, replaced by the familiar chill of apprehension.

'Why not?'

'Because the wheels are in motion,' Katie said. 'The board is so behind Nathaniel now, I don't think he could stop this thing if he tried. They want what he wants. And these people – my parents and their friends – they'll stop at nothing.'

On some level, Allie had already suspected this. But hearing it said aloud was still shattering. If Katie was right, there was no hope.

'Are you telling me you think this is all over?' Her voice was barely above a whisper. 'There's no way Lucinda can win?'

Katie's nod was reluctant but Allie saw no doubt in her expression. 'I think Lucinda and Isabelle know it, too. They're just trying to slow the process.'

'So we've lost already.' Allie felt bleak.

Losing had always been unthinkable. They didn't have a plan for failure. Suddenly she had to imagine a situation in which they were all homeless. With no family to turn to. No future. And it was awful.

'I don't understand. Why would Lucinda go through with this if it's hopeless?'

Katie's green eyes studied her with curious kindness. 'There are different ways to lose, Allie. Sometimes you lose and it's a sort of victory. I think that's what she wants.'

'How?' Allie was baffled. How could losing be anything other than failure?

'We are fighting for a lot of things here. For the school, Orion, the board, power, money …' Katie ticked the items off on her fingers like a shopping list. 'Lucinda cares about some of them more than others. If she loses control of one, can she gain control somewhere else? If she loses the school, can she find another place? If she loses Orion, can she gain power in another organisation? She needs to hold out long enough to stop Nathaniel from getting what he really wants. This is strategy.'

For some reason Allie found herself thinking about her old life. Before Cimmeria. The way her parents always took their work so seriously. Leaving every morning at seven and not returning until dinnertime. How every little thing that happened in their offices had to be discussed, analysed.

They weren't poor. They actually had things pretty good compared to some people. But everything *mattered*.

By comparison, this, treating power and wealth like it was one of those giant chess games you see on holiday – move a pawn here, a king there – seemed garish. Irrational.

Insane.

She forced herself to ask one last question. 'If she can't win, what is Lucinda trading Jerry for?'

Katie didn't hesitate. 'Time. She needs to buy some time to decide how to lose without losing everything.'

Twenty Nine

'I just don't see the point.' Rachel slammed her book shut with a bang. Nicole and Allie stared at her in surprise. 'And I hate that I can't see the point in studying. Because I love studying.'

It was Sunday afternoon and they were in the library. They had the room to themselves. Even Eloise wasn't there today. So they weren't bothering to be quiet.

'Come on, Rachel. You can't give up on normal life.' Nicole's delicate French accent made normal life sound dazzling. 'No matter what happens.'

'She's right,' Allie said, even though she, herself, had been doodling pictures of armed rabbits for half an hour. 'There might be an apocalypse but we still have to take A-levels. And that's what really matters.'

Rachel greeted this ironic statement with an eye roll. 'I'm starting to understand why you guys like fighting. It would be so good to kick something right now.'

Nicole brightened. 'That would be easy to arrange …'

With perfect timing, the library door opened, hitting the wall with a thud. Zoe swooped in and stood in front of them, disbelief in her eyes. The bruise on her face was going green around the edges. Every morning she gave them a detailed update on the colour changes and what it meant about the movement of blood beneath her skin. This had ruined everyone's appetite at two breakfasts so far.

'Why are you *studying*?' Her tone said studying was the most idiotic activity she could imagine. 'There's a meeting.' When they just stared at her, she gestured impatiently for them to follow. 'Come now.'

She led the way down the grand, empty hallway to the basement stairs, and then along the narrow, dusty subterranean corridor. As they neared Training Room One, Allie's stomach began to twist. An unannounced Night School meeting was never good.

When they arrived, the featureless room was as full as it got these days. All the members of Night School were there, along with Zelazny, Eloise and a handful of guards. Someone had taken up the exercise padding that usually covered the floor and leaned it against the walls, revealing the cold concrete below.

The girls found Carter and Sylvain standing on one side of the dimly lit room with Lucas and they hurried across to them.

'What's going on?' Allie asked, searching their faces for clues. But they both shook their heads.

'No idea,' Carter muttered. His hands were shoved deep into his pockets and he scanned the room with suspicious eyes.

'Looks serious,' Lucas said.

Tension thickened as they waited with no word. By the time Isabelle and Raj walked in with Dom ten minutes later, nerves crawled under Allie's skin like insects.

Her eyes were drawn to the American. As always, she wore trousers and a masculine shirt. Her glasses sparkled in the harsh fluorescent light. She looked so enigmatic. So confident.

With the teachers and guards arrayed around her, the headmistress surveyed the room, her head held high.

'You all know what's been happening in the last few days.' Her rich voice filled the space with easy authority. 'Jerry Cole has admitted he's been working for Nathaniel, pretending to be one of us but reporting to the man who would like to destroy this school and your future. He has been removed from the school and is being held in a safe place until we can return him to his owner.'

Quiet murmurs swept the room as the students processed this. Allie hoped Isabelle was telling the truth – she didn't want Jerry anywhere in the building.

'Now there will be a parley with Nathaniel,' Isabelle continued. 'A date and location have been set and the final conditions are being negotiated as we speak.'

A prickle ran down Allie's spine.

It's really happening. We're really going to do this.

Isabelle waited for the room to settle before continuing. 'You will all have important roles to play. The situation is very dangerous. As always, there's no way to know what he's really planning. So while we are away, the school will need to be protected. Raj?'

She stepped back, and Raj took over.

His face was hard as his gaze swept the room. 'The meeting with Nathaniel will take place in London. Half my guards will accompany me to the parley. Half will stay here with you. Between now and the day of the meeting you will be involved in intensive preparation. I think we all know now that Nathaniel is capable of anything.'

He stepped among them, eyes moving from one face to another. 'Whether you come to London or stay here, I need you to give me everything you've got. Your role will be critical in saving lives. Keeping each other safe.'

As he passed them, the students stood straighter, shoulders pulled back, heads high. Even after everything that had happened in the last year, Raj's approval still mattered.

Isabelle handed Raj a piece of paper and he held it up so they could see it.

'If I call your name,' he said, 'you will be working with Mr Zelazny and my guards to protect the school.'

He called off a list of names. One by one, the students walked over to stand with Zelazny.

When he called Lucas's name the boy looked up in surprise. Clearly he'd thought he was going to the parley with the core group. But he didn't argue. Shoving a lock of sandy brown hair back out of his eyes, he walked over to Zelazny. Carter patted him on the shoulder as he passed.

The last name Raj called was Rachel's. Noticing how she hesitated before crossing the room to join the group, Allie hid her relief. She knew how much Rachel would hate not staying with the parley group. But she couldn't be with them. She was in no way ready to take on Nathaniel and Gabe again.

Before Rachel could line up with Zelazny's group, though, Raj stopped her.

'You're not working with Zelazny.' His daughter looked up at him in surprise; he pointed to the other side of the room. 'We need you to help Dom.'

The American held up her hand, as if Rachel might not know who he was talking about. After a brief pause when Allie feared she might argue, Rachel walked to the tech's side.

Already, Allie was beginning to feel better about things. If Rachel was with Dom she had to stay at the school. Nathaniel wouldn't get his hands on her again.

When Raj stopped reading, the room fell silent.

Allie, Sylvain, Carter, Nicole and Zoe stood alone. All the other students were on the other side of the room with Zelazny.

'The rest of you,' Raj looked across at Allie's group. 'With me.'

He walked towards the door. Allie could feel the other students watching them as they crossed the room after him. Like they were celebrities.

'This is weird,' Carter whispered under his breath as they walked out the door and she almost smiled.

'Weird is what we do best.'

They gathered with Isabelle and Raj in one of the small, top-floor classrooms where the chairs had been arranged in a half-circle. Allie sat between Sylvain and Zoe. Nicole and Carter filled out the group. Raj stood near Isabelle, letting her lead.

A row of windows lined one wall. Outside, grey clouds had built up and, as Isabelle stood to speak, a clipboard held in front of her chest like a shield, rain spattered against the windows like nails tapping.

'The parley will happen Friday night on Hampstead Heath.' She glanced at Allie. 'I assume you're familiar with it.'

Allie, who'd grown up on the other side of the city, had only vague memories of vast green fields, a lavish white mansion with columns, and an orchestra playing in the sun.

'I went there once a long time ago,' she said.

The headmistress acknowledged this with a nod. 'Then let's start with the basics. Hampstead Heath is a park in the north of London. We've agreed to that location because parts of it are quite remote and likely to be empty at night. So there's less chance of an innocent person being hurt.'

The idea that she so openly anticipated violence was unnerving.

'He wants to meet on Parliament Hill.' Isabelle didn't hide her irritation at this fact. 'Nathaniel and his symbolism. However, this could work to our advantage. There are many places on that particular ridge where we can station guards. The terrain is not unlike the grounds here – hilly, forested – and we know how to operate in those conditions.'

As the students digested this, she turned. 'Allie. We will go over the conditions we've agreed to in detail later. But for now, you should know Nathaniel insisted you come alone.' Allie shook her head fiercely at this news but, before she could voice her protest, Isabelle held up her hand. 'We have refused, of course. After some resistance, he's agreed you can bring one person with you but it must be a student – he won't allow Raj or any of his guards. Obviously, we will all be there, one way or another. But only one person can travel with you and be at your side during the meeting.'

Allie shivered. It was all happening exactly as Jerry had told her it would.

Outside, the rain was falling harder now. Running in rivulets down the glass.

The headmistress stepped towards her. 'Raj and I both believe that, under the circumstances, this decision should be yours alone. Who would you like to be with you?'

Wordlessly, Allie stared back at her. She kept hearing Jerry's words in her head. *'Take someone you believe in.'*

What did that even mean? She believed in every person in this room. She would throw herself in front of a bullet for each of them. How could she choose one of them above the others?

She forced herself to look around the circle. Zoe gazed at her with hopeful eyes. But that was impossible – she was far too young. The incident in the library had proven she wasn't ready yet.

Her gaze moved to Nicole. She was both quick and skilled, and Allie knew she could stand her ground. But Gabe would find a way to use her lack of sheer physical strength against her.

That left Sylvain and Carter.

Sylvain watched her with a look of steady confidence but she knew him well enough to see worry darken his blue eyes when she didn't immediately say his name.

Her eyes moved to the last desk in the circle.

Carter was the only one in the group who didn't meet her gaze. She could see his tension in the set of his shoulders; the way a muscle worked in his jaw.

Take someone you believe in …

Indecision pinioned her.

The moment stretched on too long. She saw Isabelle frown at Raj when she didn't speak. She had to choose. She had to do it now.

She took a deep breath. 'I'll take Sylvain.'

Carter's shoulders stiffened as if she'd struck him.

The others reacted as she'd expected. Zoe muttered mutinously to herself, while Nicole seemed unsurprised. Sylvain nodded as if this was precisely what he'd expected.

But Carter kept his eyes on the ground; his face expressionless.

'Fine.' Isabelle's clipped tone gave no clues to her feelings about Allie's decision. 'The two of you will work with Raj and Dom on the details of the journey and the meeting. Otherwise, we will all work together on overall preparedness and planning.'

She set the clipboard down. As she looked around the circle, her golden brown eyes were shadowed.

'I must be honest with you. As we said downstairs, this is going to be dangerous. But Lucinda believes if we don't go to Nathaniel now he will come to us later, and that could be worse. You must be ready for anything. My *one goal* is to get every single one of you back here safely. Nothing else matters.'

Thirty

When the meeting ended, the group walked out in a hushed cluster, stunned by the speed with which it was all happening. Only a few days to prepare.

From beneath her lashes, Allie kept her eyes on Carter. He'd been subdued throughout the meeting, avoiding her gaze.

As soon as they reached the first-floor landing, she saw him drop back and peel away from the others. She hurried to follow but he was moving fast. When he reached the foot of a narrow staircase that led to the boys' dorm, she called out to him.

'Hey!'.

He froze. .

'Can we talk?' she asked.

'Sure.' His voice was even. But still he didn't turn around.

She reached for his arm. His white shirt was cool beneath her fingers but she could feel the warmth of his skin through the fabric.

Slowly, he turned to look at her. His face was carefully blank.

'Look …' She hesitated. Now that she was here she didn't know what to say. 'I … I wanted to talk to you about why I chose—'

'It's fine.' He cut her off before she could finish. 'I know why you picked Sylvain. And I don't blame you. I would have made the same decision.'

Allie blinked. 'You would?'

'Of course. He's gone up against Gabe more than once. And Nathaniel. And won.' He dropped his gaze. 'I've never done that. Probably couldn't. So Sylvain's the right choice. You need someone who can keep you safe.'

Despite his obvious attempt to sound neutral, his voice dripped with self-loathing.

Allie was horrified by how he was interpreting her choice.

'Carter, I didn't choose Sylvain because he's better than you,' she said, willing him to believe her. 'That's not the reason.'

'It should have been,' he said roughly, colour rising in his cheeks. 'All that matters now is choosing the best person to fight with you. Nothing else. And that's Sylvain.'

'That's not true,' she said, tightening her grip on his arm. Carter's gaze locked on hers with such intensity it was hard for her to breathe.

'If that's not the reason then … why, Allie? Why did you choose him?'

She stared at him, seeing the hurt in his eyes. But she didn't know how to answer his question. *Because he's my boyfriend? Because he loves me?*

Those were both stupid reasons to choose a fighter.

She had the horrible feeling she'd made a mistake.

Dropping her hand she looked up at him hopelessly. 'Don't you see? I had to. What I want doesn't matter.' Surprise flared in his eyes. But before he could ask any questions, she stumbled away, running hard into a marble statue she'd forgotten was

behind her. Flustered, she grabbed on to the plinth to right herself.
'Sorry … I should … I've got to go.'

Then she ran down the stairs as if someone was chasing her.

* * *

The next few days were a blur of preparation. Isabelle insisted they continue with their coursework, even as their physical training extended later and later into the night. By Wednesday, they were already exhausted, and there were still two days to go.

But Allie was glad of the hard work and the pressure – it kept her from worrying all day. Made her tired enough to sleep at night. Kept her mind from spinning through all the ways it could go wrong.

She and Sylvain met every day after class with Isabelle, Raj and Dom for updates on their plans for the parley.

The work was relentless. Every element of the route they would take to the park, and how they would make their way to Parliament Hill, was scrutinised and analysed over and over again until Allie knew Hampstead as well as she knew Cimmeria.

On Wednesday afternoon they gathered in a small basement office across from Training Room One and crowded around Dom's laptop, looking at a map of Hampstead Heath and the surrounding tangle of city streets. The park was a mass of dark green, the streets around it white lines that curved and angled.

This was high summer, so they knew the park would be packed with picnickers, bikers and tourists during the day. But at night it was virtually empty.

'The area around the park is very exclusive – some of the most expensive property in London. But it's also densely populated,' Raj explained, pointing at white lines just beyond the southern quadrant of the park. 'We should be able to drop you off without being noticed. The problem is getting you across the park and to the top of the hill safely.'

He gestured for Dom to take over.

With her cursor, she traced a dark, curving line. 'If we let you off here, you could walk up quite easily, but we believe this path is too exposed. It's the most popular route for tourists because it's along a gentle curving slope.' The cursor moved to a longer footpath, which came into the park from another direction. 'This one is steeper and travels through wooded terrain. It provides more cover and thus safety. However, it means you're on foot longer in the park, which increases the risk, if Nathaniel's guards are where we expect them to be.' Through the clear lenses of her narrow glasses she glanced up at them. 'Despite that, we believe the benefits outweigh the dangers, and this is the better path.'

Sylvain frowned. 'You think we can avoid Nathaniel's guards?'

'You'll have to,' Dom said.

Raj took over, pointing at a white line at the edge of the green. 'We'll drop you off here, on Tanza Road. From there you'll need to hike five hundred yards due east to meet up with this footpath here.' He tapped a slim black line on the screen. 'After that, your journey to the top of the hill should be straightforward. I will station guards in the woods along the way to provide protection but it's nearly a mile to the meeting point. You will need to be extremely cautious.'

'What about police? Civilians?' Sylvain asked.

'If you see the police you're just a couple of kids looking for a place to be alone.' Raj spoke without apparent embarrassment, but his words made Allie go red.

'Civilians?' Sylvain prodded him.

'If you see people, avoid them. That's the basic rule,' Raj said.

'Will Lucinda be with us the whole time?' Allie asked.

Raj shook his head. 'She'll take a different route. Keeping you together would be too dangerous. You'll meet her at the top of the ridge.' He tapped his finger on the screen. 'Now, our guards will be all over that hill but that won't be enough. Nathaniel's guards will be there, too. You'll need to rely on your training and your wits to get through this. Because whatever Nathaniel has planned, it isn't a parley.'

'We'll be ready,' Sylvain vowed.

Allie couldn't tear her eyes from the map, glowing green and white on the computer screen. She wished she felt as confident as he sounded.

When they came out of the meeting, Rachel was waiting in the corridor, a huge stack of papers in her arms.

Seeing her, Allie felt a sudden burst of unexpected happiness. A friendly face was just what she needed about now.

She ran up to her. 'Hi! Looking for me?' She glanced at the papers. 'How did you know I'd run out of all the paper in the world?'

Rachel peered over her shoulder. 'Not exactly,' she said. 'I mean, I'm *always* happy to see you but during this particular Cimmeria apocalypse I'm here for someone else.'

'Rachel. There you are.' Dom's voice came from behind them.

Eagerly, Rachel stepped past Allie, holding up the pages so Dom could see them. 'I got your message. Here's the information you asked for.'

She fairly vibrated with excitement.

Allie watched her with interest; it had been a while since she'd seen Rachel so enthused and animated.

'Great.' Taking the papers from her, Dom handed her the laptop case. Without a second's hesitation, Rachel draped it across her shoulder and followed the tech down the narrow corridor, skipping a little to keep up.

'We need to plot some walking routes,' Allie heard Dom explain in a brisk tone. 'We'll need to take the Ordnance Survey maps and then recalculate time and pace …'

Her voice faded as they walked down the hallway, absorbed in their plans.

'Rachel fits well with Dom,' Sylvain had walked up next to Allie without her noticing.

'Yeah,' she said, watching them disappear down the stairs. 'They're two clever peas in a super smart pod.'

As she headed down the shadowy top-floor corridor, Sylvain fell into step beside her. It was very quiet.

As they walked, Allie glanced at him. 'How do you feel about all this? Do you think we're ready?'

He looked at her, his eyes a flash of turquoise in the dimness. 'It's OK, I guess. But we'll need much more precise knowledge of where to go once we enter the park, how we'll communicate … everything.'

A shadow crossed his face. In all their training he'd never betrayed anything but steady confidence. Now, as Allie realised how worried he was, nerves tightened their grip on her.

Because he was right. This meeting was taking them out of their comfort zone. Away from Cimmeria, where they knew they had home field advantage, and into London: enemy territory.

'It's all happening so fast,' she said. Sometimes I feel like we're kind of running into something we don't totally understand.'

He met her gaze. 'I suppose we'll have more information tonight. I think that's what Rachel and Dom are working on.'

'Yes, but … there's no *time*.'

Hearing the worry in her voice, Sylvain reached for her hand. She let him pull her closer, until she could feel the warmth of his skin through their clothes.

'We'll be fine,' he said. 'I promise.'

This close to him she could breathe in his familiar scent – he smelled of coffee, spicy sandalwood soap. See how his eyes fractured the light like sapphires.

He was beautiful and kind and brave. Any idiot could see that.

At that moment, footsteps stormed up the stairs towards them. They were moving fast. Urgently. As if someone was panicking.

In sync, they both turned.

Nicole hurtled up towards them, her blue pleated skirt swirling around her legs, dark hair flying.

'Sylvain,' she said and her voice sounded strange. She was white as paper. 'Something's happened.'

Allie felt Sylvain's body tighten.

'What is it?' His voice had gone cold.

A tear ran down Nicole's pale cheek and Allie saw that she was trembling. 'It's your father.'

Thirty One

Isabelle met them at the foot of the stairs.

'Is he alive?' Sylvain kept asking. The colour had drained from his face but his voice was steady. Insistent.

All the headmistress could say was, 'I hope so. We're waiting.' She reached for his arm as if to steady him. 'But, Sylvain. It's bad.'

From then, everything took on a nightmarish haze. Allie couldn't seem to feel anything. She was numb.

The three students followed Isabelle to her office. Nicole and Allie tried to make Sylvain sit but he refused. Instead he stood stiffly by the door, his face drawn.

'My mother …?' he asked.

'She's fine. She's on her way to the hospital now to be with your father,' Isabelle said. 'Please sit and I'll tell you everything I know.'

He set his shoulders. 'I will stand. But … tell me.'

Nobody could bear to sit if he didn't, so they all stood as Isabelle explained what had happened.

His father had been at his offices in Paris. He had a meeting that afternoon elsewhere in the city with a business associate.

'It was perfectly routine,' Isabelle said. 'Someone he met all the time.'

His chauffeur drove the car to the front door of the office to pick him up.

'Everything was normal,' Isabelle said. 'He and his driver had gone less than a mile when the bomb went off. They believe it was hidden in the engine of the car. A very sophisticated device.'

A bomb.

The world swung beneath Allie's feet. She gripped the back of the chair in front of her so hard her nails dug deep pits into the leather.

Unflinching, Sylvain fixed the headmistress with a piercing look. 'How bad is it?' When the headmistress hesitated, his tone sharpened. '*Tell me.*'

'The car flipped over on to its top.' Isabelle's voice was low. 'It flew fifty feet. The driver was killed instantly.'

Nicole made a small sound of grief. Allie covered her mouth with her hands. She knew Mr Cassel's driver. He always had a smile for her when she passed him on the grounds. He was young. Normal.

Dead.

Sylvain looked suddenly older, his face sagging.

'And my father?'

He tried so hard to look in control but Allie could see how he struggled to get the words out. How frightened he was.

Nicole put her arm around him; he didn't seem to notice her touch.

Her actions seemed to release Allie from the shock that had held her in place, and she ran to Sylvain's other side, putting her arm across his shoulders. . He stood stiffly in her embrace but she didn't let go. She knew what it felt like to have fear and grief cut you off from the world.

'All we know is he is alive. He's in surgery.' Isabelle's golden brown eyes were full of sympathy. 'His injuries are grave. I wish I could tell you more.'

Sylvain nodded, absorbing this information.

'Allie, Nicole,' he said, not at all unkindly, 'let me go, please.'

Reluctantly, Allie let her hands drop to her sides. She wanted to help – she *needed* to do something. She thought of how kind he and his family had been to her and to Rachel after they'd washed up on their doorstep, pursued by monsters. She wanted to be like them – to always know the right thing to say or to do.

But there was nothing she could do that would make this moment any less frightening for him.

'Thank you.' His voice was steady and strangely formal. But she could see he was holding himself together by a thread. A slender strand of determination. For a long moment he seemed to think. Then he looked up at the headmistress. 'Isabelle, organise a plane. You know who to call. I'll pack a few things. Have a car meet me at the front door in ten minutes.'

Allie glanced at the headmistress, expecting her to object to being given orders. To try to calm him down. To offer alternatives.

But Isabelle did none of those things.

'Of course,' she said. Then she picked up her phone.

Without another word, Sylvain opened the door and disappeared into the hallway.

Allie couldn't seem to understand anything that was happening. Sylvain was going away? By himself?

It wasn't safe out there. Surely they wouldn't let him just leave.

'Isabelle …?' she said. But the headmistress was scrolling through the numbers on her phone and didn't look up.

Panic rising in her throat, Allie turned to Nicole helplessly. 'What is *happening*?'

'Come with me.' Taking her arm, the French girl steered her from the office.

Behind them, Allie heard Isabelle speaking into her phone. 'The Cassel jet, please. Number A135982. How quickly can it be fuelled and prepped?' Then after a brief pause, 'We need it quicker than that.'

This cannot be happening.

As soon as they were in the hallway, Allie wrenched her arm free of Nicole's grip. 'Stop. Just … tell me what's going on. Sylvain can't just *go*.'

'He can.' Nicole studied her with sympathy. 'He has to. And you must let him go.'

Her French accent had thickened; it was always heavier when she was under stress.

'But—' Allie began to protest but Nicole cut her off.

'Sylvain and his parents are very close, Allie. You know that. He must be there for his mother. And in case his father is alive.' Her voice trembled when she said 'in case', reminding Allie that she and Sylvain grew up together; she loved his parents. 'When his father wakes up he will need Sylvain's help. His protection.'

'Protection?' Allie frowned.

'Sylvain's father is the head of the European organisation,' Nicole explained patiently. 'The one called

Demeter. He is not just a friend of Lucinda's. He is her equivalent in France. If Nathaniel did this, it was a declaration of war.'

Allie stared at her in astonishment. She'd known the Cassels were important in the organisation but this was the first time she'd been told just how important they were.

Nicole was still talking. 'Whoever did this wants Mr Cassel dead. If he survives this attack they will try again. Someone needs to coordinate his protection and run the business. Sylvain's mother will be ...' She paused, looking for the right words. 'She might not be able to do it right now. She will be upset.'

'But he can't go alone,' Allie insisted. 'It's too much.'

'He has to,' Nicole said firmly.

'He'll be in danger,' Allie said.

'We are *all* in danger.' Nicole's tone sharpened. She shook Allie's arm with gentle firmness, as if trying to wake her. 'He has to go, Allie. He has no choice.'

Allie stared at her wide-eyed. Sylvain was about to leave. To walk straight into the aftermath of a highly skilled assassination attempt. He could be killed.

'I have to go to him,' she said.

A tear tumbled down Nicole's cheek as she stepped back. 'Go. Help him.'

Feeling cold with fear, Allie ran down the wide hallway and pounded up the stairs to the boys' dorm. Girls weren't allowed there but no one tried to stop her. All The Rules had lost their power.

When she reached the plain white door with 306 lacquered on it in glossy black she stopped, panting heavily. Through the door, she could hear the sliding sound of wooden drawers opening and the thud as they were closed again.

She knocked hesitantly.

A second later, Sylvain yanked the door open with such force she jumped back.

He stood in the doorway, frowning at her, his arms full of folded shirts.

'Allie. What are you doing here?' Without waiting for an answer he walked back across the room and set the shirts in the open suitcase on the bed, then stalked to the wardrobe.

'I ... I came to see if I could ... help.' The suitcase was sleek and black, lined in monogrammed silk. Allie had to marvel at how neatly he was packing even in a crisis. Nothing looked disturbed in his room. Everything was in its correct place.

I'd be throwing things around, she thought.

As he pulled more clothing from his wardrobe and folded them into the case, her eyes were drawn to the old oil painting that dominated one wall. It showed an angel carrying a man up to the clouds. The angel's wings were beautifully painted – they seemed to glow from inside, like pearls. He'd told her once that it had been a gift. It only occurred to her now to wonder who had given it to him and why. There was nothing in his parents' house like it.

'I'm almost finished,' he said, jerking her attention back. Picking up a small bag for toiletries he walked to a shelf by the door and picked a few items off it with deliberate movements.

He closed the suitcase, taking care to latch it. Then he picked it up as if it weighed nothing and turned to the door, his face set. Allie found herself wondering if he was in shock. He wasn't acting at all like himself. It was as if someone was operating him from far away.

'I have to go now, Allie.'

Panic made her heart race. He was really leaving.

'Sylvain …' She stepped towards him, arms outstretched as if to … what? Stop him? Hold him?

Lips tight with determination, he sidestepped her. Embarrassed and confused, she dropped her hands.

Seeing the look on her face he stopped and closed his eyes. He looked torn. Tormented.

'I can't do this, Allie. I have to go.'

But then, still holding the suitcase in his left hand, he walked up to her. Cupping her cheek in his right hand, he looked at her with such longing it broke her heart.

'I love you, Allie. I always will. Even though I know …' He almost smiled then, a terrible, sad smile. 'Well, I know.' Leaning forward he brushed his lips against hers; his touch as light and ethereal as a kiss in a dream. 'Goodbye, Allie.'

Lips parted in surprise, she didn't move as he walked away. In the doorway, he stopped and looked back at her.

'Take Carter to the parley,' he said. 'And, whatever happens … stay alive.'

Then he was gone.

'Sylvain …' Allie breathed the word, too quietly for him to hear.

The sound of his footsteps receded in the distance.

She couldn't seem to move. It was if her world had spun off its axis as she clung to it, helpless.

Nerves made her stomach burn and she clutched her abdomen as she tried to think.

Whoever tried to kill his father would surely want Sylvain dead, too. And anyone who supported Lucinda. He was just as vulnerable as his father.

'He has to go,' Nicole had said.

But he was walking into a maelstrom.

Only then was she able to move, and she ran after him, nearly tumbling down the staircase in her haste.

Tears wet on her cheeks, she skidded into the grand hallway. In the distance she could hear the steady rumble of a car engine and her heart stuttered with the fear that she'd missed him. That he was already gone.

When she reached the front door, Isabelle and Nicole were on the steps watching sombrely as Sylvain opened the door of a gleaming black car.

Allie ran down to the lowest step and then stopped, unsure of what to do. She knew she couldn't stop him. If she tried, she'd only make things harder for him.

When he turned for one last look at the school, Sylvain's eyes found her.

Choking back a sob, she raised her hand in goodbye.

For a long moment he stood still, studying her as if he was trying to memorise her face. Then he climbed into the car and it drove away.

Thirty Two

'Take a break, everyone.' Raj looked around the training room. Sweating, exhausted Night School students collapsed on to the dark blue rubber matting on the floor. 'We start again in ten.'

The students groaned.

Allie stayed on her feet, muscles tense. She didn't want a break. She wanted to fight.

'What's wrong?' Cocking her head to one side, Zoe studied her with a quizzical expression. 'You look funny.'

Allie wasn't in the mood to explain how she felt. 'Nothing,' she lied. 'I'm just thirsty. I'll get us some water.'

Without waiting for the younger girl to respond, she crossed the mat to the front of the steamy room where a cooler filled with water and ice stood open. Grabbing a bottle, she pressed the cold plastic against her forehead.

Sylvain had been gone six hours but it felt like days.

At least his father had come through surgery, although he hadn't yet woken. She couldn't imagine what Sylvain was going through. Everything there must be so chaotic and heartbreaking.

She couldn't get the look he'd given her in his room out of her mind. He'd seemed … destroyed.

Against her will, her gaze was drawn across the room to where Carter stood talking to Raj. His cheeks were red from exertion and his dark hair had swung forward to his eyes, sticking to the damp skin of his forehead.

Allie kept hearing Sylvain's words in her mind. *'Even though I know…'*

Guilt swirled inside her. What did he know? That she'd had doubts?

That she was tempted?

Her stomach twisted. If she'd made things worse for him right now with her indecision and stupidity she'd never forgive herself.

'Can I have one of those?' Nicole's French-accented voice startled her.

Allie swung around to face her. 'What?'

Her voice came out sharper than she'd intended and Nicole shot her a puzzled look.

'The water,' she said. 'Could I have one, please?'

Looking down at her feet, Allie realised she was blocking access to the cooler.

'Sorry,' she said, handing a bottle to Nicole. 'I was thinking.'

The French girl gave her a wan smile. 'It's fine – we've all got a lot on our minds.'

Hoping not to be asked what she'd been thinking about, Allie let her gaze skitter around the room, avoiding Carter. Only then did she notice someone was missing.

'Where's Rachel?' she asked with a frown.

'She's with Dom. Raj has given her a pass on physical training.'

'Oh thank God,' Allie said, relieved. 'At last.'

Nicole looked at her curiously. 'Raj says Carter's going with you to the parley now. Is that going to be OK? He doesn't have much time to prepare.'

Against Allie's will, her gaze darted back to where Carter stood not looking at her. 'We start working together tonight. Carter learns fast.'

'I just hope—' Nicole started to speak but then Raj's voice rang out in the humid air, cutting her off.

'All right, everyone. On your feet.'

Giving Nicole an apologetic wave, Allie hurried back to Zoe, tossing her a bottle of water. Zoe snatched it out of the air with ease.

'Allie, Zoe.' Raj motioned for them to come over. Carter stood next to him.

When the girls reached them, Raj spoke quietly. 'Allie, you and Carter are partnered from now on.' Zoe's brow lowered ominously but before she could speak, he added, 'Zoe can train with Nicole.'

'Awesome.' Instantly placated, Zoe ran over to where the French girl waited.

Without discussion, Allie and Carter took their places next to each other. Allie didn't know what to say. She was glad to be training with him. And she felt guilty for being glad.

She thought it best to say nothing at all.

As Raj called for order, the room hushed. All around them the students paired up, preparing to fight.

Carter squared off against her, taking the first position, arms loose at his sides, feet shoulder-width apart.

He held her gaze. 'You ready for this?'

Half turning her body in anticipation of the first blow, she met his look with grim determination. 'I have to be.'

After training that night, Allie hurried up the stairs to the top floor of the darkened classroom wing to meet with Raj and Carter. Her hair, still wet from the shower, dampened the back of her white shirt, which she wore loose over her short skirt.

It was nearly midnight. Her muscles ached a little from the workout and she walked stiffly, trying to loosen the kinks.

Her footsteps sounded hollow in the stillness. Ahead, the staircase was lost in shadows, illuminated only on the landing where the moon cast a pale blue glow through a tall window. When she reached the window she stopped to look out over the grounds – the moon was almost full and she could see all the way to the treeline. Nothing moved out there. The night was still.

The sudden sound of footsteps startled her and she spun round, fists raised.

'Hey.' Carter stepped into the moonlight two steps below her. 'Don't shoot. It's only me.'

'Oh.' Allie looked at her fists as if she didn't know how they'd ended up in front of her. 'Sorry. Instinct.'

He climbed the last two steps.

'Good instincts,' he said. 'Quick instincts. They'll save your life.'

In the moonlight his dark eyes were impossible to read. Allie hated that she was glad to see him. But she was.

'Look … we didn't get a chance to talk earlier. I just …' He faltered. 'Are you really cool with this?' He gestured at the two of them. 'If you want someone else with you on Friday don't be afraid to say so. I won't be hurt. This is important.'

His words left her so aghast, she didn't stop to think. She just told him the truth.

'I don't want anyone else, Carter,' she said. 'I want you. Please don't back out.' She paused, her lower lip trembling. 'I need you.'

If her heartfelt plea surprised him, he didn't show it. His serious eyes held hers for a long moment. Then, as if they were agreeing about the weather or some essay they needed to write for class, he nodded.

'Good. That's all I needed to know.' His voice was steady and strong. 'Let's do this.'

After the dark quiet of the stairwell, the little classroom at the top was a hive of activity and light. Dom stood at a bank of laptop computers, typing furiously. She wasn't alone.

'Rachel?' Allie couldn't keep the surprise out of her voice.

Glancing up from her computer screen, Rachel gave a wave that seemed almost jaunty. 'Helping!'

She was purposeful and in her element, and Allie felt a rush of gratitude to Dom for choosing her, making her part of the team.

Across the room, Raj and Isabelle were deep in conversation in front of a table spread with maps and papers.

Noticing them, Isabelle straightened. 'Let's get started,' she said. 'Are you ready, Dom?'

From behind a laptop Dom gave a terse nod. 'Ready when you are.'

'Carter.' Leaving Isabelle, Raj walked over to them. 'We're going to run through the plan from start to finish. It's a lot to take in but I have no doubt you can do this.' Including Allie in his gaze he said, 'Seeing the way the two of you worked together tonight reassured me. But we only have twenty-four hours to prepare. We're going to need everything you've got. Both of you.' Without waiting for their response, he turned to Dom. 'Map one.'

Behind Dom and Rachel a map of Hampstead Heath appeared, projected on to the wall in vivid green detail. As Raj explained the route Allie had already memorised with Sylvain, she stared at the cartographer's drawing. It had been coloured emerald green to illustrate its vibrancy but that only made it seem cartoonish.

She tried to remember what she knew of Hampstead but all she could recall was steep hills, big, expensive houses and tourists.

Not for the first time, a litany of all the things that could go wrong went through her mind. The places Nathaniel and Gabe could hide. The weapons they might carry.

Apprehension tightened its noose around her throat.

Taking slow breaths, she made herself focus on what Raj was saying as he pointed to the road where they'd be dropped and traced out their path into the park with steady hands, talking in a low, calm voice that proclaimed his faith in them. His belief they could get through this.

And they would get through this, she told herself.

They had to.

Thirty Three

The next morning, Allie fought to stay awake in class. They'd worked on plans for the parley until three in the morning. Carter absorbed information quickly but Raj insisted he have it all down perfectly, so they'd gone through it all over and over again.

She couldn't even remember climbing into bed.

By the time Zelazny walked into the history classroom, his arms filled with stacks of books, she was having trouble keeping her eyes open. Even through a haze of exhaustion, though, his demeanour caught her attention. He didn't shout at them to be quiet in his usual way or fix them with a glare. He'd been subdued ever since Jerry's exposure as Nathaniel's man. As if he'd believed they'd all failed.

Allie had never expected to miss his bluster, but she did.

'All this term,' the history teacher said, as the students fell silent, 'we've been talking about the years of the British Empire. But today is an unusual day.' Setting the books down on his desk, he studied the students sombrely. 'There's no point in pretending. You all know about the parley with Nathaniel.'

Allie's breath caught. Outside of Night School, none of the instructors were talking openly about it. She glanced over to where Carter sat next to her, but his gaze was fixed on Zelazny; a small frown line creased his forehead.

The other students seemed similarly surprised. Two Night School students murmured disapprovingly in the back. The non-Night School students looked fascinated. Hopeful they'd learn more.

At the front of the room, the history teacher was still talking. 'Most of your teachers will act as if nothing is happening. They want to distract you. Keep you calm. I intend to do something different.' He began walking around the room, placing a book with a black cover on each desk. When he reached Allie he paused, holding her gaze. 'I want to talk to you about surviving.'

The room filled with the whisper of pages against desks as the students hurriedly picked up the books to see what they were.

The volume was slim and light in Allie's hand, almost insubstantial. The elaborate gold letters on the front, almost gaudy against the black, read: *Sun Tzu: The Art of War*.

Zelazny had returned to the front of the class now, where he held up his own copy.

'Sun Tzu was a general in China in the sixth century,' the teacher explained. 'His theories are still taught in military schools, studied by generals, used in combat. I think they could be useful to us, too.' He leaned back against his desk. 'Carter, read from page ten, please.'

The other two Night School students at the back of the room exchanged a glance as, still frowning, Carter flipped the pages in his book. For a second he scanned the words silently.

Then he began to read aloud.

'*Which of the two sovereigns is imbued with moral law? Which of the two generals has the most ability? With whom lie the advantages derived from Heaven and Earth? On which side is discipline most rigorously enforced? Which army is stronger? On which side are officers and men more highly trained? In which army is there greater consistence in reward and punishment?*

'By means of these seven considerations I can forecast victory or defeat.'

To Allie the words felt horribly portentous. What was Zelazny trying to tell them? That he thought they would lose?

When Carter finished reading, Zelazny straightened slowly and looked out at the class.

'The two sides who will meet at the parley tomorrow are, I believe, equal in strength and in training. Because we are the same people. We attended the same schools. Followed the same course in life. Therefore, we are equally matched with our enemy.'

A rustle of disapproving murmurs swept the room. No one in that room wanted to believe they were anything like Nathaniel.

But, despite herself, Allie could see the truth in his words. This was a civil war.

Zelazny ignored the discomfort his words were causing. 'I think Sun Tzu could not say from looking at us, which would win.'

His honesty in these circumstances was breathtaking. None of the other adults were even countenancing the possibility that they wouldn't succeed. But Allie had always known failure was possible. She could see the effort it took for Isabelle to look positive. The doubts Raj failed to hide.

But for him to say this so openly was chilling.

As if he knew what she was thinking, Zelazny looked right at her. 'That is where strategy comes in. Allie, read from page twenty-one.'

Flipping through the pages, Allie found the one he'd asked for. It held only a few lines.

'All warfare is based on deception.

'Offer bait to entice the enemy. Then feign disorder and crush him.

'If he is secure at all points, be prepared for him. If his strength is superior, evade him.

'Attack where he is unprepared. Appear where you are not expected.'

The room had gone quiet again but the words rang in Allie's head.

All warfare is based on deception.

She thought of Christopher standing in her room.

Nathaniel holding a knife to Rachel's throat.

Lucinda's promises and Nathaniel's threats.

Her chest felt tight. *Who's the liar?*

'This is the best advice anyone can give you.' Zelazny's sharp voice broke through the fog of her thoughts. By now he had everyone's full attention. Every student in the room was hanging on his every word. 'When you are faced with a clever enemy, one well matched to your strengths and weaknesses, you must be smarter than him. You must adapt and innovate if you want to stay alive. Because, however technically perfect your plan might be, there's one thing I can promise you.' He thumped his desk hard with his finger. 'It will go wrong. Nothing will be as you expect. Night is always darker when you step into it than it seems when you're in a lighted room.'

As he looked out at the class, his stare was intense.

'For the rest of the lesson I want you to read this book. Commit it to memory. As if, tomorrow, I was going to make you recite it to me.' He lowered his gaze to Allie's. 'It could save your life.'

The rest of Allie's classes that day passed in a haze. Zelazny was right – the other teachers were just trying to distract them. Keep them calm.

Her mind wouldn't let go of his lesson. Whenever no one was looking, she flipped through the book he'd given them. Words and phrases floated up at her. Chilling her.

If his strength is superior, evade him.

Run away. Hide.

Zelazny was always confident. If he was worried … were they doing the right thing?

But they had no choice. Always, it came back to that.

They had to go to the parley, they had no choice.

They were trapped. *She* was trapped.

There was no break between classes and Night School training. As soon as her last lesson ended, she was back down in the training room, practising evasion techniques with Carter, Nicole and Zoe. Rachel was off working with Dom.

Just before dinnertime, Raj walked over to where Carter and Allie were trying a complex manoeuvre of whirling kicks and elbow punches.

He spoke so quietly only they could hear. 'Isabelle would like to see you both in her office.'

'Should we change first?' Allie asked, running a hand across her forehead. They were both sweating, and dressed in their black Night School exercise gear.

Raj shook his head. 'She'd like you to hurry.'

Allie's heart stuttered. It sounded bad.

When they reached Isabelle's office minutes later, her door was closed but they could hear her talking to someone inside.

Carter and Allie exchanged a look before he knocked lightly on the carved wood.

Isabelle's response was immediate. 'Come in.'

Carter turned the handle – the door swung open silently.

Inside the familiar office, Isabelle sat at her desk – the room was otherwise empty. Her desk was topped with neat stacks of papers and an open laptop.

'You wanted to see us?' Allie said.

Isabelle motioned for them to sit in the leather chairs arranged so they faced her imposing mahogany desk.

As Allie took a seat, she studied Isabelle's face for clues. She didn't appear panicked or distraught, but there was a new sadness in her eyes, and the set of her mouth.

Only when they were settled did the headmistress speak again. 'Lucinda, are you still there?'

'I am.' Her grandmother's voice emerged from the computer on the headmistress's desk, clear and strong. Relentless.

Allie's heart jumped. So it was *that* kind of meeting.

Carter swung round to look at her in surprise. Allie held up her hands in a 'sometimes this just happens' gesture.

'We're all here, as you asked.' Isabelle leaned back in her chair. 'Allie and Carter are both present.'

'No one else?' Lucinda said.

Isabelle gave her head a slight shake. 'No one.'

'Good,' Lucinda said.

Fleetingly, Allie wondered what it must be like for her. She stood to lose the most. Her position in the Orion Group and all the power that came with that were on the line. Already she'd lost her place at government meetings; her respected position as a senior advisor.

What would she do if she lost all the rest?

'I asked Isabelle to bring you both here so we could go over The Rules for tomorrow night,' Lucinda said.

The Rules? Allie thought, instantly suspicious. *What the hell is she talking about?*

'Allie, when I offered to let you go to the parley, it was on the condition that you follow the plan I set for you. I presume you recall that conversation?'

Put on the spot, Allie hesitated. She had only vague memories of Lucinda's voice projected through Isabelle's tinny phone, her own anger about Christopher. She wasn't really certain what she'd agreed to that night, but she would have said yes to almost anything if it meant she got to go to the parley and take on Nathaniel herself.

'Yes ... I think so,' she said after a moment.

'Excellent.' Lucinda's tone was crisp. 'Then I'll expect you to hold to your agreement. Carter West.'

Carter straightened. 'Yes ... ma'am ...?' His gaze shifted uncertainly from Isabelle to the blank, dark plastic of the computer.

'I must have the same commitment from you that I've received from my granddaughter. I require you to swear that you will do precisely as you are told today. That you will follow The

Rules Isabelle and I set out for you, above and beyond anything you are told by anyone else. Up to, and including, Raj Patel and his guards.'

Allie stared at the computer in shock. *Is* that *what I agreed to that night?*

She could see her own doubts reflected on Carter's face. What Lucinda was asking for wasn't small. It was like a gigantic 'just trust me' to both of them.

But this was her party.

After a short, tell-tale pause, Carter gave a helpless shrug. 'Fine ... I mean – yes. I agree to your Rules.'

They both looked at Isabelle as if she could give them some explanation but her expression was inscrutable. Clearly, Lucinda was in charge here.

'Then we are ready to proceed,' Lucinda said. 'The Rules are as follows. I will meet you on Parliament Hill in the park at midnight. I will have Jerry Cole with me. You are not to interact with him even if he provokes you. '

Allie tensed.

Lucinda was going to be in charge of Jerry?

She thought of the way the muscles in his arms bulged that night in the basement cell when he yanked at the chains holding him. She'd believed for a moment he might rip them from the wall. He was strong. Far too strong for a woman of Lucinda's age to control him. What was she thinking?

Her grandmother continued: 'Once we are all there, I will do the talking. Nathaniel will speak to you, I have no doubt. If he addresses you directly, I will indicate whether or not you should reply. The indication will be a nod. One nod means yes. Anything other than that means you must let me handle it. This is not up for discussion.'

She added the last line sternly, as if she expected them to argue, but neither of them really wanted to be Nathaniel's go-to guy, so they both sat in silence.

Taking their lack of response for compliance, Lucinda kept talking. 'You will be given the name and address of a safe house in London. You are both to memorise it. If anything happens and we are separated, you are forbidden to search for me, or for Raj or his guards. Do not trust anyone who claims to represent us. Do not attempt to find anyone from Cimmeria. Go directly to the safe house and wait. As soon as possible, someone will come for you. Is that understood?'

Allie's chest felt hollow. This was a plan for failure.

She and Carter exchanged a long look. She could see in his eyes that he knew it, too.

'Yes,' Allie said after a moment, her voice barely above a whisper. 'I agree.'

'And I agree,' Carter said.

Lucinda accepted this without comment. 'The last Rule is this. I expect something to happen. I expect violence. Any one of us could be hurt. We have done all we can to prevent such an outcome but pure practicality and bitter experience indicate no amount of preparation will prevent Nathaniel from violating all the parley rules and attempting something … unnecessary. If anything happens to me or to Carter, Allie, you must promise to run. You must leave that person, whichever one of us it is, and you must get out of that park and to the safe house. You must not hesitate. I will need your agreement.'

Cold with horror, Allie stared at the laptop. A sudden brutal memory jabbed into her thoughts like an ice-pick. Jo lying in a pool of blood on an icy road. All alone.

Pressing her lips together tightly she shook her head in mute disagreement but, before she could speak, Carter reached across the space dividing them. Prising her fingers loose from the chair arm she'd been unconsciously gripping, he took her hand in his.

Still shaking her head she looked up at him, already knowing what he would say.

'Say yes,' he said.

'No, Carter.' Her eyes pleaded with him to understand. 'I can't.'

'Allie, Lucinda's right. Whatever happens, you have to run. I'll be fine. I promise. Say yes.' His gaze was steady and his hand was warm on hers.

But how could she do it? She couldn't just leave him or Lucinda hurt. If they needed her …

'Allie.' Her grandmother's haughty voice shattered her thoughts. 'I need your commitment or the deal is off. You stay at the school and I meet Nathaniel alone. You know what that will mean for the school and your friends. You know what Nathaniel is capable of.'

On the other side of the desk, Isabelle made a small sound of disapproval but Allie didn't look at her. Her eyes were on Carter.

His gaze never wavered. 'Say yes.'

Her thoughts in turmoil, Allie tore her gaze away and let her head fall back against the cool leather of the chair. She couldn't look at him and do this.

'Yes,' she whispered. A tear escaped from beneath her lashes. 'Fine. Yes. I'll do it.'

'Good.' Lucinda's voice held no emotion.

At that moment, Allie loathed her grandmother almost as much as Nathaniel. That she could make her agree to leave Carter alone to bleed to death like Jo. And for what? For power she didn't believe in? For money she didn't want?

No. To stop Nathaniel from hurting other people.

Even then. Even for that. She knew she'd never do it. Not really.

Lucinda wasn't finished yet. Her voice emerged from the computer, cool and distant. 'Carter?'

Still holding Allie's hand, he looked at the computer as if he'd expected this. 'Yes. I'm here.'

'I will also need an agreement from you. Your Rule is slightly different from Allie's. I am told you are strong, reliable and determined, and that you care for her very much. So your Rule is this. If anything happens to me or to Allie, you are to get her out of the park. Get her away from Nathaniel at all costs and to the safe house. Do not leave her at any point for any reason. If I am injured, do not let her try to help me. Do I have your agreement?'

Allie's fingers tightened around Carter's.

He turned to meet her gaze. His eyes were dark and endless, warm and trustworthy. As familiar and loving as family. As necessary as oxygen.

Jump.

'Yes,' he said.

'Good.' Lucinda's brisk, authoritative tone betrayed no emotion. 'Then we are agreed. Now, let's go over the plans again …'

Thirty Four

The gleaming black Land Rovers arrived just before seven the next evening. They sat outside the front door like a glamorous funeral procession.

Allie noticed them as soon as she walked down from her room.

Raj had told the students to dress like 'normal' kids their age would on a Friday night, so for the first time in weeks she wore street clothes – they felt strange on her body. The jeans were stiff and itchy. Over them she wore a long, black T-shirt. Her red Doc Marten boots were laced up to the knee. To complete the picture of youthful normality, she'd encircled her eyes in heavy eyeliner and mascara. Her hair hung loose over her shoulders.

She was the first to arrive – the entrance hall was empty. The front door stood open, letting in the muggy, summer evening air. Bouncing on her heels, she waited impatiently. Nervousness gnawed at her insides as if it was trying to get out of her. She hoped the makeup hid her fear.

When Nicole and Zoe arrived a few minutes later she stared at them in amazement. She'd never seen either of them in street clothes. Nicole looked elegant with her long hair pulled back in glossy braids. She wore a snug-fitting, strappy top with black trousers and tough-looking ankle boots. She could have been any cool teenage girl on a night out with friends.

Zoe wore jeans and a striped top with trainers. The simple outfit made her look even younger than she really was.

'You look weird,' she announced, studying Allie with a disapproving wrinkle of her nose.

'So do you,' Allie fired back.

'It's a disguise,' Zoe explained.

'Are the cars here?' Carter's voice came from the corridor seconds before he and Lucas emerged into the entrance hall together, looking slightly panicked.

'Yeah but… They're just sitting there,' Allie said.

Lucas, who was staying behind, was the only one of them still in a school uniform.

'I came to see you off,' he said, answering the question no one had asked.

Zoe rolled her eyes but Allie was genuinely touched.

'Thanks,' she said. 'I wish you were coming with us.'

He gave an amiable shrug. 'Someone's got to stay and defend the homeland.'

Allie glanced over to where Carter stood in the doorway, looking out at the silent row of cars. In dark jeans and a black pullover, he looked so much like a normal person it was disturbing.

'Nice disguise,' Zoe commented. Carter gave her a puzzled look.

Lucas punched Zoe lightly in the arm. 'Whatever, Shortie.'

Zoe kicked his fist away with an effortless swing of her foot and Lucas promptly adopted a mock-fighting posture. Before it could go any further, though, Carter held up his hands.

'Let's not.' He said it with such unconscious authority that they both obeyed.

'Sorry.' Lucas said sheepishly. 'Nerves.'

'I hear you.' There was no rancour in Carter's voice. He looked at his watch. 'Where the hell is everyone? It's time.'

'Here.' Raj's voice echoed off the stone walls and they all spun round.

He walked towards them from the grand hallway, backlit by a crystal chandelier and followed by phalanx of guards. Isabelle, Zelazny and Eloise were among them.

Dom and Rachel appeared at the back, weighed down with equipment.

Allie's heart sank.

She ran to Rachel's side. 'What are you doing here? You're not coming ... I mean ...' Realising how that sounded she stumbled over her words. 'Are you?'

But it was Dom who replied. 'Don't worry. We won't be in the park. We'll be blocks away monitoring you in the best-protected car you've ever seen. Rachel will be safe. Now.' Dropping her bags on a marble-topped table she motioned for Allie to come to her. 'Let's get you all wired up.'

As Dom and Rachel began opening bags and arranging supplies, Allie's heart beat out a rapid cadence and she took gulps of air. She needed to calm down.

Rachel will be fine, she told herself. Dom knows what she's doing.

She forced herself to let it go. To trust Dom.

Seemingly unaware of her inner turmoil, the tech pulled a long, slim black box out of one of the bags and opened it carefully. Inside, Allie saw neat rows of what looked like dark pins.

'What are those?'

'This' – Dom held one up between her thumb and forefinger; it was no bigger than a freckle – 'is a tracker. Put your foot here.' She patted her bent knee. After a brief hesitation, Allie did as she was told.

'Nice Docs.' Dom tapped Allie's heavy red boot. Carefully, she inserted the end of the device into one of the laceholes in Allie's right boot. Amid the tangle of black laces it was invisible.

'Done.' Dom released her foot. 'Now, if you take a wrong turn or fall into a pond, we'll be able to find you. But … you know. Don't do that.' She turned to Carter, who stood just behind Allie's shoulder, watching. 'Your turn.'

'No comms system this time?' Allie said as Dom placed the tracker in Carter's boot.

Dom didn't look up. 'Too hackable. I'm not giving Nathaniel a toy to play with.'

When they were all kitted out, the guards began climbing into the Land Rovers. The air filled with the low growl of powerful engines.

The students huddled together by the door. They wouldn't see each other again until this thing was over, one way or another.

Allie was so nervous she couldn't stand still; she shifted from one foot to another. What if this went badly? What if they never came back? What if this was the last day?

She looked around, at the grand stone building, with its glorious stained-glass window, the grounds sprawling green as far as she could see into the darkness of the woods. This was her home. These people were her family.

There had to be another day. They had to come back.

'Well, good luck, you lot.' Lucas' earlier jovial mood had evaporated. He looked around the group sombrely. 'Kick some Nathaniel arse. Watch your backs.'

The boys shook hands and pounded each other's shoulders. Lucas paused to whisper something to Rachel. When he walked back into the school building, Allie saw her eyes were bright with unshed tears.

Rachel cleared her throat. 'Look ... you all have to stay safe, OK?' She looked around the group, her eyes pleading. 'Just say yes.'

'Yes.' Nicole pulled her into a quick, fierce hug. Allie followed suit.

'Be careful,' Rachel whispered before letting her go. And Allie fought a sudden urge to cry.

'You, too,' she said.

'Rachel.' Dom strode past. 'Let's go.'

Her tone was business-like but, as she passed, the American caught Allie's eye and gave her a nod that seemed to say without any words, '*You can do this.*'

Coming from Dom – so cool and capable – it meant a great deal.

I can do this.

After a final wave, Rachel followed her, and the two disappeared into one of the Rovers. Now only Allie, Carter, Zoe and Nicole stood on the steps.

For a long moment, no one spoke.

Then, lowering his head, Carter caught Allie's gaze. 'We should go.'

'I know ...' But she was reluctant to leave. She turned to Zoe and Nicole.

'Look. Be careful, OK? Don't do anything crazy. I'm so glad you're going to be there ….'

Nicole's answering smile was filled with understanding and affection, but Zoe, who had endured the earlier goodbyes with barely contained irritation, stared at her as if she'd gone mad.

'Of course we'll be there. Where else would we be?'

Allie's lips twitched. She tugged at Zoe's ponytail. 'Just … go, OK? I'll see you when this is over.'

At that, Zoe zipped away towards their assigned car, not hiding her relief at escaping the emotional scene.

Nicole hugged Allie quickly. 'I'll keep an eye on her,' she promised. 'She's only scouting. She'll be safe.'

'I know.' Allie forced a smile. 'Take care of yourself, too.'

'And you.'

After giving Carter a hug, Nicole ran after Zoe. Then Allie and Carter were alone on the wide front steps.

It was time.

With a shuddering sigh, Allie raised her gaze to his. 'Ready?' 'I guess so,' Carter said, but still they didn't move.

His gaze swept across her face. 'Look at us,' he said, a wry smile making his dark eyes twinkle. 'The dynamic duo. Together again.'

Her responding smile was tremulous but her voice was steady. 'Allie and Carter save the world.'

There was so much she wanted to tell him. So much to decide. But the weight of the moment was too heavy. There was too much at stake right now.

This wasn't the time for anything except fighting.

She raised her eyes to his. 'Let's go.'

The drive to London passed in tense silence.

Allie and Carter sat in the back seat, looking out of their respective windows. Two guards sat in the front. Raj's voice crackled occasionally from a radio. He was in the lead car, about a mile ahead.

The cars were to take different routes. Dom and Rachel were following their progress through the trackers, making sure none of the vehicles got clustered together and that everyone followed their assigned course.

As the evening light faded, they passed mostly farmland. Pastures were dotted with pale sheep, recently sheared and relishing their new nudity. In the distance, church steeples thrust up at the darkening sky like stone daggers. Sometimes, for fleeting moments, grand, Victorian mansions, not unlike Cimmeria, could be seen peeking out through faraway trees.

The last of the light had disappeared from the sky by the time they entered the bustling fringe of London, where torturously twisted streets made the metropolis a gigantic vehicular labyrinth. But the driver seemed confident as he took first one slow road then another.

Allie, who had grown up in the city, traced their route through the tube and train stations they passed. Richmond, Chiswick, Acton, Shepherd's Bush ... Seeing the names again was like running unexpectedly into old friends.

Next to her, Carter stared out of the window in a kind of fascinated wonder. Allie was reminded that he'd grown up in the country.

'Have you ever been to London before?' she asked, and he glanced over at her.

'A long time ago, to go to museums,' he said. 'I'd forgotten how crowded it is.'

The car stopped at a red light and a stream of people hurried across the road, women in business suits and sensible low heels, or in tiny skirts and teetering on stilettos. Men with headphones on, never looking up.

When she'd lived in London, Allie had never really noticed how many of them there were. This was just ... home. Her life.

Now she saw it differently. The people packed on pavements, in cars and in the double-decker buses that swayed past. The tall buildings filled with office workers even at this late hour. The teeming pubs beginning to empty. The throngs outside kebab stands and fast-food joints, and lingering in the shadows around bus stops and tube stations. The complaint of horns and blinding bright lights.

They were a long way from Cimmeria Academy's green fields and quiet forests now.

A siren shrieked very close by and they both jumped. Twisting around in her seat, Allie looked through the rear window. She inhaled sharply. Carter turned to see.

A police car pulled up behind them, its warning lights flashing in an angry swirl. The driver motioned sternly for them to pull over.

Adrenaline flooded into Allie's system. Her heart thudded in her ears.

Come on, Allie. Think.

What should they do? They didn't have a plan for if they got stopped on the way into town. That was stupid of them.

Nathaniel had a firm grip on the police right now. Could he have *this* much control?

It didn't seem possible.

Anything was possible.

In the front seat, the driver and the guard in the passenger seat were arguing but the screech of the siren was too loud and close for Allie to make out what they were saying.

Glancing to her right, she saw Carter studying the guards with calm alertness, as if looking for clues about how bad the situation might be. One of his hands had come to rest casually on the door handle.

Allie followed his example. She placed her fingers on the cool metal of the door handle. Her other hand lay on the catch of her seat belt.

But as the moments went by it was clear the guards were more irritated than nervous. After a moment, the road ahead cleared and the driver pulled the Land Rover up on to the kerb.

As the police car sped by it was so close Allie could see the officers inside clearly. They were both looking straight ahead, utterly uninterested in the Land Rover they were passing.

The wail of the siren bent and twisted before fading away in the distance.

Gradually Allie's heart rate returned to normal.

Carter exhaled audibly. 'Bloody hell.'

After a second, traffic began to move again. They bumped down off the kerb and turned to the north.

'This is it,' the driver said as he pulled the Land Rover to the side of the road and cut the engine.

Turning her head, Allie could see the street sign attached to the decorative wrought-iron fencing that edged the pavement.

Tanza Road was a short street on a hill that tilted gently up, as if something heavy sat on one end of it. Elegant terraced houses made of beautifully carved Victorian stone and brick lined the lane on both sides.

Now that they were here, she felt strangely calm. Focused. As they waited, she was acutely aware of everything around her. The engine ticking as it cooled. The guards talking into their phones. Carter's observant stillness next to her.

Her heartbeat was steady and even.

A sudden thunk echoed in the quiet as the doors all unlocked through some central system.

The guard in the passenger seat turned to face them. 'Now.'

Allie turned to Carter. She could see the readiness in his face. The determination. It reflected the way she felt.

We can do this.

She took a steadying breath. Then she popped open the seatbelt with a decisive click and metallic rattle. Carter did the same.

Holding her gaze, he reached for the door handle. She grabbed hers. His eyes asked if she was ready and she nodded her reply.

Their doors opened at the same time.

Allie jumped down out of the tall SUV on to the dark street. She closed the door without looking back.

It was time to be brave.

Thirty Five

On the street, the night was alive with sounds. The noise of television programmes floated softly through windows left open to the warm summer breeze. Voices could be heard in the distance – talking, laughing. From farther away came the faint song of sirens, the growl of a plane.

A normal big city on a normal Friday night. Nothing to see here.

Some of Allie's tension evaporated as soon as they started walking. Despite everything, it felt strangely good to be back in a city. In the countryside she was always the outsider. London was her territory.

The elegant buildings around them spoke of money and power. Light poured from tall windows, golden and silky, as if everything inside was gilded.

Walking side by side, like two Hampstead kids out for a stroll, Carter and Allie made their way to the top of the street. Their eyes constantly scanned the right side of the lane, peering between houses.

Allie saw it first.

'There.' She nudged Carter, tilting her head at the short, paved path running between two houses. It was unmarked, almost hidden.

They turned into it.

Instantly, they were plunged into darkness. The pavement beneath their feet soon ran out and the path turned to dirt.

They were in the Heath.

Aware that they were still visible through the windows of the houses behind them, they kept their pace languid. But they were both assessing the terrain around them.

To the left, Allie could see a scattering of trees and then thicker forests beyond. That was where they were headed.

Once the light of the houses faded, they broke into a jog. The ground was uneven, the grass high, but they were both used to that.

The route they'd chosen required them to circle the base of Parliament Hill – its widest point – and then climb to the top.

As Raj had warned them, what seemed simple on a map was more complicated at night. Once they were in the trees, it was hard to keep a sense of direction. At least in the city there was more ambient light. Once their eyes adjusted they could see where they were going without the use of flashlights.

'I'm sure I've seen this tree before,' Allie whispered, glaring at a memorable tilting pine.

'Trees all look like trees,' Carter pointed out, pulling a GPS reader from his pocket. 'We should be going north-west.' He turned his body and the device slowly until he had a reading that satisfied him. He glanced back at Allie. 'That way.'

Once they'd turned, though, the brush grew thicker. Soon they were fighting their way through thorny brambles and stinging nettles that left Allie with bleeding cuts on both arms.

'Bloody evil pissing things.' Allie swore as a thorny bramble branch slashed the skin of her right hand.

'I think it thins out ahead.' Carter pointed to a clearing they could just make out through the trees.

Clutching her wounded hand, she hurried after him. They jumped over a fallen log that blocked the path, landing on the edge of a slow-moving stream. They forded the water as quietly as they could, scrambling up the bank on the far side with their boots squelching unpleasantly in the mud.

They were just entering the clearing when Allie saw it. A flicker of movement that shouldn't be there.

At first she thought it was just a shadow. Then it moved again. And it did so with far too much intent and purpose.

Someone was there.

Silently, she grabbed Carter's arm, pulling him back into the protection of the trees. His eyes met hers, questioningly. Raising her hand, she pointed into the glade.

At first his eyes searched the area aimlessly, seeing nothing. Then his gaze sharpened.

The shadow seemed to glide across the glade – its movements soundless. Lethal.

One of ours? Allie wondered. *Or theirs?*

There was no way to know. In the dark, both sides looked the same.

They crouched down low, watching the shadow.

If his strength is superior, evade him.

Up here, the noises of the city faded away. Allie could hear only her own heartbeat and Carter's even breathing. There was almost no breeze and the trees stood still, as if they were waiting, too.

When the shadow finally disappeared, they waited for several long minutes to be certain it was gone. Then Carter caught her arm and gestured ahead. She nodded.

Rising in unison they slipped through the glade, as silently as the shadow before them.

By unspoken agreement they cut across the path it had taken and headed to the base of the hill on a diagonal trajectory. Their training told them this was the best direction to avoid running into the shadow again.

One thing was clear: this was real. These woods were full of people.

After ten minutes of cautious progress the trees thinned and they found themselves heading up a steep slope towards open ground. Raj had warned them about this section – there was no way to hide here.

His solution to this problem had been simple: move fast.

Crouching low, they burst from the woods, accelerating their pace until they were pounding up the hill. Although they kept the requisite distance apart, Allie was always conscious of where Carter was, how quickly he was moving.

In fact, she was so focused on him that it took her a moment to realise they'd crested the hill. She skidded to a stop as the view took her breath away: all of London sprawled out below them. Like a galaxy of low stars, stretching to infinity.

Overlooking it, all alone, was one woman.

Her hands were laced behind her back as she gazed out over the city. A neat shock of platinum-white hair caught the glimmer of the city lights and shimmered. She stood very upright.

It struck Allie that she would have recognised her grandmother anywhere by her posture alone.

She wore expensive trousers and an expensive trench coat. Any passer-by would have taken her for a Hampstead doyenne out for a late-night stroll.

Allie ran to her side. Carter dropped back, staying a respectful distance away.

'Lucinda ... Grandmother ...'

At the sound of her voice, Lucinda turned serenely.

'Oh good. You're here. I must say I very much admire your promptness, Allie. I'm afraid I was rather early. Carter.' Including him in her enigmatic gaze, she held out one self-assured hand.

After a brief hesitation he walked up, shaking her hand with careful deference.

'I've heard a lot about you,' Lucinda said. 'In many ways, you're one of the reasons we're here today. You are what we're fighting for.' Her eyes swept across him with a sceptical look. 'I do hope you're worth all of this.'

Before Carter could ask what she was talking about, Allie stepped forward. 'Where's Jerry? I thought he was with you.'

'He's here.' Lucinda's tone was dry. 'I can assure you of that.'

It was clear she wasn't going to reveal more. Allie let it go but worry twisted inside her.

Turning a wrist, her grandmother glanced at her watch. 'Your timekeeping may be good, but I wouldn't say much for Nathaniel's ...'

'Oh, Lucinda.' Nathaniel's familiar voice came from behind them. Allie and Carter spun round to see him walking along the hilltop path in their direction. 'Must you be so critical?'

His tone was sardonic. Familiar. He looked utterly comfortable, strolling along the lip of the hill, hands casually in his pockets.

Not for the first time, Allie marvelled at how normal he looked. How unthreatening. He was a little shorter than Carter with a medium build. His thick dark hair was neatly combed. His dark grey suit and crisp white shirt looked expensive but not flashy. He wore no tie and that made him look even more ordinary. But everything about his appearance was far too precise to be normal.

Her heart began to race but she forced herself to stay still. Look calm. Next to her, Carter hadn't moved a muscle.

She scanned the surrounding woods for any sign of Raj or his team but found nothing.

They were alone with him.

'Nathaniel,' Lucinda admonished, 'you should announce yourself. Did I teach you nothing?'

She spoke in tones of mild irritation, as if he'd turned up late for dinner at her club. Allie could see no sign of discomfort in her expression or stance. Instead, she actually looked pleased – her cheeks were flushed and her eyes bright. As if he'd done something amusing.

She likes this, Allie realised. *The game. The high stakes. This is her world.*

'Always the professor.' Nathaniel laughed, and it was not an unpleasant sound. He brushed his left sleeve twice. And then his right sleeve. His movements were identical in both cases.

She was reminded of Katie's belief that he had OCD.

He strolled up to them, as if they were friends about to have a picnic in the park.

Suddenly he turned to look at Allie, his eyes clear and interested. 'Allie. You look well.'

She'd been this close to him only once before, and that time he'd held a knife to her throat.

Her mouth went dry and she couldn't seem to speak.

Carter took a deliberate step to his right, placing his body between them.

Clearly intrigued, Nathaniel cocked his head to one side. 'And who might you be?'

'I don't think I'm required to tell you anything.' Carter didn't attempt to hide the dislike in his tone.

'Oh, I think you are, actually.' Nathaniel's gaze sharpened. He didn't look so nice any more. 'This is my party. I set the rules. Your name.' He snapped his fingers. 'What is it?'

'Nathaniel,' Lucinda interceded. 'May I introduce Carter West? Carter? Nathaniel. Now can we get on with what we came here for?'

But Nathaniel wasn't ready to move on. He studied Carter with new interest. 'So you're the famous Carter West. How intriguing. I've heard so much about you. Somehow I'd expected you to be ... I don't know. Bigger.' He paused, stroking his thumb across his cheek thoughtfully. 'Actually, haven't we met before?'

Carter didn't reply. He just stared at him with icy contempt. He betrayed no fear but Allie saw a muscle twitch in his jaw.

The last time Nathaniel had seen Carter was the night Gabe nearly killed him.

'Now I remember.' Nathaniel straightened as if the memory had just occurred to him. 'It was at the castle. I am sorry about that. Gabe went too far ... again. He is so difficult.'

Still, Carter said nothing. Allie admired his self-control, but she didn't share it.

'The last time I saw you, you stabbed me in the arm,' she said, taking a step towards Nathaniel. 'Remember that?'

'Allie,' Lucinda said reprovingly. 'Remember your promise.'

Unexpectedly, though, Nathaniel looked apologetic. And when he spoke, some of the cockiness left his voice.

'That was truly accidental, Allie,' he said. 'You moved too quickly for me to pull the knife back in time. I had no intention of hurting you. I'm very sorry it happened.'

Allie stared at him in mute surprise. If there was one thing she hadn't expected from him tonight it was humility.

'I was glad to hear you were not badly injured,' he continued. 'That night did not go as expected.'

It looked like he intended to say more but Lucinda made an impatient gesture.

'Enough, Nathaniel. Surely you haven't arranged this elaborate parley solely so you could apologise to my granddaughter for the unforgivable act of gravely injuring her?'

He turned back to her, his smile almost nostalgic. 'Oh, Lucinda. I have missed sparring with you. Despite everything.' Before she could reply, he continued quickly. 'So, we are here to do business. Such unfortunate circumstances. Such bad business indeed.'

Suddenly Allie's nervousness heightened. This didn't feel right. His demeanour was out of character; the location felt odd and vulnerable.

The hairs on the back of her neck stood on end. Something was wrong.

She glanced around at the dark heathland. They should be keeping an eye out. Anyone could be hiding in the dark.

She nudged Carter. When he looked at her, very subtly she tilted her head at the heath that sprawled out behind them in the protective shield of darkness.

Getting the message, he took a careful step back to get a better view of the land behind them. And whoever might be hiding there.

Allie was comforted by the thought that somewhere nearby Nicole and Zoe were hiding. They might be watching them now.

'Have you brought my prize?' Nathaniel said.

He seemed to have forgotten about her for now – all of his attention was focused on Lucinda.

'If by "prize" you mean "Jerry Cole", then yes,' Lucinda said. 'He's nearby. And you can have him as soon as you agree to our conditions.'

Nathaniel rocked back on his heels, warm brown eyes betraying nothing but curiosity. His tone was challenging. Even playful.

'And what might those be? Come on, Lucinda. Surprise me.'

Her grandmother's hesitation was only fractional but Allie recognised it. She was finding Nathaniel's behaviour confusing as well. He was almost … jovial.

'Nathaniel,' Lucinda stepped closer to him, 'let's end this. Let's find a compromise. A way to go forward without destroying the organisation. If you want me to step down from the Orion leadership, I will. We both know I'm finished there anyway. If you want someone else to take over Cimmeria, fine. Isabelle and I will compromise on that, too.'

Allie heard Carter's breath catch, and she stared at Lucinda in disbelief.

None of this had been mentioned before.

This was what we came here for? For Lucinda to give Nathaniel everything?

She wanted to argue, but she'd promised not to interfere. She'd promised to trust her.

So she bit her tongue and waited.

Nathaniel widened his eyes in apparent surprise. 'Why, Lucinda, how magnanimous! I'm swept away by your generosity. Are you saying you would be happy for me to take over the leadership of Orion and to pick the new leader of Night School? Because if you are, then at last we are getting somewhere.'

Lucinda's smile was lupine. 'Now, Nathaniel, you know you can't take over Orion. Whatever you've been promised by your friends on the board, if I step down, you know they won't really give it to you. A promise isn't worth the paper it's printed on. The Rules are inviolable and, technically, you're not even a member at this time. But there are many existing, long-term members whom I'd be happy to support.'

Nathaniel's gaze narrowed. 'Oh, I have no doubt there are people you would support. I know about your pathetic puppets. The handful who still cling to the hope that you'll come back from your defeats and give them all power once again.'

He took a step back, as if he couldn't bear to be so near her.

'How disappointing. I must say, I so hoped you were serious this time. That further unpleasantness could be avoided. Instead I see we're right where we started. Playing games as you try desperately not to lose control of the organisation.' He shook his head sadly. 'This is beneath you, Lucinda. You, more than anyone, should know how to let go.'

Lucinda didn't react to this. Instead she stood tall, unflinching. She looked, Allie thought, quite magnificent, with

London at her feet. Her thin raincoat fluttered like a cape as she shrugged.

'You cannot have Jerry Cole, Nathaniel, if you do not compromise. And I know how much he means to you.'

Nathaniel barked a delighted laugh. 'You figured out who he is, then? Or who he was, at any rate.'

Lucinda inclined her head.

Looking back and forth between them, Allie frowned. Neither she nor Isabelle had said anything about determining Jerry's true identity.

When did that happen?

'Gerald Barlow-Smith.' Lucinda pronounced the name with precision. 'Your manager when you first came to my offices. He was your mentor. He was fired for stealing.'

'He was wrongly terminated,' Nathaniel said. 'By you. Because of a personal disagreement he had with one of your assistants.'

Lucinda looked exasperated. 'Oh please, Nathaniel, he diverted hundreds of thousands of pounds from the corporate account. The evidence was clear.'

'The money was his,' Nathaniel began angrily, but then he seemed to change his mind. 'I don't intend to quibble over this. At any rate, it's beside the point. I don't need you to give Jerry to me. I've got him already.'

Lucinda froze.

It was the first time Allie had seen her caught off guard tonight.

Nathaniel waved a hand towards the trees behind them.

With a slow sense of dread, Allie looked where he pointed. She was conscious of Carter stepping in front of her, his body angled as if to block a blow. That was when she saw Jerry step out of the woods. Gabe stood at his side. Each held a gun pointed right at them.

Thirty Six

Jerry looked rumpled, as if he'd been in a fight. His hair stood on end and one sleeve had been ripped off his shirt, baring a muscular arm. Allie could see a bruise and a bloody scrape on his cheek.

However he'd got loose, it had involved a fight.

Gabe, on the other hand, looked fresh as a daisy. His tawny hair was longer now, hiding the scar on his scalp, and artfully tousled. He looked like Allie remembered him from the days before Nathaniel – a handsome young psycho killer.

She couldn't breathe.

Every person complicit in Jo's death was right in front of her. Nathaniel arranged it. Jerry opened the gate. And Gabe. Who thrust the knife into her.

For so long she'd wanted her revenge. Now, at last, here they all were. And she was terrified.

She wanted to tell Carter to step back. To stand beside her, not in front of her, but her lips had gone numb.

She forced herself to take a breath. And then another. Somehow her lungs kept working. It wasn't easy but, luckily, no one was paying any attention to her.

Even Carter's gaze was fixed on the gunmen.

'Gerald, I could ask how you unshackled yourself but I suppose it's quite evident,' her grandmother said dryly.

Then, to Allie's horrified astonishment, she turned her back on him, as if he didn't matter a bit. As if, even holding a gun – with life and death in his hands – he was insignificant to her.

Jerry stiffened. His grip on the gun tightened and he took a step towards them. Gabe pulled him back.

'Not yet,' he said.

The sound of Gabe's voice made Allie's skin crawl.

She stepped closer to Carter. If this was about to get ugly they needed to be ready.

'This is your plan?' Lucinda said reproachfully. 'I'm so disappointed in you, Nathaniel. You had such promise. More promise than anyone I've ever known.'

'More than Isabelle?' Nathaniel asked, and Allie could hear hurt beneath the acid in his tone. 'It would have been nice if you said it once in a while.'

It was clear this was familiar ground. A path they'd trodden many times, never getting anywhere. All the while Jerry and Gabe stood still, their guns pointed at them, unwavering.

But neither Lucinda nor Nathaniel seemed to care about the weaponry. They were too intent on destroying each other.

Nathaniel was twisting one cufflink, Allie noticed, with quick, irritated movements. Once, twice, three times.

In her head she heard Katie's voice. *'He does this thing when he's really cross. He twists his cufflinks three times ...'*

She wanted to warn Lucinda but she had a feeling she knew already. That she was doing this on purpose.

'Pettiness is so unattractive.' Lucinda shook her head. 'Your jealousy has always been your undoing. If only you could have faith in yourself.'

'Enough,' Nathaniel roared in tones of cold fury. 'I'm done with this. It isn't fun any more. Lucinda, I've been very patient but my patience has run out. Today is the last day. Your allies will not help you because, even as we speak, each of them is receiving a visitor. A very convincing visitor, who is explaining why they cannot support you any longer.' He glanced from her to Allie, feverish with excitement. 'By the time this night is over your leadership of Orion will be through. It's time for a new generation, Lucinda. We've tried it your way. Now we're going to try mine.'

Allie wasn't sure what he was saying – was he talking about blackmail? But Lucinda did seem to know. And she went pale.

'Nathaniel,' she said with quiet sadness, 'what have you done?'

Triumph blazed in his eyes. 'I've finished this. It's over. You have no one to turn to now. Nowhere to go. There's nobody left to run your little political games, to try and stop the inevitable progress of change. You're done, Lucinda.' He stepped back. 'Take a bow.'

Lucinda seemed to sag under the weight of this and, for a moment, Allie thought she might fall. She took a step towards her, but her grandmother instantly held up a hand.

'Not one more step, Allie.' Her tone was commanding. 'You stay where you are.'

'Yes,' Nathaniel said, turning to her. 'Listen to your grandmother. You are here as a witness, not a participant. I want you to see what happens if you cross me. To understand why it has to be *my turn* to run the organisation. Not yours.'

'Leave her alone, Nathaniel,' Lucinda snapped. 'She's no threat to you.'

'Oh, but she is.' Nathaniel studied Allie shrewdly. 'Her very name makes her a threat. She's Lady Lanarkshire, after all.

Your chosen heir. And who am I? I'm nobody. The bastard son of one of your cast-off husbands. Someone you were generous enough to involve in your life at one time but nobody could expect more of you.'

'Nathaniel, *stop*,' Lucinda insisted. 'This is absurd.'

He rounded on her, stepping close until his face was inches from hers. 'Don't ever tell me what to do again.'

Lucinda didn't back down but she lowered her voice. 'I would appreciate it if you would not blame Allie for what's happening. She is just a child.'

'Yes,' he said, stepping back. 'But a very unusual one.'

He rubbed his hands together, as if he was thinking things through. Then he turned towards Allie again, only this time he kept his tone calmer.

'I will need you to promise, Allie, that you will never seek to take control of the Orion Group while I am still alive. I will ultimately insist that you put this in writing but for tonight I'm willing to accept a verbal agreement.'

He took another step and Carter moved between them, one hand out in warning. Nathaniel shot him a cold look, but he stopped.

'People will come to you, soon, I think, and ask you to join the organisation. To take a post on the board. To join their faction against me. I will need you to say no to them. No matter how many times they come back, you must always refuse. Is that clear?' Nathaniel kept his gaze fixed on Allie. 'Agree to that and we all go home tonight. And life goes on.'

The alternative to going home that night was not mentioned but Allie thought it was quite clear what he meant. If she refused, someone would die.

She couldn't believe this was happening. She'd never wanted to be a part of the organisation. What did it even mean? Going to meetings? Telling the prime minister what to do?

She didn't understand what he was afraid of. Who would want her to run anything, anyway?

She wanted to scream at him: *I am seventeen years old.*

But she had a feeling that wouldn't matter. He was obsessed – like her grandmother and everyone else she knew – with the Orion Group. And with power.

'Don't say anything, Allie,' her grandmother warned her. 'Nathaniel, that's quite enough.'

'It's OK,' Allie heard herself say, and couldn't quite believe she was saying it.

Everyone turned to look at her.

'Allie …' Lucinda cautioned but Allie shook her head.

'It's fine.' She looked at Nathaniel. 'I don't want to be a part of any group you're in. I will say no. I won't be in Orion or on the board. If anyone asks me I'll say no. OK?'

Her grandmother looked pained. As if she'd done something very hurtful.

Nathaniel studied her with curious intensity. 'I have your solemn vow?'

'Sure. Yes.' She held up her hands. 'I vow it. I'll sign whatever you want. Just don't hurt anyone else.'

After she spoke there was a long pause, while everyone seemed to absorb what had just happened. Allie got the feeling she was alone in not fully understanding what she'd agreed to.

'At *last*.' Nathaniel gave a triumphant laugh and raised a fist to the sky. Then he turned to Lucinda, his expression gleeful. 'How astonishing that you ended up with such a docile granddaughter. So willing to do what you will not.'

'She doesn't understand what she's doing,' Lucinda said quietly. 'She doesn't know she's been tricked. Deceiving a child is hardly anything to be proud of, Nathaniel.'

He gave an irritated flick of his hand. 'You should have taught her better, then.'

This conversation was unnerving. They were talking about her like she wasn't there. Like she'd made a huge mistake.

Allie risked a quick glance at Carter only to find he wasn't watching the discussion at all. Instead, he was staring across the dark hilltop. When she realised what he was looking at, her heart began to pound.

Behind Gabe and Jerry, two shadows had broken free of the trees and begun moving with lethal steadiness towards them.

Absorbed in Nathaniel and Lucinda's dispute, the two men had noticed nothing as the shadows crept up behind them until they were perfectly positioned.

Allie held her breath.

The shadows pounced.

Jerry gave a rough cry of surprise as the gun flew from his fingers. He scrambled after it, but was pulled back. Gabe struggled to keep control of his own gun. Allie heard the slap of fist against face. The bone-crunching sound of metal striking a skull. Someone grunting from the pain.

Behind her, Nathaniel's voice rose. 'Is this your doing, Lucinda? You were to come alone.'

'And you were to trade fairly for Jerry Cole,' her grandmother replied with icy indignation. 'I am not alone in breaking the rules of parley.'

That was when the gun went off.

It was too dark and too chaotic to see who fired. Later, Allie would think through that moment over and over again, trying to *see more*. Had Jerry recovered his gun? Was it Gabe? Was it accidental?

But at that moment, as the retort cracked through the air, she just flinched and reached instinctively for Carter, who caught her hand and pulled her to the ground with such force it knocked the wind out of her.

Then the echo of the gunshot faded away and the night went silent again.

Allie fought to get her breath back. Cool strands of grass, soft as feathers, tickled her cheek. Carter had flung his arm across her, holding her down. But he wasn't moving.

'Carter? Are you hit?' Her voice sounded breathless and thin.

'No. Are you?' As he spoke, his hand pressed against her back as if seeking verification that she was OK.

'I don't ... think so,' Allie said, unsure. 'I don't feel shot. I think—'

'*Lucinda*?' The voice that interrupted her was Nathaniel's. He sounded strange. Frightened.

Somehow, Allie knew then. She just knew.

She sat up just in time to see her grandmother sag into Nathaniel's arms and then slowly, so slowly, slip down to the ground.

Thirty Seven

For an instant, Allie didn't move. She felt dizzy. The lights of the city at the foot of the hill seemed to spin up and around her.

Grandmother.

Stumbling to her feet, she began to run towards her. She was vaguely aware of Carter's voice calling her back but she kept going. She wasn't far from Lucinda but those few steps seemed to take forever. As if the world itself had slowed down.

She could hear Nathaniel talking to Lucinda but his words made no sense. Saw him reaching for her hand.

Then she fell to her knees beside him. The lights of London illuminated the bloom of red on the white silk of Lucinda's neat blouse. Just above her heart.

'Grandmother?' Allie was shaking now, her teeth chattering, as she reached out to the woman she'd only known a few months. Only seen a few times.

Nathaniel looked pale and drawn. He pressed both his hands against the wound on Lucinda's chest. Blood bubbled between his fingers. His breath hissed between his teeth.

'Oh God, Lucinda,' he whispered.

This is bad, Allie thought. *Bad, bad, bad ...*

'Allie.'

Lucinda's voice was unexpectedly strong. At the sound of it, relief flooded through Allie. She sounded fine. Yes, she'd lost a lot of blood but she'd be OK. They'd get her an ambulance.

'I'm here,' Allie said, fighting back a sob. 'We'll get you to a doctor …'

Her grandmother reached out with a blood-slick hand and grabbed her wrist.

'Your promise.' Lucinda held her gaze with fierce grey eyes. 'Keep your promise.'

Allie's brain wouldn't function. Too much had happened. 'My promise?' At that moment, someone grabbed her from behind, dragging her roughly to her feet. Lucinda's hand slipped from her wrist, letting her go.

'No!' Allie screamed, struggling in the unknown arms, swinging her elbow back to connect with a muscular torso. But the hands only tightened.

'Allie.' Carter's tone was grave. 'We have to go.'

She stopped fighting. At her feet, Nathaniel was still pressing his hands against Lucinda's wound and talking to her in a low voice. 'Stay with me, Lucinda. Please. You can't do this.'

'Go?' She stared at Carter. 'We can't *go*. Lucinda …'

'Your promise,' he said, holding her gaze as if to force her to remember, 'was to run.'

Suddenly she remembered the conversation in Isabelle's office. Lucinda's insistence that she swear she'd leave if she was hurt.

For the first time she paid attention to the landscape around them. Dark-clad bodies had flooded the hilltop. Guards from both sides were all around them. Everywhere was fighting and shouting.

She thought she saw Nicole, her long braid flying as she kicked a man in the face, sending him crashing into a tree. Then the two moved into shadow and Allie couldn't see her any more.

The whole nightmarish scene, she realised, was like the paintings in the Cimmeria library – crowds of people, their faces contorted with hate, trying to kill each other.

Carter didn't wait for her agreement. Holding her hand in a tight grip, he ran down the hillside through the fight towards the trees, half dragging her with him.

As they ran Allie looked back at Lucinda, still on the ground with Nathaniel hunched over her. Then fighters stormed in between them.

She saw a flash of dark blonde hair and realised it was Isabelle, fighting a man much bigger than her. The headmistress whirled and kicked, blocking his blows, then leaped into the air to aim a flying kick at his jaw that struck clean and true. The man crumpled like a toy.

Isabelle can really fight, Allie thought, dazed. But then another man came up behind the headmistress, aiming a blow at her head. The headmistress dodged at the last minute and turned to take him on.

Allie and Carter were nearing the trees now, and she dug in her heels.

'We should stay and fight,' she protested. 'They need our help.'

'We can't stay,' he said, pulling her hand. 'We promised.'

Before Allie could reply, a thick, muscular arm wrapped around her throat from behind, yanking her off her feet.

Her hand slipped free of Carter's.

'Allie!' Carter spun towards her but then someone else grabbed him and pulled him down to the ground with a heavy thud.

Helpless, Allie was dragged up the hill, towards the melee.

She yanked at the arm, clawed at it. But it was like iron. Nothing she did mattered. She could feel the hard muscles of the man's chest against her back and it made her skin crawl.

Suddenly her blood ran cold. Gabe had grabbed her like this that night in the woods with Sylvain. Was this Gabe?

She squirmed in his grip, trying to see who held her. This turned out to be a bad idea. He tightened his grip across her throat.

'I like it when you fight,' a voice hissed in her ear. 'Fight some more.'

Now she couldn't breathe. Couldn't move. Her heart hammered against her ribs as she gasped futilely for air.

Bright flashes of light began to dance in her vision like fireflies.

It's over, she thought in a cold haze of surprise. *He's killing me.*

Then, with no warning, the man shook. His arm released and she fell to the ground, gasping for breath.

When she looked up, Gabe lay on the ground next to her, blood streaming from his head. Christopher stood over him, holding a truncheon.

Allie stared at him in disbelief.

He reached out his hand to pull her up. 'You OK?'

Too stunned to argue, she nodded. 'Lucinda. Grandmother. Someone shot her.'

His lips tightened. 'I saw.'

'You get the hell away from her.' Out of the darkness, Carter hurtled at Christopher. He was drenched in sweat, fists clenched.

Christopher adopted a defensive stance with the truncheon ready in one hand.

'No!' Allie stepped between them. 'Carter. This is my brother. This is Christopher.'

'Oh?' Carter, who knew everything Christopher had done, kept coming until only Allie's body separated them. 'Then you *really* need to get the hell away from her.'

'He just saved my life, Carter.' Allie raised her voice. 'Stop this.'

With clear reluctance, Carter backed off. He turned his attention to Allie. 'We have to go, now.' Allie's gaze darted to her brother. She didn't want to leave him with Gabe who lay groaning on the ground.

'He's right,' Christopher said. 'Get out of here. I'll cover your back.'

'Will you be OK?' Allie asked, hesitantly.

'I'll be fine,' he promised. 'Go as fast as you can.'

Carter started to pull her with him but she turned back.

'I want …' Allie hesitated. She didn't know what she wanted. 'Thanks, Chris.'

His responding smile was bittersweet. 'You're welcome, Allie Cat. Now *go*.'

Turning, she and Carter ran side by side, weaving their way through clusters of fighters. As they ran, she scanned the heath for familiar faces.

She saw Zelazny shove his elbow into someone's back and then bring his fist down on the arch of a neck with brutal force. At his side, Eloise was a whirling dervish, kicking and punching.

In the distance, she thought she saw Zoe swoop across the grass like a bird of prey. At least, she hoped it was her.

Then they'd reached the edge of the woods and they were safe. They rushed into the darkness with relief.

But they'd only gone a few steps when a voice called out to them: 'Stop right there.'

A black-clad man stepped out from a cluster of trees. 'Where do you think you're going?'

Allie squinted at him in the dimness. She didn't think she'd ever seen him before.

One of theirs.

'Look –' Carter raised his hands – 'we don't want trouble. We're just leaving.'

The man walked towards them, his gaze steady on Allie's face. She'd come to know that look of recognition well. He knew exactly who she was.

'You can go,' the man said. 'The girl stays with me.'

Carter walked right up to him. 'The hell she does.'

He punched the man in the stomach in a move so quick, to Allie it was a blur. Just one minute the man was standing there staring at her, and the next he was doubled over, vomiting.

Carter walked back to her side. 'Let's go,' he said.

This time she didn't argue.

RESISTANCE

When they emerged from the park some time later, the street lights blinded them at first.

A night bus roared by and Allie looked around in confusion. She had no idea where they were. They hadn't come out on genteel Tanza Road but somewhere else completely – this was a wide, steep avenue, busy with cars and buses even after midnight.

In her mind she kept seeing the red blood pouring on to Lucinda's clean white blouse. She forced the image away with iron will.

She would have years to cry about this night.

Not now.

She could see the confusion on Carter's face, too and it helped to calm her. She was the one who'd grown up in this city. She needed to be the one to get them to the safe house. There were other people on this pavement. Normal people. She wondered how they must look to them – a couple of battered and bloodied kids wandering around Hampstead in the middle of the night. Someone might call the cops.

Smoothing loose strands of hair away from her sweaty face, she schooled her features into the bland, disinterested look every Londoner eventually acquires.

Ahead of them, a group of kids their age in hoodies swung around the corner and began walking towards them. Allie saw Carter stiffen as they neared, ready for a fight.

'Act cool,' she said, as much to herself as to him. She was surprised by how calm she sounded. How controlled.

The kids didn't even glance at them when they passed.

Allie waited until they were just out of earshot. 'Look. I don't know where we are,' she said in a conversational tone.

Slapping at his pockets, Carter shot her a helpless look. 'My GPS – it's gone. I must have dropped it in the fight.'

Allie bit her lip and looked around them, but nothing seemed familiar.

'I'm going to stop for a second,' she said. 'Just … follow my lead.'

When they reached an ancient-looking pub set back off the road, Allie walked on to its front path and crouched down, pretending to tighten her shoelaces. As she did so she checked out the signs around them.

Spaniard's Inn … Spaniard's Road …

In her head she visualised the maps they'd memorised. This wasn't any of the streets they were told to look for, and it took her a second to place it. When she did, her heart sank.

'Oh bollocks, Carter.' She stood up. 'We're on the wrong side of the bloody park.'

He held up his hands. 'Which way to the safe house?'

She pointed down the long, curving road running alongside the dark heath.

'That way,' she said grimly. 'A long way.'

He didn't argue. 'Let's get walking.'

Hampstead Heath sprawls for hundreds of acres. Nathaniel's guards were all over it right now. They needed to get away from it, fast.

Allie pressed her fingertips against her forehead as she mapped out a mental route.

'OK,' she said after a second. 'Stick with me. I think I know where to go.'

Carter didn't question her as she set off at a rapid pace. He stuck close to her side, letting her lead.

The need to plan and think of practical logistics cleared the fog from Allie's mind. She felt in control. They needed to get out of here. She could focus on that.

One foot, she told herself. *Then the other foot. One foot ...*

After ten minutes fast walking they turned off the busy road on to a leafy residential lane lined with well-maintained houses. No light came through the wide windows at this hour. No cars passed them.

It was peaceful here. Their footsteps made soft rubbery sounds against the pristine pavement. Their breathing seemed unnecessarily loud.

Images from the park kept intruding into the controlled space of Allie's mind. Lucinda's fierce expression. The suppressed glimmer of her blood-covered diamond ring.

Some part of Allie simply couldn't accept that it really happened. Lucinda Meldrum could not be shot. People like her did not get shot. They were protected. They were *safe*.

She kept seeing the haunted look on Nathaniel's face. Hearing his pleading voice. *'Stay with me, Lucinda. Please.'*

'Did he shoot her?' The words came out unexpectedly. She hadn't meant to say it aloud.

In the dark, Carter looked pale. His dark hair clung to the damp skin of his forehead.

'Who?' he asked. 'Nathaniel?'

'Yes,' Allie said. 'Was he the one who shot her?'

'I saw two guns,' Carter said. 'Gabe's and Jerry's. But there were a lot of people. I don't think Nathaniel did it though.'

'No,' Allie agreed. 'He actually seemed upset.' She shook her head. 'I don't get it ... I thought he hated her.'

'Hate and love,' Carter said. 'They're a lot alike.'

They turned on to another road, just as quiet as the first. They were halfway down it before she summoned the courage to ask the one question she was most afraid of.

'Do you think she's dead?'

Carter glanced at her; his pace slowed.

With clear reluctance, he nodded. 'I think so.'

A frond of grief uncurled inside her, taking up its familiar territory near her heart.

She'd hardly known her grandmother. But she was *family*. And she had, from the very first meeting, seemed to believe in Allie. To have faith in her.

Now there was no one left in her family who felt that way.

It took them nearly an hour of walking to reach the address Raj had made them memorise.

Number 38 Carlton Lane was a nondescript three-storey terrace building with a dingy sign hanging out front that said 'The Drop Inn B&B'.

'Bit dodgy,' Carter said, as they looked up at the front door. 'I wonder why they chose this place?'

'No idea.' Allie looked around as if the answer could be found elsewhere on this insalubrious street. Even at this hour, the bar on the corner had customers. And they seemed to be getting in a fight. 'This is Kilburn. It's all dodgy.'

'What's Kilburn?' Carter asked.

'Where we are,' she said. Then, not wanting to explain north London neighbourhoods right now, she changed the subject. 'Want to go first? I'll keep the door open in case we have to leg it.'

She was certain this was the right address but Raj had said nothing about a B&B. He hadn't mentioned that the street was scary nor told them who would be inside. Maybe he'd never really thought they'd need to use it.

As Carter walked up the stairs and pressed the buzzer, she stayed a step behind him, keeping an eye on the street.

Nothing happened.

Carter shot her a look over his shoulder and she shrugged.

He pressed it again.

This time they both heard the heavy footsteps on the stairs inside. Then the metallic clunk of three locks being opened. The door was yanked open to the extent a protective chain would allow.

A dark face glared out at them. 'It's one o'clock in the bleeding morning.'

The accent was classic north London. The man looked cross. He sounded cross. And he was big.

When Carter hesitated, Allie stepped up beside him.

'We're guests of Raj Patel.' This was what Raj had told them to say. But she added apologetically, 'We're sorry to bother you so late.'

The man slammed the door in their face.

Allie and Carter exchanged puzzled looks. Maybe this was the wrong place after all.

Then the chain slid loose inside and the door opened wide enough to reveal the tall man in a blue dressing gown.

'You better come in.'

Thirty Eight

Carter and Allie stepped inside cautiously. The man let them pass, then closed the door, flipped the three locks shut again and braced the door with a metal bar.

Allie watched this elaborate procedure with interest. One thing was certain, this place was secure.

The entrance hall had once been grand. It had a beautiful old tiled floor, stained-glass windows and carved wood. But it was run down . The paint needed touching up and two lights had burned out on the stairs behind them.

The man turned and looked them both up and down.

'I'm Sharif,' he said after a thorough inspection. 'Who the hell are you?'

'Uh ... I'm Carter,' Carter said.

Allie kept her hands in her pockets. Her eyes darted to the door now so very comprehensively locked.

Trust Raj, she told herself. But it wasn't easy.

'Allie,' she said tersely.

'That's all you need to tell me.' The man headed down the hallway, motioning for them to follow. His slippers made a scuffing sound on the tile floor. 'If you're here, something went wrong. I'm sorry to hear it.'

There was kindness in his voice. Allie relaxed a little.

He stepped into a windowless kitchen, and turned on the switch. Harsh fluorescent lights came on with an industrial buzz. It reminded Allie of a hospital: white walls, white cupboards, white floors. Everything was spotless.

Opening a drawer, he located a black key on a silver ring and held it out to them. After a brief hesitation, Carter accepted it.

'Go to room eleven,' Sharif instructed. 'It's at the top of the stairs. Lock the door behind you. Don't come out for anyone you don't know. And I mean anyone. Including me. Go now.'

They hurried to the long steep staircase that ascended into darkness. Behind them, Sharif was turning out the lights.

Halfway up the stairs, Allie turned back. 'Thank you, Sharif.'

His hand on the light switch, the man looked up at her.

'No need for that,' he said. 'I owe Raj Patel my life. I imagine you do, too.'

Room eleven was in a converted attic, three flights up. It was pitch dark at the top of the stairs, and Carter fumbled with the key for some time, trying to get it into a lock he couldn't see.

When he did get it unlocked, the door was so heavy he had to put his shoulder against it to open it.

It was just as dark inside the room as out, and they both felt along the wall until Allie's fingers found the cool plastic switch at last and flipped on the lights.

The room was small and stuffy with a ceiling that slanted steeply. A double bed took up most of the space, topped with two flat pillows and a clean but faded blue bedspread. A small window on one wall was hidden behind dark curtains. Through a narrow door Allie could see a minuscule bathroom.

It seemed unnaturally quiet.

'I wonder what he meant,' Allie said to break the silence. 'That he owed Raj his life.'

'I don't know.' Careful not to bump his head on the low ceiling, Carter went to the window and moved the curtain far enough to look out. 'Raj was in the military for a while.'

Allie hadn't known that.

The blanket of silence came down again.

Now that they were here and safe, weariness hit her like a fist. Carter still stood by the window. She wondered what he was looking at. Or if he just didn't know what to do. The bed was the only piece of furniture in the room aside from a small, battered bedside table with a lamp.

After a brief hesitation, she sat down on the edge of the mattress. It was one of those hard mattresses that seemed to be carved out of solid wood.

'That must be it,' she said, running her hand tiredly across her face.

In the light, she noticed something on her wrist, and she turned her hand over to see it better.

It looked almost like a bracelet, but she wasn't wearing jewellery.

A sudden image of Lucinda grabbing her wrist flashed in her mind.

The bracelet was her grandmother's blood.

Stifling a sob, Allie rubbed hard at the rust-coloured stain. 'What is it?'

When she didn't reply, Carter crossed to her side in three long steps. He took her hand to look at her wrist. She didn't fight him.

'It's …' But she couldn't bring herself to say what it was. That would make it all real. Besides, he must know anyway. She swallowed hard. 'I need to clean up.'

To her relief, he didn't try to make her feel better.

'In here.' He reached into the bathroom to turn on the light then moved back to the window, giving her space.

Like everything else here, the bathroom was antiquated but clean. Allie turned on the tap. As she waited for the water to warm up, she stared at herself in the old mirror. She was shiny from sweat and her skin looked greeny-yellow in the fluorescent light.

Tears ran down her cheek and she stared at them curiously. She hadn't realised she was crying.

The water was warm now. Grabbing a cracked bar of soap, she rubbed it against her wrist. The water ran pink at first. Then rusty red. Then clear.

She scrubbed her hands and arms until they burned. Then she splashed water on her face and neck.

By the time she finished, she actually felt better. Her eyes were red but she wasn't crying any more. She took a deep breath and walked back into the bedroom.

Carter was by the window again. His eyes searched her face.

'I'm OK,' she lied.

'I know you are,' he said.

He walked towards her, and she stiffened. If he hugged her she'd start crying again and then she might never stop.

Instead he went into the bathroom and closed the door behind him.

Relieved, Allie sank down on the bed. She could hear water running behind the door. She wanted Carter close but she was glad there was some space between them right now. She needed a second to think.

It struck her that he might feel the same way.

She was so tired. The adrenaline that kept her going all night – maybe all week – had abandoned her. She went to pull her feet up on to the bed but then cast a guilty glance at the clean coverlet.

Carefully she unzipped her muddy boots and slipped them off, leaving them on the floor. If they were attacked she might have to run away in her socks but ... so be it. She wasn't smudging Sharif's neat bedspread.

Pulling her feet up on to the bed she leaned back against the flat pillow.

Lying down felt good. Even the hard-as-a-rock mattress felt good.

The overhead light was brutal but she was too exhausted to care.

I'll close my eyes ... Just for a second.

'Allie ...'

Someone was calling but Allie didn't know who. It was too dark to see.

'Hello?' *she called back. No one replied.*

She looked down – she was barefoot but for some reason she couldn't feel the grass against the soles of her feet.

When she looked up again, she was back in Hampstead Heath, at the top of Parliament Hill. The lights of the city twinkled below her.

'Oh no ...' *she whispered.*

Lucinda lay gracefully at the crest of the hill. Nathaniel knelt beside her. Neither of them moved or spoke. They were like statues.

Slowly, Allie approached them. Her heart pounded. It was hard to breathe. Somewhere up here was the man who grabbed her. Somewhere Gabe waited.

So many enemies in one place. What was she doing here?

But she had to see Lucinda again. To tell her goodbye. To tell her she was sorry.

But now she and Nathaniel weren't alone. Jo was there, too. A sorrowful angel in white, her blonde hair highlighted by the city lights behind her.

'It's not your fault, Allie,' she said, reaching out a pale hand.

Slowly, fearfully, Allie looked down at her grandmother. Nathaniel was weeping. Lucinda's white blouse was soaked red with blood. Blood pooled beneath her and ran down the hillside in waves. Pouring and rushing. Engulfing the city.

'Allie, I'm serious. You did all you could. It's not your fault,' Jo said again.

Then Lucinda's eyes flew up.

'Yes it is,' she said.

Allie screamed.

'Wake up, Allie!' Carter shook her by the shoulders.

She stared up at him. 'What?'

Her gaze skittered around the unfamiliar room. No Lucinda. No Jo. No Nathaniel.

Blue coverlet. Dingy walls. The safe house.

'You had a nightmare.' Carter still held her tightly. His fingers were warm against her shoulders. 'You screamed.' Letting go with one hand, he brushed the hair back from her face, smoothing it gently behind her ear. His fingers were like feathers against her skin. 'You talked in your sleep.'

Allie's gaze shot up to meet his. Her brow creased. 'What did I say?'

Carter's fingers paused, then resumed stroking her hair. 'You said ... "Jo".'

Biting her lip, Allie nodded.

She resisted the urge to lean against him. Let him hold her and tell her everything was OK. Like the old days.

Because everything was *not* OK. And this wasn't the old days.

Her eyes searched the room. At some point, he'd turned off the overhead light and switched on the bedside lamp. She wondered how long she'd been asleep.

She glanced at him again. It couldn't have been too long – his hair was still damp and curling a little from the water. He smelled of the same bar of soap she'd used.

Unconsciously, her gaze darted down to her clean hands and wrists.

No blood.

He was stroking the strands of hair against her shoulders now. It felt soothing and electrifying at the same time. She felt each touch like heat against her skin.

She didn't want him to stop. But he had to. He wasn't hers. And she wasn't his.

With unnecessary abruptness, she sat up.

He dropped his hand as if she'd stung him.

Pretending not to notice this, she cleared her throat and scooted back against the pillows.

She glanced at the pillow next to hers. It wasn't dented – he hadn't been sleeping. He'd been standing guard.

He was staring down at his hands. Even at that angle, she could see the sadness in his face.

'I ... dream about her,' she admitted, finally. 'About Jo, I mean. All the time.' She paused, and he raised his gaze to meet hers. His dark eyes seemed as deep as the ocean. You could sink into them. Lose yourself. 'I like seeing her. It's like she's not really gone.' She searched his face for judgement. 'That sounds crazy, right? Lock Allie up in the Lunatic Hotel. She sees dead people.'

'I dream about my parents all the time,' he said simply.

Allie blinked. 'Really?'

He nodded, forcing a faint smile. 'So ... if there's a Lunatic Hotel, maybe we can share a cell. Save on the rent.'

Allie felt strangely relieved. She was new to this whole grief thing. Carter, on the other hand, was a professional – his parents had died when he was five. That he'd lived to be seventeen, and relatively sane, was one of the things she'd held on to after Jo's death.

After all, she'd only lost her best friend. Carter had lost his mum and dad and *survived*. Knowing that he'd kept it together after all of that made the idea of going crazy seem almost selfish.

'It's weird,' Carter said when she didn't speak. His hands were crossed loosely in front of him. 'Sometimes in my dreams they look like they do in the pictures I have of them. Other times they don't look like themselves at all.' He gave a sheepish smile. 'When that happens I wake up feeling guilty for not recognising them.'

He looked so shy at that moment, and so vulnerable. Allie had never wanted to hold his hand so much as she did right then. She had to curl her fingers into fists to stop herself.

'So,' he concluded, 'if anyone's bonkers it's definitely me.'

'You're not crazy,' Allie said softly.

When he looked at her then his eyes nearly broke her heart.

'You're the sanest person I know,' she said.

He smiled. 'Yeah but ... you know a lot of crazy people.'

'True,' Allie conceded. 'Birds of a feather.'

'But I'm the closest bird at the moment.'

Allie's smile faded as she held his gaze. 'You always are.'

The light moment dissipated instantly. The electricity returned, crackling unseen around them.

'Carter ...' she started to say but he spoke at the same time. 'Allie ...'

'Sorry,' he said, holding up his hands. 'You first.'

Her lungs felt strangely tight. 'I just wanted to ... I mean ... thank you for what you did tonight. You were so calm.'

Carter exhaled and shook his head. 'Someone shot your grandmother tonight and you're telling me I was calm? I'm not the cool-headed one, Allie. I've never seen anyone so steady under pressure. You were amazing. *Are* amazing.'

He reached for her hands then and she let him pull them into his, although she knew it was wrong. Knew it couldn't be anything.

But she wanted it to be something.

She could feel the strength in his fingers. And yet his thumbs brushed her knuckles with the softness of butterfly wings.

'You are the most amazing person I know.'

She needed to stop this before it went too far. 'Carter ...'

What should she say? Don't? Stop? We can't?

That would be the right thing to say.

What she wanted to say was entirely different. But she couldn't say that.

Could she?

Jump.

He studied her face intently, as if he could hear her internal struggle. As if he knew she was deciding something.

'What?' His fingers ran up her bare arm to her shoulder. His eyes were urgent. As if this was their last chance. 'Say it, Allie. Say anything.'

With her whole heart she wished that was true. Wished she could say anything. Because, if she told him the truth, what would she say?

'Carter … I love you.'

Thirty Nine

Allie's heart seemed to stop.

The words hung in the air like smoke; incriminating her.

I did not just say that, she thought, panicking. *Why did I do that?*

But it was too late to turn back. You can't recant a declaration of love. It cannot be withdrawn or stricken from the record. It's there forever.

She stared at Carter in shock, as if he was the one who'd said it, and waited for him to recoil. To look embarrassed. To tell her she was wrong. A horrible person.

A cheater.

He'd gone dangerously still – so still he didn't seem to breathe.

Then he sagged back as if some unseen force that had been holding him up had suddenly let go. His breath came out in a ragged sigh.

'Oh God, Allie, I love you, too.'

Something cold inside of her began to thaw. All of her confusion left her. Because the answer was right in front of her.

She couldn't love Sylvain because she was in love with Carter. She always had been.

They reached for each other at the same time, and then, at last, his lips were against hers and they were kissing with the pent-up desire of months of trying not to want each other.

Exhilaration made Allie's head swim. She'd wanted this for so long. Dreamed of it. But she'd thought it could never be. Now his lips were against hers – warm and familiar. His breath was soft inside her mouth, filling her lungs.

After everything that had happened, she needed this. Needed him. Needed it to be OK.

She knelt closer to him on the unfamiliar bed, twining her wrists around his neck.

He whispered words against her lips that she couldn't make out but she knew what he was saying. That he loved her. That they should always be together.

His hands slid down her spine, flattening against the small of her back, trying to pull her closer, but it wasn't necessary, she'd wrapped her arms around his neck and was pulling his body down on top of hers.

When she lay flat on the bed, he propped himself up on his arms so as not to crush her against the unforgiving mattress, and covered her face with kisses. Kissing her forehead, her eyelids, the tip of her nose, her chin.

Then his mouth returned to hers.

Butterflies swarmed in Allie's stomach. Wonderingly, she explored his body, running her hands over his shoulders, down the bare skin of his arms, up the flat plane of his stomach, the shallow curves of his chest.

He was so warm. So alive.

'Is this really happening?' she whispered. 'I'm not dreaming … am I?'

He sat up, pulling her with him with easy strength until she sat facing him, her legs tangled up with his. Cupping her face between the palms of his hands, he held her as if she were made of the most fragile glass. His eyes were as serious as she'd ever seen them.

'This is not a dream.'

'But how?' she said, still stroking his shoulders, feeling the muscles move beneath her fingers. Solid and real. 'What will we do?'

His hands slid down to her waist and he pulled her forward until she could feel his breath on her cheeks.

'We will find a way,' he promised her. 'We have to. I won't be apart from you any more. I won't pretend any more.'

It was like he was reading her mind. Saying her thoughts aloud.

'I feel like I've been lying to myself for so long …' She touched the soft silk of his eyebrows, the hard, smooth angles of his cheekbones. 'But I had to. I didn't want to hurt anyone. I didn't want to be hurt.'

He closed his eyes, letting her touch him everywhere. 'I will never hurt you, Allie. Never again.'

She believed him.

Placing her hands flat on his chest she pushed him back on to the bed. He fell back willingly and she lay on top of him, the sound of his soft laughter muffled by the pressure of her lips against his.

'I tried,' Carter said quietly, 'to make myself fall in love with Jules.'

As he spoke, his fingers traced circles on the sensitive skin on the inside of Allie's forearm. She felt that touch in her stomach.

Her own fingers were running through the soft, dark strands of his hair.

They lay side by side on the bed, facing each other. Now that they were allowed to touch each other, they couldn't seem to stop.

'It was the same with Sylvain,' Allie confessed. The thought of how much this would hurt Sylvain extracted some of the joy from the moment with the precise sharpness of a scalpel. She dropped her hands to her sides. 'I care about him – I can't seem not to. But when he told me he loved me … I couldn't say it back. I think I knew then. But I couldn't admit it to myself.'

Carter pulled her fingers up to his lips and kissed them. His eyes were sombre. 'The poor sod.'

Allie thought of the lost look on Sylvain's face when he said goodbye. The way he'd said, '*Even though I know …*' Had he meant this?

All along, had he known who she really loved?

She couldn't bear to think of that.

Taking Carter's hand in hers she pressed his palm against the skin of her cheek. This was what mattered right now. This contact.

This love.

With his other hand, Carter traced soft, invisible lines along her jaw, down her neck, along her clavicle.

His touch made her shiver.

'And Jules?' she said. 'Is she in love with you?'

His face darkened. Dropping his hand on to the curve of her hip, he nodded.

'Before she left … things were getting serious. I knew I had to get out of it before it went too far but I didn't know how. I was afraid I'd … I'd hurt her.'

He rolled over on his back, resting his head on his hand, staring up at the ceiling as if he would find the answers he needed there.

Allie sat up so she could see his face.

'When her parents took her away, the worst part was … I was kind of relieved.' He wouldn't meet her eyes. 'And I hated myself for that. But I couldn't help it. I kept hoping she'd find someone at the new school who deserved her. Then she'd break up with me and everything would be fine.'

'But she didn't,' Allie said.

He shook his head, his lips in a tight line. 'She wrote me letters, telling me she'd wait until we were both out. We could go to university together …'

Allie let out her breath.

'What a mess we both are.' Her voice was thick. 'We try so hard not to hurt anyone that we hurt everyone.' She raked her fingers through her tangled hair. 'We ought to be arrested for the good of the community.'

A wry smile quirked up the corners of his lips. 'We're not criminals, Allie. We just … can't not love each other.'

Each time he said the word it made her heart flip.

Love.

So this is what it feels like.

'What happens now?' she asked, leaning closer to him. 'I mean seriously? If neither of us can bear to hurt Jules or Sylvain …'

'We have to.' A strand of Allie's hair tumbled on to Carter's chest and he caught it, twisting it around his finger like a ring. 'You just said we tried to protect them and all we did was make things worse. I actually think we'll protect them more by being honest.'

Suddenly miserable, Allie lowered her head on to his chest, pressing her body against his. He pulled her into his arms, holding her close. As she listened to his heart beat a steady rhythm she couldn't ever remember feeling so warm and safe.

'I don't want to hurt anyone,' she murmured as exhaustion took over and her eyes drifted shut.

He pressed his lips against her temple. 'Me neither. But I am never losing you again, Allie Sheridan. And that is a promise.'

Bang, bang, bang!

Allie went from sound asleep to wide awake in an instant, sitting straight up in bed and staring at the heavy bedroom door, hoping she'd dreamed it. But Carter was already standing on the other side of the bed, his body tense.

The knocking came again, so hard and insistent the door shook in its frame.

They ran across the room until they stood on either side of the doorway.

'Who ...?' Allie whispered, looking at Carter.

He kept his eyes on the door. 'Raj, I hope. Only one way to find out.' He stepped closer to the door. 'Who's there?'

There was a pause. 'Dom. And friends.'

Hearing the familiar American accent, Allie relaxed. They were saved.

Carter moved quickly to open the sturdy locks and the door swung open.

On the dark landing, looking as unruffled as if she always roused students from guesthouses at four in the morning, Dom stood at the head of a phalanx of guards.

Her glasses glittered in the light from the bedroom as she scanned them for wounds. Finding none, she tilted her head. 'Let's get you out of here.'

Before they could move, though, Nicole and Zoe pushed through the others to get to them.

'Allie!' Nicole pulled her into a hug. Allie clung to her, relieved to see them both in one piece.

'Where's Rachel?' Allie asked, looking down the dark stairwell.

'She's safe,' Nicole promised her. 'Outside in the car. Everyone's OK.'

'Thank God.' Allie felt weak with relief.

They were all OK. Everyone was fine.

All but one.

'Lucinda?' Allie looked from Nicole to Dom, afraid she already knew the answer.

Nicole just squeezed her hand and shook her head.

'She didn't make it,' Dom said. 'I'm very sorry.'

Allie shuddered. Those were precisely the same words Isabelle had used about Jo.

She didn't make it ....

It was an awful way to say someone had died. As if they'd somehow *failed* to live. Failed to survive a bullet. Or a blade.

She was still processing how she felt when Zoe looked past her and frowned at the rumpled bed. She wrinkled her pert nose. 'Wait. Did you two *sleep together*?'

Allie froze. The stairwell went sickeningly silent. Everyone seemed to be looking at her. Or trying not to look at her.

Carter handled it. 'There's only one bed,' he explained. 'But we didn't do much sleeping.' Allie's gaze shot to his; he didn't meet her eyes. 'We were waiting for you guys. What took you so long anyway?'

'There were lots of people to fight,' Zoe said chirpily. 'Then Raj made us wait because you were followed.'

Allie saw Carter's body tense.

'Why did he think that?' he asked, his voice unnaturally even.

'When you left the park, someone was behind you,' Nicole said softly. 'But Raj's friend – Sharif, I think? – he's been watching the street all night and he saw no one so we decided it was OK to come get you now.'

Allie thought of Sharif, already tired when they arrived, staying up all night to keep them safe. She could have hugged him.

'We *think* it's safe but we're not certain,' Dom said, clarifying Nicole's assessment. 'We should go. The cars are out front.'

'One second.' Allie ran back to the room to grab her boots, hopping on one foot as she pulled them up. Carter was on the opposite side of the bed, putting on his shoes.

She could feel everyone watching them; speculating about what had happened in this room with just one bed.

Boots on, she straightened and walked to the door with her head held high. Carter was right behind her.

As they closed the door, Allie stole a quick last glance at the room where everything changed. Where she'd finally listened to her heart.

Carter's fingers brushed against hers as she turned away and she didn't believe it was an accident.

Her heart ached with love for him.

She'd lost the grandmother she barely knew but she still wasn't alone. Now she had Carter.

They descended the stairs in a precise order. Two guards in front. Then Nicole and Zoe, Allie and Carter, followed by Dom and two more guards.

Allie was sure they'd already woken everyone in the house but they moved quietly now, hustling down the steep staircase to the ground floor.

The entrance hall was dark and there was no sign of Sharif. She said a silent thanks to him, wherever he was, for looking out for them.

The guards opened the front door.

Allie stood on her toes to see, but all she could make out was darkness.

They left the building in pairs. Allie and Carter were side by side, surrounded by the others.

The street was utterly silent. The drinkers in the pub on the corner must have finally gone home to sleep it off.

It was not yet dawn. The sky was velvety black above the harsh glare of the streetlights. Allie looked up at the dark emptiness above them. Something was missing. It took her a minute to figure out what it was.

There were no stars.

RESISTANCE

You can never see the stars in London. The city is its own solar system, so bright it blinds you.

When she'd lived here, she'd just accepted that fact. But now the sky seemed empty without them.

The warm night air smelled heavily of exhaust.

A line of four black Land Rovers stood waiting for them, double parked, engines idling. Allie saw Rachel inside one of them, waving at her wildly. She waved back.

Moving as one, careful but fast, they made their way down the concrete front steps to the pavement, then out into the street. Ahead, the car doors opened for them.

Something moved at the edge of Allie's vision. She snapped around to see a skinny black cat slinking across the road in a pool of lamp light. It stopped in front of the first Land Rover, licked its shoulder then stared at her accusingly with wide, golden eyes.

Black cat crossed our path.

A sudden sense of dread made her shiver. But then Dom, talking quietly into her mobile phone ('Loading the vehicles now. All parties accounted for'), grabbed her elbow, and steered her towards the third vehicle.

Her nerves alight with apprehension, Allie went where she was told, but she kept her eyes on the cat.

Suddenly, it crouched and hissed, as if startled. As she watched, it scuttled out of the road, leaping over a low wall with impossible grace, and disappearing in the darkness.

With Dom still propelling her along briskly and Carter a half-step ahead, Allie turned back to see what had frightened it.

Her breath caught in her throat.

They came from everywhere. Black-clad bodies emerged from cars, from dark alleyways, from stairwells. There were everywhere and they were heading right for her.

Words from the book Zelazny had given her appeared in her mind with cold clarity. *'Attack him where he is unprepared. Appear where you are not expected.'*

'Carter ...' she breathed. And her voice must have scared him because he spun towards her just as Nathaniel's guards attacked.

The night exploded into sound and fury.

'*Go!*' Dom shouted, shoving Allie and Carter hard towards the Land Rover. Whirling, she called to the others, her voice straining: 'Positions. Now.' She turned back, shoving the phone into her pocket and raising her fists.

Then the silence was split with cries of pain and grunts of exertion. And the raw meat sound of fist against skin and bone.

Carter grabbed Allie's hand, pulling her close, shielding her with his body as they struggled to push their way to the car through flying fists and spinning kicks.

Fighting her way to the open door, Allie reached for the handle to pull herself up. She had one foot in when someone grabbed her by the hair and shoulder, tearing at her skin with their hands, yanking her back into the street.

She screamed and struggled to extricate herself from the unseen grip, and Carter leapt into action, kicking high and sure. His foot connected perfectly with the man's jaw and he went down, nearly pulling Allie to the ground with him.

Pain burned like fire as he chunks of hair ripped from her scalp.

More hands were reaching for her now but, spinning back towards her, Carter grabbed her by the waist and threw her roughly into the vehicle. She landed in an ungainly heap on the floor.

Nathaniel's guards were swarming them now. Too many for Allie to count. One of them reached for the door, another grabbed at Carter's shirt, yanking him hard away from the car.

'Carter!' Allie screamed, reaching out to try and pull him in after her.

But he didn't follow her. Instead he kicked the guard's hands away from the door and slammed it shut.

'Go!' he shouted to the driver, slapping his hand hard against the metal of the door. 'Get her out of here.'

His jaw was set and determined. He didn't look at Allie. It took her a second to realise what he was doing. When she did, all the breath seemed to go out of her.

She stared at him through the window, aghast. Her heart hammered against her ribs so hard she thought it might explode.

'No-no-no …' Her voice sounded odd. Terrified. 'Carter, no! Don't do this.'

She scrabbled for the door handle, nails scratching against the plastic on the door. Before she could get it open, though, she heard a *thunk*, as the doors locked through the central system.

The Land Rover shot forward with such suddenness Allie lost her grip on the door and was thrown hard into the footwell.

Dazed, she thought she heard herself groan. Every part of her body hurt. Blood trickled down her face and she didn't know where it was coming from.

Gritting her teeth, she pulled herself back up. 'Stop the car!' she said, with as much force as she could muster. 'You have to go back and get him.' But the car didn't stop. It went faster.

Sobbing now, she grabbed the door handle, tearing at it with all her strength, but the locks were solid.

She was trapped.

'We have to go back.' She appealed to guards in the front seats hoarsely, striking the tears from her cheeks with the back of her hand. 'We can't just leave him there. They'll kill him.'

In the rear-view mirror, the driver's eyes flickered to hers. 'My orders are to get you back to the school.'

Only then did she realise they really meant to abandon Carter. They weren't going somewhere to get it together so they could return and rescue him. They were *leaving him*.

'No!' She lunged for the driver, but the guard in the passenger seat was ready for her. Spinning around he caught her wrists, holding them in an iron grip.

She struggled in his grasp but he was unbelievably strong.

'Miss,' he said evenly, 'I understand how you feel, but we have no choice. Our orders are to get you back by any means necessary. Please sit back in your seat and let us do our jobs.'

Mutely, Allie shook her head. She couldn't do that. She couldn't let them leave Carter.

The guard held her gaze with cool blue eyes. 'Miss Sheridan, don't make me restrain you.' He wasn't angry or cruel and somehow that made it all worse. He just didn't care.

Allie was trembling so violently now it was difficult to speak. Still, she pleaded with him.

'But don't you see?' she said, her voice shaking. 'He'll die. And if he dies …'

…my life is over.

'I'm sorry,' he said. But she didn't believe him.

Twisting in his grip, she strained to see what was happening behind them. Already they were too far away for her to make out the faces of those they'd left behind. For a second she thought she saw Carter amid a black cloud of fighters; standing his ground.

'Oh God,' she whispered, her heart breaking. 'Carter …'

Then the car turned a corner and he disappeared in the dark of the city night.

CIMMERIA ACADEMY

Here's your chance to read the thrilling first chapter of Book 4 in the Night School series!

Endgame

NIGHT SCHOOL

C J DAUGHERTY

MOONFLOWER

One

The black Land Rovers roared down dark London streets. Stopping for nothing and nobody, they hurtled across the crowded metropolis, thundering through red lights, tearing over intersections.

Alone in the back seat of one of them, Allie Sheridan stared out the window without seeing anything. Her eyes were red and sore from crying.

She couldn't stop remembering Carter alone in the dark street, fists raised. Nathaniel's guards swarming.

He got away, she assured herself for the thousandth time. *Somehow. He got away.*

But in her heart she knew it wasn't true.

It all made sense now. Jerry Cole told her to take someone she trusted to the parley. And now she knew why.

Take someone you trust so Nathaniel can take him away from you.

Take someone you trust so Nathaniel can kill him. Like he killed Jo.

Tugging hopelessly at the unyielding door handle, she stifled a sob. She couldn't get out. Couldn't go back to him. The doors were locked through a central system.

This car was a prison.

She'd tried fighting, begging, weeping… the men in the front seats were unmoved. They were under orders to bring her back to Cimmeria. And that's what they were going to do.

Frustration raged inside her. She struck the door hard with her fist.

The vehicle careened around a corner with a screech of tyres, throwing her to one side.

As she scrabbled for the safety handle, the guard in the front passenger seat turned to look at her.

'Put your seatbelt on, miss. This is dangerous.'

She glared at him balefully.

I watched my own grandmother die five hours ago, she thought of saying. *And you're telling me this is dangerous?*

At the thought of Lucinda, everything that had happened that night seemed to hit her at once. The sour taste of bile filled her mouth. She lunged instinctively for the window, but that was locked, too.

'I'm going to be sick,' she muttered.

The guard said something to the driver. The window rolled down with a smooth, mechanical whirr.

Cool air flowed in.

Allie stuck her head out of the car, inhaling deeply. Her hair flew around her face in a tangled cloud.

Now that it was OK to vomit, though, she couldn't seem to. Still, she stayed where she was, resting her clammy forehead on the cool metal of the window frame and taking deep, steadying breaths.

The air had that city smell of exhaust and concrete. Vaguely, she considered climbing out and jumping to freedom, but they were moving too fast for her to be certain she'd survive.

She was so tired. Her whole body ached. Her scalp burned

where one of Nathaniel's goons had pulled out a clump of hair. Blood had coagulated on her face and neck, tightening her skin unpleasantly.

In her mind she went through the evening's catastrophic events step by step.

The plan had been simple. Meet Nathaniel for a peaceful parley on the neutral ground of Hampstead Heath. Hand over his spy, Jerry Cole. In exchange, Nathaniel would back off long enough for the Cimmeria leaders to regroup.

But then Jerry had a gun. And the night had spun out into an awful chaotic maelstrom of violence. In the midst of it, Lucinda collapsed, blood pouring from a gunshot wound.

And Nathaniel.

Allie shook her head, still puzzled by what she'd seen.

Nathaniel had been in tears. Trying desperately to save her grandmother.

Until that moment she'd thought he hated Lucinda. But she'd never seen anyone more heartbroken.

She could still hear his tormented voice in her head, pleading with her grandmother. *'Don't leave me, Lucinda...'*

Almost like he loved her.

But she had left him. She'd left all of them.

Now, all Allie knew was that she didn't understand Nathaniel at all.

If he didn't hate Lucinda, why was he fighting her in the first place?

What does he really want?

Letting go of the door, Allie leaned back against the tan leather seat. The guard in the front passenger seat turned to look at her.

'Better now?'

She levelled a silent glare at him.

After a second, he shrugged and turned back around.

Next to her, the window closed.

They gained speed as they pulled on to a motorway, desolate at this hour. They were nearing the city limits. Behind them London was a canopy of light. Ahead, the English countryside lay shrouded in darkness.

Allie's chest tightened around her heart. She was so far from Carter now. God knew what was happening to him.

A tear traced a line down her cheek; she reached up to brush it away. Her hand never reached her face.

A bone-jarring jolt threw her off balance. Before she could react, the vehicle swerved wildly, hurling her across the back seat. She slammed into the window with such force she saw stars.

She never had put that seatbelt on.

'What's going on?' Her voice sounded far away; her head rang from the blow.

No one replied.

Pulling herself up, Allie saw the driver wrestling with the steering wheel. The guard was talking into a microphone, his voice low but tense.

She looked around to try and see what had happened but all she could see was darkness and headlights.

The driver swore and spun the wheel. 'Goddammit. Where are they coming from?'

Allie was clinging to the door handle, but the sheer force of the turn threw her against the door so hard her breath hissed through her teeth from the pain.

'What is going *on*?' she demanded again, louder this time.

Without waiting for an answer, she reached over her shoulder for the seatbelt and strapped herself in, latching it with a metallic click.

Then she turned to look out the back window. What she saw made her breath catch in her throat. There weren't four vehicles anymore.

There were ten.

'Are those ours?' she asked, her voice faint.

No one replied to that question, either. But they didn't have to. She knew the answer already.

A large, tank-like vehicle swung up next to them, revving its engine. Suddenly the Land Rover seemed small.

Allie stared at the monstrous thing, her heart contracting. Its windows were tinted – she couldn't see who was inside.

Without warning it gunned the engine and swerved sharply towards them.

'Look out!' she cried, ducking low.

The driver yanked the wheel. The Land Rover swung right, so sharply Allie's stomach dropped.

They dodged the collision but the car wobbled wildly and the driver struggled to keep control. He clung to the wheel, muscles bulging from the effort as the tyres squealed and they swung across two lanes.

'Six to seven vehicles, affirmative,' the guard in the passenger seat said into his microphone. He was clutching the safety handle above his door to try and hold himself steady as another massive machine swung towards them with an angry roar.

'Convoy disrupted and separated. Other vehicles using diversionary tactics... Look to your *left*!'

He shouted the last words at the driver, who saw the car heading straight towards them at the last minute and wrenched the wheel hard. Too hard.

The Land Rover spun sickeningly. Allie couldn't feel the

road beneath their tyres anymore. They seemed to be flying.

The scene took on a dream-like feel. The world outside blurred. They swirled in a deadly dance towards the flimsy guardrail.

Allie closed her eyes.

Nathaniel had found them.

Acknowledgements

This new edition of Night School was an absolute joy to work on. Huge thanks to the small but mighty team at my new publishing imprint, Moonflower Publishing, especially to the multi-talented Jasmine Aurora, who was responsible for the fabulous cover and the interior design. I cannot imagine what we would do without her.

Thanks always to my amazing agent, Madeleine Milburn, who was the first person to love Night School who wasn't actually married to me. Without her, there would be no Cimmeria Academy. She is a hero in stilettos.

As always thanks to Jack Jewers. He is the first reader of every single book I write, and the first person I want to talk to when everything is great, and the first one to fix things when everything is terrible.

Most of my thanks, though, go to the readers who have supported the series from the beginning, and stayed with me on Instagram and Facebook for years. You are the Night School family, and I love you.

About the Author

A former crime reporter and accidental civil servant, C.J. Daugherty began writing the Night School series while working as a communications consultant for the British government. The series was published by Little Brown in the UK, and went on to sell over a million and a half copies worldwide. A web series inspired by the books clocked up well over a million views. In 2020, the books were optioned for television. She later wrote The Echo Killing series, published by St Martin's Press, and co-wrote the fantasy series, The Secret Fire, with French author Carina Rosenfeld. Her books have been translated into 25 languages and been bestsellers in multiple countries. She lives with her husband, the BAFTA nominated filmmaker, Jack Jewers.

Links

Follow C. J. DAUGHERTY on…

INSTAGRAM @cj_daugherty
YOUTUBE /nightschoolbook
TWITTER @cj_daugherty
FACEBOOK /CJauthor

Join her book club at…

www.christidaugherty.com

Christi Daugherty

Made in the USA
Monee, IL
12 July 2021